MAD DOGS AND ENGLISHMEN
Third book in the Brigandshaw Chronicles

Peter Rimmer

FIRST EDITION

KAMBA
PUBLISHING

Published by Kamba Publishing, United Kingdom

First Edition January 2017

Book Cover Design

Cover Design by *Hakim Julizar*

Contents

1

THE GUIDE, AUGUST 1920

The first distant call of the steam whistle made the knots of people on the railway platform stop talking to listen. Again, across the highveld. Three times. Satisfied they talked again, each with their own small story. Above them the clouds were motionless white in the African sky that had not rained for five months.

An old man watched the line of rail, watching for the train and his last opportunity. None of the others, deep in their trivial talk took any notice of him. His skin was dry and wrinkled. On his back he carried an old canvas haversack. In his right hand he gripped a gnarled stick he had made for himself long ago from a limb of a mukwa tree, harder than any Burmese teak. The old man waited patiently, alone, as he had done many times before when meeting the train from Beira, the deep water port that served Rhodesia, some three hundred miles east on the Indian Ocean in Portuguese Mozambique. The only good pieces of clothing were his boots which he had bought from the army surplus store for sixpence. In 1920 there was plenty of army surplus. The clear blue eyes that watched the train were the last sign of his youth. The three blasts of the steam whistle still echoed in his mind. Like so many other things from his past. Most of the good he was going to have from life had happened a long time ago. All but this one thing. Which made him determined.

The great iron engine with grand puffs full of energy and white steam rolled over the last of the metal track into Salisbury Station, the big cowcatcher pushed out front importantly. As the driver and his fireman looked out of opposite sides from the high, hot metal cab, the great piston of the steel turning the wheels that clanked the iron railway that had cut open the heart of Africa, the old man noticed the rotten leg of a kudu caught in the cowcatcher. When the train moved past him slowly he saw the flies had begun to eat the dry blood of the antelope and lay their eggs. The hoof of the kudu was small and beautifully made, pointing at the roof of the shed that ran the length of the platform.

More people were pushing forward to have a look at the train, the great engine, full of modern energy. Behind came the line of wooden carriages, their windows down. People leaning out. Eager faces. Looking with happy expectation. Their old sad lives left in England when they boarded the boat that had brought them to Africa. The boat train was the end of their journey. The beginning of their new lives. The excitement of new hope. For some it was the happiest day of their lives.

THE BUTTERFLIES in Jim Bowman's stomach made all of a flutter. Everyone else in the carriage had stood up. The sleepers were in first class and Jim had saved his money. He never understood how the mind dictated to the stomach. The first shellfire had emptied his bowels. The first sight of Jenny Merryl had stopped his heart. The first man he killed with a bayonet had made him vomit. And now the butterflies were fluttering, concentrating his fear and expectations. Only when the train stopped was he able to get up, certain his legs would hold him up. Then he took down his kitbag that had gone with him through the war before they gave him his commission in the field. He had been paralysed with fear but gone on in with the bayonet, leading the others so they had said. He didn't really remember except the vomiting and no one had mentioned that. And the next day the colonel had made him a second lieutenant. He thought the fact that the junior officers were all dead had more to do with it than the mentally paralysed charge across no man's land. There had been so much noise.

And then they had had to teach him which knife and fork to use in the officers' mess. By the summer of 1918 when he made his charge, the British were nearly out of the officer class at the junior level. The war was over six weeks after they made him an officer. He had enjoyed the food. One of the officers had been a Rhodesian which was why he was on the train alone with his kitbag and fifty-three pounds, seven shillings and thruppence, all after paying his passage. As a lance corporal his severance pay would have got him as far as London from where he lived in the north, next door but three to Jenny Merryl who would not even notice he had gone.

The butterflies stopped fluttering at exactly the moment he very much needed the lavatory. This time it was his bladder.

"There you are, dear boy," said an old man with a haversack on his back. Jim had never seen him before in his life.

"Where's the gents, please?"

"I see. Better follow quickly."

Surprisingly quickly, the old man led the way.

With his bladder bursting and his mind still in control, Jim Bowman stood at the urinal with the old man watching behind him. Nothing happened.

"Oh, I see, dear boy... I'll be outside when you're finished. You are Lieutenant James Bowman of the Lancashire Fusiliers?"

"Please!"

"I'll be outside. Just outside."

His flood of relief lasted a full minute and then his bowels took control. The small cubicle with the half door smelled of stale urine and there was no toilet paper. He crammed in with his kitbag and took down his trousers without wiping the seat like his mother had always told him. After ten minutes and with a smile of self-satisfaction he found the roll of toilet paper in his kitbag. The army had taught him always to carry a toilet roll.

Outside on the platform everyone had gone. Down the far end the engine driver was letting out the last of the steam. A mongrel dog looked at the driver hopefully. The fireman threw the mutilated leg of kudu out onto the empty platform and whistled to the dog. By the time the mongrel reached the meat, there was a dogfight going on and a pair of crows had flat landed on the platform.

The old man with the gnarled stick was sitting on the bench outside the waiting room watching him. Not sure of his next move, Jim smiled at the old man and went across to him.

"How do you know my name, sir?"

"Colonel Voss, at your service. You will be going to Meikles Hotel I presume? There is a delightful restaurant."

"I wasn't sure where to stay."

"Everyone stays at Meikles when they first arrive. I'll show you the way. We can walk. The weather in Africa is beautiful... Oh, and on the patio there is no dress code at lunchtime. The farmers you see. Mostly a scruffy lot until they've had a bath and changed. They travel long distances to town... I'm in the mining business but I'll tell you over lunch. Mining and rare artefacts. I'm sure you'll be interested. There is sweet music in the energy of youth larded with the knowledge of great experience. Come along. Take us five minutes, I should think. We go along Pioneer Street and turn left into Second Street. Give you a chance to see a bit of the town. We can have a bottle of wine with our lunch... Have the butterflies stopped fluttering?"

"They have as a matter of fact," said Jim, surprised at the old man's perception.

"What do we call you? Bowman or Mr Bowman."

"Call me Jim, sir."

"None of the 'sir' business... You see, you and I are going to be partners."

With the kitbag on his right shoulder he walked behind the old man with the haversack who was walking fast. Jim noticed the old man was wearing a new pair of British Army regulation boots. Suddenly Jim Bowman felt very happy.

IN THE SIDE street to the left of the hotel were a line of hitching posts. Some of the tied up horses were alone. Some were still in harness with long traps behind them. Outside the hotel entrance stood a Bentley car with a long bonnet and a leather strap over the middle of the round bonnet. Small black boys in bare feet and cast-off shorts were looking at the car. A huge black man with the biggest belly Jim had ever seen was standing on the pavement watching the small boys with distrust. A leopard skin was flung over his shoulder. He carried a shield and spear. Hung below the vast open belly was a shirt made from animal skins that had seen better days. Unbeknown to Jim Bowman, the big Zulu from the tribe of King Shaka and King Lobengula would have been an induna if the white man had not interfered. His father had been one of the last induna's of Lobengula to stay with the king at Gu-Bulawayo, the king's last kraal. Now he was the doorman at Meikles Hotel.

The Zulu watched Colonel Voss with the young man, envious of the old man's new boots. They caught each other's eye. When the old man was lucky, he made the young men give the Zulu a penny when they left. One of them had given him a three-penny piece. All the coins had on them the head of the King of England, some with the words 'Southern Rhodesia' around the bottom. A penny bought a lot of meat the white butcher called boy's meat. With a big pot of sadza it was good to eat... And always there were more of these young Englishmen coming into his country. Especially since the big war was over. White men killing white men. He would have liked to have seen that.

One of the small boys was about to touch the gleaming black bonnet of the Bentley when his half bare behind was pricked by the Zulu's spear. The small boys ran off down the dirt road together. Through the trees of Cecil Square, the church clock struck eleven o'clock in the morning.

"Why don't we have a beer on the veranda, dear boy? Still a little early for lunch and that bottle of wine."

Ignoring the mild protest of the head waiter, the old man sat down at the round table. They were in a courtyard ten feet from the kerb. A red-sashed, red-fezzed waiter came up.

"You order, dear boy," said the old man trying to make it look like a favour.

And then Jim had the message, smiling to himself. He was young but not that naïve. He comforted himself with the thought of a horse-drawn cab to the nearest hotel would have cost him more than a bottle of beer. He really felt at home. Later he would find a cheap room in a boarding house. Colonel Voss with the old clothes and new boots would know where to find him what he wanted.

The big black man with the spear and shield was looking at him with something close to pity. He gave the man a wink. The man broke into a broad smile with big white teeth. Then the cold beers came dripping condensation down the outside of the bottles onto the silver tray. He gave the waiter an English sixpence and waited for his change. English money they had said was just as good as Rhodesian. Most anywhere, English money was as good as anything. Certainly in the colonies. By the time his change came the old man had drunk his beer. Jim ordered them both another one. He was curious how the old man knew his name. And he was having fun. The first beer had gone straight to his head. Maybe he had better spend his first night in the hotel.

"Excuse me," he said getting up.

The old man was alarmed. The two new beers had been ordered but not paid for.

"Waiter," called Jim to the man's back. Hefting his kitbag in one hand he gave the bar money to the waiter and walked into the hotel.

He was quite sure the old man would still be there when he came back. At reception, they gave him a key, took away his kitbag, sealed his wallet and put it in the safe. Jim had a pound note in his pocket. It would be enough. Feeling safer, he walked out onto the front courtyard of the hotel. The old man was waiting for him. The two full bottles of beer stuck in an ice bucket with the tops off ready to be drunk.

The traffic in the wide street had built up while he was standing inside at the reception desk. A pretty girl in a flowered dress gave him a smile. Only when she had gone past him did he manage to smile back. It was hot, but the air was dry. Invigorating.

"Do you know any of the legends of Africa, dear boy?... Always sensible to find a base straightaway. You know that doorman would be an induna if Doctor Jameson hadn't chased Lobengula out of Bulawayo."

"What's an induna?"

"An adviser to the king. Rather like a minister in the British cabinet. Cheers, dear boy. Your most excellent good health. The legend brought me in the first place, not the gold or the promise of a great farm. Long before Rhodes sent up his pioneer column. In those days the white hunters got permission from the Ndebele King Lobengula to hunt the lands of the great Shona tribes. Men like Hartley and Selous, Oosthuizen and Brigandshaw. The British hanged Oosthuizen for going out with the Boers during the war. He was a British subject. Crown colony Southern Rhodesia. Sebastian Brigandshaw was killed by the Great Elephant. But I digress, dear boy. The legend was the thing."

"How do you know my name, sir?"

"I'll come to that. You see, the legend is so old no one knows when it started. The tribes of Africa never wrote anything down, but the legend lived. Father to son. Round the cooking fires over the long, long centuries. They weaved the story of their history. Their ancestors. The legend has it there was a great civilisation here when we in Europe were still climbing trees and living in caves dressed in animal skins. And the heart of the ancient empire was right here in Rhodesia. Deep in the bush are the ruins of a great city that thrived two thousand years ago. Before the birth of Christ. Before the Queen of Sheba. Only Egypt, far to the north, had anything like this great kingdom."

"What was the kingdom called?"

"Nobody knows."

"A legend without a name! Pardon me. That's silly. Nobody passes down a legend for three thousand years without a name."

"They won't tell us, you see," said the old man leaning forward and dropping his voice to a whisper. Then he took out a pipe, the bowl carved in the shape of a crocodile head. "Do you have any tobacco?...

Maybe the waiter could find us a pouch of pipe tobacco... You won't mind me smoking?"

"Not at all," said Jim laughing. The price of local knowledge was going to cost him more than he thought... Either the old man was a crook or crazy... Jim was halfway through his second bottle of beer. He had had no idea what he was going to do on his first day... He thought of the pretty girl and blushed. The old man was spinning a good yarn. The beer was cold. The sky was blue. He told himself there were times in life to talk and times to listen. Jim was sure the story was a figment of the old man's imagination.

When they had eaten a good lunch and drunk a bottle of wine, Jim wanted nothing more than his cool room upstairs in the hotel with the curtains drawn and a bed to sleep on. He paid the bill, shook the old man's hand and excused himself. The old boy was still sitting at the round table when he looked back. Either the man was drunk or bad of sight as his small wave went unnoticed.

Only in the cool of his room did he remember he had not learnt how the old man knew his name and regiment. Then he fell asleep and dreamed of the Queen of Sheba wearing a floral dress and a smile.

He slept through the afternoon and deep into the night. When he woke an owl was calling from outside in Cecil Square. He counted the clock strike three and fell back into sleep. When he woke a crack in the curtain had let a line of sunlight cut across his bed. All the blankets were on the floor.

When he got up and looked out of the crack in the curtain at his new home, he realised he was ravenously hungry. On the side table was his watch and his change. The beers, the tobacco, the wine and the lunch for two of them had cost him two and sixpence.

Downstairs there was no sign of the old man. The fat-bellied Zulu was at his work. The Bentley had gone. The small boys were back looking for something to do.

Jim went into the big dining room with the punkahs turning overhead to cool the room and ate his breakfast. He was going to have himself a good life, of that much he was certain. In time he might even forget the war. Sitting over a second pot of tea he waited for the pretty girl in vain.

The first thing he had to do was find himself a job. He wondered if Salisbury had a labour exchange for just arrived Englishmen. He doubted it and sent his waiter out for the newspaper. Doves were calling outside his nearest window from a tree in an inside courtyard.

When he had read the *Rhodesia Herald*, he looked up and found he was the last in the dining room. No one seemed to mind. No one brought him a bill. He found out at reception that the night in the room included his breakfast. He changed his mind again, walked back to the reception desk and asked the man to keep his room for another night. Then he walked out of the hotel to look around Salisbury. He gave the big Zulu a penny as the old man had told him to do. Again he was given a flash of white teeth. They were becoming friends.

"Always keep in with the doorman, dear boy. First rule in a strange country."

When Jim Bowman walked down Stanley Avenue, he was whistling. There was plenty of time to find himself a job. And the sun was shining. In France, in the trenches, the sun had rarely shone.

THERE HAD been a push that morning in which half his men were killed. They had thought the Germans were broken, but they weren't. They had to retreat to their own trench which was when he met the Rhodesian captain of artillery. The man had been sent up the line to look for new sites for the heavy guns. Once again the British generals had been wrong. The Germans had not run away but hidden deep in the earth and came out to repel the British advance. Jim thought the captain was a year or two older than himself. They were both frightened beyond fear. They sat on empty ammunition boxes in Jim's dugout he shared with his fellow officers. It was all very new to him. After the morning push there weren't any fellow officers. Only the captain with the strange accent and the faraway look.

Jim had found a bottle of brandy and two tin mugs. Their part of the Western Front was all quiet. The wounded had been taken back down the line. There were just the two of them hunched and cold in the dugout with the blanket two feet over their heads held up badly by pit poles that had been sent up a year earlier to stop the trenches collapsing inwards in the mud. They could not see the French October sky but it was raining. The blanket dripped water on both their tin hats. Their big grey oilskins covered them like tents. Jim noticed the puttees worn by the captain above his boots were rolled perfectly. Only at first did they drink in silence. Then they introduced themselves.

"Captain Nicole, Royal Artillery."

"Jim Bowman. Lancashire Fusiliers."

"Angus Nicole," said the man smiling. "You never know with the British. So forward. Even in this mess. Probably what kept them together for so long."

"I've only been an officer for three weeks. Colonel Tucker gave me a field commission."

"That explains the Jim Bowman... I'm from Rhodesia. Southern Rhodesia to be exact. There are lots of us colonials come over to help. You know where Rhodesia is?"

"I'm from Stockport. North of Liverpool. Left school at fourteen though I have read some books. Well, three to be exact. I was down in Manchester, training in the wool trade. Office boy, really. Dogsbody. Everyone's beck and call. I wanted to go to war believe it or not. Thought there could be nothing worse than a cold dingy wool broker's office fourteen hours a day. I was wrong, of course. Have you ever been to Manchester?"

"No, I haven't."

"All right if you're rich. Not much fun in a pokey room the size of a coal-hole. And damp. That room was always damp. Paradise looking back from this. No, Angus Nicole. I don't know where it is. Rhodesia."

"Africa. Central Africa. Just north of the Tropic of Capricorn. The most beautiful country on this earth. Space. Lots of space. Clean air that tastes like champagne. Animals. Big, beautiful animals. And only a thin sprinkling of the humankind. It's a place we haven't spoiled, Jim. When this is over you should come out. I'll give you my address. Can you imagine a cool, green plateau that runs for hundreds of miles among trees and tall grass where it does not rain for six months of the year? Well watered by rivers that flow the whole year round. Where the wild fruit on the marula trees are sweeter than anything on earth."

"Well, I don't know about Rhodesia for me. It seems such a long way away."

"You mark my words."

"What would I do?"

"Go farming."

"I don't have any money to buy a farm."

"There is so much empty land out there the only real cost is stumping out the trees and planting a crop... Live in a tent. Run some cattle. Live off the gun. You'll get sick of venison and guinea fowl but you'll live under the sun with a future and a great future for your children."

"Are there nice girls in Rhodesia?"

"You'll have to bring your own wife from England."

With a flash of insight Jim imagined himself in bliss under the African sun with Jenny Merryl, his next-door neighbour but three. The smile on his face vanished as quickly as it came. Jenny Merryl had long forgotten Jim Bowman even though he had waved to her the last time he was home to see his mum.

A runner put his head through the side curtain of the dugout from the main trench.

"Mr Bowman. Colonel Tucker wants to see you."

"Now?"

"Yes, sir."

"What about Captain Carrington or Mr Trent?"

"They're dead, sir."

When Jim Bowman entered the colonel's dugout ten minutes later a lone German gunner was ranging in on the British front line. From behind the British reserve line a battery of British gunners ranged in on the lone German gun. The German gun went silent. Colonel Tucker smiled grimly.

With the new orders in his hand to be ready to attack at first light Jim went back to find his sergeant. He hoped the colonel had not smelled the brandy on his breath. Then he returned to the dugout.

There was nothing there. The lone German gunner had dropped a shell through the dripping wet blanket. Bits of Captain Nicole were imbedded in what was left of the pit propped walls.

The armistice came at eleven o'clock in the morning of the 11th of November, three weeks later. All the guns went silent on the Western Front. It was all over. Jim Bowman still had no idea what it had all been about.

He had found out the address of the Rhodesian captain from the adjutant of the Royal Artillery. The war had been over a month. It was the last job he had as an officer, sending the gold cross of Christ back to Angus Nicole's parents in a place called Hartley in Rhodesia. Mr and Mrs Nicole had been listed as his next of kin. He had told them Angus had been thinking of his home in Rhodesia minutes before he was killed. He told them about their conversation. The fact he had not known where to find Rhodesia. It was all he had known of the man. All he had in common with the dead man's parents.

WALKING DOWN Stanley Avenue on his second day in Rhodesia, Jim still had the address of Mr and Mrs Nicole in the wallet in the safe at Meikles Hotel. Angus Nicole had been killed nearly two years ago, so he thought it best to leave them in peace. He was going to find his own way. Maybe later when he was established in the new country he had first learnt about in the dugout, he would make a social call.

He had gone back to the job with the wool broker after visiting his widowed mother. Jenny Merryl had moved away. Her mother said she had gone to London. Someone else in the village said she had gone to America. Someone else Canada. She had been a nurse at the end of the war. Nursing officers. Someone else said she had her nose stuck in the air and good riddance to her. Jim was going to hit the man. The village would have laughed at him, defending his next-door neighbour three doors away who would not have given him the time of day.

Jim had three sisters and a brother so his mother would be all right. His father was a fisherman drowned at sea. The boat had washed ashore without the crew. His brother sailed the boat with two of his brothers-in-law. He had thought of joining them but gone to Manchester instead. He had put his money from the army carefully in a bank at three per cent. After learning how to use a knife and fork properly he was back in the damp coal-hole with the wool broker still calling him boy. At the back of his mind was always the place called Rhodesia where for six months of the year it did not rain.

He could either fish for cod, wait ten years to become a wool clerk or get out of England like Jenny Merryl. He imagined her rich and married to an American in California where he had read it was warm all the year round.

At the end of 1919 he went back to Stockport for Christmas. His brother knew he still had the fifty pounds, and they argued.

"Together we can buy a bigger boat. We can share the catch as owners. It's a good life. Look at you, Jim. You look like a slug. Never seen the sun or the rain. Be a man and be a fisherman. 'Tis a grand life."

"Has anyone heard from Jenny Merryl?"

"You still on about her? Don't be daft. She never so much as looked at you." He had never liked his brother.

"I'm going to Rhodesia," he blurted out.

"What the bloody hell for, and where the bloody hell is that?"

"A captain gave me his address. And it's in Africa, Central Africa."

His brother laughed and walked away down towards the jetty. "A captain, no less. Blimey! What's his name?"

"Angus Nicole. And he's dead."

"That's not much good to you."

"He gave me the idea. I've been to the colonial office. They say because I was an officer I could apply for a Crown land farm once I have farming experience."

"You were only a bloody officer for weeks."

"Doesn't matter."

"Then piss off. If you don't want to put your money in a boat, piss off. And good riddance. When you goin'?"

"After Christmas."

"Told your boss?"

"No."

"You're a fool, Jim Bowman. Never come to nothin'. Our dad would spit in your face."

No one seemed to care much what he did. Once they learnt he was not going to put his capital in the family business, they lost interest in him. They talked over him. He was no good to them. When he went to the train station no one saw him off. Even his mother knew which side her bread was buttered. Their indifference made up his mind. If he meant so little to his family he might as well go.

His landlady demanded an extra week's rent. His boss docked his last pay packet for something called breakages. He had become invisible.

Getting on the boat at Tilbury docks in London Jim could hear the door to England slam behind him. He was strangely exhilarated. Like he now felt, walking down Stanley Avenue six thousand miles away from where he was born. Even the two and sixpence he had spent the previous day seemed a good investment.

All morning he walked around the wide streets of Salisbury, wide enough to outspan a team of oxen. Along the tree-lined streets people moved about their business. Passers-by smiled at him. When he reached his hotel, it felt natural for him to head for the front courtyard to drink a cold beer. He felt good. He was smiling. He was happy.

"There you are, dear boy," said a voice behind him. "Didn't think you'd run away from such a good proposition."

When he turned, knowing full well it was going to cost him another two and six, he was pleased to see the shabbily dressed colonel. At least the man did not want him to plunge around the North Atlantic in the rain and howling wind fishing for cod in ice-cold water.

"Have you thought about the legend, dear boy?"

"Of course," said Jim Bowman, lying. "Will you join me for a glass of beer?"

"Very civil of you. Delighted. I trust you had a good sleep?"

"The best I ever had. A wonderful breakfast. Walked all around Salisbury. Now I'm starving again."

"I'm so glad to hear that. Fact is, so am I, dear boy. Did you tip the Zulu? The doorman, dear boy."

"As you said."

"Shall we take the same table?"

"Quite splendid. It shall become a tradition. We will come back to this table when we find the Place of the Legend."

"So there is a place for the legend. But still no name?"

"Exactly. As the Jews will have it. There is a place for heaven but no name for God. He is too almighty. High almighty... You do believe in God and heaven?"

"And hell, Colonel Voss."

"Yes, hell. The place that is all the way paved with good intentions. I rather hope I don't go there."

"Do you think you have a chance?" After two and sixpence he had the right to gently pull the old man's leg.

"We all have a chance, Jim. Frankly, I think we all end up as dead as mutton."

"So you DON'T believe in God?"

"Of course I do. Especially for other people. Where would we be without somewhere to go? And people need the fear of God in them to behave themselves. A man who believes in hell and damnation disciplines himself. He doesn't need a policeman to tell him what to do. God gives us our conscience. No, believe in God, dear boy. Without the belief in God there will be no civilisation. Why there are so many missionaries pouring into Rhodesia. To bring everyone God and civilisation... Which is otherwise known as the British Empire. And if you think you hear a tweak of cynicism you are wrong. God and civilisation make life a lot more comfortable for everyone. Goodness gracious me. Before we brought in God and civilisation the local tribes were constantly killing each other. We stopped all that but I doubt if we will be thanked for it. You never get thanked for doing a man a favour he didn't ask for.

"The rains won't break for another three months so we don't have much time to waste. We need a small, covered cart with two salted horses. Horses that have been bitten by the tsetse fly and recovered from the sleeping sickness. They become immune... Some food for three months though most we will find on the way. A good compass. Though the stars will help too... And some good blankets. In the high mountains of the legend it is very cold at night. Twelve thousand feet above sea level. Good clean air. No flies. No sickness. Why I think the Arabs went there three thousand years ago... You do have enough money, I hope? You see I don't have a penny. Not a penny. Rich in intention. Rich in the knowledge of the legend. So far as I have been able to find out, of course. They clam up when a white man talks to them. Even in Shona. I did tell you I speak Shona? A delightful tribe. Came down from the north end and chased the poor Tonga into the valley of the Zambezi River. Very hot and swarming with tsetse fly so most of them died of the sickness.

"All this business outside Fort Victoria is not what it is all about. The archaeologists found some old ruins I have no doubt. With an Arab connection. But not the Place of the Legend. The Arab influence manifested at what the Royal Archaeological Society are calling Zimbabwe, is much later. Part of the slave trade. Anyway, someone else stole the best artefacts years ago. The archaeologists found those stone carved birds and sent them down to Cape Town. But nothing of real worth. Nothing really old... That is my opinion. Everyone else disagrees with me. Everyone else is wrong. You come with me into the high mountains towards Mozambique and I will prove it. Both of us will be rich. In money and prestige. We will go down in history as the men who found the Place of the Legend. The Valley of the Legend. Voss and Bowman. Our names shall live forever. Now that's better than a good chance of going to hell don't you think, dear boy?"

"How much will all this cost me?"

"Ten pounds including a second-hand rifle and a shotgun. The only thing we have to make sure about are the horses. Damn long way to walk back."

"Did you ever look before?"

"Not for the Place of the Legend. Not for the Valley of the Legend that pocket of ancient civilisation in the heart of darkest Africa. An empire to rival the pharaohs."

"Are we looking for pyramids? A sphinx?" Jim Bowman was trying hard not to smile.

"Maybe. Maybe not. Who will know until we find it? Voss and Bowman. Sounds so grand. Now I'll have a bottle of beer if you don't mind?"

"Not more than ten pounds?"

"Not a penny. After lunch we can walk among the exotic trees in Cecil Square and look at the goldfish. They had to put a wire mesh over the ornamental pond. The herons found the goldfish much to their liking. Goldfish and palm trees where none had been before. There are palm trees on the banks of the Zambezi but not on the highveld. Why do people not put up with what they've got?"

"How'd you know my name?"

"I asked immigration. Friend of mine. We used to travel together until he got a job. They have a photograph on the form. Not a very good one. You can't go anywhere in this world without someone knowing who you are."

"Why me?"

"Because you have fifty pounds. Says so on your form. The one you filled in at the colonial office. Why they probably said you would be offered a Crown land farm. Though they most likely said it was about being an officer. The one thing the British government likes is for the private citizen to pay for the British Empire. Look at Cecil Rhodes, for goodness' sake. Gave him a royal charter. Didn't cost the taxpayer a penny. Queen Elizabeth did it with Raleigh. Royal charters to plunder the Spanish Main. Turned pirates into model English citizens provided they gave half their plunder to the Queen, God bless her. What the king gave you for fighting his war, the king shall take away again. And leave you labouring with the soil for the rest of your life, God bless my soul as well. It is a wicked world in which we live. A wicked world. Be careful."

"Ten pounds."

"Not a penny more. A friend owns the horses and the cart."

"We could sell the horses and carts when we come back?"

"We could. We could also deck them in gold and feed them on the

finest grass. We will give them names so they too will be famous. Like Pegasus."

"Will our horses have wings?" The smile spread right across his young face.

"Our horses will have the hearts of lions. The bravery of Ulysses. They shall travel just as far."

"Ten pounds?"

"Not a penny more."

"Are you really a colonel, sir?"

"No."

"Does the Valley of the Legend exist?"

"It's like heaven. It exists so long as you believe in it. And I believe with all my heart and soul. Otherwise, what would be the point of looking?"

"Waiter!" called Jim, raising his hand.

"We shall leave half an inch of beer in each of our bottles. Libations to the gods. Very important. Just as important as giving the Zulu doorman another penny. They came from the south, the Zulus. Mzilikazi ran away from Shaka when he failed in battle. Tore into the Shona. Made them vassals. The Tongas probably thought it rather poetic. Now the poor fellow is draped in a leopard skin, opening and shutting an invisible door. Why do they call a man outside a hotel the doorman when he has nothing to do with the door? You shall have to buy yourself a large bush hat. The leopard skin band and the feathers can come later. When you have earned them... Thank you, dear boy. Ching-ching. I learnt that in Singapore."

"You have been to Singapore?"

"A long time ago. I was about your age. Just after Raffles by a few years. He was the merchant sailor who became governor of Sumatra for the British. Didn't cost the taxpayer a penny. Or none they did not get back afterwards. Sir T Stamford Raffles. With a name like that no wonder he was a rubber baron. Jolly good seaport, you see. Right on the trade route. Singapore. I believe they named a hotel after him. The island was a swamp. Hong Kong was a rock. A large rock. So there you have it."

"What were you doing in Singapore?"

"Like you, looking for my future. Why are we so sure we will find it when we are young?"

"Did you find it?"

"No. Why I came to Africa."

"Straight to Africa?"

The old man had poured his beer into the glass, leaving a small amount in the bottle. Jim did the same.

"Oh, no. There was China until the Boxer Rebellion. Chinese Gordon sorted them out. With my help, of course. General Gordon. Now there was a man."

"So you were a soldier?"

"Everyone has to be a soldier sometime or other in his life. The world is fluid. Darwin had it. Survival of the fittest. We are all the product of rape and pillage, dear boy. Including you and I. Kill the fighting men, take their woman for your own and re-educate the young children. Vikings. Saxons. Normans. And tribes we shall never know. The world evolved from rape and pillage. The same world we know and now call civilised."

"Don't you have to pour the libation to the gods on the floor?"

"I leave that to the waiter in the kitchen."

"He may drink it."

"He may drink it. Whichever way, the gift is ours. To the gods. The gods are very wise. They have to be."

The old man's eyes were full of laughter looking at him. He liked the old man. He asked himself, for ten pounds, how much could he lose? To see the new country in the hands of an expert guide. For ten pounds and still own the horses! If there was a catch, he was young enough not to worry.

"I have a better idea," said the old man. "We shall take some sandwiches into the park and look at the goldfish. There is a bench near the pond. I have slept upon it many a night under a moon. Sometimes the fish reflect the moon but not very often. The hotel will give us a luncheon basket. Many of the guests like to visit the country. To look at the animals. The plains are rich with animals. All kind of antelope. Elephant. Buffalo. We are so near to heaven. I'm very partial to hard-boiled egg and lettuce sandwiches. If you ask they will make the tea from China tea. Not all this stuff from Darjeeling. Tea is the Chinese word, for goodness' sake. A thermos flask of tea in a picnic basket. Some hot scones folded into a linen cloth to keep them warm.

"We can have one more beer while they are warming the scones, making the tea and cutting the sandwiches. I will ask them for you at reception while the waiter brings our beer. They know exactly how I like a picnic. Once, when I came to Rhodesia for the third time, I was quite rich. It was I who started them making the picnic lunches. I stayed in the hotel for three months soon after Thomas Meikles built his hotel. Better I ask them. I like everything just right... Then we can take a walk and look at our horses. They have names but we shall give them new ones. That Zulu is ready for his penny."

The old man got up abruptly and made for the interior of the hotel. Jim watched him go in his new boots, wondering how old he was. The gait was strong, the face deeply lined, the skin wrinkled, scored with liver spots. He wondered how much of anything was true. Whether the old man knew himself. Even parts of the war were so frightening he was not so sure if they happened to him.

THE GOLDFISH were mostly hiding under the large, green lily pads. There were small white flowers among the pads. A frog with a rich red *V* on its forehead, the size of his thumbnail was sitting looking at him where Jim sat on the bench.

The large picnic basket was between them. The birds in the trees were new to him. Except the doves. The rule was to eat their lunch without talking, silent in the shade of the jacaranda tree. Jim thought he would buy the old man a new pair of trousers before they went. He was going, that much he had made up his mind. He had thought of asking the big-bellied Zulu about the old man but gave him another penny instead. The large smile, open mouth with the white teeth was comforting. The egg and lettuce sandwiches were much to his taste as well. The tea was too weak, without any milk. There was no sugar. Each of them had a nice big piece of cold roast chicken. Celery sticks. Radishes. Two bananas each... He was full when they had finished everything including the scones with butter and strawberry jam and the frog had plopped back in the water. Water boatmen were skating on the clear patches of water between the lily pads. The clock in the church some way behind them struck three o'clock with considerable authority.

Jim packed up the luncheon basket putting back the china plates that tucked into neat places next to the cups and saucers. Everything buttoned down. There was a little tea left in the thermos flask that he left where it was. They sat for a long while in comfortable silence digesting the food. The colonel, as Jim still thought of him despite the denial, let out a deep sigh of contentment.

"Well, to work," he said. "Without work there can be no pleasure. And that, dear boy, was indeed pleasure. I have greatly enjoyed your company not saying a word. I dislike people who talk during meals... You can take the basket back to the hotel and I shall wait for you here.

I may even take a snooze. A good snooze after a good meal is one of the last great pleasures left to me. You may take as long as you like. Going and coming."

THE OLD MAN was sound asleep when Jim Bowman returned half an hour later. He had taken the precaution of speaking to the young girl at the reception desk. She had a nice smile which made up for the fringe and glasses.

"Do you know the man who ordered this basket in my name?" he had asked.

"Colonel Voss! Everyone knows Colonel Voss. You must be off the boat train. He waits at the railway station looking for a grubstake. The young ones fall for it."

"Do you think I should fall for it?"

"Depends on you. What's he looking for this time? Emeralds? Gold? Diamonds?"

"Does he ever find anything?"

"You only have to look at him."

"Have you heard of the Place of the Legend? Somewhere in the high mountains."

"They found it just outside Fort Victoria."

"Colonel Voss says that was not the right one."

"He wants you to help him look for the right one? Well, at least that is new."

"You never heard him looking for the Place of the Legend before?"

She gave him a queer look that spoke of many things. Her own frustration at being single. A young man on a fool's errand. The general stupidity of the world.

"Thank you," said Jim. "You have been most kind. Please add the cost of the picnic basket to my bill."

"I already have... You won't run off without paying your bill! Some of the young men just go off into the bush and we never see them again."

"You have my wallet. Locked in your safe... Has he ever killed anyone?"

"Colonel Voss! I'm sure he has. He fought with General Gordon during the Boxer Rebellion in China."

"He says he is not a colonel."

"I can't vouch for everything people say."

"Are you sure he fought with Gordon?... Do the people who give him a grubstake come back again?"

"I have no idea."

"You have been a great help."

"Just pay your bill before you go, Mr Bowman."

"What makes you think I'm going?"

"According to the Zulu on the door, they all do. And he's been here since Mr Meikles built his hotel."

"That explains the penny."

The young girl with the fringe and glasses turned her back to help another guest.

Jim walked away. It would seem disloyal to ask the doorman if the man they called Colonel Voss was honest. There was something about Englishmen sticking together far from home. And they were both Englishmen. Something deep inside was telling him to be reckless. That strange and good experiences were few and far between. That boredom knocked more often at the door. He was young and strong. He could look after himself. The worst thing the old man could do was leave him in the bush to find his own way home. He would always hobble the horses at night. The only source of small wealth worth stealing. He would keep the compass in his own pocket. Alone in the African bush with the wild animals, sounded much more comfortable than the British front line on the Western Front. And a lot safer.

He had to wake up the old man from his dreams. They were to go and have a look at the horses. The old man had been sleeping bolt upright on the wooden bench.

As they passed the big church while walking up Second Street, the clock struck the half hour.

"Did the reception desk tell you anything?" asked the old man. They had stopped to look up at the clock tower of the stone built church... "Churches are sprouting all over British Africa. Do you think that a good thing?"

Jim Bowman blushed to the roots of his dark brown hair. Even his ears were burning. "No, sir," he managed, answering the first question.

"At least you're honest. We shall get on. Always be honest. The rest does not matter. Lies, dear boy, are the ruin of man. Cut out their tongues, I say."

THE HORSES when they found them half an hour later were the sorriest sight Jim Bowman had ever seen. Skin and bones. Unshod. Lethargic. Their owner, a man much older than Colonel Voss, much the same. The owner of the horses' bare feet was gnarled and his front toes clutched the earth like the toes of a chicken. The old man had a lazy eye that looked over Jim's shoulder while the other fixed him with a stare. The man lived in a shack with a paint peeled door but no windows. Jim could make out a bed in the dark inside but nothing else. The floor was unswept dirt. A dog with its tail firmly between his legs guarded the door. A big wooden cart with high sides and a tailgate stood in the yard with the chickens. The canvas top had long shredded in the wind, the shreds of canvas bleached by the African sun. The colonel handed the old man a leg of roast chicken he had kept in his pocket. The old man ate the chicken. His teeth were surprisingly good. The dog got the bone.

"The roan we shall call Hamlet, dear boy. That big, dark beast shall be Othello... They need some food, Bert."

"Don't we all," said Bert. The dog, having eaten the chicken bone without mishap, had its tail back between his legs.

"I'll do you a favour feeding the beasts, Bert. Why don't you take them into the bush and let them graze?"

"Then they run away."

"Don't blame them," said Jim.

"What you say, young whippersnapper?" The straight eye had fixed him again.

"I didn't mean to be rude."

The one eye stared him down.

"How about hiring them for three months?" said Colonel Voss. "Five bob the lot, including the dog. We'll need a dog. Does he have a name?"

"Not that I'm aware of. He's a stray." The old man was well-spoken.

"Gout still killing you?" asked Colonel Voss.

"Why I keep off the shoes."

"Five bob? We'll fix the canvas and the front right wheel. Mr Bowman, please give Sir Robert the five shillings. Then we'll be off. At least the horses are salted."

"They won't go ten yards," said Jim Bowman.

"Oh yes they will," said Colonel Voss. There was steel in his voice for the first time. "We leave for the mountains in a week. During which time Hamlet and Othello will be fed on the best food a horse can eat.

You shall see. New horseshoes. A good brush. Lots of food… Oh, yes. And that dog could do with something to eat, too. The dog shall be King Richard the Lionheart. We mount the expedition, dear boy. Indeed we do."

"You think a week will be enough for the horses?"

"Maybe two."

Jim Bowman was convinced a lifetime of good fodder would have no effect on the horses.

The front wheel received attention. Jim gave Sir Robert the five shillings. The horses were harnessed into the big double shaft. The dog was coaxed into the cart by Sir Robert's bare right foot lifting the dog violently up over the dropped tailgate. The reins needed repairs. The wheels creaked ominously. There were chicken droppings thick on the floor of the cart.

"Where are we taking them?" asked Jim seated on the high bench above the skinny rumps of Othello and Hamlet.

"I have a friend who runs a stable. For two shillings and sixpence we shall have a great change. I shall sleep with the horses. A man mounting a great expedition can never be too careful… We five shall meet again in two weeks. At the place of the stable. I shall need a shilling."

To Jim's surprise the horses moved off at a trot. Colonel Voss turned and waved at Sir Robert standing in his doorway. Jim Bowman felt a long way from his home in Stockport.

"We had better shake hands," said Colonel Voss. "On our agreement. Remember, an Englishman's word is his bond."

"What is our agreement, Colonel Voss?"

"Together, we go in search of the Place of the Legend. Now, do we shake hands?"

Reluctantly, Jim Bowman took the gnarled hand as they trotted back down the road into Salisbury. The old man's grip was strong. Jim looked back over his shoulder to find King Richard the Lionheart looking at him with pathetic eyes. He put a hand out to the dog which snarled at him. Bravery was overcoming the dog's fear. Never in his life had he ever found himself in such a peculiar position.

They parted company at the stables and Jim walked on to Meikles Hotel without any idea of what he was going to do for two weeks. Like any young man with time on his hands he headed straight for the bar. He wanted to talk to someone. He wanted to tell someone. Most of all he wanted reassurance.

2

DECEIT, AUGUST 1920

*J*im Bowman felt flat. There were a few more desolate experiences than sitting in a strange bar alone. Everyone else seemed to know each other. The barman smiled at everyone else. How the old man had drawn him into spending money was beyond his comprehension. Instead of getting on with his life. Looking for a job on a farm to give him the experience in five years' time to apply for a Crown land farm. He was about to gallivant off into the bush with an old man who had picked him up at the railway station. Ordering his second beer from the unfriendly barman he wished he had put his damn money in the fishing boat. Until that moment he had no idea he was so gullible. The old boy was clever, he had to give that to Colonel Voss. Making him shake hands.

A young couple came into the bar laughing and settled at a table. He had chosen the first bar he found. The ladies' bar. The rest were reserved for men only. He thought for a sweet moment the girl smiled at him and looked quickly away. After a few moments his eyes strayed back to the young couple.

They were in their early twenties, he guessed. The girl had big brown eyes and was dressed in the latest flapper fashion. She was smoking through a long, black cigarette holder held up high when she was not taking small puffs of the cigarette. The long, tight dress gave the impression of a flat chest. Jim knew the modern girls tied themselves down with something they wore under their dress, to make them look flat-chested. The girl was obviously not flat-chested and the fight between nature and fashion was more erotic than anything he had seen before. This time he was sure she smiled at him, reading his mind, and he blushed a deep crimson. He could see the colour of his face in the bar mirror, behind the bottles of whisky. She had close-cropped wavy hair in the London fashion with a small tight hat that hugged her head.

To add to his consternation, the man got up and came towards him. He could see clearly what was happening in the mirror behind the whisky bottles. The young man was elegantly dressed in a double-breasted blazer and grey flannels.

"I say, don't I know you from somewhere? Army, probably. You were in the war? Barnaby St Clair, at your service. I can see you're on your own. Come and join me. Silly for an Englishman to sit on his own where there's another Englishman... You're not waiting for someone?"

"No. No I'm not. My name is Jim Bowman."

"You were an officer?"

"For the last six weeks."

"Jolly good. That settles it. Come and meet Tina. She was the one who thought we knew you. She's quite a girl, Tina. Leave that beer. I'll have the barman make us a sidecar. I rather like these American cocktails. You are staying in the hotel?"

The combination of the liquid brown eyes and luscious, slightly open mouth at close proximity caused Jim to want to cross his legs with embarrassment. Under the tight strapping beneath the red dress he was now sure large, full breasts were trying to come free. As he sat down in a hurry at the table and crossed his legs, the girl took an elegant puff through her cigarette holder, sending an erotic ripple across her chest.

"This is Mr Bowman, Tina. He's come to join us. Miss Pringle, Mr Bowman."

Before Jim knew fully what was happening a fancy cocktail was put in front of him. He had drunk down the last of the beer before leaving his bar stool, not being a man to waste beer.

The girl put an elbow on the table and leaned towards him, smiling. The tip of a small pink tongue appeared and retreated. They all raised their new tall glasses and Jim managed to say 'cheers'. He was acutely aware of the girl's thighs under the pencil-thin dress. The material smoothed its way to her ankles. Her fingernails were painted bright red, accentuated by the ebony black of the long cigarette holder. He had never felt more out of place in his life. Both their accents were languidly upper class, the man's tie clearly from a good regiment or an even better public school. Jim hoped the girl could not smell Hamlet and Othello's manure. All thought of Colonel Voss and their handshake fled with his embarrassment. He had no idea what to say. Both of them were just smiling at him, as if he were a long-lost friend. He was quite sure he had never seen either of them before in his life.

The girl very beautifully put out her cigarette in the ashtray and placed her cigarette holder on the table, all the time sending waves of sexuality across her chest.

"You had a bad war," she said sympathetically putting a hand with red fingernails on his hand. "Your hands are shaking. The worst part of war is afterwards. Barnaby lost his eldest brother to the war. Frederick was heir to the title. Now little Richard is going to be the eighteenth Baron St Clair of Purbeck. They came over with the Conqueror. Very old family. Known them all my life. And poor Robert had his foot blown off. You must have heard of the novelist, Robert St Clair. He had a great success with *Keeper of the Legend*. Both in England and America. America is where the money is. Poor Mr Bowman. Was your war really bad?"

His erection under the table, not far from his hand was so stiff Jim thought it would poke through the table or worse. The hand with the red nails went back to the cigarette holder. She lit another Turkish cigarette. He knew the smell of the tobacco. The thought of another legend coming into his life so swiftly after the first sent his mind flashing back to Colonel Voss which relieved the pressure under the table. He had not seen anyone order but another tall drink replaced the one he had just finished. They were both looking at him with sympathy, something he had never experienced before, not even as a small boy growing up. The drink had gone straight to his head.

"I was in Palestine. With Allenby," said Barnaby St Clair. "You were on the Western Front?"

"Yes I was and commissioned in the field, you see, so not a proper officer."

"Oh yes you are. Did you lead a charge or something?"

"Yes, I did."

"Then you are a very brave man," said Tina Pringle. "I hope they gave you a medal as well as the commission."

"The Military Medal."

"Jolly good," said Barnaby St Clair with deep satisfaction. "We are lucky, Tina."

After the second sidecar on top of the two beers, Jim lost his inhibitions and his tongue began to wag. He even told them about the fishing boat and his fifty pounds in his wallet in the safe of the hotel. They listened with consummate interest to every word he said. Somewhere in the wonderful conversation, the wonderful girl with brown eyes that never left his face told him Barnaby also had a title. The Honourable Barnaby St Clair. Jim had never met anyone with a title before.

When his friend Barnaby suggested they all went through to lunch together he was the first to rise to his feet in anticipation.

They were passing the reception when Barnaby stopped abruptly and felt in the inside pocket of his blazer.

"Oh, dash. I must have left my wallet on the farm… I say, old chap. Can you lend me ten quid? Damn silly of me. Left it at Elephant Walk. You must have heard of the Brigandshaws. Harry Brigandshaw's my brother-in-law. Frightfully nice chap… You do have some money here, don't you? Money is such a bore. Someone should invent a way of paying for things without having to cart around all that money."

The girl at reception with the fringe and glasses pulled his wallet from the safe in a matter of seconds. The girl was not as plain as she was in the morning. Jim took out ten pounds and gave it to his new friend. Everyone smiled, and they went into the dining room for lunch. Jim saw that Barnaby ordered the most expensive French wine on the list and appreciated the gesture.

"Can't have cheap South African wine for our friends, can we Tina?"

Barnaby watched his wine glass for him and kept it full with his own hands. All his new friends talked about was the rich and famous. When the head waiter brought the bill, Tina distracted him for a moment. The bill was put in front of him. There was a pen on top of the bill for one pound, three and sixpence.

"Oh, that's jolly good of you, Jim. Really is. Lovely lunch. You can just sign the bill seeing you stay here. That will be all right, Williams?" he said to the tall thin man dressed in tails.

"Quite all right, sir."

"You can just add on a tip," said Barnaby helpfully. "Well, this has been a pleasure meeting a fellow Englishman. We would stay for another cup of coffee but Tina has an appointment with a hairdresser. And you know what women are like with their hairdressers."

Jim had no idea what women were like with their hairdressers but before he could say anything they were shaking his hand and Tina gave him an almost kiss on both cheeks. Then they were gone leaving him standing unsteadily at the table.

"Ten per cent is usual," said the head waiter in a business-like voice.

Jim wrote 'add ten per cent tip' in a barely legible hand. He was drunk. The signed bill disappeared with a 'thank you, sir' from the head waiter. Then he was alone as he had been at the bar. Alone and drunk. He was smiling. They were such nice people. He touched his right cheek where the girl had almost kissed him. Then the left cheek with the other hand. He only just managed not to bump the other chairs when he left the dining room.

If he had known better and not drunk too much wine, he would have sworn the head waiter called Williams gave him a look of pity. Why pity, he had no idea. He had never enjoyed a lunch so much in his life.

He went up to his room where someone had thoughtfully drawn the curtains. He fell asleep on his bed without taking off his clothes. In the dark of the night he woke with the instant picture of Tina in his mind. Then he remembered the bill... And the ten pounds. And felt sick.

When he eventually drifted back into a troubled sleep he had decided for the rest of his life to avoid anyone with a rank or a title.

When he enquired the next morning after the Honourable Barnaby St Clair, the girl with the fringe said he had left that morning for Johannesburg.

"Did he leave a note for me?"

"No, he didn't."

"Why did he go to Johannesburg when his wallet is at Elephant Walk? There is a farm near here called Elephant Walk?"

"Yes, there is."

"Is it owned by a chap called Brigandshaw?"

"Yes, it is."

"Will Mr Brigandshaw be at home do you think?"

"He left to look for his brother-in-law over a year ago. No one has heard of him since."

"The man I lent ten pounds to was his brother-in-law."

"The other one. Married to his sister Madge, Barend Oosthuizen."

"You are a font of knowledge."

"Thank you."

"You did see me give that chap ten quid?"

The girl with the glasses and fringe moved off to help another guest.

"You'd better wake up, Jim my boy," he said out loud to himself. "They must have seen you coming."

UPSTAIRS IN HIS room again, Jim Bowman took a good look in the mirror. Hands on the dressing table he leaned to within a foot of the mirrored glass.

"Do I really look that naïve? Can they see the wet behind my ears?"

A boy's face looked back at him. Only the eyes were older, staring hard at the reflection of himself in the mirror. The nose was well shaped and slightly flared at the nostrils. When Jim turned his face to try to take a look behind his ears, the jawbone was smoothly curved from the hairline round his jaw. The skin was clear and healthy, slightly blushed red on the cheeks. He had not shaved that morning though nothing showed.

"Smooth as a baby's bottom," he told himself. "No wonder. Just look at you. Lamb to slaughter, Jim my boy. Down to under forty quid within a couple of days. My, oh my."

Then he laughed. A good, strong laugh, his young face shining with humour. A knock at the door stopped him looking at himself. A lock of soft brown hair fell over his forehead as he turned sharply. Standing upright he pushed the lock of hair off his forehead and marched to the door. He had locked the door, so the cleaner was unable to use a master key. Fumbling the doorknob and the safety catch he turned the handle expecting to see a black face. The man at the door was white and did not carry a dustpan and brush. The man had a notebook in his right hand and was reading something written on the pad.

"Can I help you?" said Jim Bowman, making his voice sound as cold as possible. He had promised himself the next confidence trickster was going to get a punch on the nose.

Instinctively the man stepped back a pace before recovering his poise. He put the notebook back in his side pocket and held out his hand.

"I'm Simon Haller from the *Rhodesia Herald.*"

Jim ignored the hand and set his face.

"The local rag, you know. You are Mr James Bowman?"

"What's that got to do with you?"

"You don't have to be rude." His hand was still out unshaken. "Do you mind if I come in for a moment? Well, more than a moment if you agree to my proposition."

"I've had quite enough of your propositions. Now, will you be kind enough to leave me alone?" Jim had tried to put some menace into his voice.

The man in front of him was lightly built in his late twenties. Jim had clenched his right fist and was going to throw a punch if the man took a step forward.

"Easy. Easy, now. I know you had a bad war but…"

"How do you know what war I had?"

"It's my business to find out things. I'm a newspaper reporter. Not a very good one, probably but…"

"Everyone in this damn country knows my business, and I only stepped off the train the day before yesterday."

"You did win the Military Medal on the Western Front?"

"Yes I did, and that's my business."

"And Colonel Tucker recommended you for the Victoria Cross after giving you a commission in the field?"

"So now what do you want? Free drinks and a tenner? Lunch of course. Out. Get out, I've had enough of you lot."

"All I want is a story. We are doing stories in the *Herald* of new immigrants who are war heroes… You'll have your picture in the paper… A little fame never hurt anyone. You are looking for a job? Probably a farmer to give you an apprenticeship with a small income. I can help, Mr Bowman. All I want in exchange is your story. The paper will pay you two pounds. I may even squeeze five pounds from my editor if there are lots to write. Now, may I come in?"

"We can go downstairs and sit in the lobby. Where there are people around."

"You don't trust me?"

"No, I don't."

"This is my press card. You can see the photograph is a picture of me."

"I don't damn well care. I've been robbed once, probably twice, and it isn't going to happen a third time."

"You really did have a bad war."

"Not really as bad as the last two days. Have you ever heard of a Colonel Voss or the Honourable Barnaby St Clair and his girl with the cigarette holder?"

The man in front of Jim began to laugh. Jim found he could not stop himself. The laughter was infectious. He began to laugh till the tears poured down his face.

"I INTERVIEWED Barnaby St Clair a year ago," said Simon Haller.

They were downstairs in the small men's bar and drinking their third beer. Jim had told his story of the previous two days.

"He had been demobbed in Cairo. His war was in Palestine. We thought he had been with Colonel Lawrence blowing up trains and by the time we found out the truth he owed my editor twenty pounds. He had never actually met T E Lawrence. The girl was not with him then but I heard about her. St Clair had gone from Egypt down the east coast of Africa where he had a boyhood friend in Johannesburg. The brother of the girl, Tina, of the ebony black cigarette holder. The brother is smart. And rich. His family lived on the St Clair estate for centuries as farm labourers, mostly. Albert Pringle made a fortune out of munitions during the war. Pringle is smart, like his sister and saw clean through St Clair. The bullshit didn't work so St Clair came up here. Has a brother-in-law. But you know that. Even Mrs Brigandshaw, that's old Mrs Brigandshaw, wouldn't give him a job. I heard Tina Pringle joined him a few months ago. Put simply, the St Clairs don't have a bean other than an old ancestral pile and a few surrounding acres. All the rest he told you about Brigandshaw's new bride being killed and the brother writing a book is true. Everything he told you was true except for leaving his wallet in Elephant Walk, the Brigandshaw farm. He's a very charming con man. The youngest son. He's out in the colonies to make his own fortune. Trouble is he doesn't like work. Why she doesn't find herself a rich man in Johannesburg with her brother's connections, I have no idea. Rumour has it, the brother hired a tutor to give the girl the right airs and graces. To bring her out of the working class. Wasting her time on a penniless charmer."

"Maybe she loves him."

"You're a romantic, Jim Bowman. No wonder you lost your ten pounds and paid for the lunch. Don't worry. There are worse failings in life. Far worse. I wouldn't mind being a romantic."

"You don't think I'll see my money?"

"Not very likely... Colonel Voss is another cup of tea. If I had the time I would go on that journey. You won't find a valley full of anything. You won't want to believe too much of what he says about himself. But the experience, the experience you will tell to your grandchildren. I don't know what rank he was. Whether he fought with Chinese Gordon. But his knowledge of the African bush is worth a lot more than ten pounds. He's lonely, poor old boy. You'll be the grandson he never had. He'll tell you stories. Many stories. What you believe is what you want to believe. There will be plenty of time to find a job when you come back. You've been in a terrible war. Let the horror seep out of you in the African bush. It will be a wonderful therapy. Maybe you can tell me the story and I'll write a book like Robert St Clair. I recommend you read *Keeper of the Legend.* I hope he writes a lot more books. Even a modern one. About his living family. Not the dead...

"Now, do you want to tell me your story?" he finished.

"There's nothing to tell. I ran for my life with a fixed bayonet that ended in a German. It was a blur. They needed new officers. I was yelling at the top of my voice for the others to follow me because I was so scared... Didn't know anything else to do. I was quite sure I was about to die and the yelling would somehow keep the bullets away."

"But they did make you an officer. Tell me about that. How it felt? How you fitted in? Tell me about your family. Readers like to read about real people. You must have done more than you say for Colonel Tucker to put you up for the VC."

"I don't remember. I don't bloody well remember."

"You'd better leave that bit to me. Maybe my editor can go to ten pounds. All this coming out of the ranks so suddenly makes a wonderful human story."

"Why me?"

"'Cause they gave you the MM and made you an officer. Have another beer. And I promise, Jim, you will not have to pay for anything today. All I want is a good story."

"Can I trust you?"

"Of course you can... Mr Barman. Two more Castle beers, please... Did I tell you Rhodesia was named after our paper? First came Cecil Rhodes. Then came the *Rhodesia Herald.* Then came Rhodesia. We newspapermen coined the name, you see. We gave this country its name. I think only Bolivia was named after a man. Simón Bolívar. What I want from you is a really good story we can sell to the papers down in South Africa. I've never syndicated one yet round the world but there's no reason why we shouldn't."

"You won't tell any lies."

"Of course not."

By the end of the fourth beer Jim Bowman was spilling his guts. Telling his life story. The codfish. The drowned father. The small house in Stockport and the poverty. He even told how his heart stopped whenever he saw Jenny Merryl, the girl next door but three in the row of council houses. He didn't want to leave anything out for such an attentive listener who listened so well and wrote in his notepad covering page after blistering page. At one point Jim asked to read back the notes.

"Sorry, old chap. You couldn't read a word. All in shorthand. Pitman's. Let's have another beer and you can tell me again about that wonderful charge. So brave of you. I was never in the war. Wouldn't have me, more's the pity. I so admire such bravery. You say you don't remember but you must have killed many more Germans than you say. Why Colonel Tucker put you up for the VC, don't you think?"

"I don't know. Maybe. I thought afterwards he was just short of officers. The average lifespan of a second lieutenant was only ten days."

"There must have been much more to your story. You were just too busy bravely leading the men to remember your personal details... I wish I had been in the war."

"No, you don't."

"Well, maybe not. I might not be here listening to such a wonderful story. A true story. They are always the best. To hell with fiction. Can you describe Jenny Merryl to me? Was she very pretty, Jim?"

"She was the prettiest girl I ever knew."

"And she went off to Canada? America? You don't know where? Why, if she knew this story she would run right back to you. A good-looking brave young soldier and a beautiful girl. What a lovely ending. What a lovely story. Five pounds. I'm now quite sure my editor will go to five pounds."

"You won't mention Jenny will you?" said Jim alarmed. "She doesn't even know I exist."

"Of course not. Now let's have some jolly old lunch. We can order a bar lunch right here. I hate those fancy dining rooms. This has been a pleasure. No, Jim, don't look at me like that. Here, Mr Barman. Take my money now. Friend here thinks he's going to land up with the bill... Now, Jim, does that make you happy? They do good cheese rolls, with pickled onions. My favourite... You do like pickled onions?"

"My favourite, too."

"Now go on with your story, Jim, I want to hear everything about you. Just everything."

An hour later Simon Haller left for his office. Jim had been talking all that time. About himself. For the third day in a row he found the curtained coolness of his room and lay down on his bed. He had managed to take his shoes off and his jacket before he fell into a dreamless sleep.

THE NEXT DAY a man with a camera found him in his room and gave him five pounds. He signed for the money.

"Usual indemnity and receipt, Mr Bowman. Now, do you mind if I take some photographs? I think it is best we go down to Cecil Square. The light is better. You do have your Military Medal so we can get a shot of it? You can hold it out to me to see when I take the photograph... You must have one hell of a story to get five quid. The editor is usually as tight as a fish's arse."

"I'd like to see the story before it's printed."

"I'm sure you would."

"When will it come out?"

"Don't ask me, mate. I just take the photographs."

"Tomorrow, maybe?"

"Shouldn't think tomorrow."

"Tell Simon I want to see his article."

"I'm sure you will. Come on. Got your medal? Good lad. Got another job in half an hour. Work me to the bloody bone, they do. How long you've been in Rhodesia?"

"Four days."

"And you're going to be famous. Missed the war, I did. Bloody shame I don't think. Never catch old Solly Goldman as a hero. Not bloody likely. Moment war started I scarpered. Before the bloody toffs made us join up. Straight on the first boat. I came to Africa in '14. First boat sailed to Cape Town. No flies on Solly Goldman, I can tell you that."

"You a cockney?" asked Jim. He had heard the accent during the war.

"How you guess, china... China plate, mate. Got it? Cockney rhyming slang. Come on. Solly Goldman don't 'ave all day. Even for a bloody hero."

"You didn't miss anything."

"I know I didn't."

They both knew Jim was talking about the war.

For three days Jim bought the *Rhodesia Herald* and looked for his photograph. Having been given five pounds he felt confident and kept his room in Meikles Hotel. With a good breakfast and a cheap bar lunch he needed nothing else. The fact the beers he drank in the small men's bar cost more than the cheese rolls did not figure in his reckoning. There was no sign of the article but he had their five pounds so what did it matter, he told himself. He had made back half the loan to Barnaby St Clair. He rather hoped they would come back again. Every time he thought of sex, Jim Bowman thought of Tina Pringle. Every time it happened in public he was forced to cross his legs and think of anything mundane. He now knew he had lied to Simon Haller. The best-looking girl he had seen in his life was Tina Pringle. The red fingernails. The ebony black cigarette holder and the way she held it up. The cloth she tied unsuccessfully across her chest in an attempt to make her look flat-chested under the dress that hugged her skin. He even went in to the ladies' bar three times a day to see if they were there. Each time he was thinking of Tina Pringle and not his ten pounds.

Every day Colonel Voss presented himself with a progress report. Hamlet and Othello were doing well. King Richard the Lionheart was not doing so well. The dog had twice bitten Colonel Voss but fortunately not broken the skin.

"Rabies, dear boy. Terrible thing. Send you quite bonkers. Heard of a chap who bit his wife after he contracted rabies. She died too... We must buy the guns today. When I show that dog a gun he will understand. One more bite and he is dead, or we take him back to Sir Robert. Can't have the leader of such a great expedition dead of a dog bite. Not even if he is a king, Richard the Lionheart."

"Is Sir Robert really a knight?"

"Does it matter?"

It was Monday and Jim had been in Rhodesia ten days. They had bought two second-hand guns for nine and sixpence. Colonel Voss proved a champion negotiator. With the nine and sixpence came three boxes of shells for the .375 rifle and two boxes for the hammer-action twelve-bore shotgun. Neither gun displayed the name of the maker. Jim had fired both of them outside the back of the shop in Pioneer Street to make sure they worked. The charge that had led to all his yelling and the Military Medal had started with his bolt-action Lee Enfield having jammed a shell in the breech. All he had was the bayonet stuck on the end of his rifle. He did not want the same thing to happen in the bush when he was facing a lion.

The guns had been oiled and wrapped in oilcloth before being put back in their leather cases. For another shilling he had made up the stock of ammunition to a thousand shells a gun. The war had at least taught him something… For some reason he never told Colonel Voss about Simon Haller and the article that had still not appeared in the paper. Even on the day before they harnessed up Hamlet and Othello, Jim had looked.

This time the dog jumped over the tailgate into the wagon. The tattered sun-bleached canvas had gone replaced by a new canvas roof. The horses looked no better and had the same look of great trust that shone in their big brown watery eyes. Jim stroked Hamlet's ears very gently and whispered in his ear.

The horses trotted into Salisbury and stopped outside Meikles Hotel. The big Zulu shouted something Jim failed to understand and two porters came out with his kitbag carrying it together. The Zulu took the kitbag and shooed away the porters. Jim gave the Zulu another penny. To Jim's surprise the girl with the fringe and glasses had left her reception desk and came outside to see them off. She neither smiled nor waved. Jim thought she was making sure he had not stolen anything. He waved just the same.

As the horses took the load forward, Jim looked back over the high box where he was sitting with Colonel Voss. He could just see over the canvas hood. The girl was smiling. She had a surprisingly pretty smile and Jim smiled back.

"May the expedition commence," called Colonel Voss grandly to anyone who happened to be listening. Then they were on their way up Second Street having done a complete turn in the street that was wide enough to turn an ox wagon thanks to the long ago foresight of Cecil John Rhodes.

Jim Bowman had been in the country exactly two weeks.

FROM HIS VANTAGE point looking through the window of the ladies' bar, Solly Goldman watched the horses and the cart go up Second Street where he hoped the cart would soon turn east and head into the bush. He finished his beer and went back to the offices of the *Rhodesia Herald*.

"He's gone," he said to Simon Haller. "Now you can print."

"Such a shame we have to embellish a story to make it sell. What we now need is for the girl to come forward and claim our reward of fame. If she does, we can turn the story into a serial. Grab the readers. Make them buy the paper to see what happens. I can see the billboards next to the newsvendors all over the world. 'HERO FINDS HIS GIRL'."

"Can I come with you when you interview Jenny Merryl?"

"We'll have to think about it, Solly. So far only the *Cape Times* and the *Rand Daily Mail* have bought the story. And that's only the start of the search for Jenny Merryl. Let's hope young Jim stays away his allotted three months. By then the story will be so big there will be nothing he can do to stop it… Why is it people believe what they see in print?"

"You think all the stories in the Bible are true?"

"The Old Testament, cock. Remember, I'm a Jew. Nothin' matters what it is in life. Only matters what it appears to be, my china."

"You should have been a philosopher."

"Every Jew is a philosopher."

"Where's all this going, Simon?"

"I have no idea… I'll just go and tell the editor he can print tomorrow. Still hopping mad he paid five quid… You sure they've gone?"

"Absolutely bloomin' certain."

"Who said the truth is fiction and fiction the truth?"

"Simon Haller?"

"Even the truth needs help. No, it wasn't me. Some Greek, probably."

IN CAPE TOWN a week later Barnaby St Clair was looking at a picture in the *Cape Times* of Jim Bowman, the man from whom he had stolen ten pounds and an expensive lunch. He smiled to himself with the recollection of a job well done. Every morning in the Mount Nelson Hotel with the early morning tea came a copy of the local newspaper. Barnaby had picked up the paper with nothing else to do. The next day he was due to go on board the *SS King Emperor* and sail back to England. In his pocket was even less money than when he arrived at the port of Lorenzo Marques in Portuguese East Africa, from Egypt where his army career had come to an end.

Tina Pringle had stayed in Johannesburg with her brother. Barnaby was twenty-three years old, trained for nothing other than war and would be penniless when he arrived at London docks. Unless he found a way of making money, he was well and truly on the skids. Not even Granny Forrester could lend him money. She was dead. Financially, so was his father.

He had last been in England in 1914 having aborted his second year at Royal Military College, to go straight to war. Since arriving in Africa he had lived on his wits for over a year and knew it was time to get out. Albert Pringle, whose family had been vassals of the St Clairs for centuries, had called him a sponger and that was the last straw. Not only was the man as common as dirt, he had once been a gentleman's gentleman, a common valet to Jack Merryweather before making a fortune that Barnaby heard started with a whorehouse. Now the man was a member of the Rand Club and effected an upper-class accent. Tina had at least got the accent and manners right but not her brother Albert. The man would have been an embarrassment in London. And there he was with all his money in Johannesburg looking down his nose at the Honourable Barnaby St Clair just because he did not have any money. It was a disgrace. The man could at least have put him on the payroll and given him a salary to fit his position as an English gentleman. Which had been Barnaby's whole idea of coming to Africa in the first place. He was going to use his childhood friendship with Tina, a friendship of young children where rank did not matter, to find himself an easy billet commensurate with his title. The letters they wrote to each other during the war, Tina's mostly illiterate until Miss Pinforth had taken to giving her an education, were nostalgic for the innocence of their youth. Men alone in war conjure pictures of women. Men wrote things in letters they would never say to a girl's face. The idea of marrying Tina Pringle had never entered his mind. She came from the lower classes. That was that. A fling, an affair and later on maybe, he might have made her his mistress. Never a wife. Mingling the St Clair and Pringle blood was laughable.

Over the years of intermittent letter writing he read of the rise and rise of Albert Pringle, rand baron. From owning a small gold mine to making boat-loads of ammunition for the Allied war effort. By living with the man in his Parktown home, Barnaby had thought he was doing him a favour. Adding some tone to the place. Giving him a name to drop in the Rand Club. In the end he had had to come right out and ask Albert Pringle for a directorship of Serendipity Mining and Explosives Company. To Barnaby's horror, which quickly turned to rage, the man had laughed in his face.

"My dear chap. What do you know about business? Every one of my co-directors, not the least my wife and partner in business as well as life, give something valuable in return to the company. You have to earn a directorship in Johannesburg. Not just be given one. Start at the bottom. I could maybe find you something as a clerk but you'd then be on your own. Company clerks, however senior, don't live with the two major shareholders of the company. Goodness I'd have thought you of all people would understand such a position. Even if you did marry Tina."

"Whoever said anything about marrying Tina?"

"You are a guest in my house, Barnaby. You have been here nine months. I suggest you go and look for something to do with your life."

"I'll go to Rhodesia. The British Africa company are offering Crown land farms, company farms, to British officers."

"Now that does sound like a good idea. You always did like the country."

"I'm sure Tina will come with me."

"You just said you did not wish to marry my sister."

"We don't have to be married to travel together."

"I wish you luck. I will speak to my sister."

"She is over twenty-one."

"If she goes with you, Barnaby, there will be none of my money going with her."

"We are not incapable."

"I never said you were. Merely illiterate in the art of business."

"One day I'll show you Albert Pringle."

"I sincerely hope you do."

WHEN BARNABY put down the *Cape Times* after reading Simon Haller's exaggerated account of Jim Bowman's war record he could still hear the sarcasm in Albert Pringle's voice.

Barnaby had lasted three whole days on his return to Johannesburg from Rhodesia.

"You're a sponger, St Clair. You want money but you don't want to work. You have to work with your hands or your head to create wealth. Clever talk and sleight of hand don't count for work. You borrow money, I hear, without the intention of ever returning the loan. That is stealing. Throughout my life I have always had respect for your family. I still do. For you I have none. This time my sister will not be joining you on your next journey. Here is a single ticket to England. On the train. Two nights at the Mount Nelson. First-class inner cabin on the *SS King Emperor*. An old but splendid ship. I sailed out third class when I came to Africa as a manservant."

"I'll be back."

"Bad pennies always do have a habit of turning up again... Please give my regards to Lord St Clair and your mother. If you should take the time out to see my parents give them my love. They were both very fond of you when you were a small boy."

"Where is Tina?"

"She has gone down to Natal with my wife. Sallie and I keep a house on the coast."

"You are a bastard."

"No. No I'm not. I was born in wedlock. As shall happen to Tina's children."

"And you never even fought in the war. You made your money from war. I even hear from whores further back."

"All that is true. I even thought of going back and joining up to be killed like my brothers. Instead I made munitions to fight the war. None of that changes anything. Now, if you'll be so kind, Bill Hardcastle will drive you and your luggage to the railway station. Your train leaves in three hours. You will have to wait on the platform. Have a good voyage... Now one more thing. Please tell your brother Robert both Sallie and I enjoyed *Keeper of the Legend*. It's a great legend, Barnaby. The St Clair legend. Don't you be any part of destroying it."

"I wish I had died in the war."

"But you didn't. Do something with your life. It may be an old cliché but it is still the only one we ever get on this earth."

Sitting in the bay window of his room in the Mount Nelson Hotel, Barnaby looked again at the picture of Jim Bowman in the newspaper and began to cry, not sure if he was crying for Tina, himself or his lost honour.

Half an hour later when he had stopped feeling sorry for himself he thought of Merlin. There was always his brother Merlin who had bought shares in Vickers Armstrong at the start of the war with borrowed money and sold them before the war ended. Merlin was the man to go to. They had been friends before the war. Brothers and friends.

By the time he walked up the gangplank of the *SS King Emperor* he was feeling like his old self. The cabin did not have a porthole, but it was in first class. He would tell them he booked too late. His clothes were good and his title would appear in the passenger list. Albert Pringle had been too well trained by Jack Merryweather. He would have automatically given the shipping line his title. He briefly wondered if any rich widows were sailing back to England. Maybe even he could make money out of the war. There was Albert Pringle's ammunition for the big guns. And the machine guns of Vickers Armstrong that had made Merlin his fortune. To his surprise he caught a picture of Tina Pringle in his mind's eye and almost lost his footing on the wooden gangplank. The idea of someone else touching her body made his stomach boil and his mouth go dry. Barnaby St Clair was jealous. Violently jealous.

THE BOAT SAILED out of Cape Town harbour towards a storm. In the lee of Table Mountain everything was quiet in the harbour though the line of the 'southeaster' ripping the sea was clearly visible from the deck of the *SS King Emperor*. A violent storm in the Cape at the end of August was quite normal but not the wind coming from the south-east. The captain's welcoming cocktail party had been cancelled and Barnaby had wondered why they had not stayed in port. There was a sprinkling of old dowagers on board who could easily break a limb if they fell.

The boat sailed to the east of Robben Island. The captain was apologetic over the loudspeaker saying storms around the Cape were normal for the time of year and that once they were past Walvis Bay, they would be sailing into spring.

Barnaby's first meal in the dining room was lonely. They had seated him at the captain's table. His rank had appeared in full in the passenger list, Captain the Honourable Barnaby St Clair. It always happened which he liked. He and the captain of the ship were the only two sitting down to dinner. An Indian army colonel on his way home from leave had tried his luck and had gone quickly. Barnaby had never been seasick and thanked his luck. They were seated at opposite ends of the white cloth table from which almost everything had been removed. The flower vases splendidly full of the first Namaqualand daisies were somehow attached to the table and leaned precariously with the roll and pitch of the ship. The lurching steward served them a Malay curry. Barnaby's plate moved on the tablecloth with the lurch of the boat. With all the concentration on the food in front of them there was no chance of a conversation.

When Barnaby first sat down, the captain gave him a hearty smile and introduced himself. It was part of the captain's job to be polite to the passengers. After the captain with a full beard learnt his name, the smile left his face. The captain gave a nod and got on with his food.

Barnaby felt his stomach sink. He had hoped he had left his indiscretions back in Africa. Albert Pringle was a bigger bastard than he thought, passing word to the ship's purser. After the curry, having been warned by the steward against first trying to eat the soup, Barnaby settled for a bowl of trifle.

They sat on alone in silence but it made no sense. If he was to be a pariah on the voyage why had they seated him at the captain's table? Neither of them had ordered wine.

"If we want a drink, St Clair, we'd better go and stand at the bar. You do have good sea legs?" The captain was looking straight at him, challenging him to refuse the suggestion. There were flecks of grey in the man's beard. Barnaby put the captain's age at over fifty. It was going to be the headmaster warning a pupil to behave himself, that what he did elsewhere was his business, but anything he did on board ship he was accountable to the captain. Barnaby knew he was about to get an ugly dressing down.

"Very good, thank you," said Barnaby keeping his mental balance. He would brazen it out. Stare the man down. Unless there was someone on board to whom he owed money, there was no proof. The thought made him nervous, and he looked around.

"A drink then. Had enough of plate chasing."

"Splendid," said Barnaby trying hard to keep his voice normal.

"You do drink, St Clair?"

"Oh yes. Rather fond of these newfangled American cocktails." He had a swift vision of the sidecars served in the tall glasses in the ladies' bar of Meikles Hotel and wanted to bite his tongue. Could the young man be on board ship?

"I was thinking more of a glass of port," said the captain.

"Splendid." Barnaby clenched his jaw.

The captain got up and marched out of the dining room past the thin sprinkling of passengers still able to put up with the pitch and roll of the ship.

Barnaby felt himself back at prep school. Following the headmaster with the long cane held in the headmaster's right hand ready for retribution.

The boat lurched and Barnaby clutched the back of a dining chair. The captain in front of him swayed through the tables as if nothing was moving his ship. The terrible thought struck Barnaby. The captain was going to make him drink all night and tell the bar steward to put the drinks on his bill for which he had two pounds to last him the voyage. The idea of borrowing money while on board swiftly left his mind. He had an idea the guardroom on board a ship was called the brig where they put thieves and miscreants to be handed over to the police when they reached England. He was not sure of the naval name for his jail but it did not matter now.

The bar was almost empty: a young man with a military moustache and the Indian army colonel who mumbled to the captain that drink never upset a stomach, only food. Barnaby suspected the man was already tight. The colonel's face was bright red behind the full set of white whiskers. The captain marched straight to the bar with Barnaby a yard behind him.

"We have a special guest on board tonight," the captain announced. The captain seemed to be talking to the steward in charge of the bar but he spoke loud enough for everyone to hear. There were two officers seated at the table within earshot. Barnaby now knew he was going to be given his warning in public. The captain was going to make a fool of him. He would have to spend the rest of the voyage in his cabin, ashamed to show his face. He had never hated anyone more than Albert Pringle. The man was living proof it was impossible to make a gentleman out of new money even if it was dressed in new clothes.

The blood had drained out of his face. He was as white as a sheet when the captain turned round to confront him in front of everyone at the bar. By breakfast the whole ship would know he was a thief. Then the worst thought struck him like a hammer blow. They would tell his father. They would tell his mother. He would never be able to face his parents again. For the only time since Granny Forrester died he was glad she was dead. It would have killed that wonderful love he had always seen in her eyes to know her grandson had become a thief.

"Make sure, Hopkins, that all the drinks tonight are entered on my card. This is Captain the Honourable Barnaby St Clair and I want you to look after him, Hopkins, while he is in our care."

"But you don't know me, sir," blurted Barnaby.

"Not you sir, personally. But your brother-in-law, Harry Brigandshaw. May I say how terrible we felt at Colonial Shipping when we heard your sister had been shot by that madman Braithwaite. They should hang him, I say. Not keep him in an asylum where he can escape again to kill. Now tell me how you found Harry

Brigandshaw?... Are you all right. You don't look well." A huge smile spread over Barnaby's face. He was not dead after all.

"I don't know. After Lucinda died Harry vanished into the bush to look for his sister's husband. No one has heard from him since. In over a year... How'd you know Harry Brigandshaw?"

"Don't you know his family own this shipping line? When London told us we had a family relation on board, they said to look after you properly. Your bar bill will be paid by the company in respect to your late sister."

"I only met Harry when I was a small boy. He stayed with us when he came down from Oxford with my brother Robert in '07, I think it was. I must have been around about ten years old. I was in Palestine for the duration of the war. Fighting in the desert."

"Did you meet Colonel Lawrence? Lawrence of Arabia the papers call him now."

"Many times," said Barnaby lying. He was quickly recovering. Back on his feet. Confident. The old Barnaby St Clair everyone loved. Mentally he thanked his dead sister for somehow saving his bacon.

By the time he drank the second glass of port with the captain he was laughing. Telling stories of Lawrence of Arabia. The fact Simon Haller had proved he never met Lawrence in person quite forgotten, along with the twenty pounds he owed the editor of the *Rhodesia Herald*. The two ship's officers had got up from the table to join them at the bar. Even the old colonel seemed to be listening to his stories. He was back in his element. Charming. Listening when spoken to. Smiling deep into each person's eyes. The resolution to God he had made following the captain to the bar to never lie again quite forgotten. He was back on his wits. He was back in control. And they were loving him. He was going to make some money out of his forced sea voyage after all.

When he staggered to his cabin, he was not sure if the boat or the drink made him lurch. Just before he fell asleep he thought the room was going round and round. On his face was a smile of deep relief.

"Tina, my darling, I'll be back," he said aloud.

He gave out two alcoholic wind burps through his windpipe and fell asleep.

WHEN BARNABY woke in the morning, the sea was calm, the storm over. He shaved very carefully and went down to breakfast in the first-class dining room. He had on his blue blazer with the right hand tucked just inside the coat over his heart. He had thought of wearing the old Harrovian tie he had stolen in Damascus during the war from a fellow officer and changed his mind. Living on his wits needed cunning. In a bar or a restaurant on land he could walk away from an embarrassing situation. On the ship he could be asked by a genuine old Harrovian the name of his house, and he had no idea of the names of the houses at Harrow School. The dining room was only half full. Some of the passengers were still recovering from seasickness. He was charming to everyone he met. The captain had not come down to breakfast as was his custom, the ship's purser had explained. Only in the evening did the captain sit down with his passengers. Otherwise he ate his meals in his day cabin.

After breakfast he took a constitutional round the deck to see what there was among the passengers. The thought of Tina Pringle had left his mind. It was a new hunt. A new day. A new confidence.

Barnaby was thinking.

DURING BREAKFAST, two of the passengers had been talking about the stock exchange, something Barnaby knew little about.

Without appearing to take his mind off the bacon and eggs he listened to the conversation carefully. They were speaking softly, so he had to strain his ears to catch every word. An old woman was talking loudly about how much better she felt. No one was listening to her. A young girl without one ounce of sex appeal was trying to catch his eye from the other side of the breakfast table. The Indian army colonel looked in the pink. Barnaby was sure the old boy had had a drink or two before his breakfast.

"The trick is to know what's happening before the public," he heard the younger man confide. "You need a friend on the inside. In accounts. With an ear to the ground. I have a chap in one of the merchant banks. A junior, but he is good. Going to be a rich man one day. I pay him for the information. Half his firm's clients are listed on the London Stock Exchange. You can make just as much when you hear a company has some bad results coming out. I just sell a block of shares I don't have knowing I can buy the stock a couple of days later at a cheaper price before I have to give any broker the share certificates. When I tell him to sell, he doesn't know if I'm holding the stock. He only wants to know ten days later when I pass him the share certificates. When I buy, of course, I use another broker. They all know but they don't care. Both of them make their commission. All you need is inside information and you can get rich without starting with a penny. I started with a hundred quid after the war and now look at all this."

The man waved a hand at the first-class dining room and smirked. Barnaby was deeply impressed. When the man changed the subject, Barnaby changed direction and gave the ugly girl his sweetest smile. If she was sitting at the captain's table her parents had to be rich. Barnaby had heard a rude but accurate statement from a drunken fellow officer during the war. He remembered it now as he smiled. 'You don't have to look at the mantelpiece when you poke the fire.' Men without women could be so crude. It made him smile again. The ugly girl blushed right down her skinny neck where Barnaby had a quick look. 'That one doesn't have to tie her tits down.' He quickly put the new picture of Tina Pringle out of his mind and concentrated on the girl at the table. Going back to what was on his plate, he decided not to start a conversation. He would let the captain introduce them at dinner. The captain would use his title and hopefully mention in front of her parents that the family of his brother-in-law owned the shipping line. He would be aristocratic which he was. From a rich family which he wasn't. And doubly eligible. Then he would find out if there was anything in it for him.

BARNABY SMILED thinking back over breakfast. His world was beginning to look much better. He decided to take another turn round the deck.

The storm had been left behind though the sea swells still made the ship pitch and roll. The shore of Africa was a thin line on the starboard side. They were sailing up the Skeleton Coast, a coastline that had torn ships apart from the time of the earliest Portuguese explorers. If Barnaby had been able to see ten miles to the dunes of the Namib Desert, he would have seen the lonely camp of his brother-in-law, Harry Brigandshaw. Barnaby would have seen Harry alone with his horses round the roaring fire, cooking his breakfast.

3

FINDERS, KEEPERS, SEPTEMBER 1920

*H*arry Brigandshaw stood up to his full height to get a better look at the ship passing far out to sea. It made him think of people which made him think of Lucinda and the pain came back again. The single shot that killed his new wife on the train at Salisbury Station had been fired by Mervyn Braithwaite the previous year. After sixteen months he could still hear the shot.

They were going to have a second wedding in Rhodesia. At the church his Uncle Nathanial had built outside Salisbury as a missionary, soon after Harry's father had taken up the farm he called Elephant Walk. Harry had sailed home on the *SS King Emperor*, the family-owned liner. His party on board with him had been his new wife Lucinda, his two brothers-in-law, Robert and Merlin St Clair, and the American Glenn Hamilton who had found the publisher for Robert's *Keeper of the Legend*.

He had tried to run away from himself soon after his wife's murder. He had said he was going to look for Madge's husband Barend Oosthuizen but that had only been part of the truth. The excuse. The reason he gave his mother to run. Lucinda had been pregnant so Braithwaite's revenge had killed two people not one. Other than Jack Merryweather, only he and Lucinda had known she was pregnant. The doctor on board the ship had given them the news that lit Lucinda's face. Harry had not told his mother. Initially he had not told Barend after he followed him into the African bush. Barend had always been a silent companion, and this had suited both of them as they went on towards the Atlantic coast of Africa, alone with their troubled thoughts. Not even once had Harry asked Barend about Barend's marriage to Madge. Or their children left behind on Elephant Walk. Years before, Harry had heard an expression in Afrikaans that translated badly into 'no man knowing what was in another man's head'. He had learnt from life that what people said and what they thought were mostly two different things. Harry hoped it was what made them individuals, having thoughts no one else could see, man's own privacy. It always gave him comfort.

They had not found the source of the diamonds. They had found the rock on the coast where Barend had marked his initials. They had walked the same piece of beach where the seven diamonds had been found. There was nothing but sand and the sea. They were too far north up the coast. The big diamond strike had come just north of Alexander Bay far to the south. After nine months of diligent searching they had wandered off on their separate ways. Before parting, he had then told Barend about Lucinda. The big man had crushed him tight in a bear hug without uttering a word. They had been friends from childhood. The three of them. Harry, Barend and Madge.

"Are you going home?" Harry had asked.

"Some day. Now you look after yourself."

They had been speaking Afrikaans, the language of the Boers. Sometimes they spoke in English. It did not matter.

HIS GEOLOGY degree from Oxford had been worthless in the search. Either a prospector had dropped the seven uncut gem diamonds, or they had been swept ashore from the sea, both highly unlikely in Harry's opinion. Nowhere in the world had diamonds which were heavy been washed ashore in a rough sea.

Amber which was light, came ashore on many an English coast. Diamonds were tumbled down rivers from sources far inland. Gold was washed down rivers. Men panned for gold and sometimes diamonds. Where the rock stood with Barend's initials carved bold and clear in the grey granite, there was not a river mouth for miles. And never had been through all the millenniums. Harry had looked for signs of an old river mouth. Nothing. Just the seven diamonds Barend had brought back to Elephant Walk from his first wanderings while he mulled the hanging death of his father by the British for being a Boer patriot. Harry was Barend's only English friend. Their bonds from childhood had withstood the seeds of hatred soured by the Anglo-Boer War.

Harry watched the liner through the field glasses he had brought back from his own war. They were German and good. His only trophy from a crashed German triplane.

HARRY HAD SHOT the pilot in the air. The plane had drifted down and crash-landed through the fence at the end of a French field, the German slumped in his cockpit. Harry had landed his biplane in the field. The dogfight had broken his squadron into lonely personal flights. With his adversary slumped forward in his seat Harry had looked for his pilots. They were alone, he and the German. His intention had been to help the pilot, but the man was dead. A young, good-looking man with a bullet in his head from a Vickers machine gun. The long leather case that contained the field glasses was on the dead pilot's lap, the case unopened. They had been made by Zeiss. They had the German's initials carved into the leather. 'H B'. French peasants were running over the field. They would steal the field glasses. His own initials on the German case was too much of a coincidence. He had taken the case and left the rest of the plane to the looting Frenchmen. He had stood to attention and saluted the dead pilot. Then he had taken off back down the field to fly back to the temporary airfield of the 33 Squadron and report his kill to the commanding officer, Major Mervyn Braithwaite.

"WELL I'LL be damned," Harry said out loud. "It's the *King Emperor*." Ridiculously, he waved his wide-brimmed hat, soaked black at the rim from sweat, as if they could see him in the sand dune. The fish he had caught earlier in the morning was sizzling in the pan on the open fire. "Well, I'll be damned," he said again as if to convince himself.

Smiling, he wondered who had become the new captain. Captain Hosey had been due to retire. Strangely, the knowledge of a friendly crew so near and yet so far made him lonely for the first time. Even his dogs were home on Elephant Walk.

He turned the fish in the pan and stood staring at the ship for a long time. Then he ate his breakfast and fed the horses the fodder he had collected the previous day, the thin patches of long grass between the sand dunes watered by the mist that rolled in from the sea. The roots of the grass were imbedded deep in the sand, white and tubular, and came up when he pulled. The roots were good for the horses even if the animals looked at him with pain in their eyes.

"You want to go home too?" he asked them. "Maybe we should."

The last time he had seen the *SS King Emperor* he had been with Lucinda at the port of Beira. Then they were alive and happy. The three of them. The secret baby that no one knew about except themselves and Jack Merryweather. They had caught the boat train into the interior and their destination, Salisbury, the capital of Southern Rhodesia. The destination that had ended his wife's life when Braithwaite killed her for vengeance. As he had killed Sara Wentworth.

HALF AN HOUR after finishing his breakfast the last smoke from the ship's funnels washed away in the distant wind. He could no longer tell the difference between the black smoke and the receding black clouds of the storm.

"I did love you, Cinda. I did. In the end... We would have had a good life on the farm... You never said what you would call the boy."

Ever since Barend had gone off alone, he had started talking to himself out loud. He hoped Barend had gone home to his family. To Madge and the three children.

Gulls were crying in the storm-free sky as he walked down to the beach to pick the long, brown mussels from the rocks. It was low tide. Harry began to whistle. The ship had told him. He had to get on with his life. He had done enough of mourning. They were dead, and he was alive. Whether Mervyn Braithwaite was mad or sane was irrelevant, he tried to tell himself. Hopefully, this time the British authorities would keep him locked up in the lunatic asylum. If his old commanding officer was sane, then he still had to live with himself.

HIS MIND DRIFTED away from the south-west African coastline and stood alone on the beach thinking back to the first time he had met Sara and Jared Wentworth. Jared was now dead, lost at sea when his ship went down, sunk by German torpedoes in 1917. Jared dying and Sara wanting to tell Harry that he had died, had started the events that killed her and Lucinda St Clair, the girl who eventually had been Harry's wife for just a few weeks.

The Wentworths, brother and sister, had taken an African safari before Sara was going to be made to marry Mervyn Braithwaite. For his part, Jared was going to be forced to settle down in the City of London as a stockbroker.

They had all met in the African bush by chance. It had been 1907. Harry and Robert St Clair were back from Oxford but Harry was forced to travel back home to Rhodesia on hearing of the death of his father, Sebastian Brigandshaw. Travelling with Harry on the SS King Emperor, Robert and Harry had made friends with Jack Merryweather and Jack was subsequently invited to Elephant Walk.

Harry and Robert had known Mervyn Braithwaite at Oxford. When Sara had mentioned her engagement to Mervyn Braithwaite, they had both exclaimed 'FISHY BRAITHWAITE' at the same time. The man had a face like a codfish, something he had been tormented with since a boy at prep school. Mervyn's family were rich. The senior Wentworths thought wealth a better reason for marriage than love.

Mervyn Braithwaite was besotted by Sara with the long red brown hair that came down to her waist. The brother and sister had dallied on Elephant Walk longer than they should have done, putting off their destiny dictated by their parents.

Through the years, Jared and Harry intermittently wrote to each other. Jared's letters always mentioned Sara. Always mentioned Sara was still not married to Mervyn Braithwaite... As he found out later to his cost, Sara was as besotted with Harry as Mervyn was with Sara.

Seven years of being put off by a fiancée should have ended the engagement. A rich woman can look like a horse and get married. Rich men thought they could have what they wanted. The possession of money was the god of most people on earth.

All the time Mervyn Braithwaite had the name Harry Brigandshaw dropped into his ear even though Harry's letters were not written to Sara but Jared. The idea of a great African romance had stayed vividly alive in Sara's mind all unknown to Harry.

When Mervyn Braithwaite had him posted to 33 Squadron, Harry thought it was because they had known each other up at Oxford, not because Mervyn wanted him killed in combat and out of the way.

Harry had survived as a novice pilot in 1916 despite being left alone in the sky by Braithwaite. His hunting skill and intuition from the African bush had kept him alive and made him an ace pilot.

The war had made Fishy Braithwaite a killer. The war had possibly made him mad. Harry was not so sure about the man being mad. Everyone on the Royal Flying Corps station had known their CO's peculiarity. Whenever he killed a German, he jeered at the dying aeroplane. Yelling at the top of his lungs at the dead pilot as if anyone could hear over the scream of his engine. 'I'm not a wet fish. And you're dead.' They all knew he yelled but only when he killed a German pilot whilst shooting from their own runway at a German low-level attack. It was then they heard the words. Some pilots like Harry vomited after they killed. Mervyn shouted an obscenity. The ground crew and pilots of 33 Squadron said it was the war. When the war was over, they would all return to being normal. Everyone shrugged their collective shoulders. Colonel Braithwaite was the CO. Colonel Braithwaite was a fighter ace. Colonel Braithwaite's tactics in the air battle had kept most of them alive. There was a war on, they said.

Only after Braithwaite went absent without leave did everyone know something terrible was wrong. He faked his own death. As by luck, a ground engineer tried to fly out the plane with Mervyn's number on the fuselage while in a German advance, and the engineer crashed and burnt. When Mervyn killed Sara in London in front of Harry, he would have killed Harry too with the second shot from the pistol but Harry who was on sick leave had hit him with his crutch. Then they said he was mad. Having escaped from Banstead asylum after the war, Braithwaite took a boat to Africa, waited for Harry to return home with the girl the papers said was his bride. And killed Lucinda.

THE TEARS FLOWED down Harry's face as he looked out over the empty sea, the mussels he was going to collect forgotten. After all the horror of the war in France he had thought to have left behind him, the war had found him again as the train pulled in to Salisbury railway station. To the peace of home. To the hope of happiness. The future of a child.

Without thinking any more, Harry sat down on the wet sand and cried.

Only when the lonely call of the gulls brought him back to the lonely beach did he understand. The name they had all called Braithwaite from a child, Fishy, laughing in his squashed face, tormenting him, had hurt more than any German bullet could have done.

"How would you liked to have been jeered at all your life?" he said out loud.

He walked on down to the edge of the sea where it was calm. A buttress of rock swept out and round, making the sea calm in the small cove. The rock buttress was wet and black, jagged. The rock had fought with the sea and errant ships for thousands of years. Under the lee of the ten-foot high rock, the mussels were growing. They were longer than his hand. Harry bent down to pull off enough for his lunch. He was going to eat them raw, tasting the salt from the seawater. He could hear the boom of the sea. The swell crashing the other side of the rock wall. Sea spray came over and drenched him as he worked.

The sun slanted into the pool below the dripping wet mussels that clung to the rocks. A sharp reflection from deep down in the pool caught his eye. With his right hand he swept aside the froth on the surface of the pool, left behind by the angry sea swirling round the buttress. Then he put his hand into the water and pulled out the small rock that had been reflecting the mid-morning sun. The sides were smooth like cut crystal. The water ran off from the stone that sat looking at him from the palm of his right hand.

Harry began to laugh. With a cluster of mussels in his left hand and the rock in his other, he turned his back on the sea and walked out of the pool and ran up the beach. The gulls flew away in alarm. Then he stopped. Turned round and looked out over the vast, lonely expanse of the South Atlantic ocean.

"The diamond pipe is out to sea, you fool. That's where they are. Deep in the ocean. Only a freak storm brings them up on the beach. Just the odd one."

The thought that many more might be buried deep in the sand never entered his head. What he had in his hand was worth a fortune. The small rock covered most of the palm of his hand. Like the oysters dislodged by a rough sea it was big enough for the waves to tumble up the beach and round the buttress into the pool. Only a diamond cutter would determine the true value of the gemstones that would fall from the rock in his hand. If he took the rock to Amsterdam, to the diamond cutters, he would be rich for the rest of his life. Slowly, Harry walked back to his horses, to the stallion he rode and the mare who carried his pack. They watched him with big, wet brown eyes, soft as velvet. They had been his only companions for months. Despite his sorrow he had been happy, alone in the wilderness. The rock in his hand would make no difference. It could even take away the peace he had found on the shores of the Skeleton Coast. For a moment he had the urge to run back to the sea and throw the rock as far out as possible. Elephant Walk was more than he needed to provide his food and shelter. Only a good woman would want to live with him on the farm. Too much money attracted the wrong type of woman. A gold-digger would never be content to live on an African farm.

He was going to marry again as he was going to have children. He owed that to his ancestors. For their struggle to survive. They had not given up. Not one of them. Or he would not be standing on the beach… He stroked the stallion's head, and the mare moved up for her share of the attention.

"You don't have to sell it. You don't even have to tell anyone. In the history of every family there has always been a rainy day."

Slowly and carefully, Harry packed his belongings onto the packhorse. He was going home to Elephant Walk. To Madge and hopefully Barend. To his mother and grandfather. He would make himself forget the rock in his saddlebag and get on with his life.

He was thirty-five years old. When he looked in the sea pool's reflections he was slim. Nearly six feet tall with long hair that fell down his back under the wide-brimmed hat. The exposed parts of his body, his face and hands, were burnt the colour of mahogany by the sun. His green eyes, flecked with grey, could count a herd of buck at two thousand yards. From the horror of war on the Western Front he knew he stared for long periods without seeing anything. Only the same pictures playing out the past in his mind. The other pilots had called it the thousand-yard stare. The stare that only saw the past.

At noon, when the sun was right overhead he began the journey home. He was going to surprise them. He was going to be home for Christmas. It would take three months to navigate his way back into the heart of Africa. To the high plateau of rich grassland watered by many rivers they now called Rhodesia.

If a man could ever be happy then Harry Brigandshaw was happy. The past would always be the past. It was the future he wanted now he was at peace with himself and his ghosts... Or so he hoped.

MERLIN ST CLAIR was a year older than Harry Brigandshaw. At first meeting people found him uncomfortable to be with. Dogs ran away. Cats arched their backs. Women stood transfixed like a rabbit caught in headlights of the new motor cars that were noisily powering themselves further and further afield.

His mother and his siblings had seen the look and called him Merlin after King Arthur's magician. On closer regard, the strange look of the small baby and the grown man was simple. Merlin's eyes were different colours. The right was a soft, clear blue. The left a darker blue, almost black. The first reaction of anything alive that looked into the two eyes staring back was to run away. The twisted smile that came shortly after the shocked recognition did not help either. But it gave Merlin power, and he knew it. Even the Germans on the Western Front were unable to kill him, and they had tried very hard for four years. Merlin was one of the few officers to go right through the war without a scratch. His men said nobody dared kill him, for fear of a terrible retribution. Merlin, smiling was never heard to make a contradiction. Not out loud, anyway, he told himself. Merlin knew perfectly well that no one was immortal.

Over the years the left eye that had started only a little different to the right became darker and darker compared to the soft sky blue of the right eye. Something to do with pigmentation, the doctor told him. Two eyes surgeons had looked and shrugged. There was nothing wrong with his eyesight.

To make the effect more dramatic, Merlin began to affect a monocle over the left eye. The single eyeglass hung round his neck on a red cord. When he wanted to put someone off their stroke, he peered at them with his eyeglass screwed into his left eye socket. The glass in the lens was clear glass though the effect on the stared at was sometimes dramatic. Robert, his younger brother by a year, liked him to stare at elderly ladies holding teacups. To see how many of them rattled their saucers. It became a constant game for Robert though they were careful to try the experiment only when their mother was out of the room. It had worked quite well even before the advent of the monocle.

The strangest thing was the birds. The birds loved Merlin. They were more inclined to fly to him than fly away. By the age of five, he had had robin redbreasts eating from the palm of his hand. His father, Lord St Clair, had said the birds knew something nobody else did, but he never said what.

His flat in Park Lane overlooked London's Hyde Park which he liked to walk in when it was not raining. His clothes were made by a tailor in Savile Row and fitted him perfectly. The cravats were always his old school or his old regiment the Dorset Fusiliers that had been affiliated with his family for two hundred and forty years.

His old flat in the Barbican had been given up towards the end of the war, a couple of years after Esther went off and married a corporal who soon after got himself killed. Esther had been the barmaid at the Running Horses at Mickelham where he had found her on a walking holiday in the Surrey countryside. He still gave her a small allowance but had no idea where she lived. Once his trust in Esther had been broken, there was no going back. She had said a week before running off with the corporal that he had no intention of ever marrying her which was perfectly true.

Ever since he had employed a manservant to look after his needs. That was after he sold his main block of Vickers Armstrong shares shortly before the Americans came into the war spelling the end of hostilities. The war had gone on into 1918, his shares had risen further but it did not matter. Afterwards he said greed was how people lost money on the stock exchange. 'When you see a good profit, sell, old boy. It worked for me. Look at the price of Vickers shares now. They can't even give away Vickers machine guns to the revolutionaries in South America.'

With some of what he thought of as his ill-gotten gains he had sent in the best firm of builders to repair Purbeck Manor, the family home of the St Clairs for centuries. When the builders left, he bought for his father a pedigree herd of Sussex cows and a bull that even chased Merlin over the fence. That happened just before Christmas 1918. Then he had gone off to Africa with Robert, Lucinda, Harry and the American Glenn Hamilton on what was meant to have been his safari.

He was a confirmed bachelor with a predilection for girls in the theatre which was why he had taken his flat in Park Lane on a sixty-year lease, thinking that should be enough to last him. London's West End theatres were close at hand. His one rule was no girl stayed overnight. That had been the start of the problem with Esther. In those days he had no money to send her home in a taxi all the way down south to Mickelham. She had arrived and stayed. Cooked his food and cleaned his flat. Esther had been plain comfortable. Being away at the Front most of the war had kept the flame of lust burning for both of them. Merlin believed in lust which he told his male friends should never be muddled with love. So far Merlin had never been in love and wondered if he ever would be. To marry just for lust he found quite ridiculous. After two years it was all expended and then what did you do for the rest of your lives? Too many people tried to make up love that was going to last the rest of their lives. In Merlin's mind, romantic nonsense could never take the place of reality. Love was rare. Few knew it.

Breakfast was always at nine o'clock. Exactly nine o'clock. The ritual was repeated every day. The newspapers were presented to him by Smithers, the man who looked after him. Always on the same silver tray with the same clear coat of arms that Merlin had commissioned from Asprey's. All the morning newspapers. It amused him to read reports that purported to be about the same subject. How different they looked depending on the newspaper's politics. Anything important, he read in all the papers to find a balanced view. It was the only way he could form his own opinion.

He kept the *Daily Examiner* until last as it made him laugh. Not that what it said was not true very often. It was always a sensational headline. A quick, sure-fire encapsulation of yesterday's events. If two men heckled the Prime Minister in the Commons, the *Examiner* shouted 'Parliament in Chaos'. They were currently having a heyday with the rights of all women to vote from the age of twenty-one, instead of only married women from the age of thirty, which Merlin interpreted as women bought the *Daily Examiner* and not only those who were married and mature.

He turned over the first and second pages to get away from the previous day's social politics. Then an article caught his eye. A soldier living in Africa, a war hero who had won the Military Medal and had been made an officer in the field, was looking for his childhood sweetheart or rather the newspaper was looking for the girl. The headline had caught his eye. '£25 for Anyone Finding War Hero's Sweetheart'. Reading the short article brought back the war and the terrible noise. The constant bombardment with the silence at the end feared more than the incoming shells. After the silence of the big guns often came the German attack bringing his machine-gun nests into action. It was the job of his unit to stop the German infantry reaching the British trench.

Merlin put down the *Daily Examiner* on the white linen cloth of his breakfast table. The table was comfortably situated in the nook that looked out over Hyde Park. He wondered if the war would ever leave his head. He hoped the man the paper called Jim Bowman found his girl. He hoped they would be in love. Maybe they would be the lucky ones.

He was still staring at the ceiling when Smithers put the plate of eggs, bacon, one sausage, one kidney and one spoonful of kedgeree in front of him, the exact same breakfast he ate every morning.

"You think I'm getting into a rut, Smithers?"

What Merlin most liked about Smithers was his habit of never replying when there was nothing to say.

Smithers poured tea into the large breakfast cup and added the milk last. Merlin never took sugar in his tea. The triangular pieces of toast with the crusts cut off rested in the silver toast rack at his right elbow.

Merlin buttered himself a piece of toast and began to eat his breakfast.

He had not returned to Cornell, Brooke and Bradley at the end of the war, the firm of Lloyd's insurance brokers who had been his employer before the outbreak of hostilities with Germany. He had nothing of importance to do until the evening when a new musical was opening at Drury Lane. With his money safely invested in British government gilt-edged stock his income would be sufficient for the rest of his life. He had chanced his arm once in the share market and made his fortune. He had quite enough money for his tastes. He never understood his friends who had enough but always wanted more.

When he was a little bored, he never admitted it to himself. Which was why he kept strictly to his daily routine. With a routine there always was something he had to do. It made his trivial life seem more important than it was.

When the front doorbell rang he was standing looking out over the park with his third and last cup of tea held in both hands. In ten minutes he would take his coat, hat and cane from the stand at the front door and go out for his constitutional in the park. He was surprised and annoyed at the doorbell ringing. No one had been invited and all his friends knew perfectly well not to call on him unless they were invited. It was the front door, he knew by the ring, and not the smaller door into the kitchen that was used by tradesmen. Merlin waited frozen for Smithers to answer the summons. Never, ever, had he opened his own front door to its ring.

"Can I help you, sir?" he could hear Smithers's voice from the front door.

"Is this the home of the Honourable Merlin St Clair?"

"Indeed it is, sir."

Merlin heard the disapproval in Smithers's tone of voice with approval.

"Please tell him Mr Barnaby St Clair wishes to speak with him."

"Barnaby. BARNABY!" shouted Merlin. "Is that you?"

Forgetting his routine and the walk in Hyde Park Merlin put down his teacup, spilling tea into the saucer in his haste.

"Come in, dear boy, come in. Smithers, it's my brother. You were in Palestine. Then Africa. How long have you been in England? Goodness, what a lovely surprise."

They had met in the corridor that separated two bedrooms from the dining room and the kitchen. Merlin did not notice the stack of suitcases at the front door or the cab driver waiting to be paid.

"This morning, Merlin. London docks. Didn't you once sail on the *King Emperor*?"

"Yes, yes. The first time it must have been five years ago, the second when Lucinda died. I was on home leave. 1915. Then you were sent out to the Middle East, and we never saw you again. Didn't you sail straight from Cairo to Africa? Come in. Come in. Let me have a good look at you. You were just a boy. Only shaved twice a week, I remember. The favourite son returns. You are, you know. Granny Forrester always said you were the best of the bunch... Who's that man at the door? What are those cases?"

"They're mine, Merlin. As I said, straight from the dock. I say, can you pay the cab driver? Jolly silly, but I don't have any money."

"Where are you staying in London?"

"Well, I rather hoped with you Merlin."

"Of course. Come in. Have a sherry or is that too early? It's after breakfast. Smithers, give that chap some money and put the cases in the spare bedroom. My, but you've changed. You're a man. Filled out. Why didn't you write to me, you scoundrel? Or did you? Yes, I rather think you did once. Just before the war was over."

"I'd like a glass of sherry."

"So we shall then. When are you going down to Dorset?"

"Well, that depends. Met a charming girl on the boat."

"You old rascal. Are you going to marry her?... Smithers. Please hurry up and close the front door. There is a draft going through the flat. It's now the end of September, you know. Bring me the sherry decanter and two glasses. Some biscuits... Come on, Barnaby. I just finished my breakfast."

"You don't work in insurance any more?"

"No I don't..."

Merlin fixed the monocle in his left eye to give himself time to think. The boy who was now a man had not been able to look him in the eye. The cuffs of his shirt were slightly frayed and for some reason his brother was wearing an old Harrovian tie. All the boys had gone to Radley, a small, less expensive public school that had given their father a discount for sending them four boys. Richard, the eldest had never gone to school. There had been something very wrong with his mind from birth. Merlin always thought Richard dying young was a blessing in disguise.

"What's going on Barnaby? You never went to Harrow."

"Oh, my God!"

To impress the girl's father, the girl with the scrawny neck from the captain's table, he had worn the tie the last day at breakfast. Hoping the father would invite him for a visit. He had intended to take it off when he left the ship. But Barnaby was more afraid of taking a taxi without being able to pay the fare and not knowing if Merlin was at home to receive him. The fear had made him forget. To add to his woes when they came off the boat, the girl who was still as ugly as sin had cut him dead. The damn girl had seen through him all the time. Had been polite while they were all bound to the captain's table on board ship.

He put his hand up to his neck and blushed. Something he had not done since he was ten years old. He had never before seen his brother wear a monocle and it frightened him. He was sure the left eye had not been that dark in 1915.

"What's wrong with your left eye?" he asked to cover his embarrassment.

"Nothing except the colour... Come in!" he called to Smithers who had knocked on the door. "Please bring me the whisky decanter instead, Smithers."

They waited in silence, Merlin looking out of the window.

"You're broke, aren't you?" he said into the silence.

"Yes I am."

"Well, we'll just have to do something about that."

"I hoped you'd say that."

"Probably not in the way you wanted. There will be no gifts. You will work. And take off that damn tie. I don't like confidence tricksters at the best of time. And certainly not in the family. You could always get your way as a boy. I watched you and hoped you would grow out of it. You always knew how to get round people but it was always calculated. You have the charm all right. Charm can be very useful in life. When it is genuine. You had better start from when you left the army. And don't lie. I can see right through lies."

"What are you going to do?"

"Take you home to Dorset. Leave you at home. Then I will think. You don't have any skills other than the army?"

"None."

"Can you go back into the army? Back to Sandhurst?"

"I'm too old."

"And they probably won't have you."

"No they won't."

"What did you do?"

"Borrowed some money from the mess funds in Cairo. I was in charge of them."

"Stole some money. Why you were demobbed so quickly?"

"Something like that… Why don't you give me a hundred pounds and I'll get out of your way?"

"What will you do?"

"I have an idea. There were some chaps on the boat. Stock exchange types."

"Stockbrokers?"

"No, investors. They both gave me their cards."

"Why don't you go back to Africa?"

"I can't."

"Burnt your boat there too? Who paid your passage home?"

"Albert Pringle, Tina's brother."

"Oh, my God! Can this get worse?"

"I hope not. Maybe five hundred pounds will give me a better start."

"Buy yourself some new shirts." He was being hoodwinked, but he did not care.

"If you don't mind I'll skip the drink. I never drink during the day." Barnaby said sarcastically.

"What did you do to Tina Pringle?"

"Nothing. And that's the absolute truth."

"Thank God for small mercies."

"So we're not going to Purbeck Manor?"

"No, not today, not after what's been said. Why don't you try America? They love a title. Even an Honourable."

"Maybe. Thank you, Merlin. I knew I could rely on you."

"There's always one in every family."

"Yes, I rather think there is. Five hundred pounds and you won't see me again."

"Like hell."

Barnaby waited patiently for his brother to write out the cheque.

"You can make it out to 'cash'. I don't have a bank account."

With a small satisfied smile on his face, Barnaby put the cheque in his pocket and turned for the sitting room door.

"Smithers can let me out. I'll send for my suitcases… And Merlin, don't you think it a little early to start drinking? Just after breakfast! Really!"

JENNY MERRYL'S family had been shrimp fishermen in Neston for generations. The shrimp boats lay on their sides on the mudflats of the River Dee down by Parkgate when the tide went out. The fine-mesh pots hung out to dry next to the houses. No one had ever got rich, and no one had starved. A few moved across the Wirral to Liverpool to make a better life so they thought. Some, like Jenny Merryl, went further afield and were quickly forgotten.

NEVER ONCE HAD anyone heard of a cod fisherman changing to shrimp or a shrimp man to deep-sea fishing. They were tough, independent and loyal to each other. The men were men among men. The women fed, cleaned and looked after the broods of children. Nonsense was sorted out with a clout round the head. Words were sparse and family honour as valuable as the catch that came in from the sea. They were private people who lived in the small stone cottages that littered the shore of the estuary in rows.

Had it not been for the parish vicar, no one would ever have heard of the reward in the *Daily Examiner* for finding Jenny Merryl. The word spread like wildfire from cottage to cottage. Twenty-five pounds would buy a small boat.

"Do we know where the little cow went to?" said her mother who lived next door but three to Mrs Bowman, Jim Bowman's mother.

"She never but looked at 'im," said Jenny's brother, Len.

"Don't bloody care. All they want's our Jenny... You think that Jim Bowman's rich?"

"Some say the boy had fifty pounds when he came out of the army."

"Fifty pounds! Don't be daft. Bloody corporal 'e was."

"Not at the end... What's all palaver about? Made 'im an officer, they did. Got a medal so vicar says."

"What's the vicar know?"

"More than us, Mum."

"You say they want a photograph of our Jenny?"

"Maybe we tell 'em who we are. Vicar can write the newspaper. You think they'll like our photo in paper? Better than nothin'. Might give us a bob or two. You think our Jenny will be famous when they find 'er? Hero, vicar says. Jim Bowman. Gave me a clout once, so I clouted 'im back. Made 'is bloody nose bleed. Serve 'im right. Must have been ten or eleven. Now he's famous. Whatever next. You think Jenny will write? She can write, you know. How she got the job as nurse in the war. Well, I never. Our Jenny famous."

"Shut up, Len Merryl, or I'll give you a clout."

"I'm goin' down the Pig and Whistle. Someone might buy me a drink now I'm Jenny Merryl's brother what's in the paper."

"Why they want to buy you a drink?"

"Because my sister's famous. Everyone likes to be associated with the famous. Somethin' to talk about."

"You're bloody daft... What we want's that twenty-five pounds. Best you go down to London, Len. Look for Jenny. First she went to see our Cousin Mildred. One that got herself pregnant. Little bugger must be two years old by now."

"Little bastard you mean... You goin' to lend me the train fare, Mum"

"Might do. Then you'll owe me that twenty-five pound less a quid for your trouble."

"That's daylight bloody robbery."

"She's my daughter."

"First, I'm goin' to the pub."

Dolly Merryl watched her son put on his overcoat. The days were drawing in. The feel of winter was in the autumn sun. A cold wind came into the kitchen parlour when Len went out the door. She was thinking. Most times she only thought as far as her next job. Five sons and Jenny was what she had to show for it. Arms the size of hams from manual work. A blotched red face. Chilblains on her toes and fingers. Hair going streaky grey. Nails broken. Feet swollen from standing all day. She was an old hag when she looked in the cracked old mirror someone had given her grandmother. Thrown out of some fancy house. Grandma bringing it home like the first prize she had ever won in her life. By then, Grandma had no teeth, only gums. She died soon after. She was fifty-two years old. Dolly remembered, looking out of the window.

The tide was out. The mudflats stretched into Wales, black and cold, waiting for the sea to come back and cover its sadness. The shrimp boats were all out waiting for the tide to come in. The two boys would be hungry when they came back in the dark and she should get on with the cooking. Instead, she was thinking. Len would put his half in a shrimp boat. The three boys would work together. Got on with each other without fighting. There would be more than potatoes and onions on the table. Bread with no butter. It filled their bellies but after fishing, pulling in the heavy nets, they deserved a good meal when they came home tired to the marrow of their bones. In her mind's eye she could see a nice boat with nice new nets and shrimp aplenty.

The Welsh coast was pretty with the green. Even the mud had a strange prettiness of its own with the yellow late sun showing pockmarks where air blew holes in the surface coming up from down below, air pockets caught by the rush of the sea when it came in with the morning tide. She was dreaming and standing and doing nothing for a rare moment in her life. Jenny by now would have collected the twenty-five pounds for herself and spent it on fancy clothes. They had never got on. She remembered. Jenny had always been different. Never wanting to be a shrimp fisherman's wife like the rest of them… The best she could hope for was a postal order for a few shillings and a letter. She hoped Jenny was all right. Doing well. Found herself a bloke.

Len had brought the dirty washing for her to do from the vicar's wife along with the strange tale of Jim Bowman. A boy like the rest of them, gone off to war and lived, not like her older boys and what was the thanks. The older boys and Da. Blown to bloody pieces, two of them. Da shot dead in '15 and she told him not to volunteer… Dreams. She should stop the dreams and peel the potatoes. She had some stock from the fish bones to pour in the mess. Some greens from the small fenced garden, salted by the wind from the sea, stunting everything that tried to grow… She needed another load of horse manure from the farm back of Neston.

She was pretty once like Jenny. Her mind wandered away and went off into the past.

FRED MERRYL HAD been a lovely young boy that summer before the Boer War started when Queen Victoria sat on the throne of England. Not a big man like some of the others, but beautiful. When the beautiful young boy looked into her soul through her eyes, she drowned in his beauty. He promised her a boat would soon be his own. He promised her eternal love. Eternal devotion. Always promises that he meant at the time he wanted her body. She could see that now. She smiled. Young and in love. One true year before the babies came and the drudgery. Never the boat of his own. Never the eternal love as his soft brown eyes that women loved strayed around the village. He had been unfaithful to her the second year of their marriage. Again and again. They made up, again and again, bringing them the children.

DOLLY BEGAN peeling the pile of potatoes, still thinking back, reminiscing, remembering the good times never the bad. She even smiled to herself alone in the kitchen at the scrubbed white table where the sharp knife took off the thinnest peel from the potatoes. At the beginning a pretty girl was in control. Once the pretty had gone, the women were servants for the men and the children. Some women fought out their frustration by nagging their men and shouting at the children. Which made it worse. Life was hard work and there was never getting away from it she told herself for the umpteenth time.

Dolly finished the potatoes and started on the big onions, making her eyes water. She got up to look out of the window and rest her eyes away from the onions. The tide was coming in flat like a mirror spread on the mud. The sunset red and pink from the sinking sun on the underbelly of the clouds was pictured in the water flooding the wide estuary of the Dee. The hills across in Wales were purple red. Dolly had never been to Wales and wondered why. She had never been out of the counties of Cheshire and Lancashire.

The sails would be up and the boat the older boys worked would be moving into shore. They were good boys. If they had the twenty-five pounds and the boat, her boys could find a wife and start the cycle of life all over again. She hoped their wives would not nag them.

She sat down again at her work and finished the preparation for the family supper. On Sunday, they were going to look for blackberries in the hedgerows behind Neston, along the fields of old farmer Bill. She liked picking blackberries. Liked making jelly in the big preserving pan. She always made enough to last her family through the long winter, the jars of bramble jelly reminders of the summer and the sun. She made up a picnic lunch for all of them when the sun shone and they laughed their way along the lanes. She had the boys if nothing else in life and that was all that mattered to her now.

She was pleased when Len came back after drinking only one beer.

"Everyone's talking about our Jenny."

"I'm glad."

"Jim is in a place called Rhodesia."

"Where the 'ell is that."

"Africa."

"Hope our Jenny don't take idea of goin' Africa?"

"Don't even like Jim Bowman."

"She will if he's rich."

"How you know he's rich?"

"Stands to reason. Why all the fuss? Papers don't fuss over poor people. We're goin' blackberryin' on Sunday."

"Thought I was goin' to London?"

"Wild goose chase. Anyway, I don't have the train fare."

THE NEXT DAY Len Merryl started his odyssey by catching the milk train to Chester. Regardless of what his mother said, he was going to find his sister. He had left his mother a badly written note under the teapot in the parlour. He felt like Dick Whittington off to be Lord Mayor of London, the only book he had ever read, struggling to the end.

He was frightened more than excited. When he got off the train at the old Roman city of Chester, in his pocket were two shillings. In his hand a small bag with a change of clothing.

WHILE LEN was working out how to reach London on two bob, Mrs Bowman, Jim Bowman's mother, was talking over the fence of her narrow piece of garden to Mrs Green next door to hear the startling news that her son Jim was in the paper. Mrs Green had heard over the fence from Mrs Trollop who had heard from Mrs Snell who had been told by Mrs Merryl with the full authority of the vicar that Mrs Bowman's son Jim was a hero. Jenny Merryl was his sweetheart and everyone was looking for Jenny including the vicar and his wife and the newspaper that wanted the picture for the story they were going to print. Mrs Merryl had also informed Mrs Snell over the fence that her Len had gone to London to find her Jenny to get the photograph for the vicar.

Mrs Bowman was still alone in the house as her son and sons-in-law were unloading the cod having come in with the shrimp boats on the eleven o'clock high tide. It was twelve hours after high tide and the boys were still taking cod out of the hold, gutting the fish, packing it into boxes of ice to go on the three o'clock train to Manchester. The deep-sea boat that had sailed three days earlier full of blocked ice had returned with full holds of fish. Only once before had every boat landed a full catch. The boys would be dog-tired but would still go straight to the Pig and Whistle to get drunk. She had sent down food to the boat twice since they landed.

"Didn't know my Jim was walkin' out with 'er Jenny."

"Don't think they was," said Mrs Green. "You never know with youngsters these days. It was the war. Quite a thing bein' in the paper. Hero, the vicar said. What did your Jim do to be a hero?"

"Never said nothin'. Made 'im an officer, I know that. Never said much my Jim."

"Better read the paper Mrs B. The *Daily Examiner*."

"You know plain well I can't read, Mrs G."

"Go and see the vicar."

"I've a mind to go and see the vicar. Doesn't Mrs Merryl do 'is laundry?"

"'Ow she 'eard... Did I tell you about the reward?"

"What reward?"

"Twenty-five pounds."

"'Ow bloody much?"

"Go and see the vicar Mrs B."

"I've a mind, I 'ave... My son in the paper. Well, I never. No one tells me nothin', Mrs G."

"I told you somethin', didn't I?"

"I'll get my Terry to see the vicar. That's better."

"They'll be drunk for two days. Did you get some of the money?"

"Told the fishmonger not to give 'em more than three bob each... Twenty-five quid, you say. What for?"

"Findin' Jenny Merryl."

"Doesn't Mrs M know where she is?"

"Seems not."

"What's the bloody world comin' to?... You better come round through the fence gate for a nice cup of tea."

They both went into the small house with the small garden. There were ten semi-detached brick houses in the row. All exactly the same. The two women were talking at the same time, neither listening to the other. Mrs Green had her arm in Mrs Bowman's. They were happy with their day.

4

VALLEY OF THE HORSES, OCTOBER 1920

*I*t was the most beautiful country Jim Bowman had ever seen. From the dry, rainless winter came the colours of spring. Not young green on trees; tulips and daffodils in his mother's garden; wild flowers in the woods over Neston. The trees, flat-topped as if pressed down by the African sun, came out in russet brown and russet red, the colours of an English autumn. They had travelled on slowly, day after day, never seeing a living soul.

Two months into their lonely journey, the tops of the distant mountains came out of the moving haze of building heat, the prelude to the rains, the high mountains were blue above the shimmering heat. Colonel Voss brought them to where he was going by using the compass and following the Southern Cross that each clear night gave him due south to let them travel to the east. The Chimanimani range reached to heaven so high above the plateau.

Never once had they travelled more than twenty miles in a day. Hamlet and Othello put on weight, the rich, red of Hamlet's coat shining in the blinding white of the midday sun. King Richard the Lionheart had taken on a whole new look on life and sat between them on the high bench above the horses' rumps, surveying all before him. Except at snakes, predator cats, hyenas and wild dogs, he neither barked nor snarled, waiting patiently for the leftover meat and bones. Then with a full belly lay under the wagon to dream and snuffle through the night.

For Jim it was a time of deep comfort away from the pain. Whether they found the Place of the Legend was now of less importance. He was content, at peace with himself, free of the ravages of war. The days could go on to the end of time as they journeyed through the msasa trees, circling the tall red, peaked anthills, crossing small rivers running through the valleys that wound between the miles of woods and hills, peace on earth with the birds and animals. Even the one terrible sound of man, the gun, failed to frighten the herds of buck, the elephants, the buffalo and the tall, eye-catching heads of the giraffe above the flat-topped trees. Only the birds in the trees burst cover as if they knew something and had seen something, knowing then to fly away.

The days went on and still the great range of high mountains stayed far away like a distance mirage, lying above the haze of the African heat. Sometimes the two men talked, most often they journeyed on in silence, listening to the calling doves or in the day under the pressing heat of the noonday sun, they listened to the sound of silence. The two horses, the two men and the dog.

They had camped for the night next to a small river of pools, barely flowing, waiting for the new rain to rush the water along on the journey to the distant sea. Jim had collected the firewood for the night, enough to keep it burning to the dawn. During the long night they would wake in turn to feed the fire. The horses had gone to graze the new shoots of the grass. Later, Jim would tether them close to the fire. King Richard had gone off sniffing in the bush. Colonel Voss was skinning an impala ram with consummate ease. He seemed to Jim to be enjoying his task, the hunter in his ancestry playing out an old rhythm. The day was cooling at last, the sun blood-reddening the western sky, reflected in the river pools in front of them. Jim watched a fish rise and break the reflection of the clouds in the pool. A pair of warthogs came down to the water from the opposite bank and frolicked in the pool, ugly but beautiful.

Colonel Voss had taken his canvas chair from the wagon and was seated watching the colours of the setting sun with deep satisfaction. The old pipe with the bone carved in the shape of a crocodile's head was being drawn at slow intervals, just enough to keep the tobacco alight. The smell would always stay in Jim's mind. Jim whittled away at a stick that would skewer the venison over the embers of the cooking fire. As the meat roasted on the spit, they would carve the cooked meat on the outside. Near the fire stood an iron pot filled with wild spinach. Colonel Voss rubbed fresh leaves of wild sage into the meat. Jim put the heavy stick through the carcass and hung it over the fire and watched until it was starting to splutter small drops of fat into the hot embers flaring up in flames to singe the meat. Later Jim got up from where he sat against the fallen log watching the meat and went to the wagon. In a second iron pot he mixed the maize meal he had ground from the corn that morning to make the pap. They would eat with their fingers, dipping chunks of cut meat into the pap and then the spinach.

The sun went down suddenly, darkening the bush. The pair of warthogs scurried away into the night. Jim turned the meat on the spit and placed the pot of pap under the spit where some of the fat would drip into the pot. Then he sat down again with his back to the log. He could make out the features of the old man in the last glow of the sunset.

"Did you really fight with Chinese Gordon?"

"General Gordon? Yes, I think so. At my age so many things blend together. The memory and the story. I don't think it matters. Yes, I think so... Did we really score that hundred runs at school or was it only thirty? A good score for a young boy. At the time a fine, fine innings. Later told by an older man and not a boy, thirty would sound a paltry affair. So we adjust, I think. To gain the same impact on our listeners. In truth a lie but right. Yes, I fought with Gordon of Khartoum though it might have been on the River Nile and not the Yangtze. He rescued the Chinese emperor... You won't remember all your battles, dear boy."

"Oh yes, I will."

"They'll look very different in forty years."

"They are burnt on my mind."

"So thought I, dear boy. By the time you tell your grandchildren there will be more than one German on the end of your bayonet. It won't change your bravery, or your fear."

"So we all embellish our deeds?"

"I rather think so. Human nature. Sam's rather a dull boy so we have to do something about it. Make a life seem worth the living. You can't tell a grandson about watching that sunset. Though you should. You'll tell how the lions' roar in the night and King Richard shivers under the wagon and the horses snicker with fear. Then you'll have him listening. But not about a sunset... You'll remember me for that later on and I shall be alive again in your memory. I thank you in expectation. My word. I'll be well over a hundred."

Jim heard the old man chuckle with gleeful anticipation of the memory. A patch of sky turned from duck-blue to black as he watched the last of the sun now sink below the horizon.

"Have you ever been married, sir?"

"Why this 'sir', all of a sudden?"

"The question is impertinent from a man of my youth."

"Ah, youth. Someone said youth was wasted on the young. Oscar Wilde, I think. Or Bernard Shaw... I don't think so. Not everyone. Depends what you do."

"Were you married? Do you have children?"

"Are you the surrogate son? All that kind of thing? Yes, you are in a way. I prefer youth to old men. They have a future. Old men just sit and suck on a pipe."

Only the fire gave them light. Jim got up again to tether the horses. Hamlet and Othello had come back with the fading light. King Richard the Lionheart was back sprawled near the fire watching the meat. In the pool, now dark, an elephant was squirting water over its head. Jim could tell by the echo of the falling water off the elephant's back... The crickets were singing in a low key, dulled by the heat of the day, woken by the cool at the beginning of the night.

"She was very beautiful. And she died. She gave me a son. He died. I'm sure. More sure than I am of General Gordon."

"Did you love her?"

"I'm not sure."

"Where did you come from?"

"Two months and now the questions! Really, Jim."

"I've told you everything."

"There wasn't much to tell."

"Will we find the Place of the Legend in the mountains?"

"Probably not. You needed a rest. The soft balm of the African bush... So did I."

"So we're on a wild goose chase."

"Maybe. Maybe not. Does it matter?"

"Not really."

"Now you have buried something. The times we accomplished nothing are also important."

"Have we accomplished nothing?"

"You can only tell yourself that. Did that man with your ten pounds accomplish anything? I think so. Did I with your ten pounds, Jim?"

"Oh yes."

"Then you see what I mean."

"Did you ever marry again?"

"No, but I loved another woman deeply. We don't write to each other, but we have a daughter."

"Do you write to your daughter?"

"No."

"I'm sorry."

"So am I, Jim. So am I."

"How old is she?"

"About your age. Older, I think. Though I mostly try not to think of her. It's not easy for a father to think of his daughter without being able to give her protection."

"Why not, sir?"

"There is that 'sir' again. Look at me. I can't protect myself. Look for young immigrants to give me a grubstake. Do you think a daughter would be proud of a man like this?"

"There's more to being something in life than money. You told me that."

"Well it's not true in society. Here, yes, when wealth is a gun and a pair of horses. You won't get far in England with a gun and a pair of horses. People are very cruel to the poor. They despise them. A daughter would not like that. They want to be proud of their fathers. The truth can be as cruel as poverty… And you'd better turn the spit… With the fire so low I can see three layers of stars through the branches of the trees… Are you going to marry your Jenny Merryl?"

"She doesn't even know I exist."

"A young man liking a young girl never gets unnoticed."

"You DON'T think that newsman will talk of Jenny?" Jim said in alarm.

"You said they never printed the article. I hear publishers buy books and never publish them. Happened to Jane Austen. When she wanted the book back for another publisher, she had to buy it back."

"You think I should return the money?"

"Only if you want to give the story to someone else."

"Do you think she noticed me?"

"Oh, yes."

Jim got up, cut a slice of meat with his hunting knife, waited for it to cool and chewed.

"It's the wild sage and the salt you rubbed on. Marvellous… Will you dine, Colonel Voss?"

"I shall."

"Are you really a colonel?"

"Are we back on that tack? What difference does it make?"

"It might to your daughter."

"That's unkind."

"What's her name?"

"Justine."

"That rings with the truth."

Jim cut thin slices of the meat onto a plate. Red blood oozed from the uncooked meat closer to the bone. He pulled off the pot of spinach and pap and sat down with the venison at the colonel's feet. Pulling the end of his log around he sat down in the silence.

"I'm sorry, sir."

"Old wounds still hurt... Oh, how they hurt."

Jim had turned the spit, exposing the uncooked meat to the flames. Juice sizzled onto the fire. King Richard the Lionheart watched patiently. Jim could see the reflection of the red embers in the dog's eyes.

"That dog's learnt some manners," said Colonel Voss. Often they thought of the same thing. "How awful to always be waiting on someone else for what you want. I like being able to take what I want... Some people can wait. Some people wait all their lives and never got anything."

"Justine is a very beautiful name."

"Yes it is."

"We had better find the Place of the Legend."

"It's too late now. Once when I had money and stayed in Mr Meikles's hotel I thought of going home. But it wasn't enough. Just a flash in the pan as they say. You need a great deal of money to cut a dash in London society."

"So that's where you come from!"

"Not me, oh dear, oh dear. Not me."

"Then she?"

"Maybe she."

"Your lady?"

Colonel Voss made a display of smoking his pipe to stop it going out.

"Please cut more meat and stop being impertinent," he said sharply.

"I'm sorry, sir."

"I know you are."

Jim cut the meat onto the communal plate and sat down again on the end of his log. They dipped pieces of meat into the pots using their fingers. It had been a young impala ram, and the meat chewed easily.

The dog was still watching him. The night around them was as quiet as a mouse. The elephant had gone off away from the river. Even the crickets had fallen silent.

"The worst thing in life is for someone to feel sorry for you," said Colonel Voss. "Especially when you're old with nothing left you can do to change your life."

"I'm sorry."

"Please never say that to me again."

Jim cut four plates of meat during a leisurely supper. The old man had a good appetite. Jim would have asked him his age but knew he had gone far enough for one night… Justine! He'd have the story out of him in the end. 'My word I will,' he thought smiling to himself. 'The old dog. With a daughter my age.' Far away a lion roared. King Richard the Lionheart began to shiver. They could both see the dog shivering in the light of the fire. Another lion roared from behind them in reply.

"More than a mile away," said Colonel Voss. "We'll keep the fire banked up tonight… That poor dog's gone off under the wagon without its supper."

"He can eat in the morning. Nothing will touch the carcass close to the fire. Not even the ants."

Jim got up and put a pot of water on the fire. Later he made the tea. The lions had been quiet after the one frightening exchange.

"They're hunting," said Colonel Voss.

"What are?"

"The lions."

In the night they all woke to the terrible cries of a dying animal. The animal took a long time to die and then there was silence all night. Once the old man forgot his turn and Jim stoked the fire before going back to sleep. They both slept on the ground round the fire. King Richard the Lionheart had come out from under the wagon. Jim had cut him a chunk of cold meat and the dog had smiled at him with his eyes.

When the fake dawn brought light back to them, the dog was asleep between the two men. The fire had died down. In the long grass on the other side of the fire, thirty yards from the horses, a large animal had lain down in the night. Colonel Voss had a look and said it was an elephant. Jim put another pot of water over the last embers of the fire. When the water boiled, he made them their morning tea. He had dreamed of Jenny Merryl whose name was Justine.

When the sun rose through the trees they continued their journey, on towards the high mountains, far away in the new heat of the day, shimmering in a haze of soft purple.

Jim had carefully covered the embers of the fire with dry earth. Pieces of wood still smouldered from under the soft layer of earth.

The day camp was in a grove of tall trees that gave them shade. At three o'clock they went on again, making camp for the night when the sun went down.

Jim collected wood for the fire and that night they ate cold venison. The lions did not hunt in the night full of stars.

A WEEK LATER they began the slow ascent of the mountain. The foothills rose gently as the horses pulled on the wagon. The men and the dog walked beside the wagon to lighten the load. They took a path that wound up higher through the wooded hills. Again they saw no sign of man. Only the animals and the birds. Looking back, they had a view of the plain they had crossed.

The third night of the climb they heard thunder. They could see the forked lightning away towards Mozambique, behind the high mountains. On the fourth day of the climb it rained. The road they had taken would take them no further. They turned the wagon wheels with difficulty and began the journey by another route.

That afternoon they found a valley. In the valley was a herd of wild horses. Colonel Voss studied the grazing horses through his field glasses.

"The legend is true! Those are Arab horses. Have a look, Jim. I wonder if anyone has seen them before?" The old man was agitatedly excited.

"Is this the Place of the Legend?" Jim was looking at the herd of horses, trying to count them but the animals kept moving.

"Maybe. There are no indigenous horses in this part of Africa. Those horses are the living presence that the Arabs came. Came and stayed."

"Can't we catch a horse?" asked Jim.

"Not in a million years, dear boy. Those Arabs are the fastest horses on this earth. CAN you imagine Hamlet racing after one of those? We'll make camp and watch them. There's no tsetse fly this high up. No sickness. Why they survived all these years in Africa."

"Then why aren't there any people?"

"I rather think the tribes killed each other. The Shona, the Tonga.

The Matabele. Before that, tribes with no names. In this part of the world, man fought himself to extinction."

"Why do we always want to kill each other?"

"Man likes to go to war. It gives him a purpose. To be brave. To pay homage to his God. To champion the downtrodden, to bring him glory. The real reason? Conquest is the easy way to riches... Some even think dying in battle is the only true fulfilment. To die for a cause and for God. Maybe there's something in it. Only God knows."

"So much land. So empty."

"Maybe there's a curse on it. For man but not those horses."

"You think we shouldn't have come? The British, I mean, Cecil Rhodes?"

"Probably not. History will tell. Civilised, Christian Africa? A dream? Or should we have left it all to the free men and the animals?... Are they not beautiful, those Arabs? Free for thousands of years. You'd go like the wind on the back of one of those, Jim my boy. Like the wind. Ah, but then the horse would have a master."

They made camp in a grove of mukwa trees. Having travelled for so long, when the sun dipped into the plain, they made a fire. The entry to the Valley of the Horses, as Colonel Voss was calling it, gave them the view over the plain, the great sea of flat treetops and grass.

Long after the trees down below were in darkness the light still played in the mountains. The colonel had said they were thousands of feet above sea level. They were halfway up the mountain range. They wondered what the horses would make of the firelight, flickering in the night. They had not approached the horses for fear of frightening them. When the light went completely, they were alone again, the horses no longer existing for them.

Just before the light faded Jim had clubbed two guinea fowl out of their roost for the night in a tree. Once the birds found a perch, they stayed till dawn. The cackling they made flying up to their perch had told Jim where to go.

Jim plucked and gutted the birds and put them over the fire on the spit. He gave the dog some rotten meat that was three days old. Hamlet and Othello had disdained to notice the horses in the valley, not associating themselves with the Arabs. Only the bed of the valley where a river ran through, was grassed. The one slope was well-wooded, thick with trees.

"I'll catch some fish tomorrow," said Jim. He was on his haunches by the fire. Colonel Voss was seated on his chair, preparing his evening pipe. There was a wind coming down the valley towards them from the horses. Jim thought he could smell the Arabs but was not sure. The start of the night was silent and pitch dark away from the flickering light of the fire. The moon had waned. It would be dark all night with the clouds hiding the stars. There was thunder over towards Mozambique, behind the great range of mountains.

"What makes you think there are fish in the river?"

"My stomach. I'm sick of meat. I'm sure a man could eat only so much caviar."

"How do you know?"

"I don't… I love the sound of the night winds going through the trees. Why isn't the dog sick on that meat?"

"You should learn to smoke a pipe."

"Maybe I will… Where will we look for the ruins of your great, lost civilisation?"

"Anywhere here. And don't mock me, Jim dear boy. Depends if the horses migrated. We got into their valley so they can get out. What if the ruins are under the trees? In Asia and South America whole cities were lost in the jungle for centuries… How many of them came and stayed? They bring their building skills?… In two thousand years they will find Salisbury under the trees and nobody will have heard of the English. Or will we still be here like in America and Australia?"

"You're rambling, Colonel Voss."

"I like to ramble. Let me just enjoy my Arab horses. Youth is so important. Gordon was too impatient. Took a train from London for the Sudan with one officer to salvage British pride among the heathen. Should have taken an army. Pride and impatience cost him his life. He believed in God. I envy him. A man of honour. There was a German mercenary who wanted to defect from the Mahdi. He had denounced Christ and become a Muslim. Gordon would have nothing to do with the man on principle. Would have saved his life and Khartoum. Honour. Some men prize it more than life."

Jim waited for more, for some time. The pipe glowed intermittently.

"Were you there?" asked Jim into the silence. He got up and turned the guinea fowl on the spit. With a small shovel, he heaped more coals under the birds. He was thinking of the fish in the river. A pair of owls were calling to each other from somewhere in the darkened trees. He was content, at peace with himself. Only conscious of the now. The old man was a wonderful companion.

"In a way. Kitchener tried to get to Khartoum. He was a major, then. The glory of Omdurman was thirteen years away."

"Were you with Kitchener?"

"I think I was for a while. Oh yes. In the desert. Riding camels. They are the nastiest animals on this earth."

"Tell me."

"We rode and rode. Gladstone thought Gordon could hold Khartoum on his own. The lines were down. It was all politics. British and Egyptian. The Anglo-Egyptian Sudan. That bit of the Empire we took with a partner. To stop the slave trade. Then the Mahdi rose from obscurity and declared a Jihad. A holy war… They were much the same, the Mahdi and Gordon. Or so Gordon thought. Men of God. Men of honour. Like everything there was truth and lies. We never got to Gordon. To Khartoum. Not that time. But we did in the end. And blew the tomb of the Mahdi to pieces. They were both dead by then. Gordon and the Mahdi. Revenging a dead man. Killing a dead man. Pride. Honour. The British public demanded revenge. Took Kitchener two years the second time. Though then he came with an army. They'll still be slaving and still be fighting in that part of the world for a thousand years."

"Were you there?"

"Yes, I was there. I watched the last British cavalry charge. The 21st Lancers. Stupid pride. All they had to do was sit their horses and watch the infantry with their Lee Metfords shoot down the dervishes. The Lee Metfords were the first rifles to have magazines."

"I know them well."

"I forget. You had those rifles in your war… Lost five officers and sixty-five men. A glorious charge. Pride. Stupidity. They'll remember that charge of the 21st Lancers to the end of British history. Winston was there. A young lieutenant. He saw the charge… Did I tell you I knew Winston Churchill?"

Jim waited in silence not wishing to interrupt but the story had stopped. Some of the claims were too preposterous. How could this old man have known a British cabinet minister by his first name?

"He wasn't famous then?" asked Jim, trying to get the story going again.

"No he wasn't. But his father was Chancellor of the Exchequer. His first cousin the Duke of Marlborough."

"Did you ever meet him again?"

"Once."

"What happened?"

"Nothing. He did not recognise me. He would have done, were I important but I wasn't. Politicians. He liked the limelight. You have to be important to be recognised by politicians. Unless they are just shaking hands, courting votes."

"Did you try to speak to him?"

"Of course I didn't. You can't just remind a man he was your friend."

"Why didn't he recognise you?"

"It didn't suit him at the time… Like your noble friends with your ten pounds. I'd bet he'd cut you dead and not just because he owes you money. He forgot the money when it was spent."

"I'll ask him for my money."

"And he'll make you feel like a fool. To him, just giving you the time of day let alone lunching with you, was worth more than ten pounds. If he remembered, which I doubt, he'd just laugh at you. Right in your face. I spared Winston from laughing in my face."

"You make me feel very small."

"Good. It never hurts. Feeling small."

"Doesn't worry you?"

"Not any more."

There was no more mention of General Gordon or Winston Churchill or anything else from the colonel's past. Jim respected the silence. He wondered if Barnaby St Clair would cut him dead when he asked for his ten pounds. He had been a fool that day. It was much clearer now. It made him blanch thinking about his naïvety. She was the prettiest girl he had ever seen. Or the sexiest. In future in his mind he would blame the girl and the erotic movement of her breasts. Men gave away money to girls without feeling foolish. Even if they got nothing in return. He could still see her wavy cropped hair and the dress that clung to her legs. He was glad it was dark but crossed legs just the same. It happened every time he thought of Tina Pringle. In daylight he tried not to think of her. The thought of the embarrassment made him blanch again. He no longer needed to cross his legs.

He got up and turned the spit, tripping over the dog. While standing in the glow of the firelight he forced himself not to think of the girl. In half an hour the meat would be cooked. It was better to cook the bird slowly, so they cooked right through to the bone.

He put on the three-legged iron pot with the pap stirred up inside. He had not found wild spinach in the valley. Just some mushrooms that he had added to the pot with the pap. The colonel knew which ones to eat. They had eaten the same brown mushrooms twice before. The tops looked like the top of a small bun when it came out of the oven.

There was wild fruit in a bowl beside the colonel's chair. Monkeys had been eating the small fruit. There were discarded husks under the trees. The colonel had said if the monkeys had eaten the fruit so could they. The pips were large and there were four of them. More like nuts. Jim tried to crack one with his teeth and gave up. The thin-film of flesh round the four pips that fitted together to make the fruit was sweet and tasted like lychee.

The water he had taken from the river was sweet and tasted of minerals. There had been hoof marks in the river sand and Jim hoped the tart taste in the water was not from the horses. The taste went when he poured the hot water over the tea leaves… They had brought a whole chest of tea from Salisbury. The chest was the size of a very small trunk and Jim had laughed then but not any more. The tea was precious. They enjoyed it twice during the day and once after supper. If he had had his way, Jim would have brought enough to last them a week.

They heard the horses run once during the night. To Jim, it sounded like the whole herd thundering in the valley. Then the sound stopped as quickly as it started. In the silence Jim fell back into sleep.

Both of them missed their turns that night to stoke the fire. When Jim woke, stiff from sleeping on the hard earth, he got up to put the big, black kettle on the fire. He had to blow up the embers with dry kindling to get a flame hot enough to boil the water.

Far away at the end of the valley that ended up against an unclimbable cliff were the horses. He looked at them through the field glasses. They were grazing peacefully. Jim wondered what had spooked them during the night. The wind was still in the same direction, blowing towards him directly from the horses. Again Jim thought he could smell the Arabs. They were further away, but the smell was strong. Jim told himself the wind must be stronger. The horses were in the gully. A dead-end gully with high cliffs on three sides. Jim and the colonel would be able to get up close. The horses would have to run back past them to escape. With second thoughts Jim saw the idea as not such a good one.

When the water boiled, he put in a heaped spoonful of tea and let the tea stew, resting the kettle on the ground a little way from the fire. They would drink the tea without milk or sugar.

The colonel was still asleep, snoring gently when Jim took him his morning tea. All sign of the thunderclouds had gone. It was a beautiful morning where they were halfway up the slope of the great range of mountains. It was cool and fresh. Back down on the plain Jim knew it would be hot and humid. The sun had just reached the flat tops of the trees in the plain down below through the cleft made by their valley. That view was as beautiful to Jim as looking back up at the purple-topped mountains. The sun was touching the one side of the valley that was without trees, bathing the long grass yellow. Strangely, Jim thought there were terraces following the contours of the valley, rising in undulating rings above the river to halfway up the slope. It was a trick of the light, when he looked again all he saw was flowing grass, the heads pushed towards him by the oncoming breeze.

When he finished his tea, he found his fishing rod in the wagon and walked down to the river. He had taken maggots from the dog's meat to use as bait. Then he had buried the meat. Behind him at two paces distant followed King Richard the Lionheart. Jim was whistling in the dawn. To show no favouritism he had stroked the soft mouths of Othello and Hamlet. The horses had watched him for a moment. Jim walked off down towards the small river that flowed from the source in the high mountains back through the Valley of the Horses to a waterfall that spilled out over the plain, thousands of feet below. By the time the river water reached the flat tops of the trees down below Jim thought the river he was going to fish would be nothing but a damp mist from heaven.

For the first time since the war ended he didn't hear the guns of the Western Front in his head or smell the stench of the trenches, the sickly smell of decaying men blown up again and again in the putrid mud of no man's land. He reached the small river that was really a stream before he realised it. Then he smiled. The colonel was right. The filth of war was washing from his mind like the oil from an anointed king. And he felt like a king. King of all he surveyed.

The horses were still grazing peacefully down the end of the valley half a mile away. Jim baited the hook with a squirm of maggots and forgot the horses. The dog sat down in the grass that came to halfway up Jim's legs and fell asleep on its side. The dog had eaten the remains of the guinea fowl, bones and all, without choking. The bones had been soft and full of marrow, a soft red marrow.

To Jim's surprise he felt a bite. Striking the second time, Jim hooked his first fish, the size of a dinner plate.

By the time Colonel Voss had drunk a second cup of black tea, Jim was back with their breakfast. He had never seen such fish before. They were more like a carp than a trout. Like a trout and salmon there were no scales. He was not sure if any freshwater fish had scales. There were more bones than a trout when he cut down the length of the fish before putting them over the fire on a wire mesh he had made at the stable before they had started the journey. The flesh of the fish was white. Jim lightly sprinkled the fish with salt. The sun had risen in the sky.

The wind had changed since Jim went down to fish and was now blowing across the valley. The old man had released the horses from their nightly tether. Hamlet and Othello were grazing the spring grass below the line of trees that covered the one side of the valley for five hundred yards of the steep gradient. They seemed content. When he had muzzled their mouths earlier, their flanks had been shivering. Jim thought the shivering had gone with the warmth of the morning sun. He went halfway towards the horses to check but neither of them took any notice. Surprisingly, King Richard was chewing a bone from the rotten meat that Jim had tried to bury. He let the dog alone. If the dog wanted to be sick, it was the dog's business.

When the fish was cooked, they ate them from the wire grill with their fingers. Jim burnt the tip of his third finger and sucked out the brief pain. The fish cooked quickly and was eaten down to the bone and turned over by Colonel Voss. Neither talked as they ate the under halves of the fish. They each took the choice pieces from behind the gills at the end.

Then they sat back with satisfaction. General Gordon and Winston Churchill, along with the Mahdi, were forgotten with the night.

A pair of martial eagles were circling the valley, high in the sky on the morning thermals. They were strangely quiet, riding up to heaven on their six feet wingspan. The birds were usually silent in flight said Colonel Voss. Jim took his word.

"This morning before tea, when the sun came up, I could have sworn the grass slope of the lower valley over there was contoured. As if someone had grown a crop there." Jim was pointing to the valley slope on the opposite side to the trees where the horses were grazing below the tree line. "Then the light changed, and the impression changed. Did the Tonga or the Shona ever irrigate crops and contour the land to evenly spread the water at different heights down the valley to stop erosion?"

"Are you sure?"

"Not really. Have a look yourself tomorrow when the sun comes up. It's your turn to make the early morning tea."

"I'll do my best to be up in time. As far as we know, the black tribes till a little soil round their huts and move every year to new hunting grounds. Most of their sustenance comes from hunting and gathering. They rarely store food for the future. There's so much land and plenty of game. Look at us. For weeks we've lived off the land. Just tea, maize meal and salt was all we brought with us. No, I'm sure the black tribes never built contours and farmed in one spot as we know it. Why they never built a town or a permanent village in this part of Africa. But the Arabs would have done. Oh, yes. They would have done. So none of your tricks with an old man just to get up to make the early morning tea."

"Suit yourself."

"See, young Jim, you are grinning."

"At the pleasure of eating fish."

Both horses whickered in fear at the same time. They were fifty yards away and even from that distance Jim could see their flanks shivering. The wind had changed again. He could distinctly smell the Arab horses.

Colonel Voss looked at the Arabs and then followed back on the line of the wind that was blowing directly into his face. He rose from his chair slowly looking towards the Arab horses.

"Jim, pass me my field glasses... Do you smell them?"

"The Arab horses?"

"No. The lions. Can't you tell the difference?"

"I can now. I thought those Arabs smelled strong."

"Get the guns. I'll get Othello and Hamlet. Put that damn dog in the wagon." He passed Jim the field glasses. "Have a look before you go. Over there... And over there. And there. They have the mouth of the valley sealed."

"Where?"

"Just the ears above the long grass. The females. That's the largest pride of lions I ever saw. The old man and his sons will circle round behind the horses and chase them onto the females. Mostly the females do the killing. The old man has the fun and eats first. When they get behind the horses at the top of the valley, the horses will smell them on the wind and bolt this way. They'll stampede right through our camp."

"Won't the lionesses face them off?"

"Maybe... There they go! They're turning. They've smelled the lions. I can see one of the males. We've got ten minutes to make ourselves secure with the wagon."

"Can the Arab horses defend themselves against lion?"

"I don't know. Ours couldn't. Those Arab stallions are big. There are lots of horses. They'll run first and then we shall find out. They can't see or smell the lionesses yet... Even after all those years they're still fighting for survival. In front of us, Jim, you see the power of life. There's nothing stronger on this earth. Why we've survived so long for some damn reason."

Jim pulled the shafts, to make an angle with the old wagon. Colonel Voss caught Hamlet and Othello. The horses were terrified, rooted to the spot. Colonel Voss dragged them by the harness still attached to their heads.

Jim took the shotgun and his .375 rifle from the wagon, each with its own box of ammunition. The spread of buckshot from the twelve-bore over the shaft might wheel the stampeding Arabs around the wagon. Running in with the horses in each hand, Colonel Voss tethered them to the back of the wagon. He had run as fast as Jim despite the difference in their ages.

When they stood up in the long grass, there were seven lionesses, their big tails whipping with anticipation as they readied to spring. The leading stallion made a terrible noise and changed direction straight for the nearest lioness. From the thundering herd more stallions broke heading for the lionesses. They could now see. The lionesses had six galloping horses coming straight for them. All but one of them broke, turned tail and ran back down the valley. They passed the laager without looking in Jim's direction. Jim was cheering on at the top of his voice, jumping up and down waving the rifle over his head. He was as much frightened as he was excited at the swift turn of events. The lioness that had not broken with the others faced the oncoming stallion without flinching. The hunter had become the hunted. The big horse reared up on its back legs and kicked the lioness in the head with both hooves, splitting open the head, killing it instantly. Jim watched in awe. With the rest of the big cats bounding away, the stallions wheeled the herd and headed back up the valley from whence they had come. Jim counted three lions as they ran into the trees where the horses would be unable to follow at full gallop.

The lion hunt was over. None of the animals had taken any notice of the human spectators. By the time Jim and the colonel, both visibly shaken, went back to the fire, the Arabs were grazing peacefully. Colonel Voss glassed the valley in all directions with his field glasses. It was as if the lions had never been. Except for the dead mother of the pride. She had stood her ground to save her less experienced offspring.

Colonel Voss took the rifle from Jim and went forward to look at the carcass. Jim expected to hear a shot which never came. The doves began to call to each other as if nothing had happened.

"Kicked to death," said the colonel on his return.

Jim put the big black kettle back on the fire, freshly filled with river water. His heart was still pounding with fear and excitement. They had both forgotten King Richard the Lionheart. Jim looked inside the wagon. The dog had buried its head under the empty sacks of maize. Its bottom was sticking out. Jim gave a friendly whack on the dog's behind. The dog buried himself further into the sack pile. The wind was still blowing in the same direction, bringing the scent of the lion. The dog had no means of knowing the lioness was dead. Calling the dog made no difference. Jim left him where he was and made fresh tea in the kettle.

THEY STAYED in the valley all day. There was no way forward except into the dead-end gully. Neither of them thought it wise to approach the wild horses. They would have to go back down the valley where a path lead to the right of the waterfall that plummeted over the cliff into space. Colonel Voss had fruitlessly searched the surrounding mountains through his field glasses to find a way to go higher. Jim thought they had gone as far as they were going.

"All good things come to an end," he said philosophically.

"Yes, they do."

"I'll never forget what we saw."

THAT NIGHT the scavengers came to the Valley of the Horses. Colonel Voss liked wonderful names for everything. The horses. The dog. The Place of the Legend.

The night sky was clear, their valley domed by millions of stars. Jim felt himself at the centre of the universe, the heart of the great dome of heaven. He was the living mind that made the heavens visible.

The scavengers had come out of the trees and waited where Hamlet and Othello had grazed earlier. Wild dogs. Jackals. Hyenas… Above, the vultures had circled high at first, falling lower circling the carcass as the birds grew confident.

All through the night of a million stars, the scavengers snapped and snarled at each other, tearing the dead lioness to pieces, ripping into her belly. The jackals chased off the wild dogs. The hyenas chased away the jackals. Jim could see them by the pale light of the stars.

Their fire was kept burning brightly all night. When far away the lions called it was late in the night. None came back to protect the carcass.

IN THE MORNING King Richard still had his head buried in the sacks. Vultures walked on top of what was left of the carcass of the lioness, flapping out their black wings to keep balance. Jim thought how beautiful the birds had looked in flight, circling on the thermals. There were birds inside the gaping belly of the lioness. The wild dogs had taken a turn after the jackals and gone back into the trees with full bellies.

Jim put on the kettle with the first light. The colonel still asleep next to the fire. Jim had not had the heart to wake him. Anyway, he liked looking after the old man. He missed his father, drowned those years ago in the Irish sea, and Jim's grandfathers had both died before he was born… It was going to be a beautiful day. Most of the Arab horses were grazing peacefully, or some were drinking at the river. He untethered Hamlet and Othello. They went off to graze, no longer fearful of the carcass still being cleaned by the vultures. The wind had changed taking the scent of the dead lioness back in the direction of the wild horses.

The morning sun came up and flooded their valley. Jim thought he saw the contours again and called across to where the colonel was still fast asleep. As the yellow sun concentrated on the side of the valley away from the trees, it was at an upward angle to the slope of the hill. Jim was this time certain.

"Look!" he shouted. "Look! Those are contours."

"Dear boy, I rather think you're right. Here we have it." The old man was sitting up on the ground blinking his eyes. As the sun moved, the long grass on the slope undulated with the wind washing the contours from the hill.

"Did we really see anything?" asked Jim. "Or was it just in our heads?"

"Maybe God was showing me what I wanted to see. This one time an omen of death."

"Don't be silly."

"There was nothing there. Only our imaginations."

"We must search the valley."

"We will. Diligently. Then we will go home. Some things we want so badly, Jim, we can never have. However much we want them. Sometimes wanting them is more important than having them. When we find what we want it mostly turns to dust."

"How long do we go on looking?" asked Jim.

"Till we die. Now, make an old man his tea and then go off and catch us our breakfast."

"Aren't we going to stay?"

"For a few days. We'll walk that slope. Make sure. There is always something else to look for... Where's that damn dog?"

"Hiding in the wagon."

"I love that dog."

"So do I."

5

JOHNNY LAKE DECEMBER, 1920

L en Merryl found Cousin Mildred with one foot bent back against a lamp post in Piccadilly. It was December in London and cold. The gaslight at the top of the lamp post shone down the bare knee and the girl's breasts as it was meant to do.

"Looking for some fun, dearie. You got to 'ave a room, see. No bloody taxi and going round Eros... What's the matter? Cat got your tongue?"

"Hello, Mildred."

"Blimey. Look what the cat brought up. What you want?"

"Where can I find my sister?"

"How the 'ell should I know. Anyway, what's in it for me? Be quick about it. I'm losin' business."

"Don't read the newspapers?"

"You know perfectly well, Len Merryl, I can't read. If I could read and write, think I'd be leaning against a bloody lamp post? What she done? Someone killed 'er?"

"Now would I ask if she was dead?"

"How do I know? Had it comin'. Fancied 'erself, that one. Stayed two nights and buggered off. Months ago. Now, piss off there's a bloke over there lookin' at me... Oh, shit it's a copper in plain clothes! You can walk me to the pub in Greek Street and buy me a port and lemon... Cold enough to freeze the balls off a brass monkey... What you doin' in London, then? Thought you was shrimpin'... Evenin' officer. My cousin Len Merryl from Neston, up north. That is."

"Is this woman your cousin?"

"What's it to you?" said Len.

"Seeing you talk with the same accent I'll let you go."

"Sweet of you, officer," said Mildred.

"Don't give me lip."

"Give you more than lip had my way," said Mildred.

"Mildred, shut up," said Len.

"She really is your bloody cousin!"

"Boyfriend killed end of war," said Len. "She was pregnant."

"I'm sorry, miss."

"So am I," said Mildred.

Len took her arm firmly at the elbow. His cousin was crying. Brazen whore to crumpled mess at the mention of Johnny Lake. They walked away.

"How's the kid, Mildred?"

"He's all right."

Len could see the sign over the entrance to the Elephant and Castle. He had been one of the lucky ones. He was still in basic training at Aldershot when the war had come to an end.

MOST OF THE girls were off duty whores and took no notice of Mildred. Mildred was still shivering despite the log fire in the alcove where Len Merryl found a seat. The whores were welcome, Len found out later, provided they did no soliciting in the pub.

"It's so humiliating," said Mildred.

She was crying again and Len put his arm round her shoulders. Her whole body was shaking. He ordered their drinks from a barmaid without letting go of his cousin. The shivering went on for a long time. No one took any notice of them.

"I'd a made a good fisherman's wife. Why they want to go and kill my Johnny? I'd made my mind up when I was four, Len. Never was no one else."

"Come home, Mildred."

"How can I, with Johnny's bastard? Anyway, 'alf of them are dead. Them dead boys don't suffer no more. I got to suffer for the rest of my life... And if I don't do better than this so will little Johnny." She was crying again.

"Don't the army give you somethin'?"

"Course not. We wasn't married, me and Johnny. Waiting for the bloody war to end. My mum was ashamed of me. Couldn't talk about it to the others. That Mrs Snell's a right bitch. Your mum never talked to me with the baby on the way, let alone when it was born, poor little bastard... And Johnny would 'ave loved him... In the end, they'd have gone fishin' together on the same boat... What am I going to do, Len?

In winter, there isn't much business for a whore."

"Where's the kid?"

"Three of us share a room. A bed too. Eight 'ours each. Lucky we all do shift work. We all got kids like me. We'll be all right... You got any money, Len?"

"No, I 'aven't. But I'd give you if I had."

"Now tell me. What's all this about your sister?... I always thought she'd marry that Jim Bowman. He was sweet on 'er. Never said nothin'. Just watched 'er with them big sheep eyes. And 'im an officer at the end... Without a bloody scratch."

Len took his arm away from her shoulders to find what was left of his money for the barmaid... Mildred gulped half a port and lemon. Len could not keep his eyes away from the girl's exposed breasts. He knew he should not be looking. Even when he sipped his beer, he was surreptitiously looking. To take his mind away from her body, Len told her about Jim Bowman and the reward in the paper. When he finished, his cousin had stopped shivering. He would have liked to have bought her another drink.

LEN MERRYL had left Neston three months earlier with his two shillings. By the time he reached the capital he had to find a job or starve. He had found no sign of his sister or Cousin Mildred. He went from hotel to hotel looking for a job as a dishwasher until he found one. A man on the train down from the north had told him about dishwashing in a good hotel.

"What them toffs leave on their plates would 'ave fed the whole bleedin' British Army. You work hard but you eat. That's what counts. No money, so to speak but you can eat."

The little pay went to Len's landlord for the room he shared with an Italian. The Italian could not speak English properly. The Italian was very efficient at cleaning dishes. After the first two weeks in London Len had given up looking for his sister.

The week before he found Cousin Mildred he had bumped into a school friend from Neston. The best of Neston left to go to Liverpool, Manchester or London.

"I fucked your cousin Mildred the other day." His friend had told him as an introduction. "Always did fancy her bosom."

"I've been looking for her since I came to London."

"Don't blame you."

"Where can I find her?"

"Piccadilly. Not far from the Elephant and Castle. Works the night shift."

"What does she do?"

"She's a whore, silly. Cost a bob to fuck your cousin Mildred."

It had taken Len a week to find the courage to look for his cousin. He had always liked Mildred.

"That bloody war never stops," he had said and walked away from his friend from school without wanting to know his address in London.

WHEN LEN reached his room in Lambeth, the Italian was fast asleep. It took Len half an hour to fall asleep. He was thinking of his cousin Mildred. If he had had a shilling, he knew he would have paid her. Which made him the same as his friend from school.

In the early hours of the morning he was vividly dreaming of a girl with big breasts. When he woke in the dark of his room, he was sweating despite the winter cold. He lay awake for the rest of the night.

In the morning he went to work, walking the four miles through the cold streets of London to the hotel in Park Lane. Inside the hotel it was warm and full of light. The kitchen smelled of good food.

The Italian had still been asleep when he closed the door of the room. The Italian worked the late shift which was why they shared the same room. He was still thinking of his cousin Mildred and hoped she was warm in her bed. There had been a cold east wind blowing through the streets of London when he walked to work over Vauxhall Bridge.

WHILE HER brother Len was washing the breakfast dishes, his sister Jenny Merryl was walking down the gangplank of the SS *Carmarthen Castle* in Cape Town. London was not much kinder to Jenny than to her cousin Mildred. Most of the trained nurses were out of work two years after the end of the war. An officer she had nursed in France had given her a job as a maid. The job had lasted six months until the young man had brought home a wife. Jenny had lived in the young man's family town house in Park Lane, not ten doors from where Len worked in his posh hotel. It had taken the wife two weeks to put Jenny out on the street. Young wives never tolerated pretty young maids in the same house as their husbands. Jenny was out the same day the young woman found out Jenny had nursed her new husband back to health in France.

Jenny's mother had told her from a young age that necessity was the mother of invention. The husband had slipped her a pound note behind his new bride's back. Then she was on the streets of London with her suitcase, an old coat and a new pair of shoes that hurt her feet. The wife had given her the new pair of shoes as a parting gift that Jenny surmised was to salve the young woman's conscience. The wife had not liked the shoes after wearing them twice. She was a size smaller than Jenny which caused Jenny's feet the problem.

That first morning she found a cobbler who stretched her shoes and gave them back to her wrapped in an old newspaper. After walking half a mile to find the cobbler she had taken her old shoes out of her case so she could walk. The cobbler said to leave the new shoes off her feet until the blisters went away. She had stuffed the wrapped up new shoes in her old suitcase and gone to look for a room. She still had the pound note in her pocket which was comforting.

She found a room in Soho above a Greek restaurant. Twice she saw Cousin Mildred without being seen herself. It was apparent to Jenny the poor girl had become a whore to support her little Johnny. Jenny kept away to save her cousin's pride. The first time after seeing Mildred soliciting, Jenny's heart had thumped all the way home. In her mind she kept saying over and over again, 'there but for the grace of God go I'. She felt guilty being in possession of the pound note.

For two weeks she had looked for any kind of job that was not prostitution. She had not broken the pound note, living off the little she had saved as a live-in maid. The wife had magnanimously given her a week's wages in lieu of notice. Everyone had to protect themselves in life and Jenny felt no grudge. In a moment of honesty she knew she would have done the same thing if their roles had been reversed. Life was tough at any level. She had liked the officer and mentally had wished him well in his marriage.

Autumn had turned into winter and Jenny was still out of work when she took the new shoes out of their newspaper wrapping, the shoes that had caused her feet so much pain. When she tried them on she found the old cobbler was right. He had stretched the good leather perfectly to fit the size of her feet.

Smiling to herself at even a small victory over life she bent down to pick up the old newspaper from the floor of her small room to find herself looking at the picture of a very familiar face grinning back at her. Quickly she read the name Jim Bowman. In a heart-stopping moment her own name leapt out of the paper making her plonk down on the bare boards of the floor next to the crumpled newspaper. Again she looked at the photograph taken by Solly Goldman in Meikles Hotel. There was no mistake. They were looking for her. Jim was a war hero. She was his sweetheart.

Jenny Merryl had begun to laugh, hugging herself as she rolled around on the floor. Like Cousin Mildred, she had seen the sheep's eyes but nothing had ever come of it. Jim Bowman had been too shy. They had never even properly spoken to each other, not even as friends despite having grown up in the same row of council houses. It was not the twenty-five pounds that was making her laugh. Ever since she had turned thirteen she had fantasised about Jim Bowman. When they made him an officer she felt so proud. She had wanted to tell him. To give him a big, fat kiss. Instead, she put her pretty little nose in the air and gave him the cold shoulder.

When life for Jenny turned on its head, she no more thought of going to the newspaper for her twenty-five pounds than flying to the moon. There it was in print for the whole world to read. Jim Bowman loved her. She knew where he lived. She was going to Africa. She was going to find her Jim. And when she did she was going to throw herself into his arms and live happily ever after.

Colonial Shipping, the holding company and the merchant shipping line owned by the Brigandshaw family from the time of Harry Brigandshaw's grandfather, had taken over three British shipping lines during the war naming them the Empire Castle Line. The new ships of the line were all to be named after British castles. Only the older ships like the *SS King Emperor* retained their names. Just off Piccadilly in Regent Street, Empire Castle had opened an office. In the front of the office through a large plate glass window were models of all the ships of the line. Harry's uncle, Sir James Brigandshaw Bart, had commissioned the works that showed potential passengers the ships they would sail upon in exact detail without having to go to the docks. Jenny had more than once passed the big window and looked at the model ships.

In the new shoes that no longer hurt, Jenny had walked as quickly as possible, her excitement bubbling up inside of her. She had to take the cheapest berth in the boat, sharing a dormitory cabin with eleven other girls. The pound had just been enough to buy a ticket on the boat to Cape Town leaving enough for the third-class train ticket from Cape

Town up through South Africa and Bechuanaland to Salisbury in Rhodesia. There she was going straight to the offices of the *Rhodesia Herald*. It was all in the London paper that came with her shoes from the cobbler. Even the name of Simon Haller who had written the syndicated story.

When they had showed her Salisbury on the map in the shipping office, she had felt no fear. If Jim Bowman lived in Salisbury, there was nothing to be frightened about once she was there.

AT THE BOTTOM of the gangplank in her lucky new shoes that were now well used and scuffed at the edge, her old suitcase from Neston firmly in her right hand, it was a beautiful summer day. For the rest of her life the sun was going to shine. Everyone was helpful. The ship had docked on time. The train was due to leave on time.

She walked to Cape Town station to save a penny. She would largely be out of money when she reached her destination which did not worry her. At the end of her journey was Jim. Nothing else could possibly matter.

All thought of Cousin Mildred had gone from her head.

EVER SINCE buying her the port and lemon in the Elephant and Castle, Len Merryl had known the address of the room Mildred shared with the other two whores and the children. The week before Christmas when the weather was particularly cold his conscience overcame his fear. Many nights since finding her with one foot back against the lamp post, Len had dreams of big breasts. When he woke, he likened his lust to wanting his sister. Never once had Len allowed himself to think of his sister Jenny as a woman. Mildred was Len's first cousin. They both had the same grandmother. Sleeping with Mildred would be incest in Len's mind, even if he paid her a bob.

From the warmth of the Elephant and Castle, and unseen by Cousin Mildred, he watched her until she went home. Then he followed at a safe distance. He wanted to be sure she was the only girl in the room even though he would not have time to walk back to Lambeth and get a night's sleep. Len had deliberately left his meagre savings in his room, hidden in the toe of his spare pair of shoes.

Cousin Mildred had gone off with one trick all the time Len sat in the alcove of the pub that gave him the view of the street and the girl in the flimsy dress that showed off her exposed leg and breasts. Len knew his cousin had to be freezing. He nursed each pint of beer for as long as possible. When she had gone off with her man, coming back half an hour later, Len had been sickeningly jealous.

"What you doin' here?"

"I've got money for you, Mildred."

"You want to fuck me too!"

"No, Mildred," Len stammered. "It's for little Johnny."

He had approached her at the front door of the seedy lodging house while Mildred was fitting her key into the door. The girl was visibly shaking and even though it was bitterly cold, Mildred's brow was sweating. She had an old shawl over her shoulders she had not had before.

When the door opened Len could smell boiled cabbage mixed with the stench of stale urine from the downstairs toilet with its door wide open to the badly lighted hallway. The old, three-storey house was at the back of Soho, away from the restaurants frequented by Londoners looking for good cheap food.

"You'd better come up."

"Are you all right, Mildred? You're sweating."

"No I'm not all right, Len. The girls think I've got pneumonia. The girls think I'm going to die. I won't be the first Piccadilly tart to die in winter. Cold enough to freeze the balls off a brass monkey." She tried to laugh and ended up coughing violently, fighting for breath.

"Why are you out then?"

"And starve! Little Johnny starve!"

"Couldn't you get some help?"

"Who bloody from? Fat lot of help you've been, Len Merryl. And us cousins."

"That's the point. If we wasn't first cousins, I'd have wanted to walk out with you, Mildred. We're Catholics. You can't marry a first cousin."

"But you can fuck 'em."

"Please, Mildred."

They had reached the third landing up the top of the stairs. The whore that took the previous eight hours in the bed had passed them on the stairs, giving Mildred a look that mixed despair with sympathy.

Len had never seen a room more tatty, more sordid.

Mildred was of little use to her son or the other two mites in the room that was as cold as charity. The oldest child in the freezing cold room Len guessed was six years old. All three children Len saw later had extended, bloated stomachs. All thought of sex with Mildred went when she opened the door to a room little bigger than a large, walk-in cupboard. One of the children was grizzling. All three were in one large bed. The room was filthy and smelled of urine. The light bulb was a red glow from a bad power supply. Len's first impulse was to be sick. His second was to cry. The tears flowed down his face as he witnessed the human degradation. Just the single, naked bulb hung from the ceiling. Mildred got into the bed with the children, too sick to feed them. She lay on her back, her large, fever-filled eyes looking through the single source of weak light. She took her arm out from the dirty bedclothes and held out her hand to him, palm up. On the palm of the small hand was a shilling.

"Can you help, Len? I can't do no more. I'm goin' to die. Mind my Johnny. I did do my best. Weren't good enough."

"I'm goin' for a doctor. Don't you move."

"I can't."

Mildred's eyes were shut when Len closed the door and went in search of a doctor in the early hours of the morning. One of the children had begun to cry softly. Even in the minutes Len had been in the room he had seen there was no gas fire or any means for cooking. He had the shilling firmly gripped in his right hand. He would have killed anyone who tried to take it away. He just hoped the doctor would come for a shilling. Then he was going to get them hot food from his kitchen. The Italian was on duty. The walk to Park Lane would take him fifteen minutes. They would find a way to keep the food hot. One of the cooks had a thermos flask that he filled with coffee when he went off shift. They would fill the flask with hot soup.

THE ELEPHANT and Castle was just closing. The barman gave him the doctor's address.

The old man was going to bed when Jim knocked. Jim tried to explain.

"I know. It'll be pneumonia. They can't whore wearing overcoats. The weak die in the first winter. What's her address?"

Len gave the doctor the address and the front door key. He offered the old man a shilling. The doctor smiled thinly.

"There is a law against making money out of prostitution. Go and get the food. I'll wait with Mildred. You did say Mildred?..."

"What will happen to the kid if she dies?"

"You can have him. How the hell do I know?"

"I'm sorry... Do they have orphanages in London?"

The old man had on a thick overcoat and carried his doctor's bag. They went out into the street together. Len was loath to badger the doctor again.

"Thank you, Doctor."

"To hell with it! Why do they bother being born?"

"That's the easy part. Her boyfriend was killed in the war."

"That bloody war again. I was retired. Now look at me. If she survives, get your cousin out of London. Go home. For the likes of you, there's nothing but pain looking for a new life here. Go to the colonies. Just don't stay in London. Now bugger off and get that food. I'm sick and tired of young girls dying on me."

"You've done this before?"

"Twice a week this time of year. And all that wealth just round the corner... We call ourselves civilised. First, we slaughter each other in the millions. Then allow this to happen."

The old man was still talking to himself as he walked away, his head bent down against the icy wind. Len watched him, to make sure he took the turn in the road to Mildred. Len walked as fast as he could to the hotel where he worked. He was not due to go on duty for five hours. All the people passing in the street knew nothing of his plight. He was only thinking of Cousin Mildred.

The shop windows were full of Christmas cheer. There were fancy lights in the rich windows. Len was the only one walking really fast. He wanted to run but thought a policeman would stop him. A couple, arm in arm, got in his way. The girl had her head on her man's shoulder.

"'Ear! What's your bloody 'urry," she spat at him.

Len still had the shilling clutched in the palm of his hand. He went on threading his way through the Christmas window shoppers. Carol singers were singing *Silent Night*. Len could not see them. The singers were somewhere in a group off Oxford Street. He would turn left at Marble Arch.

Then he saw them. It was the Salvation Army in their uniforms, the women wearing Victorian caps on their prim heads. For a moment he thought of talking to the man with glasses who seemed to be in charge. The man ignored him. A young girl held out at a box. Len went round her.

Len could hear the indignation mixed with righteousness in her voice as the sound of it was swallowed by the crowd. He could smell roasting chestnuts. A man was playing a barrel organ by winding the handle. Len had to sidestep the man's monkey on its chain. Cars and carriages passed both ways on Oxford Street. Mostly they were cars. Two policemen rode on horses high above the heads of the crowd to have a better look at what was going on. Len slowed his pace to be inconspicuous. He was going to save her life. That much he had determined. He and the old man who was a doctor were going to save Mildred's life.

"She's not even twenty," he said out loud, quickening his pace.

No one took any notice of him.

When he reached his hotel, he passed the grand front entrance before going round the back to the tradesman's entrance and the kitchens. All the guests had appeared to be wearing evening dress. They were likely to be back from theatres preparing to go for supper. The women were heavily jewelled as they stepped from the cars dropping them at the entrance.

THE ITALIAN took charge. Ten minutes after reaching the kitchen Len was on his way out again with the food. This time he walked more slowly. He was more confident. Everyone in the kitchen had helped. There was always soup left over in the tureens when they came back from the dining room.

Len had three large flasks full of hot soup. One was full of lobster bisque. The other shark-fin soup. The third had been made from the flesh of a turtle. To add to the feast were half eaten chops, cut bread and dry toast the cook had called Melba toast. The swag was slung over his shoulder in a tablecloth with a black cigarette burn in the middle.

Halfway to Soho a policeman stopped him. Len explained and showed him the half eaten chops. Dropping to his knees on the pavement to open the tablecloth the kitchen manager had thrown away.

"You'd better hurry, lad, carry it over your arm. Less conspicuous. Like Christmas presents. No one carries presents slung over the shoulder. What made me suspicious like."

Len had never thought of it.

With the tablecloth wrapped around the food again Len hurried on his way.

WHEN LEN reached the lodging house, the front door was locked. Shut in his face. He looked up at the top floor and shouted Mildred's name in panic. He had put the swag down on the top step. Twice he shouted at the top of his lungs. It was worse than ever. Now he couldn't even get to his cousin Mildred dying in the bed with the children. Len banged on the door hurting his hand.

The doctor himself opened the door.

"Careful, laddie." The man was a Scot. For the first time Len recognised the accent, he was so pleased to see the man.

"Is she going to die?"

"Probably not if you look after her. I gave her penicillin."

The old man pushed past Len with his doctor's bag and walked down the steps into the street without looking back.

"Where are you going?" called Len.

"Home. She won't be the only one wanting to die on a night like this. Christmas is a bad time for the lonely and destitute. Half of survival is wanting to survive. Look after her. You know my address wherever you take her. A good nurse can save her. The lungs are inflamed but not collapsed. Are you a good nurse, laddie? The children are starving. Why they have extended bellies. Good food and warmth for all of them. Can you manage that?... Good night."

"Can't I pay for the penicillin?"

"No. I'm an old man with few needs. Gave up tobacco and drink. I was one of the lucky ones. My father was rich."

"Why do you live in Soho?"

"Some people use young girls. Make them into whores. My pleasure is making them live to change their ways."

"You're a good man, Doctor."

"There isn't such a thing on this earth."

"Thank you, anyway."

Len was crying again when he closed the front door. The doctor had given him back the key.

All through the night he fed spoonfuls of soup to his cousin. He had thought of the spoon and borrowed it from the hotel kitchen. The children had eaten all the bread and meat and gone to sleep.

To keep his cousin warm, Len got into bed with her. She was skin and bone. When he wasn't trying to feed her soup, he had his arms around Mildred. Whatever the doctor had done made her drowsy. Len didn't think she knew who was holding her body.

In the morning a strange girl let herself into the room.

"Out you go, Milly. My turn."

"She's sick."

"Who the 'ell are you?"

"Her cousin."

"Well bugger off. I'm tired. She knows better than bring johns back here."

"I'm her cousin, Len Merryl."

"And I'm the Queen of England. Now bugger off."

"She's going to die."

"So are we all. Now bugger off. I'm dog-tired. One bloody trick all bloody night. Being a whore ain't what it used to be."

Len got out of bed fully dressed.

"Which clothes belong to Mildred and Johnny?" he asked the whore.

"You are her cousin. Sorry. You takin' her home?"

"Something like that. She's got pneumonia. A doctor gave her penicillin. Can you pack for her? You can use that tablecloth."

"Got any food left?" she had seen the thermos flask.

"There's soup in the flask. Help yourself."

"Blimey. It's still 'ot. I'm starvin'."

"Can you help?"

"Course I can… You are taking the kid? Funny that the kids don't want to wake up."

"I had them full last night."

"That'll be a first. You are a bloody angel, aren't you? Milly never mentioned no relation. Never said where she came from."

"I'm going to get a taxi. She can't walk. Will you put the things in the tablecloth? I have to take the thermos flasks and spoon. They belong where I work. What's your name?"

"What the fuckin' hell does that matter… Go on then. Sooner you lot have gone, the sooner I can get some sleep. She ain't paid this week's rent, neither."

"I bloody did," said Mildred.

Len looked down on her in the bed. The girl had again closed her eyes.

When Len came back and carried her down to the waiting taxi with her few clothes in the tablecloth and little Johnny straggling behind. Mildred was delirious.

THE ITALIAN had brought back a thick vegetable soup the cook had made from leftovers on the plates. First, they bathed Mildred in the bathroom that served all the boarders in the Lambert house. Neither looked at her body as Len washed her clean. By the end her hair was matted but it was clean. He thought he knew how his sister Jenny felt nursing the officers during the war. He was unaware of the body, only the cleansing. Then they dunked young Johnny in the same water. The boy squealed with excitement, revived by the bread and half eaten chops and a good sleep.

Len put Mildred and little Johnny in his own bed. There were two beds in the room he shared with the Italian. Then he went to work. The cab driver had agreed not to charge them for the return journey. Len was five minutes early for work. Once he fell asleep face down in the washing-up water which brought him back to earth. Nothing had ever happened to him like this before.

FOR A WEEK they fought for her life. The doctor came twice more all the way to Lambeth at his own expense.

All through the years of the rest of his life, Len Merryl took comfort from having met one good man in his life. In all he only saw the old doctor three times but the old man stayed in his mind forever.

"You're going to marry that girl," the old man had said on his last visit. This time he was smiling.

"I can't. She's my first cousin."

"Change to the Church of Scotland. We marry first cousins, I wish you both a long and happy life... Merry Christmas."

WHEN MILDRED was up and about everything changed again. The crisis was over. They had helped to save a human life. They had all felt good.

"You can't go on taking food out of the kitchen. It was Christmas, and the girl was going to die. Now that is over. You work by the rules. Eat what you can of the leftovers behind my back but don't take it home. Someone outside the kitchen finds out, I'll get the sack. Tell her to get a bloody job."

"She's a whore."

"Whore's work. How they feed themselves. People help in emergencies. Not for the rest of their bloody life. This kitchen ain't no charity. Watch yourself, Len. You're twenty. Far from 'ome and done a good thing. But it is over. Back to normal. The rules. Don't fuck around with the rules and fucking regulations."

It had been a week since he fell asleep in the dirty washing-up water. The kitchen manager knew what he was talking about. The rules could only be bent in an emergency.

Little Johnny kept them awake at night now he was full of food and energy. The Italian had become short-tempered. Now Len had to find food for Mildred and Johnny out of the three pennies that were left to him from his pay after paying half the rent of the Lambert room... The man on the train had been right. Washing dishes in a good hotel filled the belly and nothing else... So far as Len could find out without asking too many questions of his fellow workers, the pay never changed from one year to the next. They fed from the crumbs that fell from the rich man's table. Scrap. Scrap that otherwise the rich would throw away in the ignorance of poverty.

LEN THOUGHT the Italian must have spoken to Mildred. When he came home on New Year's Day, Mildred and little Johnny had gone. Len supposed Mildred would have written a note if she could have written. For the time she had stayed with them in the room, Mildred had slept in Len's bed with Johnny. He had slept on the floor.

That night Len slept a dreamless sleep in his own bed. He never went back to Soho or the Elephant and Castle. He had done his best, he told himself. There was nothing more he could do. He tried to hope she had gone back to Neston. There was no point in writing to his mother to ask. Mrs Snell had to read his mother any letters. Mildred had been right. Mrs Snell was a bitch.

When he looked at girls, big breasts sticking out of blouses made him think of Mildred. Now there was no arousal. When he had washed the big breasts of the smell of Mildred's room she shared with the whores, it was just a large envelope of skin that floated out on the scummy bathwater. Little Johnny had sucked it dry and empty in his desperation.

Len knew he should go and look for her but he didn't. Even if he wished to be he did not have the wherewithal to be his cousin's keeper. The old Scot doctor had been wrong. The idea of marrying Mildred had never entered his head. Being cousins was an excuse. Lust came and went. Len's lust for Cousin Mildred had gone while he washed off the dirt into the bath. The war that had been over for more than two years had found another victim. Two victims... He wondered if the other two whores had let them back into the room in Soho. He wondered if she still leaned against the same lamp post of the Elephant and Castle.

Cousin Mildred was the first of many people who became for a while so central to his life. As the years went by he was to think of her less and less and always with sadness. Most people survived somehow through their lives.

IF NOTHING else it made him think of the pitfalls of life. A wrong turn. Bad luck. The wrong friends. All could cost him his life. Most of all, it taught him there had to be more to life than washing dishes or being a whore.

In the hope of finding work and a dream he was unable to see in the kitchen of the Park Lane hotel, Len Merryl took himself off to the London docks. The fog was thick over the estuary to the River Thames, the trade route to the capital from the time of the Romans. He was an Englishman which was better, he told himself, than being a lot of other less fortunate nationalities on the earth. He was British. The British had an empire. In the colonies he would find himself something better to do than washing dishes.

A MONTH AFTER Mildred walked out of his life, Len took a ship for Singapore. The boat was a tramp steamer that traded from port to port around Africa, down the west coast, the east coast, across to Bombay from the port of Mombasa in Kenya, round India to Singapore with a stop in Ceylon. Somewhere on the way he determined, he was going to find himself a better destiny. Mildred's life had frightened the wits out of him.

He was twenty years old when the old tramp cut loose from Woolwich docks and edged out into the estuary of old father Thames. He was going to see the world. The fact that his job in the ship's scullery was washing dishes just made him laugh.

He would miss the Italian who after so many weeks together seemed to speak a better English. The Italian said it was better. Len was not so sure. They had wished each other a good life for the future. Neither thought he would ever see the other again.

The fog swallowed up Len and the boat.

FROM INSIDE the corner of a long shed that was packed high with bales of cotton destined for the mills of Manchester, Mildred watched him go. She had on a thick overcoat pulled tight across her thin body. Little Johnny had his hand tucked deep in Mildred's right hand. When Mildred waved to the ghost-like ship, little Johnny waved with his free hand.

She had wanted to thank him. To say so much. She knew better than Len what washing a whore could do to a man's sexuality. She knew he was a virgin. She had sensed that. She hoped his experience of her would not make him cold to other women. That first night in his arms. Filthy in the filthy sheets in the filthy bed had been the nicest thing anyone had ever done for her before. She had been ready to die, too tired to fight any more for little Johnny.

Then he had washed her clean of dirt and sin and put her in his own bed while he slept on the floor... As soon she was strong enough she had removed the burden from his life. She hoped that some day they would meet again in better circumstances. She doubted it. Their ships had passed in the night. Len and the old Scot doctor had given her back her life. It was now up to her.

Mildred had also seen the Salvation Army singing Christmas carols on the street. When a month ago she had walked from Lambeth with Johnny back to Soho, her luck had changed. She found them in Regent Street. The young girl that had shaken the poor box at Len heard her story to the end. The girl had taken them to a shelter where they gave her the coat.

Later, the girl had found out for her from the Park Lane hotel where Len washed dishes that Len was sailing on the steamer from Woolwich docks. She had wanted to see him off. To thank him. To tell him how she felt... She had seen him walk to the ship not twenty yards from where she stood just inside the shed. The fog had been her friend. She had hesitated for a moment, wondering if she was doing the right thing, fearful he would turn back to them out of guilt and not go forward on his journey.

It was the best thing she did to let him go. He would think of her as a whore for the rest of her life but it did not matter. Mentally, she called out to him God's blessing. She was going to make a life for herself. They were teaching her to read and write. She was going to give herself an education if it meant reading in every spare moment for the rest of her life. She owed Len Merryl more than that.

Little Johnny began to fidget. She waved at the rolling fog now empty of the ship. Then she turned and walked briskly along the wet railway line to where a man at the gate had let her see off the boat. She was crying.

"Did you find him all right?" the man called as she walked through the gates that led out of the dock.

"Yes, I did. And thank you."

"He'll be back soon. His boy will miss him. Boys always miss their fathers."

"Yes they do," said Mildred. The tears began again. This time for Johnny Lake.

6

LONDON, JANUARY 1921

*B*arnaby St Clair laughed out loud. It was easier than backing the only racehorse in a field of carthorses to win the Epsom Derby. The racehorse could still stumble or die before reaching the post. In four months he had turned the five hundred pounds extorted from his brother Merlin into five thousand pounds, enough to buy himself a country house in the new stockbroker belt that was spreading over the fields of Surrey.

The first hundred pounds had been invested in exquisite clothing. Perfectly tailored suits and evening dress from Savile Row. Handmade shirts from Jermyn Street with pucker-free hemlines and French seams. Handmade shoes. A cane to match Merlin's with a thin sword at its heart should there ever be trouble. Hats. Gloves. An opera coat with a gorgeous maroon interior that flowed behind him manifesting his glory. Only the cufflinks and shirt studs were made from fake sapphires that looked the same as the real thing. Barnaby at just twenty-four was the quintessential man about town. The three years under the desert sun of Arabia that had scorched and dried his skin gave him the air of maturity. He never gave his age. He had even given himself the rank of captain. Major sounded too old. Captain the Honourable Barnaby St Clair was always at their service. Provided they were rich and gullible. The piercing blue eyes smiled at everything rich while the mind behind them calculated the worth of everything he saw... Best of all, which surprised Barnaby the most, every penny he made so easily on the London Stock Exchange was perfectly legal. All was fine as everyone was making money. There were no losers to squeal. How it was possible was beyond his mental means to understand. As it was with everyone else. The market was going up by the day. Money was made in large quantities without having to work for it. Barnaby just wished Tina Pringle was in London to see what he had done. He wanted to tell her what he was going to do. How rich he was going to be. He needed Tina to appreciate his cleverness.

FIRST BARNABY had reserved his membership of the Army and Navy Club that only officers could join and women were allowed to enter through a side door between certain hours once a week. The women were allowed no further than the ladies' cocktail lounge. They were not permitted to dine in the restaurant. Barnaby would have preferred the Cavalry Club at 127 Piccadilly, close to Buckingham Palace. Despite having ridden a camel it was not a horse. The second-rate regiment he had joined in Palestine was laughed at by the cavalry. Only cavalry officers could join the Cavalry Club. When anyone asked his regiment he replied with a knowing smile full of secrecy that he had been with Lawrence in the desert. The mysteries of Lawrence of Arabia were enough to shut up the inquisitive and the sceptical. He told them even his captaincy had been kept a secret just in case they looked him up in the army list and found his captaincy missing.

With the right calling card and the perfect clothes, Barnaby called on the two gentlemen he had met on the boat back from Africa. They had both given him their calling cards. The three of them were a perfect match. A young, good-looking, dashing ex-officer from a very old family with a minor title and the two unscrupulous investors who knew how to make a fortune out of the system.

When a company listed on the London Stock Exchange was due to announce its results, it was important to the two gentlemen to know those results before they were known by the public. As Barnaby worked his way through London society he listened for information, and passed it on to the two men for money. Being so simple it was all so beautiful.

"Vickers are due out soon. They'll be down with the war over but we want to know by how much their profits are down. Then we'll short the shares. Here is a list of their directors and managers. Rolls-Royce are also due. There is a rumour. They want to make engines for aeroplanes. Probably a lot of nonsense if you ask me but it will kick their shares if the press get hold of it. If the story has any truth we can leak it to the press after we buy a block of their shares. We only have to settle with our stockbroker at the end of the month. By then we will be out with a profit and not put a penny on the table. Here is their list of directors. Remember their names."

"I know one of the daughters. Ugly as sin."

"Never mind. Tell her she's pretty. Get her drunk. Pump the bitch… Of information, Barnaby."

"She's thirty or more."

"Better still. She'll be grateful for the attention."

"Max, you sure this is legal?"

"You can ask your solicitor."

"I will."

"Nothing wrong with using good information."

"No, of course not. Never thought of using women." Barnaby was still smiling.

"Don't be bloody daft, Barnaby. It seems to me you've been using women all your life without knowing it. Now run along and find out what you can. Don't forget you are not our only source of information… Aren't those cufflinks fake sapphires?"

"How do you know?"

"I just know. Change them. The rest is fine."

"Thank you, Max."

"Be careful. Never be too smart to learn. Always keep your wits about you. Reputations take a long time to build and one stupid error to go down the drain. This may look like easy money to you but it is not. Money can only be made, real money, by using your brains. Society will throw you out as easily as they welcomed you in… Does your father ever come up to London?"

"Never."

"That's good. Any other relations in town?"

"Merlin. Brother Merlin. The writer, Robert St Clair, is a recluse in Dorset. Doesn't like showing off his one good leg."

"Keep away from Merlin."

"You don't have to worry about that. Merlin keeps well away from me."

"And don't go home to Dorset for as long as you are working for me and Porter."

"I have no intention."

"Do you have a girlfriend?"

"She's in Africa."

"Leave her there. Never confide in anyone. There is no such thing as a secret. You made a fortune in Africa. That's all they have to know."

"How did you know I said that?"

"As Max said, Barnaby," Porter interrupted, "there is no such thing as a secret. Everyone loves to talk. You just do the prompting and the listening. For the moment, stay at your club. You can look for a flat later on."

"Will I earn that much?"

"Probably," said Max.

BARNABY HAD done what he was told for the first month. Max and Porter had paid him twenty pounds for his information. The social circuit, spending money as carefully as possible, always deferring to another man who wished to pay the bill with the right amount of persuasion but not too much to land him with the bill, had cost Barnaby ten pounds. He had lived well and made a profit. Max and Porter had made a fortune if they did half what they said they were going to do. Only one of the shares failed to perform in the way it was meant to perform. One share out of ten. The odds were well loaded in their favour. Soon after Vickers came out with their results, the shares on which Merlin's fortune was once based, fell seven per cent. Max and Porter had sold short. Selling Vickers shares they did not have. When they bought the shares at the end of the month to give the stockbroker the shares they had sold, they pocketed the seven per cent difference in the share price without laying out a penny. Their only cost was the broker's fees for selling and buying the shares.

"And if the shares had gone up?" Barnaby had asked trying not to show too much interest.

"We would have had to find the difference on one hundred thousand Vickers's shares to pay the stockbroker."

"That would have been a fortune."

"But we made a fortune, Barnaby. From your information."

"For which I received five pounds."

"You took no risk. We took the risk. Money is only made by those who take the risk."

"But their profits had dropped in half! They had to go down!"

Max and Porter had smiled smugly. Barnaby had shaken his head in frustration.

His first reaction was to go out on his own. Buy and sell shares on his own account. With the four hundred pounds now left over from Merlin's cash cheque for five hundred pounds.

He thought about it all that night, thinking of Vickers. In the morning he saw the light, as he told himself. Most men went wrong by being too greedy. He would give his new employers their information. After all, they asked him to look out for the right information that he otherwise would not have been aware.

Instead, he opened a bank account with Cox's and King's, who had been the bank the army used to pay his salary during the war. He deposited the four hundred pounds. He spent half an hour polishing the bank manager's ego, dropping names and being terribly deferential to the man's position as manager of the bank.

"My father, Lord St Clair, does not believe in owning shares. Something about being in trade. Came down the centuries, you see. Now that's old rubbish, of course. You would know that better than anyone, sir. Well, I want myself a few shares. Nothing more than what I have, you understand. But I want to buy them in a name other than the Honourable Barnaby St Clair so my father can't trace the transactions. He's quite eccentric you see. My grandfather was much the same. They check up on you. Father will go to the registrar of companies and demand to see the list of shareholders if he suspects I own shares in the company. You know how people talk. One of the problems of having such a well-known name. You know what people are like talking about old money."

"Well, that would be quite difficult for your father. How would he know which shares to look for?"

"But not worth the risk, sir. You see, I love my father very much."

"Then you could use the bank as a nominee. The shares will be registered in our name. Only in our books will they be for your account, Mr St Clair."

"Is that legal?"

"Of course, Mr St Clair. You don't think the British Army would use us as paymasters for its officers if we did anything dishonest… All the shares are going up rather nicely. There's another thing the bank can do for you, Mr Barnaby. We can lend you eighty per cent of the value of the shares you buy. That way, with your four hundred pounds, you may buy two thousand pounds worth of shares."

"And if the shares go down?"

"We have your four hundred pounds to cover the twenty per cent drop. The shares are in our name. We only sell when the bank is at risk."

"And if the shares go up?"

"You may borrow another eighty per cent of the profit. You take the risk. You take the profit. We are bankers, Mr St Clair, not gamblers. You have banked with us for three years as a serving British officer. Welcome back to Cox's and King's."

"You really are a remarkable man, sir."

"Is there anything else I do for you?"

"Would you be kind enough to purchase these shares? There are ten of them. Ask your man to buy to the maximum of my credit in equal proportions. In the name of your nominee. This morning would be a good time. If your man is unable to buy any of these shares before lunch, he is to leave them alone."

"By lunchtime? You mean one o'clock?"

"Exactly. Please to understand any purchases made after the hour I give you be for the bank's account. Please be kind enough to give me that in writing."

"Yes, sir, would you care to wait for the letter?"

Outside in Pall Mall, Barnaby had felt better than at any time in his life. It was much better than he thought. Two thousand pounds worth of shares instead of four hundred pounds. He doubted if his father had ever seen a share certificate. He certainly would have no idea about the registrar of companies. It was Max and Porter Barnaby wished to keep in the dark for as long as possible. The only person he wanted to tell was Tina Pringle. She knew how to keep a secret. Had always known. Since they were young children. He wondered where she was. What she was doing. Which made him jealous. The very idea of Tina Pringle with another man made him jealous.

Walking away from the bank he was smiling to himself. How typical of the British Army to keep its misdemeanours to itself. The bank manager had had no idea he stole from the officers' mess account in Cairo. It was the one risk he had had to take. He needed the army's years of backing with Cox's and King's to be to his credit. Being an army officer was the only way a man under twenty-one could have a bank account. He was going to write to Tina. He was solvent. By the end of next month he would be worth a thousand pounds. Instead of writing to Tina he would send her a cable. Ask if she wanted to come home. He hurried down towards the club. The doorman would be a good chap and send his cable. There were forms in the club. His days of being poor were over. Tonight he would go out on the town. For himself. There was a young girl at the Embassy club he had had his eye on. He needed his own flat. He would give his shares a week to rise. Then he would sell. And find himself a flat where he could take the young girl from the Embassy.

He was still thinking of Tina Pringle and the girl from the Embassy when he reached the Army and Navy Club. He decided to write to Tina after all. A cable might sound too strong a message. He would write to her in the morning, a long letter, and tell her everything. Maybe the girl at the Embassy had her own flat or a place to go. Unlikely. He just hoped so. The Embassy was very expensive, and the girls were always getting tips. First, he would have a drink in the bar to celebrate.

"You look very chipper, St Clair. Very pleased with yourself." Barnaby had seen the man twice before on the social circuit.

"Can I buy you a drink, Fortescue?"

"Let me buy you one."

"As you wish, old boy."

"Have you come into money?"

"Nothing like that, I'm afraid."

"Anyway, have a drink with me."

BY THE TIME Barnaby was worth five thousand pounds he had still not written to Tina Pringle. He had forgotten all about the idea. The girl from the Embassy did have a small flat in the West End. Barnaby used it half a dozen times. He thought the girl sometimes charged for her services. The flat was expensive. She never asked him for anything and he put it down to his youth and charm. The girl only mixed in the right circles so he did not think there would be any problems. Her father was a colonel in the Indian army. Barnaby doubted the father knew his daughter waited tables. Or charged the older men for her services. If she played her cards right, Barnaby thought, she would find herself a rich husband. She was very pretty. Old men liked young pretty girls. Barnaby had even checked the Indian army list. The father was half a colonel. Lieutenant colonel. But he was an officer.

When Barnaby grew bored with her, he suggested she go back to India on the fishing fleet. To find herself a husband. Young girls of good families went to India looking for lonely bachelors. The single girls out from England were known in India as the fishing fleet. Englishmen never married the natives. It was just not done. If they did they were thrown out of the regiment.

Barnaby had given the Embassy a miss for a month. When he went back, the girl had gone. There were so many young pretty girls in London. They were the flappers dancing into the small hours every night. With money, Barnaby was having a wonderful time. The war was over. He was rich. Everyone was having a good time. It was right everyone should have a good time after such a terrible war. No one thought too much of the future. They were too busy enjoying themselves. The ones like Barnaby spending their money and their youth.

ON THE SAME morning Len Merryl sailed for Singapore watched unbeknown by Cousin Mildred, Barnaby St Clair decided to call on his brother Merlin. To add to his brother's annoyance, he decided to call unannounced. There was a thin fog in Hyde Park which was not uncommon on a winter's morning in January. Barnaby passed the opulent entrance to the hotel where Len had worked as a dishwasher and found his brother's block of flats. Barnaby had them ring his brother's flat from downstairs in the foyer. There was a telephone system between the desk in the foyer and the flats. The man at the desk made the call on Barnaby's behalf.

"There is a gentleman to see Mr St Clair, Smithers, Mr St Clair's brother."

Barnaby waited, giving the desk man his best sardonic smile. He was dressed, he thought, to perfection but without the old Harrovian tie. The sapphires in the cufflinks of his handmade shirts were now genuine. He wore a tailor-made overcoat with lapels of black fox fur. He carried kid gloves and a trilby hat that he held in his hand with the light cane that hid the rapier blade of his sword. Barnaby had always wanted to walk around London with a sword disguised in a walking stick. It gave him a feeling of daring. A cut above the rest. In his pocket was a cash cheque for five hundred pounds which is what made him smile. If his brother had been poor, he would never have given him back the money. One of Barnaby's new golden rules was never to upset anyone who was rich. The poor did not matter. The rich mattered very much.

"Mr St Clair is on his way down, sir." The man was giving him a queer look. Barnaby smirked back at him and waited, exuding confidence from the top of his head to the bottom of his well-made leather shoes. Gently, with the tips of his fingers, he tapped the top of his felt hat, the latest fashion from America to rage through London, along with the cocktails he copiously drank on his social rounds.

As Barnaby expected, his brother Merlin was scowling when he stepped out of the lift into the foyer. Barnaby smiled sweetly and gave his brother the cheque for five hundred pounds.

"Sorry it's been so long, old chap."

Merlin stared at the cheque for a moment. Then he grinned up at his brother.

"You'd better come up to the flat," said Merlin.

"Breakfast would be nice. It's ten minutes to nine o'clock. Maybe even a glass of whisky."

"Isn't it too early to drink?"

"It's never too early to drink," said Barnaby.

The brothers were now laughing. The man at the desk watched quizzically as they got into the lift. They were arm in arm. He rang the same number again.

"Make it breakfast for two Smithers, they coming up. Bloke gave him a bloody cheque."

Nothing was secret in a small block of flats, however exclusive. The servants had to do something to alleviate their boredom. So they gossiped. About their employers. Usually while drinking the employer's whisky when the employer was out of his flat. It gave the servants the satisfaction of getting even for having to know their place and play the game of master and servant. Smithers had said so succinctly to the doorman the night they first drank Merlin St Clair's whisky.

"Never piss in your own whisky glass. Play them along. If they want to speak with a plum in their mouth and a stick up their bum that's fine by me. Have another drink."

"Won't he mind?"

"The man has far too much breeding and manners to ask. It's like adding up the bill in a restaurant. If you have to add up the bill, you should not be there in the first place. If you have to watch the level of your whisky bottle, you shouldn't have a servant."

"You speak just like 'im."

"Makes him feel comfortable. Cheers, old boy. I hope this will not be the last time we drink good whisky together."

"So do bloody I, mate. So where you from, Smithers?"

"Lambeth. East End. I'm a cockney."

"Don't sound like none."

"Don't get me started."

TINA PRINGLE had found out soon after Barnaby St Clair had been kicked out of her brother's house in Johannesburg that being a rich man's sister was of very little use. She was never going to get any of it. The house on the beach at Umdloti in Durban had had all the attributes of a jail for a girl of twenty-two. Otherwise everything was perfect. The sea was warm, the seafood rich, the servants polite, the conversation with her sister-in-law relaxed. She had tried to suggest going back to Johannesburg the day they arrived. There was this beautiful house right on the beach with nothing on either side. Durban, that might have provided some fun, was seventeen miles down the coast. There were no neighbours. No restaurants. No people.

"Isn't it lovely?" Sallie Pringle had said.

Tina said nothing. She wanted to be with Barnaby. Even if they had to live off their wits and their own good looks.

A week passed before her brother phoned his wife and told her to come home.

"Barnaby has sailed for England," Sallie had told Tina. "He's on the water. We can go back to Johannesburg, Albert has paid his passage. Albert loves you, Tina. Wants the best for you. Barnaby is a rotten apple."

"How DO you know? Why can't Albert mind his own bloody business?"

"When a man sponges off of him it is his business, Tina." Sallie was doing her best to control her temper.

"He can afford it."

"Your looks won't last forever."

"How do you know?"

"Don't be rude."

"I'm sorry. I really am, Sal... Blimey, can we really go home? This place is a bloody mortuary."

"Remember how Miss Pinforth taught you to speak. Please, Tina."

"Bugger Miss Pinforth. I love Barnaby. Always have. Since we were little kids. Is that really such a bad thing? Loving someone. Without Barnaby life doesn't happen. Doesn't exist. Where's he gone to?"

"London."

"What's he going to do in London?"

"I don't really care."

"But I do. What am I going to do?"

"Find yourself a rich husband."

"I wish Barnaby was rich. Solve all our bloody problems."

"Please don't swear, Tina."

"I can't help it. You wouldn't help it either if your lover was on the other side of the world."

"Are you really lovers?"

"'Course we are."

"Be careful you don't get pregnant."

"You're a fine one to talk."

"But we got married. Barnaby won't marry you. He's far too much of a snob. You would be his mistress for as long as it suits him. Men like Barnaby like to be seen with very pretty young girls. It boosts their ego. They try to keep young girls as long as possible. Look at Benny Lightfoot. You were going out with a man thirty years your senior. Those kind of men don't want a wife and family. They want to think they are still young with everything ahead of them. In the end it's desperation when they discover they have missed out on life. Sex is more important to them than family. They are very unhappy people. So are the girls that love them."

"You can't stop loving a man just because he's a rotter."

"There are lots of men in Johannesburg. I promise to help. I'll find you a man you can really love. Who will fulfil your life."

"Do you really love my brother?"

"Not in the way you might think. I love his mind. That will last us forever."

"Don't you like sex?"

"Of course I do. But it is not the predominant need in my life. In a man. Can't you understand?"

"No I bloody well can't. I'm a physical person. So is Barnaby. Why I love him so much. Don't you understand?"

LITTLE JULIA PRINGLE has been born seven months after Tina's brother married Sallie Barker, as she was then. Even Tina's maths worked that one out. Everyone she had ever known, starting with her mother, knew the way she should live her life. In criticising her, telling her what to do, they implied their own lives were perfect. Even at twenty-two, Tina knew that was a lot of rot. Her mother had spent her married life breeding children and cooking for her family. Nothing else. She was an old woman before she was thirty-five. She had had less fun than the family cat. And as to Sallie loving a man's mind rather than his body, Tina thought in that case it would be better not to be born. Where was the fun in a man's mind!

When they arrived back in Johannesburg at her brother's house at Parktown Ridge, Tina looked for a letter from Barnaby. There was nothing. When she calculated the boat he was sailing on had arrived in England she waited for a telephone call. There was nothing. She moped about the house and read cheap novels all day. She began to eat too much and put on weight. None of the men Sallie paraded through the house sparked in Tina any interest. She sulked. Tina knew she was good at sulking. There was nothing anyone could do about her sulks. It infuriated the whole household. Silent sulking was her best weapon.

The weeks went by without a word from Barnaby until the truth struck fear right through her body and mind. She knew him too well. If he was having a hard time he would want to talk to her. Want reassuring letters from her that he was still the most important man in the world. He must have landed with his feet on the ground and it made her want to scream. Without her he was having a good time! Without her help he was making money out of someone. The weeks and weeks of silence told her everything. The thought ate deep into her soul. She wanted to strangle him: kill him with her bare hands. Most of all she wanted to make him lust after her body so she could make quite certain he never had enough. Never be satiated. Never be free of her power to make him lust. She wanted to tantalise Barnaby St Clair into total submission to one Tina Pringle.

She got the money from Benny Lightfoot. He owed her that much. A man getting a really good young body when he was well past his prime had to pay. One way or the other. If the age difference had been a lot less, she might have tried again. He was rich enough. Now she saw him as an old man with wrinkled hands and a soft pot belly. She did not want the man to even touch her any more.

"Thank you, Tina."

"What for?"

"Your youth. That was what I wanted. Have a good life. I hope you find him."

"I'm sorry, Benny. It's just the age thing."

"I know."

TINA LEFT Albert and Sallie a letter on the silver tray in the hall, next to the front door where visitors left their calling cards. She had not wanted an argument.

Christmas had come and gone but it wasn't the same in Africa. No one sang carols. Christmas trees ablaze in the sun looked fake. There was no snow. Eating hot turkey in the sweltering heat of an African summer seemed ludicrous. The church bells didn't sound the same without penetrating the cold and frost of an English winter. She was miserable. Everyone in the Parktown Ridge house knew she was miserable. It was better she left. She was old enough to fend for herself.

When the train left Johannesburg railway station for Durban, she had felt the spark come back into her life. She had bought new clothes for the boat and Barnaby. She was going up the west coast through the Suez Canal. 'Through the Med', the sign had said at the ticket office. Round past Gibraltar. It was exciting. Life was exciting again. She would even make herself some fun on the trip. She could not expect her brother to keep her any longer. She was right. She was doing the right thing. She would find Barnaby in London and give him the surprise of his life. Finding him would be easy. Barnaby St Clair always made a lot of noise.

THE MORNING Barnaby was eating nine o'clock breakfast with his brother, the boat bringing Tina Pringle back to England docked in Southampton. It was a warm day for January when Tina found a cab. With her luggage safely in the cab, they drove to the railway station. Tina hugged herself with excitement. She could just imagine the expression on his face. She would stay at the Savoy. Give a nice tone to her arrival in London. Benny Lightfoot, bless his heart, had been very generous. The small, close-fitting hat on her head had made a perfect picture in the mirror of the cab. She was as pretty as paint. The close-cropped hair suited her. Her brown eyes were soft and full of seduction. Her figure was back to perfect.

She pulled the trim fur collar of her white coat up to her small ears. She was enjoying the ride. The cabbie smiled to her in the mirror. She smiled back. She was back in England, well-dressed, well-spoken and with money in her purse. She would plan her pursuit of Barnaby like a military campaign. When the time was right, he was going to want her so badly nothing would get in their way. Other people could go to hell. Not only was she going to win the battle, she told herself, she was going to win the war. She was going to marry him. Become Mrs Barnaby St Clair. She was that determined.

ONCE ENSCONCED in her room at the Savoy Hotel, it took half an hour to find out where he was. She knew him so well it made her laugh out loud. A pretty laugh that made the bellboy with the sweet little chocolate-coloured box-hat turn back from the door with her shilling tip in his hand. The boy smiled back at the pleasure he could see in her face. The boy was little more than twelve years old but cute as a button.

The first thing she had done when her luggage was safely in the room was to send off for the *Tatler*, the gossip magazine that followed the aristocracy. Barnaby needed people to make money, to survive. The *Tatler* needed good-looking young men with titles to sell their subscriptions. If Barnaby had done what Tina expected, the two would have found each other. To succeed in parting fools from their money, Barnaby would have tried to make himself a minor celebrity. To be talked about. Sought-after by the social hostesses of London society. Chased after by horsy young girls with family titles and young rich girls looking to marry into the aristocracy. How Barnaby had got money out of Merlin or Robert was the puzzle in her equation. They had talked about it more than once. Merlin from the wealth he made during the war buying Vickers Armstrong shares and Robert from the sale of his books. Barnaby would have needed something to set himself up in society. Albert had paid his passage with a small allowance that would have lasted the boat trip and no longer.

When the twelve-year-old bellboy shut the door to her room gently, Tina looked again at the picture of Barnaby in the magazine. The girl he was with had a face like a horse which pleased Tina no end. The one fear since leaving Johannesburg was Barnaby finding a rich girl as pretty as herself.

Licking her lips with the tip of her tongue, Tina began planning her campaign. The first thing to do was set herself up with a photograph, a big one in the *Tatler*. She was going to battle her Barnaby in the columns of glossy magazines that followed the rich and famous. In the end, Barnaby would want to find her. Only then would she start the fun. Like so many things in life it was a lot more simple than she had imagined.

She called the manager of the hotel, affecting the speech tones taught her by Miss Pinforth with such difficulty in the little cottage in

MAD DOGS AND ENGLISHMEN

Johannesburg. The name of the society photographer was mentioned twice in the *Tatler* issue that had the photograph of Barnaby and his nag. Tina had chuckled to herself thinking of the girl as a nag.

Tina had dressed carefully before making the call.

"I have a problem, Mr Bennett. Would you please come to my room?"

"Right away, madam."

Tina thought the poor man was probably frightened of his guests. Everyone who stayed in his hotel thought themselves superior to the manager. He was only there to make them pleased.

It took the poor man three minutes to tap on her door. The man nearly fell over his patent leather shoes when he came through the door at her command. Tina thought rightly, few young girls stayed at the Savoy and none with her kind of looks. The man started wringing his hands, he was so subservient. Tina put on all her hard learnt airs and graces.

"As you know, my brother, Mr Albert Pringle of Johannesburg, is chairman of the London listed company, Serendipity Mining and Explosives Company which of course he owns. He wished me to see London but was himself unable to afford the time to leave his gold mines in South Africa. Mr Barry Jones of the *Tatler* will want to take my photograph as I wish to announce my London arrival. Be so kind as to telephone Mr Jones, Mr Bennett, and tell him. I loathe talking to the press but sometimes it is a must. Men like to announce their presence. We women only have to be seen."

Tina had deliberately worn a loose dress, leaving her large, firm breasts with little constraint. The poor man's eyes popped out of his head at the sexuality oozing from the movement inside the top of her dress. It was a trick she used on every man she wished to seduce. The same way she had seduced Jim Bowman in Meikles Hotel. The day Barnaby had tricked him out of ten pounds. Then she had been fashionably strapped up but the trick had still worked perfectly. As the manager went out of her room to do her bidding, she had remembered Jim Bowman for some strange reason. She thought the trick and Barnaby had brought Jim Bowman to her mind. She remembered their lunch together. Just the three of them. The poor naïve man would never get his ten pounds back again but that was life.

Three hours later Barry Jones was taking her photograph. The issue was due out on the Friday. The manager had done a perfect job. Tina knew her sexuality would photograph well. The society photographer had come to her room with a lady journalist who knew all about the share price rise and the rise of Serendipity Mining. Albert if he ever came to London, which she doubted he would, would be an instant celebrity. She changed her dress twice in the large bathroom to give Barry Jones a choice. In the article the girl would mention Tina was staying at the Savoy. The journalist owed that much to the manager for her story.

When Tina dined alone in the grill room of the hotel that night, she was well pleased with her progress.

Alone later in her room she would have phoned her mother in Dorset in the cottage by the railway line where her father had worked checking the line of Corfe Castle every morning if her mother had had a telephone. She would have liked to laugh with her mother at the incongruity of her situation. Tina Pringle from the railway cottage staying at the Savoy.

"You've come a long way, girl," she said to herself in the mirror. The one glass of wine from the half bottle she had allowed herself at dinner had gone to her head. "Just you wait, Barnaby."

Tina turned out the bedside lamp and drifted towards sleep. She could hear a ship's horn coming from the River Thames outside her window. Then she was asleep and back in Africa in her dreams. All night, for some strange reason she dreamed of Jim Bowman. In the morning she remembered. Even in her sleep, Barnaby was being evasive.

THE NEXT DAY, keeping her room at the Savoy and asking the desk to keep her messages, she caught the train to Dorset to see her parents. It had been a long time and lots for her to tell. Only when the article appeared in the *Tatler* would the phone in her hotel bedroom begin to ring. She had the time to spare.

By the time she reached Corfe Castle station and home, she was just as excited as a child. The fact that her mother was old, fat and harassed made no difference to Tina. Her mother was her mother and she would only ever have one of those. She chose not to wear her smart new clothes and roughed up her hair.

When she ran into her mother's ample arms, she was just Tina. Both of them were crying they were so pleased to see each other. Standing waiting his turn her father looked fit to burst.

"I've got plum pie just ready. Cable came from village two hours ago. Look at 'er! Look at 'er. Ain't she a picture? My Tina. Come here, lovey. Give your mum another hug. Pleased to be home?"

"'Course I am."

"Where you stayin'?"

"London."

"Where in London?"

"Savoy Hotel."

"Don't be daft. Now, you want a nice cup of tea first or slice of your mum's plum pie?"

"Don't you ever stop looking after us?"

"What's gives me pleasure. Where's your luggage?"

"Left it at the hotel."

"Pull the other leg. How's Bert? How's my granddaughter? Little Julia."

"They send their love."

"Bless 'em. Now give your da a big hug like you gave me."

Along the way from the railway station she had looked up at the ruins of Corfe Castle, once the home of Barnaby's family.

Everything was so separate. The ruined castle on its hill torn down by Oliver Cromwell. Her paid for empty room at the Savoy Hotel. The tiny cottage with its garden where she was born and had been so happy.

She wondered if she would ever be that happy again. In her mind there was a small boy standing in the vegetable garden waiting for her. They would join hands and run together to the river that was really a stream. To each other they were Barnaby and Tina. To the rest he was the Lord of the Manor's youngest son and she the barefoot daughter of a vassal. Tina knew she was able to have one world or the other. But not them both together.

For a brief moment in her mother's warm kitchen that smelled of freshly baked plum pie she was not so sure of which world she wanted. The Victoria plums had come from their own tree outside in the garden, bottled in the autumn into Kilner jars with her mother's own hands. From the high picture skirting, dried herbs hung, cut during last year's summer. The store cupboard was full of home-made jams and jellies, jars of pickles and hazelnuts in string bags. The old ginger cat was giving her the eye without moving an inch from his perch on the wooden stool next to the Dover stove piled on either side with dry cut wood ready to burn. The square table, big enough for all the large family was scrubbed white. The sweet smell of wood smoke was somewhere in the air, mingled with the fainter smells of the dried herbs. Tina began to cry uncontrollably. Her mother folded her back into arms.

"What's the matter, pet?" asked her mother.

"I'm just so happy to be home."

MERLIN ST CLAIR suspected he was being manipulated by Barnaby but could not see how. Neither had shown the slightest outward emotion once they had eaten breakfast. The fact he had put up his arm through his brother's getting into the lift had been impulsive and out of character. Even Granny Forrester had found herself doing things for Barnaby she would never do for the other children. It was so often the unexpected, the nice things he did when least expected that caught people off guard and had them doing favours for the likeable young man without thinking. That was it, Merlin had told himself. When he wished to be, Barnaby was so likeable. He did what you wanted him to do. To turn from being a parasite to being generous. Only afterwards did Merlin remember the generosity was the return of his own money. But before that thought had clouded his mind, he had had Smithers go off in the car and retrieve Barnaby's possessions from the Army and Military Club and bring them back to the Park Lane flat. The fact he was nearly thirty-six and living on his own in lonely splendour was a secret he even kept from himself.

Barnaby had straightaway lit up the place. Smithers had somehow first produced breakfast for two. Smithers had smiled. Smithers had laughed, something Smithers never did on his own. Everyone felt better. The breakfast tasted better. The illicit morning glass of whisky was a shared naughtiness that would have been letting the team down on his own; a man drinking on his own after breakfast was highly suspect. Instead it was the best whisky he had drunk in years.

The invitation for Barnaby to stay with him in London for as long as he liked came with the euphoria caused by the whisky after the sudden appearance of his perfectly dressed brother with a cash cheque for five hundred pounds, money that he had written off for the rest of his life. They had had a second and third whisky, swapping all the lovely stories from their youth and family in the old home. Purbeck Manor in Dorset was a place of happy memories they had all shared together. By the time they went off to lunch, Merlin was slightly tight, something he had never been in his life before lunch.

"Come and have lunch with me, old chap," Barnaby had said with an all-enfolding smile. "I still have to tell the club secretary what I'm doing. Just polite. Super chap. Maybe he'll lunch with us. Least I can do after such a splendid breakfast is buy you a bite of lunch. Food not bad... It really is jolly good of you inviting me into your home. I'm going to be so happy. We can go out on the town together, introduce you to some jolly good people. London is so much fun if you are part of the set. You'll see, Merlin, you'll see. What you've been saying leads me to think you've not been getting out enough. The theatre is fun but there's more to London and going to see a play... I know some splendid gals. There are so many the fun never stops. London's so gay, Merlin. You should enjoy it living here. We will. What fun. The two of us. Two brothers. Out on the town."

THE 'GALS' as his brother had called them were indeed a lot of fun. Merlin thought the night-long plunge into hedonism would lead them straight to perdition at the worst, a sanatorium for people who drank too much at the best. None of the 'gals' were looking for a husband. Just a good time with as many men as possible. The 'gals' danced to ragtime all night, drank all night and slept all day, their only daily workload dressing themselves up for the night ahead. They seemed to Merlin young and inexhaustible.

AFTER A WEEK Merlin took a night out alone in the flat with a pot of China tea and a glass of milk to make him go to sleep. When he took breakfast in the alcove overlooking Hyde Park in the morning Barnaby had yet to come home from his night on the town. Merlin thought the thirteen-year difference in their ages had something to do with it. He simply could not keep up. Smithers had even given him a sympathetic look with his bacon and eggs. He had not even bothered to lay breakfast for Barnaby, Merlin's life had been torn apart. So had Smithers's.

With the plates cleared away and the fresh pot of tea on the table, Smithers put down the silver tray from Asprey's. In it lay the morning's mail. Smiling at the pleasure of his own company, Merlin looked through his letters.

There was a letter from his bank that he hoped would not have been there. He went cold. His stomach turned. With the first good night's sleep having restored his senses since Barnaby's arrival, Merlin had intended making discreet enquiries concerning the source of his brother's new-found wealth. He had met Max and Porter during the social swirl. They had been introduced by Barnaby as his business partners. Porter had raised an eyebrow. Merlin had taken a dislike to the pair of them on sight. They were too well-dressed. Too well-spoken. Too emphatic. Their speech was as smooth as silk. Porter had given Merlin his calling card as his grand gift.

It was as if Porter knew more about the St Clair family than Merlin wished him to know. The gesture had been slightly condescending, a rich man giving a poor man a crumb from the table.

Before he had sat down to breakfast, he had made a call to his old firm in the City where he had worked as a Lloyd's insurance broker before the war. An old friend was now a senior director of Cornell, Brooke and Bradley, Lloyd's of London insurance brokers.

"Philip, old chap, did you ever hear of a chap in the City called Porter? C E Porter to be exact. Doesn't list any club on his calling card."

"Nasty piece of work, so I hear."

"So you know him?"

"Know of him, Merlin. How are you?"

"Not bad, considering. Young Barnaby staying with me."

"I see."

"What do you see, Philip?"

"You'd better come over. Maybe nothing."

"What are you doing this afternoon?"

"Always fit in a friend. Make it four o'clock. Then we can go off to the club for a drink. I'm not surprised Porter doesn't list a club on his card. He was thrown out of the Cavalry Club for talking business on the premises. More than once, so I hear. Asked the members too many questions. Club rule, no shop."

"Is this about Porter or my brother?"

"Both of them, I'm afraid."

When Merlin opened the letter from his bank, expecting to find the cheque from his brother returned, it was his monthly statement. The cheque which he had deposited the day Barnaby arrived had been credited to his account. He had written on the back for the bank to check the funds, backing the five hundred pounds cheque, before it was presented to Cox's and King's. Bouncing a cash cheque was fraud. Once perpetrated the fraudster went to jail. He had had no wish to put his brother in jail for a five hundred pounds loan he had never expected to see again.

For a moment he thought of phoning Philip Spence and cancelling his appointment. There was always a snag with Barnaby.

"Better to find out now than later," he said out loud while he picked up that month's copy of the *Tatler*. He liked to know who was out and about. Old friends from school. Old friends who had survived the war. The magazine kept him in touch, he told himself.

It was strange that Barnaby, the penniless member of the family, had been so welcome in high society, something Merlin knew he would never be fully part of himself. Neither was he going to be the next Lord St Clair of Purbeck, nor was he going to be truly rich. The *Tatler* gave him a window on a world he sometimes touched but never entered. In the simpler moments of his life, walking the woods, the stream, the hills of Purbeck, he had known it was a world he never wanted... Or had he just told himself that? Convinced himself. 'I can't have it so I don't want it.' The *Tatler* was his proxy to that other world. The glamour. The wealth. The power of money. The seduction.

The third page had a full-length photograph of the most beautiful woman he had ever seen. She was smiling straight at him, straight into his groin. The fact she was smiling at him from the page of the magazine made it no different.

There was a full article written about the girl. Merlin read the article twice, constantly turning his eyes from the words to the picture. Nowhere did it tell her age as it was expected. She was young. Much younger than most of the pictures of the girls he had seen before. The name Christine Pringle meant nothing. Albert Pringle meant nothing, the brother the article said was rich. The girl was staying at the Savoy. Merlin determined he and Philip would take their drink in the Savoy Hotel. He wanted to see the girl. Catch a glimpse. There was a chance. There was always a chance in life. If anyone had said he had met the girl as a child many times with Barnaby he would have laughed in their face. He had known a little girl called Tina. A small boy called Bert. They were the same to him as any other of the servant's children. Unimportant... The name Pringle had rung a bell. Merlin thought it a boy from school. A boy from prep school.

When he left to go to the City and his meeting with Philip Spence, he had left the magazine alone on the table.

WHEN BARNABY came home at four o'clock to change and ready himself for the night, he just had time to phone Porter and report the business news of the day. Then he picked up the new *Tatler* and took it to the bathroom where Smithers had run his bath.

Wiping his hands with a towel and making sure not to wet the pages, Barnaby settled back in the hot bath to read his favourite magazine. First, he flipped to the social pages, the chit-chat, the photographs of couples. There were two photographs of himself with different girls. Neither would mind the other girl. He liked looking at the pictures of the prim young girls and remembering his manhood thrust in their mouths. They had both looked so different. Animals. Their eyes screaming for more, their legs stuck back around their ears. The thought gave him an erection which he found a surprise. The one woman had been married. About forty, insatiable. Probably not had sex with her husband for years. He smiled at his erection. Like money, if there was more to be had he wanted it. He had escaped a war alive. Life was shorter than anyone knew. The older women were so grateful. They knew young, virile studs were rare to come by. He liked the older women. It gave him a feeling of power. He always made sure they never got enough of him. He did it well once. Maybe twice. Then he left them alone.

He was hoping he would find what he wanted again. At the party. At the theatre. At the after-theatre dinner. At the nightclub. Where did not matter.

Then he turned back to the magazine, to the photograph of Tina Pringle and his heart began to thump in his chest.

"Damn you, Tina. I was having a good time."

MERLIN HAD his back to the entrance to the lounge of the Savoy Hotel when Philip Spence licked his lips slowly and lost the thread of their conversation. Merlin knew who it was without looking round. The eyes of every man taking drinks or having tea at the round coffee table set apart in the lounge were following the same direction. Merlin thought it was like a draft of warm air that had swept between the pillars of the big room where a man on a dais in evening clothes was playing the piano, his black tails hanging over the back of the piano stool. The conversation subsided and then rose again as the men tried to remember their manners. Merlin stopped himself from looking around.

"Sorry, old chap. What did you say?" asked Philip Spence.

"Is she very pretty?"

"Exquisite. There was a photograph of her in this month's *Tatler*. I'm sure it's the same girl. I wonder who the lucky man is. Her name is Christine Pringle. I remember that from the article. Brother owns Serendipity Mining. Frightfully rich. I think we're in luck. They are heading for that empty table in front of you... Don't turn around. Shouldn't be rude. I'll be damned! The same girl in the flesh. I think the article said she was staying in the hotel so it's not such a coincidence. What a stunner... Now, where were we? Yes. Mr C E Porter. There should be a law against what he does. Totally unethical. The man's a rotter. Finds out what's happening in companies before the chaps publish their accounts. Knows what's happening before the rest of us. Damn unfair, I say. Not cricket. We all wait for the figures and then buy or sell. Not Porter. I rather think your brother Barnaby's a leg man, I think they call it. For Porter. Specialises purely to mine information... Are you listening Merlin?"

"She's exquisite," sighed Merlin to himself. "Absolutely exquisite... What did you say again about Barnaby?"

TINA PRINGLE HAD seen Merlin St Clair when she stepped out of the lift. She had returned to the hotel the previous day from Dorset and wondered if the light was playing tricks. Having been so close to the St Clairs for days she spent with her family, suddenly one of them was walking through the same hotel. The man with him was bald and tall but there was no mistaking Merlin, right down to the monocle he affected in his left eye to dramatize the different colours of his eyes. As a child she had always been frightened of Merlin after the ginger cat shot out the kitchen window when Merlin come looking for Barnaby. They had been eating her mother's best apple and bramble pie. The cat was only young then, she recalled. Probably a year old. She was seven or eight. It was long before the war. She saw Merlin a few times after that but never said a word in his presence. Barnaby had wanted to know why. He had told her more than once that Merlin was his favourite brother. Even his sisters came in for praise. Everyone loved Barnaby and Barnaby loved everyone.

Tina doubted if Merlin would know who she was. What he would know was where she could find Barnaby in London.

There had been many messages when she got back to the hotel. The article in *Tatler* had been a great success. The manager, he was very sweet, had presented her with a diary, so she could keep all the invitations in order. Lord and Lady, Mr and Mrs, General and Mrs, invited Miss Christine Pringle to the coming of age dance of their sons Lance, George, Frederick. She had clapped her hands at all the invitations, certain one of them would bring her face-to-face with Barnaby St Clair. Tina was very determined with what she was going to do to Barnaby for not even writing her a letter.

The man she was to meet at the reception desk had been sent to escort her to a coming out dance for a girl she had never heard of before, let alone met. There was clearly a shortage in London of rich young girls who did not look like the back end of a bus... Recovering from her surprise at seeing Merlin, she walked gracefully as taught by Miss Pinforth towards the chinless wonder waiting for her at the desk. There was no doubt it was him. He kept changing feet and looked most uncomfortable, poor boy. He was older than she expected. His parents must be desperate. Tina smiled. She was dressed in a silk sheath that tried to make her breasts look as flat as a pancake which she knew was impossible. The fur stole hung round her neck. Diamond and pearl earrings, given to her by Albert for her twenty-first, sparkled in the light from the chandelier. The black cloche hat fitted perfectly. She had what she knew was a sweet black bag in her right hand that went with the long black gloves that came up to her elbows. Over her left arm trailed a fur coat given to her by Benny Lightfoot at the same twenty-first. She knew better than anyone she looked a million dollars.

"You must be Mr Willoughby-Smythe," she said to the chinless wonder. "I hate getting to a party early. Why don't we take a small drink in the lounge before we go? I do like to be naughty. I hope you do, Mr Willoughby-Smythe."

"You are even prettier than the photograph in the *Tatler*," the man stammered.

"You see the man sitting with his side to us, wearing a monocle. There's a table next to him. Please lead the way. Then I have a favour to ask you."

"Anything, Miss Pringle."

MERLIN REMOVED the monocle with the plain glass from his left eye as he did not wish to be seen staring. Their eyes had met and locked soon after the girl sat down at the vacant table next to them. Merlin thought the man with her looked like a perfect twit. The girl smiled at him and then leaned towards the twit. Philip Spence was also speechless. To their surprise, the twit got up and came to their table. Merlin screwed his monocle in his left eye to frighten the man.

"Miss Pringle, the lady I am escorting to the dance, requests the pleasure of your company, Mr St Clair. I'm afraid we have not had the pleasure. Willoughby-Smythe. You may have heard of my father. Textiles."

"I'm sorry. There must be a mistake."

"Your name is St Clair?" persisted the twit. The girl was smiling at him and moving the long silk dress by recrossing her legs. "Miss Pringle tells me your families are old friends. From the same part of the world. Have you forgotten, sir?"

"Of course not," said Merlin standing up, the memory of Tina Pringle suddenly returning. "Spence, please meet Willoughby-Smythe... Would you mind, old chap, if we change tables?" he said to Philip Spence.

"Not at all." Philip was leering at him. "Old friends?"

"Well, more of an old friend of my brother, Barnaby... How are you Tina? I did not recognise you at first. How old were you the last time we met?"

"The first time I was eight. The cat bolted through the kitchen window."

"They do that, I'm afraid. How's Bert?"

"Very well. He has a little girl."

"What can I do for you, Tina?"

"Where is Barnaby?"

"Ah, Barnaby. Please may I present Philip Spence? Miss Christine Pringle. Our families grew up together. It will be a pleasure to join you. I'm sure the waiter will bring across our drinks."

Merlin sat down quickly without being asked further. He was reduced to water. Something no woman had ever done in his life.

"May I say you have become a very beautiful woman?"

"Why thank you, Merlin."

"Barnaby is staying at my flat. When would you care to come to dinner? My man Smithers is a passable cook. You'll come of course, Willoughby-Smythe?"

"I'll have to check my diary," said Tina. "Please remember me to

Barnaby. I live at the hotel. Africa was very good to me... You may remember a mutual friend of Robert's. Brigandshaw. Harry Brigandshaw."

"You met Harry!"

"Oh, yes. I meet a lot of people."

"I'll ask Barnaby to phone the invitation to your hotel."

"Why not yourself?" said Tina.

WHEN SHE LEFT twenty minutes later with her chinless wonder she was chortling inside. She had struck lightning in Merlin St Clair. She would play Merlin against Barnaby. Her revenge was going to be sweeter than she thought. "Dear oh dear," she said to herself, "Merlin!"

It was strange. So often the older men fell at her feet... There was still something about Merlin that gave her the shivers.

All through that night she thought of nothing but Barnaby. She did not remember saying goodbye to the chinless wonder.

MERLIN TRIED HIS BEST. He went to the theatre that night where a girl he had taken twice to supper was playing a minor part. When he asked, the girl was otherwise engaged for the night. He knew where Barnaby was going to for the last part of his evening. They had both received an invitation to join a group of friends at the Embassy where there was a small dance floor. The Prince of Wales sometimes joined the group, Barnaby had said.

When Merlin arrived the Royal Prince was nowhere to be seen. To Merlin's surprise, Barnaby was drunk. Not enough to be embarrassing, even Barnaby was well bred enough not to make a fool of himself in public. Only a brother or a close friend would have known he was drunk. His eyes were watery. His speech measured. He sat too quietly.

Merlin had joined the party without any fuss. His usual glass of whisky was put in front of him, which came as a surprise. He thought he was not that well known. Everyone knew each other. There were no introductions. He heard somebody say to someone he was Barnaby's brother. The music changed to ragtime and the girls all got up as one. Luckily for Merlin there were more men than girls. Barnaby stayed seated. Merlin moved to sit next to him.

"You're all right, Barnaby?"

"Why can't she come from the right family? Why can't she be rich?"

"I have no idea what you are talking about but I do know you have drunk too much."

"I love her, Merlin. I always have. Our mother would be ashamed. Our family. What can I do?... She's back in England. The photograph was in the *Tatler* you left on the table."

"I know. I had drinks with her earlier tonight."

"What are you talking about my dear Brother?"

"Tina Pringle. Christine Pringle. And if you asked me she looked rich enough. The diamond and pearls were real, and the coat was mink. I want to talk to you about C E Porter. Philip Spence says he's a bad egg."

"You can't be serious?"

"Philip knows what is going on in the City."

"I'm talking about Tina."

"She's staying at the Savoy. I said you will give her a ring. She wanted to know where you were. Mother always said your childhood friendship should have stopped a lot earlier than it did. You can't get involved with the staff."

"She's not the staff."

"Her father was. The Pringles have worked for the St Clairs as far back as anyone can remember."

"So what."

"You are drunk, Barnaby. I'm taking you home. Come along."

"I know a small bar that stays open. Against the law but who cares? I need a drink, Merlin."

"All right. But come on before this music stops. Have you paid your bill?"

"I have no idea. If I haven't, they'll keep it for me. Did I tell you you're a jolly good chap, Merlin? Be a sport and get my hat and coat. And my cane. It's a swordstick, but I didn't tell you... Just in case. You never know... You're a splendid chap... Why did she have to leave Africa? I was quite fine. Quite fine. Now I'm going to be quite miserable."

"No you're not. In the morning you won't remember a thing."

"I've got to phone her. Where is the phone?"

"Not now, Barnaby."

"All right. We'll go and have a drink. You and me. The two brothers. I wish Robert was in town. If he was, I'd invite him. He's a dear chap is Robert... Please don't push my elbow, Merlin, or I may fall down. I don't wish to fall down in the Embassy. Had a girlfriend here once.

Went to India, I think… Yes, that is my coat. And my hat. I promise not to pull out the sword. Might frighten the gals."

"The taxi is waiting, Barnaby."

"Good."

Barnaby fell asleep in the cab and they went straight home. The doorman was asleep at his desk.

Merlin put his brother to bed and poured himself a whisky. The most vivid recollection of his evening was Tina Pringle recrossing her legs.

"There is no fool like an old fool," he said out loud. Then he took himself off to bed.

7

ECHOES FROM THE PAST, JANUARY 1921

*T*he next day when Barnaby found out Tina was not going to return his call let alone speak to him, Harry Brigandshaw reached home. It was the end of January, the temperature well over one hundred degrees Fahrenheit and he was two months late. There was no sign of his sister Madge or his brother-in-law Barend Oosthuizen. His mother looked ill, his grandfather was detached and Harry wondered if his grandfather had gone senile. For some reason there was a note for him from a man called Jim Bowman who was looking for a job. It seemed that only the three dogs were pleased to see him. The old ginger cat was still up to its trick on the windowsill in the kitchen, lying fast asleep both eyes wide open. Tembo was nowhere to be seen.

After giving his mother a kiss on both cheeks and shaking his grandfather's hand he had taken the horses down to the stable and rubbed them down himself. There was just nobody around. He could smell the distinctive smell of curing tobacco coming from one of the tall, red-brick curing barns so the farm had not died while he was away. He could see people in the compound and smell their wood smoke from the cooking fires. The gang must have been given the afternoon off.

Feeling dejected from his welcome he walked down to the river, leaving his two horses in the stable with water and a bail of fresh lucerne. The two dogs and the bitch followed him.

The Egyptian geese were still there, noisily chasing each other down the full flow of the Mazoe River. The rains had been good as he knew to his cost too well. The female ridgeback allowed him the privilege of tickling her behind her ears, looking at him with soft brown adoring eyes.

It had been a long journey. He had been away too long. Almost two years. He had not brought back Barend to his wife and children. He had not reached home for Christmas. He had been wrong to leave home, he knew that. But to be almost ignored on his return was more than he deserved.

It had been nearly five months since he had looked at the SS *King Emperor* through his field glasses as it sailed on its way to England ten miles off the Skeleton Coast in South West Africa.

He sat down on the high riverbank and thought back over the journey. Somewhere from far away on the other side of the river, Harry heard a lion roar. From the dark building clouds to the west he could see it was going to rain again, but he did not think it would come for a while. Were it not for the crocodiles lurking in the muddy waters of the river he would have gone in for a swim. He missed the sea and the Skeleton Coast. He felt lonely. Totally lonely. Something frighteningly new in his life. As if no one in the whole world wanted him. He was thirty-four years old behaving like a child and he did not care. He was alone and if he wished to cry and feel sorry for himself it was no one else's business. No one was looking.

His intention of reaching home for Christmas had gone wrong on the north bank of the Chobe River. Thirty miles downriver, the Chobe flowed into the Zambezi forty miles west of its violent drop over the Victoria Falls. Normally the main rains broke after Christmas in that part of the world. Or so Barend had told him. That year when he had to cross the river with the horses the heavens opened in October and rained for a month, leaving Harry stranded and suffering from malaria. At one point he thought he would never see home again. Never see Elephant Walk. He had thought deeply of his father and the farm he had inherited when his father was killed by the Great Elephant. He had been lucky. He still had had one small bottle of quinine. It saved his life.

He spent two months by the river waiting for the floods to subside. He built a reed house that kept out the rain and made his cooking fire in the centre of the one room. In the worst of the storms he brought the horses into the hut. They were his only companions. Far up river in Angola where the rain fed the Okavango which fed the Chobe the sun came out. It was the start of a long drought that was to kill half the native population but no one, including Harry, knew that at the time. They were all too glad to see the end of the rain. All over the plains the grass was rich and green. There were many flowers. The horses fattened as they grazed on the good grass.

He had finished the quinine and had slept each night in the smoke-filled hut. The smoke hurt his eyes and burnt his throat. He hoped it would keep away the mosquitoes. In the first light of day when the mosquitoes stopped their main assault the tsetse attacked with venom. Harry was more worried about the horses who were both salted and thought to be immune from the deadly bite of the tsetse fly. If the horses died, there would be no way for him to get home.

All through the weeks Harry saw no one. It was as if he was the last man on earth. Once in his delirium he thought he was. God had forsaken him. God had forsaken man. There was not to be any more life for man on earth. The species had died out. Extinct.

He was too weak to fish. The trap caught the fish as they swam into the calm waters of the small oxbow lake made by the flood close to where Harry camped. The fish brought back his strength. When he was strong enough to shoot a waterbuck, he cut it laboriously into thin strips and hung the strips from the river trees to dry. He had run out of salt and the meat dried badly. He had found wild sage which he had rubbed into the meat. Before the meat was fully cured a leopard ate most of it during one night.

For the rest of his stay in the reed hut, Harry slept with one hand on his gun. During the worst nights of his dreams he dreamed of Lucinda. At the end of each dream she was always dead and Fishy Braithwaite always got away. Sometimes Lucinda was dead in the cockpit of a German aircraft he had chased and shot down. He only saw her face when he removed the dead pilot's flying helmet. When he woke from those dreams he went out of his hut and was sick in the bushes clutching his gun again, against the leopard's attack. Once he had dropped the Purdey in the pitch dark of the night. There was total cloud. The heaving had come right up from his coccyx, making pain shoot through his body. He had panicked in the rain and mud and for a moment when he found the gun was not sure which was back or front. He had stayed awake in the hut with the horses for the rest of the night for fear of falling asleep and dreaming again. There were many nights alone when he thought he was going mad in his mind. Only the light of dawn brought him sanity.

Slowly the water went down until it was possible for Harry to ford the river and continue on his long journey home to Elephant Walk.

"WHO ARE YOU?"

When Harry turned, a small girl was looking at him. She was sure of her ground. There was no fear in her eyes.

"I might be your Uncle Harry," he said returning from the reverie in his mind.

"You can't be. Uncle Harry went away. My daddy went away. They are never coming back."

"I am your Uncle Harry."

"Then where is my daddy?"

"I don't know, Paula. He said he was coming home."

"You saw my daddy? How do know my name! Who are you?"

"Is that your brother Tinus?"

"Yes, he doesn't say much."

"Where's your mummy?" asked Harry, smiling gently at his niece and nephew. They had grown.

"I heard from Mother you were home. The children wanted to have a look at you first."

"Didn't he come back?" asked Harry. His sister Madge came up behind him from the other side to her children.

"Not yet."

"He will. He said so. He said so last time we spoke."

"So you found Barend... Was he all right?"

"He never got over the British hanging his father in the Boer War."

"I know... Mother has a letter for you from London solicitors."

"What's that got to do with me and solicitors?"

"We don't know. We never opened the letter. It came almost a year ago. Mother is ill. She is pining away. Now you're home, she'll get better. Oh, Harry. Hug me, Harry. It's been so terrible."

"Why is Mummy crying?" asked the boy Tinus.

"Mummy always cries, silly. Let's go and see Grandfather. He won't be crying. Grandfather never cries."

"You're silly... He's at the tobacco barns. Come on. I'll race you."

The dogs left the river with the children. The dogs were barking all the time. The Egyptian geese took flight and flew off downriver. Harry hugged his sister for a long while.

Then they walked up to the house over the lawns that now went right down to the river, the lawns flowing through the msasa trees, each tree ringed with a bed of flowers. The stockade, built by the children's real grandfather, Tinus Oosthuizen, during the Shona rebellion in '96 had been removed while Harry was away. The man the children had gone looking for at the barns was their great-grandfather.

THE BIG ENVELOPE when they gave it to him was addressed to Group Captain Henry Brigandshaw, Royal Air Force, MC and Bar. No one ever formally addressed him as Henry even though he had been named after his maternal grandfather, Sir Henry Manderville, Bart.

"This looks ominous," said Harry.

Quietly he sat down in his father's old chair in the lounge of his mother's house and opened the big brown envelope. The dogs came back from running with the children and took up positions round the armchair. Harry began to read, watched by his mother and sister. Harry could hear the third child, a girl, that had been born at the end of the last war, crying from somewhere within the house. Then the child stopped crying and Harry finished the solicitor's letter without interruption.

"Uncle James is dead. He's made me his heir. Not the title, he can't decide that. Colonial Shipping. Hastings Court. They want me to go to England."

"You can't," cried Madge. "It's hell here on our own, Harry, please. Stay with us. This is your family. Damn England. It's only ever given us pain. They don't need you any more. Why can't they leave us alone?"

"There's more to it than that," said Sir Henry Manderville from the open door to the veranda. "There's history."

"Damn history," said Madge.

When Harry put the letter on the coffee table he looked round at his family. His mother Emily was crying to herself. His sister was looking at him with a look of panic bordering on fear. Sir Henry was smiling philosophically. All three dogs were watching him. The ginger cat had woken up and came in from the kitchen. Tembo had appeared from nowhere and was standing in the doorway that led from the dining room into the lounge. He was grinning from ear to ear. Harry got up and gave him a hug. Harry had known Tembo all his life.

"Shall I bring the whisky and ice," said Tembo as the two men stood back and looked at each other. "Welcome home, Baas Harry."

"A drink's the answer... Bring the tray, Tembo... I'll worry about England later," he said back to the room. "Much later. They waited a year. Probably forgotten me. Or think I'm dead. They must have asked you by now, Mother?"

"Yes, I wrote to them saying I didn't know one way or the other. I told them you had gone into the bush. Far away."

"Good. What's for dinner?"

"Cold roast duck and salad," said Tembo.

"That sounds delicious… How was the tobacco season?" Harry asked his grandfather.

"The price is down after the war."

"To be expected."

"The yield's up. Six hundred pounds of dried leaf to the acre."

"Now that's something."

"When you are settled, then we can talk about the farm."

"Where's Aunt Alison?"

"She prefers living on her own at New Kleinfontein."

"Are they growing any crops?"

"Maize. Just maize."

Harry had thought his grandfather was going to marry the woman he had always called his Aunt Alison, the widow of Tinus Oosthuizen, the man who had befriended Harry's father. Tinus Oosthuizen had been Harry's father's mentor. Together they had become the most famous white hunters in Central Africa after Selous and Hartley. The one had been hanged by the neck. The other killed by the Great Elephant.

"Let's have a drink," he said, not wanting to think about the death of his father. He wanted to change the subject. Looking at his grandfather's expression, Aunt Alison was obviously a sore point.

With the flow of good whisky, the tension flowed out of the family. Madge went off to put the children to bed. They talked of everything that was not important. When Madge came back they went into the dining room to eat their cold supper. They sat down formally at the dinner table. Sir Henry said grace which had never happened before. The tension had come back again. Harry was glad of the bottle of wine produced by his grandfather. They drank two bottles without saying what was in their minds.

When Harry found his old room, a servant had made up the bed. He was just drunk enough not to dream.

IN THE MORNING the birds were singing outside his bedroom window. He knew he was home. He got up and looked through the window. He could now see the river down through the trees, the view no longer blocked by the stockade and he liked what he saw. He sighed with pleasure, smelling familiar smells, hearing familiar sounds from the native compound. The village, a mile downriver was waking up. He could hear their dogs bark and the cockerels crow. There was a lot of noise. He thought a buzzard was trying to steal the newborn chicks. In his mind's eye he could see the scurrying balls of yellow fluff and everything else making a noise to protect them from the birds of prey. He smiled broadly.

Then Harry remembered, they wanted him back in England.

WHEN HE went to join his family for breakfast, he was still trying to make up his mind where his duty lay. Life was never simple. Even back in his own house. He shivered as if someone had walked over his grave.

After breakfast he went with the children to check on his horses. He loved his horses. They were his friends. His horses were never complicated.

"I LIKED JAMES," said Henry Manderville to Harry later in the day. "He was a stuffed shirt but they all were in the army. Part of being a regular officer. Sandhurst. Good regiment. Did everything he could to save Tinus from hanging. He was a major then. Don't think he had made colonel. It was all politics, the hanging. The Boer War should have finished when Roberts marched into Pretoria in 1901. A small contingent of Boers wanted to fight on. Smuts. De la Rey. Louis Botha. They fought a guerrilla war and ran us all over the highveld of the Transvaal and Free State. Then they invaded the British Cape Colony from where the Boers had trekked in the last century. Not all of them, of course. Not all of them wanted to get away from British control. Many stayed and prospered, becoming British subjects.

"After Tinus and your father split their assets, Tinus went to the Cape, to the farm Kleinfontein in Franschhoek. Even by then he was a British subject. He had lived most of his life in what became Rhodesia. Tinus thought himself a true Boer wherever he roamed. In the land of Lobengula or Rhodes.

"When the Boers called on their Cape brothers to fight the British Tinus went out with G J Scheepers, the Cape rebel. To stop the Boers being further replenished with Boer men from the Cape, the British said they would hang all captured rebels for high treason. Tinus, a Boer general by the time they caught him, was in British eyes the epitome of a rebel. They hanged him as an example. To stop the war. It was politics... Damn politics... Now I'm right off the subject and probably want to be. You're going to ask me what you should do. What is your duty, Harry? The reason you were born. Your responsibility to those of your family who came before you and those of your family that will come after you. From generation to generation... What we want to do in life is rarely what we should do. Most of us run away. I ran away. I regret most of the things, important things, that I did in my life. I don't want you to do the same."

They were seated in the small house in the family compound that was Harry's grandfather's. Harry had waited till the middle of the afternoon to find him alone.

"Much of my life's regrets have to do with you, Harry. The truth is bitter. Full of human frailty. We are all the product of that frailty from time long gone by. Some say it is what makes us human... I'll give you a large whisky when I'm finished... What you do is up to you. First, I have to tell you the truth about your birth and upbringing. Do you want to hear, Harry? Or do you want me to shut up? You've been through a terrible war. You are not a boy any more. You have the right to say now you don't want to hear."

Harry was white in the face, dry in the mouth and for some absurd reason wanted to go to the toilet. He thought he wanted to run away. Anywhere. The toilet was good as anywhere.

"Please go on, Grandfather," he said formally.

"Your mother and father were childhood friends. My estate, Hastings Court, or what was left of it was near The Oaks, your paternal grandfather's home. He was evil. A man only concerned with himself. He cared nothing for any of you, least of all your father and you. He hated being self-made. Building Colonial Shipping first out of piracy I suspect. I always called him the Pirate. He probably called me the Fool. He surely thought of me as a fool right up until the time he died alone at my dining table in Hastings Court. You see he got what he wanted. Whether he died happy only he could know. I would prefer not to have lived than to have lived his life. And that is not sour grapes.

"Emily was my only child. My wife died very young. I've never even looked at a woman to breed from again. Never. Alison and I hoped to be companions. We Mandervilles, like your friends the St Clairs, came over from Normandy with William the Conqueror. My ancestor, your ancestor, fought at the Battle of Hastings. The French won. In exchange, William gave his knights land. Land to defend for the King.

Rather like Cecil Rhodes gave his pioneers land to occupy and defend for him in Rhodesia. Through the centuries we fought as knights for the King. Now the English king. The de Ville had become Derville. We were now English and proud to be English. We fought at Agincourt, Crécy, Poitiers, Blenheim, Waterloo. In the Crimea against the Russians. We have just again fought in France, Group Captain. We are an old line of knights and proud of it, something your Grandfather Brigandshaw desperately wanted to be part of. And even that he thought his money could buy, and I sold it to him. I did business with the devil. Sold the soul of the Mandervilles. Sold my only daughter in holy matrimony to the eldest son of the Pirate."

"Grandfather, you don't have to go on."

"We had run out of money. Hastings Court was down to a few acres round the old house. Promised to bring it back to its old glory. He was going to live there with his eldest son and my daughter. He was going to buy himself a baronetcy which any fool can do if they approach the right politician with enough money. The Tories sold him his. With his blood mingled with ours, you, his grandson would have been rich and Lord of the Manor. He would have made himself and his family the owner of an old home and the blood of the ancient Mandervilles would run in the veins of his grandchildren. In his obsession the old Pirate would have made himself legitimate. And his heirs for a thousand years.

"He paid me two hundred thousand pounds for my daughter, your mother. There were conditions. The money had to be left in my will to my grandchildren. That way in his twisted mind it would not cost his family a penny... I knew your father and Emily had always been friends. I did not know they were lovers. I swear to you. She was sixteen. He was seventeen. On that subject I say no more. That is for your mother to tell you. I do know she has not told you. Many times she has agonised to me what to say to you and what not to say. Are some secrets better taken to the grave? If James had not left you Hastings Court and all the Pirate's ill-gotten gains, I would have let it die with me and your mother. Now I can't. You are the Manderville heir though your name is Brigandshaw. The current knight in our meander through history. You will not be Sir Henry Brigandshaw, Bart. That will go to your Uncle Nat, the Bishop of Westchester and one-time hopeful Archbishop of Canterbury. You will never be the next Sir Henry Manderville, Bart, that will go to Cousin George in America when I die. But what you will be is Lord of the Manor. That goes with Hastings Court. The bloodline will not be broken even though I never had a son."

"So you want me to go to England?"

"You must."

"Even if I don't want to?"

"It is your duty."

"Did Uncle James know all this?"

"Yes. Arthur, his elder brother, never consummated his marriage to your mother. I used the two hundred thousand pounds to make him annul his marriage to my daughter. All he had wanted was money. They had your father in a Cape Town prison for abducting you and your mother. The authorities were going to send him back to England. Your grandfather had bribed enough people to make sure of that. No one was going to dirty his plans. In those days, kidnapping was a capital offence. The Pirate was going to have them hang his youngest son to keep his direct line free of scandal. To let them walk freely in the highest society. You see your Uncle James is now trying to make amends for his father by leaving you his estate."

"I always knew who was my father. I believed that all through the war. He flew with me in the cockpit. Much of my instinct came from my father. The instinct to hunt and know when I was being hunted in the air. I just never understood why Arthur was married to my mother... I wonder what my father would have done now?"

"It is your decision, Harry. You have to work out where your duty lies. I did all I could to preserve Hastings Court."

"Was it worth all that?"

"It was to the generations before us. We are the product of their lives."

"My mother was pregnant with me when she married Arthur?"

"Yes."

"She didn't tell you then."

"She was frightened. Society dictated what she had done was a mortal sin. She was sixteen years old."

"You didn't ask her?"

"Whether she was pregnant? Fathers don't ask daughters such questions."

"No. Whether she loved my father?"

"Duty comes before young love. Young love dies early in life. Duty remains. I foolishly thought your mother deserved the wealth and privilege that would come with marrying the heir to a fortune. I thought I was doing the right thing."

"You didn't think my father would come to anything on his own?"

"I didn't. We usually judge other people by ourselves. How was I to know he would do all this? How was I to know they would go on loving each other? Most people hate their wives and husbands a few years into their marriages. Love dies, Harry. Money stays behind. I may be a damn old fool but that much I know. Look around you. Look at your sister. Look at the whole damn world. Mostly they hate each other. Envy. Greed. Jealousy. All the human frailties. Love is the precious one and, it's as rare as hen's teeth. How was I to know? How was I to know they'd love each other all their lives?"

Harry stood and looked at his grandfather who was holding himself across the chest, rocking backwards and forwards in the armchair. A wretched old man at the end of his life with nothing to show for it. Harry looked around the small cottage. Outside there was only the African bush. Inside on the display tables were his grandfather's butterfly collections in neat, glass-topped wooden display boxes. There were his books on the shelves. But not even a portrait of his wife, Harry's grandmother he had never met. Harry wondered about that. There should have been something. He had heard throughout his life how much his grandfather had loved his grandmother. Were there more skeletons in the family cupboard?

"What happened to Arthur?"

"He died of debauchery in 1901. Drink. Food. Fat as a pig, they said. Heart failed him. He was forty-four. Then that self-righteous uncle of yours, condescended to marry your mother and father. The Bishop was only a missionary then. The same church he built where you and Lucinda were to repeat your English vows of marriage... Oh, I'm sorry, Harry. I'm a mess. You do what you think is right. Maybe none of it matters. Maybe there is no truth to life."

"So, my parents were not married in the Salisbury Magistrate's Court?"

"No, they weren't. They put that out for the likes of Jeremiah Shank and the rest of the locals. The colonials believed it I think. No one cared about that sort of thing in Africa during the pioneer days. Too busy surviving to gossip. There were so few of us in a vast and hostile country. Prowling lions in the cattle. The Shona rebellion they called their Chimurenga. War of liberation. Some witch doctor with power in jeopardy. Told them to kill us… No, they only married in 1901."

"So all of us are bastards."

"You could put it that way… Do you know the witch doctor was a woman? May have been a rumour. Propaganda. We hanged the ringleaders. Been quiet ever since, I think. You never know. You never know what they are thinking."

"George, dead in France. Little James buried next to little Christo Oosthuizen in the graveyard here on Elephant Walk. Madge. Me. All bastards. Well, that's something to think about."

"Please, Harry."

"Oh, I don't care. What I don't understand is why everyone is suddenly so interested in some bastard in the middle of Africa. Why me? Why not the Bishop's son? He has one, I remember. Must be twenty-one by now. Cousin Archibald. Even named after my paternal grandfather. Far more appropriate, I would have thought… Why did Uncle James not leave it all to Archie? In the end he'll be the one to get the Brigandshaw baronetcy. He'll be Sir Archibald. Why couldn't Uncle James let the ghosts lie peacefully in their graves? We were all right in Africa. We have our own place. A great future, I hope."

"He thought he was doing the right thing, like me."

"I love Elephant Walk. This is my home. The only home I've ever known… Bishop's son. Even the Archbishop's son will have nothing of material wealth. Just a hollow title. It doesn't make sense."

"Archibald's a fool."

"Who told you? He's only twenty-one the poor sod."

"Don't swear, Harry."

"I'm sorry. Yes, I'm sorry for swearing. I'm sorry for a lot of things."

"So am I."

"I'm going to take a gun and walk the bush."

"You won't have a whisky?"

"Not now."

"Don't hate me, Harry. I couldn't stand that. I would die now of loneliness. Emily hates me. I'm sure, underneath it all. Wouldn't you?"

"She loves you. As we all do. Madge. The children. George loved you. Life's the mess, Grandfather. Not you. We are what we are despite ourselves, not because of ourselves. We all have sins. Did I ever tell you mine? I made love to Lucinda before we were married. She too was pregnant when we married. That bloody Braithwaite killed my son.

I'm sure it was a son... Don't blame yourself. Let me just go and walk. If I had an aeroplane, I would go up in the sky. The clear sky and the African bush have a lot in common, Grandfather. Both the virgin bush and the sky in heaven are unsullied by man."

"You don't hate me?"

Harry put a hand on his grandfather's shoulder, looking down on the bent nearly bald head. He was silently crying for the old man. Unable to speak any more, he squeezed the shoulder and left the house. The Purdey was locked in a gun safe in the main house. He walked across the lawn seeing nothing, tears blinding his vision.

HARRY LOOKED up at the sun. It was three o'clock with three more hours of sunlight. No one had been around when he unlocked the gun safe. It was not going to rain. Hot and humid with the thunder far away. He wondered if Madge knew the truth. He certainly was not going to tell her.

For the first time in his life he knew why people told so many lies. The truth hurts. The truth was mostly better hidden.

HALF AN HOUR later and deep in the bush, Harry began to laugh.

"Whatever the truth, without the old Pirate you wouldn't be alive," he said out loud to himself. "Life, despite everything, is good."

The thought made him feel a whole lot better. Who was he to judge? To ever think he was different to the rest of them was absurd. If only he had known his paternal grandfather, he might have understood him. The man must have been something to come from nowhere to be what he was. For good or evil. His Grandfather Brigandshaw had been a success if money were the criteria.

When he called back at his grandfather's house, the sun was laying long shadows from the msasa trees on the lawn up from the river. He was much better. Knowing the truth was good after all. He would give it a while and then make up his mind as to what he was going to do with his uncle's will.

The drinks tray was on the side table with a bucket of ice and the tall soda siphon. They were back to normal, he and his grandfather. He knew neither of them would ever speak of his birth again.

"Your mother's coming over for a drink." The old man was smiling at him. "She's cut some flowers. Putting them in vases. You know how your mother loves flowers."

Harry had unloaded the bullets from the gun before reaching the family compound. He rested the Purdey in the corner and took the glass of whisky from his grandfather.

"Cheers," they said in unison.

The rules were back in place. They were two civilised men about to enjoy a sundowner. Harry smiled with a wry smile that nothing could be less normal, stuck in the middle of Africa. He wanted to laugh.

WHEN HIS MOTHER and Madge came into the room, they were both smiling. Outside on the lawn, the children were playing with the dogs.

He and his grandfather drank too much after supper sitting on the veranda. Tembo had put the fly screens in place before the sun went down. The oil lamp threw flickering shadows out towards the black of the African night. Bugs battered the fly screens to get at the lights. The crickets were singing loudly all around the house. From the village came the beat of the drums. It was Saturday night and there was no work to be done on the farm in the morning. The sound of the African drums was therapy to the frayed nerves they were hiding from each other and themselves.

When Harry found his bed he was quite inebriated .

They had all survived another day Harry drunkenly thought to himself. Much like everyone else in the world. He was verging on the philosophical. Drink usually did it to him. He was still smiling when he finally went to sleep. Outside it was pitch dark. There was no moon. Thunderclouds obscured the stars. He woke once in the night with a splitting headache and then fell back into sleep.

THE NEXT MORNING everything looked so different. Brilliant sunshine outside Harry's bedroom window. No one had drawn the curtains the previous night. The children were shouting with excitement. Tinus was spraying his sisters and the dogs with a garden hose, the pressure from the header tank letting the boy spray a long distance. The dogs ran in front of Harry's window in a race away from the water. All of them were barking. Standing only in his pyjama bottoms at the open window, Harry felt cold water drench his face and chest.

"Do that again!" he shouted.

"Spray Uncle Harry!" screamed Paula. She had her bare back to Tinus who had turned the hose on his sister, soaking her small naked body. "Not me! Uncle Harry!"

Harry felt the full force of the water on his chest and considered getting out of the window to give chase. All three children stamped on the wet grass and screamed with excitement. They could have run away but didn't. They were bursting with the anticipation of Harry coming through the window and racing after them.

"Breakfast is ready," called Madge.

The children stopped the game in mid-flight and ran for the house, the hose left spurting water on the grass.

"Turn the water off, Tinus… Now!… Harry. Make him turn off the hose."

Harry got out through the low window of his bedroom as he had done all through his life. At the tap under the msasa trees he turned off the water. He made up his mind to build the children a small, shallow swimming pool where they could play without wasting the water. Harry knew drought was more common than floods on Elephant Walk. The children had to be taught the preciousness of water.

By the time Harry got back in through his window he was dry. The hangover had gone. He was thirsty. The smell of fried bacon made him hurry into a pair of khaki shorts. He then put on an old shirt and walked barefoot to the kitchen. It was the rule in the Brigandshaw house that the servants had the day off on Sundays. Madge was doing the cooking, leaving the dirty pans for the next day. Mondays were always bad days for the cook, a Kalanga whose family and village had died from some disease. Harry had asked and found out little more than the cook's family was dead. No one asked further questions. Madge had taught him how to cook. They called him Smiler. No one in the house could pronounce the name he gave himself. He was always smiling, showing big, perfectly white teeth. The whites of his eyes were as white as his teeth.

"Does Smiler regret being off on Sundays?" asked Harry. He could see the kitchen was going to be a mess by the end of the day.

"Probably. Sleep all right?"

"Passed out. Grandfather not in for breakfast?"

"I take him a tray. He's getting old, Harry. Sit down at the kitchen table. Scrambled eggs. Devilled kidneys. Bacon. Tomatoes. Kudu chop. Toast. Coffee. All at your service, sir."

"They should have made you a wife and mother years ago."

"I wanted to be his wife before he ran away the first time… I'm grateful now though. I have three of his children. Will you take the tray in to Mother? Tea and toast. She doesn't eat properly."

"We'll see about that."

"Are you going away again?"

"Not for a while. We'll get in the tobacco crop. I have to work for my food. I'll think again what I have to do after the grading. Let's have a pact, Sis. No talking about Uncle James. No talking about Barend."

"Suits me. With Barend there's nothing to talk about. He doesn't want to come home. I can't force him. If he doesn't want us what can I do?"

"We're starting to go round in circles... Who is this Jim Bowman bloke who says he wants a job? Why's it addressed to me?"

"Barnaby St Clair owes him ten pounds. Gave him your name."

"He WANTS me to pay?"

"He wants a job. To learn farming. Mother talked to him. It was just after Christmas. Said he would come back. Another drifter. There are so many drifters after the war. He said something to Mother about being commissioned in the field, whatever that is about."

"When they make you an officer without putting you through an officer's training course. They did it a lot at the end of the war. Jerry always picked off the officers first even when they weren't wearing insignia. In an attack you can usually tell which are the officers. Junior officers were in short supply... He might be useful. Did he have a contact address? Is he married?"

"You'll have to ask Mother. There was something about a girl from England but I wasn't listening... You can take Mother her tray... Tinus, if you don't stop making that noise you won't get any breakfast! Get those dogs out of the kitchen!"

"He's always naughty, Mummy."

"You're a wicked little girl, Paula. One more word like that about your brother and I'll give you a clip round the ear. Girl or no girl."

"Doris is crying," answered Paula.

"She's always crying. She's a blubber," piped up Tinus.

"Tinus! Get those the dogs out... Now!"

"Is it always like this?" asked Harry happily. "The place is bedlam."

"They bully Doris. Just because she's the youngest. She's three next month. I wanted twelve of them. Can you imagine?"

"You love it."

"They keep my mind off other things. When you've eaten breakfast I want to sit under one of the trees on the lawn and have you tell me everything. Everything you've done since you've left."

"And especially the bits that include Barend."

"Especially the bits about Barend."

"The pact is not going to work."

"Then you can use me as a sounding board about England... Oh, and Mother is rebuilding the fireplace in the lounge. It's cracked from the heat, Grandfather's going to supervise. They start tomorrow. I just wanted to warn you. Welcome home. I've missed you. We all have. Why did you stay away so long?... No. Don't answer that."

"He'd gone a long way. Wanted to go further. The Skeleton Coast. We were looking for the source of the diamonds."

"Did you find any?"

"Not one," lied Harry. "Boil an egg for mother. I'll make her eat it."

The idea had come to him with the fireplace. The old, cracked fireplace came to a small pyramid at the centre. The mantelpiece over the fire topped the pyramid. It was a perfect spot. He would tell them the big rock was a crystal he had picked up on his travels. The best hiding place for the big diamond was right in front of everybody. No one would cement a diamond into the mantelpiece of the fire. Even if it did sparkle in the firelight, no one would think of the stone as other than a worthless piece of rock. Just a pretty crystal. Rose quartz. There was a slight rose tint to the diamond when it came into the light. Even if the house burnt to the ground, the heat would do nothing to harm the diamond.

In his mind's eye he thought it would take a year or two to sort out the mess in England. Then he would come home. In a year or two he would find a buyer for Colonial Shipping. His responsibility would be over. Cousin Archie could have Hastings Court. The idea of leaving Africa forever was too appalling. He would split the proceeds of the sale among his grandfather's descendants. In equal proportions. The children now screaming again on the lawn would be rich. Harry thought further. He would create a family trust with the senior members of the family as trustees.

Harry picked up the breakfast tray and took it through to his mother's bedroom. Somehow what he now knew about his mother made her even more precious to him. She was half asleep. Harry kissed her on her brow.

"You have a mischievous look in your eyes, Harry."

"I love you, my mother. Your breakfast is served. I will leave you in peace."

"Thank you, Harry."

"My pleasure, Mother dear," he was trying to be flippant.

"Ah, he told you."

"Yes he did."

"I'm glad... Did it hurt?"

"Not at all. It has made me very happy."

His mother was smiling at him from where her head lay on the pillow. For the first time Harry realised what a beautiful woman she must have been as a girl. His father had been lucky. It was nice to be born of both of them.

"I made Madge include a boiled egg. Eat it, Mother dear. That's an order."

"Yes, sir."

"Can I pour your tea?"

"Please."

"Did Jim Bowman leave an address?"

"I have it somewhere. He's in Salisbury. You will like him. From the North. Where your father's family came from. How long are you going to be away?"

"I'll go at the end of the tobacco season... One, maybe two years. However long it takes for me to find a suitable buyer and sell Colonial Shipping. Don't you worry your head... We'll have to stop them bullying little Doris."

"Go and have your breakfast." She was still smiling at her son.

When Emily tasted the egg, it was rich and good. She finished all the egg and two pieces of toast. Then she drank a full cup of tea.

Later, and for the first time in a long time, she was happy to get out of bed. There were things to do. Things to look forward to in her life.

8

NEW HORIZONS, JANUARY 1921

*J*im Bowman watched the touring cars arriving outside Meikles Hotel. He was eking out a pot of tea in the courtyard, conserving what was left of his fifty pounds, seven shillings and thruppence that had started him on his journey to Africa from England. There were four cars with long bonnets making powerful noises in the street. The big Zulu doorman dressed in animal skins watched the entourage arrive. He was not carrying his usual spear and shield. To Jim, the leopard skin over the big Zulu's shoulder looked shabbier than when he first arrived in Salisbury back in August. They had returned from the Valley of the Horses a month ago. Colonel Voss was living with the original owner of Hamlet and Othello along with the dog, King Richard the Lionheart. The cart they had travelled in was back in the squalid yard of the man Colonel Voss called 'Sir Robert'. Jim had doubted the knighthood from the start. There had not been a penny returned of his money. Once money left Jim's hand it never seemed to come back again. The horses and the dog were happy to be home. There was grazing round the old shack. The bush grass had grown again. Jim had made up his mind to check on the animals once a month to make sure they were all right. None of the animals had let him down.

What Jim needed most was a job. A real start on something in Africa. There was no doubt in his mind he would never go home to live in England. Colonel Voss had told Jim he had bush fever with no sign of a temperature. Jim was not sure how a man had a fever without being sick. Fact was, he felt very well.

"Some get it, dear boy. Some don't. You've got it. Bitten. Incurable. Marvellous."

155

Jim knew the old man was right. The codfish in the Irish Sea would likely not be troubled by one Jim Bowman. He certainly hoped not. Life in Africa was nothing else but interesting.

Behind the four open tourers arrived a five-ton truck. Jim had seen many of them in France. They were army trucks. Hard on the bones of the driver. Rugged. He had travelled in many of them. What it was doing behind the smart cars was at first a mystery. They were all together. Jim could see that from his vantage point at the courtyard round table. He had already ordered a second pot of hot water which he had poured into the silver teapot. There was now little colour to his tea, and the milk had run out. There were three other men doing the same thing inside the lounge which was why he had chosen to sit outside... They were all out of work. The others probably couldn't even afford a pint of beer. The only thing going for them was being English or Scots or Welsh or Irish. One of the down and outs with frayed white cuffs and no cufflinks was a Scot. Jim could hear his accent. None of them ever seemed to speak to each other. Silent islands with two hot water pots for their tea. Jim had learnt the extra hot water pot trick from the Scot. It added half an hour to sitting in the comfort of the hotel.

In the front of the touring cars, the driver and the passenger were white men. They wore new pith hats. In the back seat plush with red leather were black men, two to each car. In the front of the truck, in the cab, were a white man and a black man. The white man who was the driver wore a cloth cap. The pith-hatted gentlemen were the first to get out. The black men in the back sat rigid, upright and Jim thought rather frightened of the roaring car engines. The Zulu had thought better than trying to open all the car doors at once. From somewhere he had found his shield and spear and stood aloof. Jim caught the Zulu's eye. The pith-hats wore long khaki shorts and long socks and every one of them had knobbly knees. They were all well into their fifties. The knees were as white as snow. The black men sat on their seats regally not knowing what to do next. The Zulu winked at him. There was no doubt in Jim's mind. Jim let out an involuntary laugh and put his right hand over his mouth. The pith-hats did not look at him, which was fortunate. To distract himself, Jim caught the eye of the only waiter attending the courtyard. He ordered himself the first beer of the day. Appearance in Africa counted for everything. A man drinking a beer was not a drifter. The two 'hot water pot' men in the lounge were drifters who would not be drifters if they sat long enough in the lounge of the hotel and got themselves a job.

By the time the beer came the luggage had been removed from the racks of the back of the tourers. The truck had been sent off round the back to the tradesman's entrance. Jim had heard the hotel day manager give the instructions.

It was twelve o'clock so drinking a beer was now all right. The men's bar next to the courtyard opened at ten in the morning but Jim knew better than to drink before twelve. Colonel Voss had said drinkers before twelve in the morning were drunks. After nearly a month waiting around looking for a job, Jim knew Colonel Voss was right.

Jim had a small room six streets from the hotel which was cheap. The beers were cheaper in the men's bar. Anyway, the beers were cheap. There was now a local brewer in Salisbury which was what made the beer inexpensive. Jim had looked up the brewer in case he had a job. The idea of a Crown land farm of his own was fading as fast as his money. To get a farm, he needed five years' experience of farming. He had none.

When the group of men from the tourers came back from booking into their rooms in the hotel, they were without their pith hats. Three of them were mostly bald on top. They took tables in the courtyard surrounding Jim and ordered beers. The black men from the back of the tourers had gone off with another black man who worked for the hotel. The hotel had servants' rooms at the back so Jim had been told by Colonel Voss. There was a small courtyard under trees in between the servants' rooms in the hotel where the servants were given their food. One of the trees in the courtyard was covered in blue flowers. No leaves. Just blue flowers that matched the sky. Jim had seen the flowering tree over the wall from the road when he walked from his room every day.

They were very loud. Jim soon learnt the men were on a hunting safari. They kept saying the truck was full of their equipment. The driver of the truck with the cloth cap had not joined them. Jim thought the man was a servant from England. The pith-hats said they were going to kill elephants. They repeated this to each other and for anyone else to hear within a hundred yards. Jim was about to get up and take his beer into the men's bar when he stopped. He had half risen from his wooden chair. They all had plummy accents which made him irritated. He felt sorry for the elephants to be killed by people so crass.

He had heard the name Brigandshaw. Then the name again. They were going to visit Brigandshaw. Brigandshaw was going to take them out and show them the elephants they were going to kill. One of them asked another how far it was to Elephant Walk. Jim was unable to resist.

"Twenty miles," he said. "He's not there. Been away for over a year."

They all stopped talking to look at him. Jim wished he had kept his mouth shut.

"I say, do you know the way?"

"Of course." He had the bottle of beer and a half empty glass in his hand and was on his feet. They could see he was on the way to the bar, trying to get away from them.

"Give you a fiver if you take us there. You do know Brigandshaw?" They were treating him like a servant. His accent had told them he was working class.

"I know his mother." Jim wanted to turn his back on them.

"Good. Splendid. Tomorrow then. Ten o'clock sharp. If we go on from there, you'll have to walk back."

"Make it ten pounds."

"That's a bit steep."

"Not if you think of the petrol for all those cars if you don't know where you're going. Easy to get lost in the bush."

"Done. Ten o'clock. What's your name?"

"Jim Bowman."

"Lord James Worth, Bowman. Now don't forget."

Jim went on his way to the men's bar.

"Ten pounds is preposterous," he heard one of them say.

"So's a fiver," said Lord James Worth.

They both had the same name, Jim thought. Probably the only thing they had in common. He wondered if it would be worth his while. Whether he was going to be lucky.

"You never know," he said to himself. "Some people have money to burn. Usually someone else's." Then he laughed to himself. He was getting the hang of Africa. He had lost ten pounds. Now he was going to make ten pounds. Probably ten shillings by the next morning but never mind. The idea was enough for him to order a second beer. And a third.

By the time Simon Haller found him he was well on his way. The pith-hats had gone.

158

"Found you at last. They said you had a room in the Avenues. Moved out of the hotel. We've managed to find a dress uniform of the Lancashire Fusiliers. The tailor will have to do some work. For the wedding photograph."

"What does Jenny Merryl have to say about that?"

"The photograph or the wedding?"

"Either. You wrote a pack of lies. The poor girl thinks I have been in love with her for years."

"The wedding story and the photograph will be syndicated round the world."

"We don't even know each other."

"You lived next door but three."

"Are you that desperate for a story?"

"The world loves a good love story. Hero and sweetheart. You can't sell a story and then renege on me, Jim Bowman. Do you remember my five pounds? That cost me sweat to get out of the editor."

"You lied, Simon Haller."

"I made the story more vivid. Colourful. More readable. Basically, it was true, of course. I should be a novelist. And rich. None of this nonsense."

"Why did the girl come all this way?"

"Because she loves you, Jim boy. She's beautiful. Young. In love with you… We'll pay you again for the story of your wedding. How's that? A happy ending. Everyone loves a happy ending. There haven't been many of them recently."

"She doesn't love me. She loves your story of me. Girls are all romantic."

For Jim Bowman, the whole thing had got out of control. The journey to the Valley of the Horses with Colonel Voss had made him wiser. More realistic. He had no money. He had no job. It was just some newspaperman in pursuit of the story. He had not even seen the girl for ten days. Once her picture appeared in the *Rhodesia Herald* she was meeting one man after another. There was a shortage of English girls in Salisbury. No one cared in Africa where she fitted into the English class system. She was English. That was good enough.

"Would you like another beer?" said Simon Haller. "Have a whisky. Buy you lunch. A bottle of wine. Just as long as you get into that uniform for Solly to take a photograph. We can go to the tailor after lunch."

"You're not going to photograph us together then?"

"We might not."

"You want them as wedding photographs?"

"The bride to be. The groom. That sort of thing. Five pounds."

"Just for a photograph of me in uniform?"

"Yes."

"Whisky! Lunch! Wine! And five pounds! How many papers have pre-bought your syndication?"

"One hundred and twelve."

"Why?"

"It caught on. The twenty-five pounds reward to find Jenny Merryl. The fact she read our article and ran to you. They feel part of it. They love it. All those lonely lost souls without a hope in hell of falling in love with a war hero. Through my story they feel part of Jenny Merryl. In their hearts they too came to Africa. Africa, with lions and elephants they've never seen in Milwaukee or Manchester. Mill girls. Poor mill girls. Living their dream through Jenny Merryl who went all the way to Africa from Neston. We can't leave them hanging, Jim. We owe them more than that."

"You should have been a novelist…"

ON THE FOLLOWING day Sir Henry Manderville had just told the barn worker to increase the heat by ten degrees in the number fourteen barn when the first tourer car came into view. The number fourteen barn was three from the end of the row of red-brick barns that rose thirty feet above his head. From where he stood at the back of the barns Sir Henry could see the hills over which the dust road from Salisbury wound its way towards Elephant Walk. One after the other the cars came into view and they disappeared into a dip. Last over the ridge came what looked like a five-ton truck he had seen in photographs taken during the war in France. The same type of truck that transported ammunition and men on their way to the Western Front.

"Now what the hell's going on?"

"What you say, Baas Henry?" asked Lucas, the black man who worked the barns during the day.

"Nothing. Someone's arriving."

"That big, big machine. Bigger than tractor." Like Henry, Lucas had never seen anything like the truck before in his life.

Curious, Sir Henry began to walk towards where the road from

Salisbury ended among the sprawl of buildings he had mostly built himself with farm labour. There were twenty barns in two rows of ten attached to each other side by side. A large grading and bulk shed combined. A tractor shed for two tractors and a small workshop that he was slowly filling with useful equipment from the profits he made from selling his Virginia tobacco, the seed for which came from his cousin George in Virginia, America.

He could hear the powerful engines of the cars as they drew nearer the barns. The truck made a different sound, lower in key but just as powerful. When Henry reached the gate at the end of the avenue of young jacaranda trees to open the gate to Elephant Walk, the big bonnet of the lead car was pointing directly at him. Two men were looking at him through the square windscreen. The morning sun was dappling them through the sky-blue flowers of the jacaranda trees. Henry swung open the gate. A man not much younger than himself took off a pair of goggles and smiled at him. The smile was false. Put on. The man was covered in red dust from the road. To Henry's surprise, the man in the passenger seat was the young man who had been looking for a job just after Christmas. The man who was not much more than a boy.

"Brigandshaw?" bellowed the driver.

"He's up at the house."

"Jolly good." The clutch was let out and with a flourish of clutch and gears the car moved forward leaving Henry still holding open the gate. Three more cars followed the first. No one even looked at him. In each of the red leather seats at the back of the cars sat two black men. They looked terrified. Henry waited for the truck before shutting the gate.

"Thanks, old cock," shouted down the white driver of the truck. The man wore a cloth cap. There was another white man next to him. The other man looked straight ahead. He had a clipped military moustache.

"My pleasure. My pleasure."

The driver barely slowed down in his pursuit of the four cars. Dust had risen all round Sir Henry.

One of the dogs appeared from somewhere and looked up at him with a look of sympathy before walking off down the road between the jacaranda trees. The dust did not worry the dog.

"Where are you going?" he shouted.

The dog took no notice.

Harry, who had been in the grading shed with the dog, came out to look.

"What was that all about?" he asked.

"Better go see. They headed straight for the houses. Mentioned your name and ignored me when I said you were up at the house. Anyway, what are you doing in the grading shed?"

"Having a look. Asking questions. I want to know all about this tobacco crop. It's the thing for us. High price. Low weight. We might just make a fortune."

"I doubt it... That chap looking for a job was in the front car."

"Jim Bowman! Save me a trip to town. Wonder what they want?"

"That young chap came on an old horse, last time. Called the horse Hamlet. Whoever calls a horse Hamlet? Chap barely needs to shave he's so young... How's the hangover, Grandson?"

"Terrible."

"We'll have a beer together at lunchtime."

"Maybe. Whether in flower or in the curing, this tobacco has a lovely smell... Where's that damn dog going?"

"That's what I asked him."

The dog was far down the tunnel made by the jacaranda trees where it was cool.

THE EGYPTIAN GEESE took flight before the first tourer reached the family compounds. The car engines went dead. Only the truck was still moving forward. When it stopped, the passenger got out quickly. It was apparent he resented Jim Bowman being given his front seat in the leading tourer. Even if the young man with a common accent was showing them the way.

The three houses and the one rondavel remained silent. There was no one in the houses, not even a servant. The man thought he could hear children's voices down by the river. The river trees were taller than the other trees. Dogs began to bark down by the river.

The white men got out of the touring cars, taking off their goggles. The black men sat rigid where they were. The mid-morning silence of the surrounding bush enveloped them. The man with a military moustache put a white pith hat on his head against the sun. The cab in the truck had not allowed him to wear his hat. The others were covered in red dust and were beating their clothes. A ginger cat was watching them from the windowsill of the larger house. When the man went up to the cat, he found it fast asleep.

"I say, this cat's asleep with its eyes open." No one took any notice of his observation. A dove called from the bush behind the houses. Another answered shortly after. The crickets were singing in the long grass, green from the good rains. The white men looked around them, less arrogant. The black men stared ahead less frightened now the cars had come to a stop.

"You looking for me?"

The white men all turned as one to look back the way they had come. The old man who had held open the gate was walking briskly towards them. With him was a younger man. The man was slim and tall, his face and arms darkened by the African sun.

"My name's Brigandshaw. My grandfather says you're looking for me."

"You can't be Sebastian Brigandshaw," said Lord James Worth, the false smile back on his face. "You're too young."

"My father died many years ago," said Harry, coldly. He did not like the man's attitude. "He was killed by an elephant... Can I help you?"

"We want a guide, Brigandshaw."

"What for?"

"To hunt elephant. My name is Lord James Worth. You may have heard of my father. My father is the Duke of Portland."

"I haven't I'm afraid."

"Probably not. You're a colonial?"

"A Rhodesian, Worth. And proud of it. My grandfather, Sir Henry Manderville. The title goes back to the Conqueror... Does yours?"

"Not quite that far."

"I didn't think so." It was the only time in Harry's life he had laid any importance in his grandfather's title. "And no. We don't hunt elephant on Elephant Walk. Or anywhere for that matter."

"We'll have to do it alone. This young man showed us the way to your farm. He can walk back to Salisbury. I gave him ten pounds."

Jim Bowman got out of the car. The man in the military moustache got back into his front seat. The engines were started by the black men turning a cranking handle in the front of each car. A black man had got out of the back of the truck to do the same job for the truck.

The convoy did a wide turn and went back the way it came.

"They want to hunt in the Zambezi Valley," said Jim Bowman lamely. He had on a good pair of boots for the walk back and wished he had brought a water bottle.

"Harry Brigandshaw... I was coming into Salisbury to find you. My grandfather needs an assistant for the tobacco. Come and tell us all about yourself... Would you like a beer? My mother tells me you were in the war. In the trenches. I had an easy war by comparison. In the air, so to speak."

"Good Lord! Are you the fighter ace?"

"Well, I wouldn't go that far... You won the MM?"

"Yes I did. I was so frightened I ran towards the Germans, instead of the other way... My name is Jim Bowman."

"I know... You met my grandfather."

JIM WAS in the middle of telling them about the Valley of the Horses when the guns went off. They were all seated on the veranda with the screens down. A breeze had come up the veranda where it was dark and cool. There were trees interspersed all over the lawn that went right down to the river where he could see the children playing with the dogs. The dog that had gone off down the avenue of jacaranda trees had trotted back and was sprawled on the cool stone of the veranda.

His hosts jumped up simultaneously.

"The giraffes!" they said.

Harry ran into the house and came back with two rifles. His own Purdey and a Lee Enfield .303 he had brought back from the war. He gave Jim Bowman the .303.

"It's loaded. If they've killed my giraffe, I'll kill the bastards. How dare they shoot on my farm? Better you stay here, Grandfather."

They ran out of the house to the stables. The stables were next to the barns. It took them impatient minutes to saddle the horses. There were no cars on Elephant Walk. Only the two tractors were mechanised, and they were too slow.

By the time they reached the avenue of jacaranda trees they were at full gallop. Lord James Worth had left the gate open. Jim followed Harry, the heavy rifle thumping his back. Instinctively he had checked the safety catch before getting into the saddle.

They found the dead giraffe two miles from the homestead. The animal was lying on its side in the long grass with its head missing.

"They've chopped off her bloody head as a trophy." Jim could see Harry Brigandshaw wanted to kill. Next to the carcass stood two small foals looking at their dead mother.

"She was tame, for God's sake."

They could both hear the car engines faraway, the sound fading into the bush. The cars and truck were headed back to the main road. Harry thought of chasing them on the horses and knew it was futile. He got off his horse and bent down to the dead giraffe and buried his head in her side. The carcass was still warm.

"A lion had killed her mother. I was fifteen. Back from school in the Cape. Carried her back from the Zambezi Valley over my saddle. Gave her cow's milk warmed up in a bottle. Slept in the stalls for a week. A giraffe never hurt anyone. I swear I would have shot that bastard and gladly hanged for it. They'll stick my beautiful giraffe on some bloody wall in some bloody mansion in England and have it stare at them for eternity through glass eyes."

"You've got her babies. How old are they?" Jim was not sure what to do.

"About two weeks. The father was wild. My grandfather saw him for a few days when Gabby was on heat. Then he left again for open bush."

It took them half an hour to truss the twins. Jim had watched Harry cut lengths of vine that climbed one of the tall trees. The baby giraffes were strong. They left the mother where she lay without her head for the jackals and hyenas. The birds of prey. Jim was now sure there were tears down Harry's face.

"Soon the vultures will be circling," said Harry. "A lion only eats its own kill. There will be nothing but bleached bones in a week. I loved that animal. As much as I have loved any human... You any good at bottle-feeding?"

"Never tried it."

"There won't be much cash salary. You can have old Peregrine's rondavel if you want a job. Eat with us until we have built on a kitchen. Tobacco is going to be the crop of the future. Later, we'll cut you a bonus out of the tobacco sales. If it goes the way Grandfather thinks it will, you'll have enough capital to apply for a Crown land farm. You'll be a landowner, Jim Bowman. In a country with the best future in the world."

"Are you offering me a job, sir?"

"If Voss approves of you, so do I. How is the old scavenger? Did you learn anything? About the bush? The rest you can take with a grain of salt. Did he tell you about Gordon? That's his favourite story."

"Is it true?"

"In everything in life there is a grain of truth. It's knowing which part is true. He knew my father. Father said he was the nicest old rogue roaming the bush. There was a scandal in London. He has a daughter. Her mother's family have kept her away from him. I rather think if he ever went back to England they would put him in jail. What for, we have no idea out here.

"My mother says you have a lady friend from England. Are you getting married? The rondavel with a kitchen would be big enough. It's easy to extend houses. We make our own bricks on the farm. The soil from the giant anthills fires well. There's something in the ants' saliva, I think."

"No, I'm not getting married."

"Sorry. None of my business... We'll give it a three-month trial and see if we all like each other. The farm is one big family. Black and white. The elements are our enemies. One day we will put in a big dam across the Mazoe River and never have to worry about the rains again. In Africa, it's all about water. A dam big enough to sail a boat on. So Voss told you about his daughter?"

"Yes, he did."

"About your age. Maybe a bit younger... You can take that one over your saddle. I'll take this one."

"Can't you report him to the authorities?"

"I could. It would be a waste of time. Mostly we look after ourselves. People like Worth have to live with themselves. I'm glad I don't have to live with him. Looked like a perfectly miserable sod if you ask me. Men with lots of money can always buy company. Buy their friends... I hope they try the Zambezi Valley on their own. That should be fun."

"Won't the black men help them?"

"That depends. If they treat the blacks like they treated me, Worth and his English friends will find themselves alone. One morning they'll wake up and find the blacks gone. The chap can't even close a bloody gate. Oh yes, I really hope they go into the valley. At this time of year it's so hot their brains will boil in their heads... Lions are not so easy to kill and they are not the most dangerous to man. It's the buffalo. A buffalo can charge oblivious to bullets, there's so much bone in the front of his head. What you say we just forget Lord James Worth? People like that are best ignored."

"Do you get the *Rhodesia Herald* on the farm?"

"Newspapers! I haven't read a newspaper since the end of the war. Anyway," Harry said with a chuckle, "they don't deliver out this far. Why, do you read the newspapers?"

"Not if I can help it."

Having at last landed himself a job he did not want the embellished war hero story making him look a fool. He did not want Harry Brigandshaw looking at a photograph of him slightly glassy-eyed from whisky and wine leering into Solly Goldman's camera lens while stuffed into a dead man's uniform, even if the uniform was from the right regiment. As they rode back, Jim took stock. In two days he had almost made up his losses. He had a job. A home. People he knew he was going to like. The story of Jim Bowman and Jenny Merryl was best left to the mill girls of Manchester. The story was over. Jenny would have her last photograph in the paper. With luck, the story would never come up again in his life.

Before reaching the avenue of jacarandas Jim turned in his saddle to look back. Vultures were circling high in the sky. Death for one was life to another. For the first time since going to war, he felt at home. At the end of the avenue of trees he got off his horse and closed the three bar gate behind them. The small giraffe was looking at him on the slant where she was tied to his saddle.

After safely stabling the baby giraffes, they walked through the barns and buildings to the houses.

The children had come up from the river with the dogs. An older woman he remembered from before was looking at him.

"There you are," said Emily. "Did my son offer you a job?"

"Yes, thank you, ma'am."

"Welcome to Elephant Walk. This is my daughter Madge. The monsters are her children."

"We are not monsters," said Paula, Tinus and Doris in unison... "Who are you?"

"I'm Jim Bowman... Can you help me with the baby giraffes?"

"What baby giraffes? Where are they?"

"In the stable."

"Oh, please!"

Catching the nod from the mother and grandmother, Jim found himself walking back to the stable with three children and the dogs. He was happier than he could ever remember being in his life. When he reached the stables, he could still see the vultures circling in the sky. The birds looked very beautiful in the air.

WHILE JIM BOWMAN was finding his feet with the children, Jenny Merryl was finding life equally sweet. All thought of early marriage to Jim had gone with her new popularity. Being the centre of rich male attention was new to Jenny Merryl, even if the African sun had shaded the colour of her young skin to a soft brown making her look exquisite. Not once had she peeled. The suntan suited her. She was a natural blonde brushed a rich brown by the morning rays of the sun. She had learnt to stay out of the sun after nine o'clock.

She was nineteen years old, almost twenty. Her body was firm and full. Good, childbearing hips and high breasts. Surprisingly, her eyes were brown among the blonde hair she let grow despite the new fashion for close-cropped hair. When she looked in the mirror, she knew she had never looked more beautiful.

Her best attribute was her ability to flirt with her eyes. To give the man a glimpse of a darker soul that wanted more than pretty words. A brief glance into a man's eyes sent a shaft of heat straight to their sexual organs. The ability which she could turn on and off at will, had come with hours of practising in front of a mirror. Too long a look was cheap. Too short would not have the desired effect. Everything was in the flash. It worked for Jenny even at a distance. Across a crowded room she could draw men towards her as surely as pulling them with a string. In England the trick had been of lesser value. In England when the right type of men came across to her they left soon after hearing her speak. They knew she was common. Or they made a crude proposition. In Africa, her north country accent was said to be cute. No one cared. Her power worked on everyone.

The attention went straight to her head. She had found out she had something to sell. Something rare in Rhodesia. Something all of them wanted. A young, pretty girl, a girl with sex appeal.

THE CRUSH she had built up over the years for Jim Bowman had vanished when they had met again. He was just a boy. A sweet young boy, but still a boy. He had been as shy as ever he had been in Neston, barely able to speak. She had given him her best look when they met in Simon Haller's office at the newspaper. The man had given her the twenty-five pounds reward a week before. Jim, she learnt, had been away somewhere in the mountains. Jim had stammered, stuck to the floor. The war hero who had found his girl was meant to sweep her up in his arms, not stand rooted to the spot.

"Hello, Jenny. It's so nice to see you again." They had stared at each other, an unlikely pair caught in a charade. "Did you have a good journey?" he had put out his hand. They had touched hands. There was nothing. They were strangers in a strange country, far from home.

"Would you like to go to lunch?" he had asked.

"I can't today," she had answered for no reason.

"Well, maybe another day."

"That will be nice."

"Mr Haller has your address in Salisbury?"

"Yes, he does."

"Good. How is your mother?"

"I don't know."

"And Len?"

"We don't write."

"How are you liking Africa?"

"Very much."

"I hope it wasn't me what brought you here. The newspapers, you know…"

"In a way. Not really. Things are different when you arrive."

He had not even said she looked pretty. He had barely smiled. She had thought the distance from Neston would push away his shyness. It was just the same. If someone had not told her through a newspaper that Jim loved her she would never have guessed in a million years. The fantasy exploded like a child's balloon, leaving little on the floor of its former glory. Just an old, worthless piece of shrivelled coloured rubber that would never blow up again. Were it not for the comfort of Simon Haller's twenty-five pounds she would have been frightened. Her young girl's dream of perfect love had vanished from her mind. All the little children. The little house. The perfect home. The perfect love.

"Goodbye, Jim."

"Goodbye, Jenny."

When she walked down the street from the *Rhodesia Herald*, she knew she was a much harder woman. Quietly, walking on her own, she shed a tear for her youth. The dream was over. More than France, more than her wounded officer, more than the sight of poor Cousin Mildred plying her trade, the reality of Jim Bowman had brought her down to earth with a crash. There wasn't going to be any happiness in her life, certainly not the type she had imagined.

"One door closes. One door opens," she said to herself, changing direction for Meikles Hotel. She wanted a drink. She wanted a drink very badly.

IN THE LOUNGE of the hotel she sat down at a table and ordered herself a gin, caring nothing of what anyone might have thought. There were three men in the room drinking tea. One ordered a fresh pot of hot water in a Scots accent. Jenny ordered a second gin that came with ice and quinine tonic water. She ignored the three men at their separate tables. She could see they were poor. She hoped Jim would walk into the big room. Jim, smiling and confident. A man about town. Above, the punkahs were turning slowly in the high ceiling.

Ten minutes later a message was delivered to her by the head waiter, a big black man with a red sash round his ample waist. On the card was strong handwriting in a jet-black ink, in perfect calligraphy.

The Count Le Jeune D'Alment requests the pleasure of the company of Miss Jenny Merryl to lunch.

RSVP. Philemon. Meikles Hotel head waiter

"May I show you the way to the dining room, Miss Merryl?"

"Thank you, Philemon."

For the life of her she had never heard of the count before.

He was waiting for her at the reception desk. The small lectern stood at the entrance to the dining room. The English maître d'hôtel was hovering at the man's elbow. She had never seen the man before in her life.

"Your picture was in the paper. I saw you were alone in the lounge. Excuse my taking such liberty with such a beautiful woman. I think you English have a small saying. 'Faint heart never won fair lady'. Please be my guest for lunch, Miss Jenny. I'm Pierre Le Jeune. It will be my greatest pleasure. The food is good, I assure you. Isn't that so Cuthbert?" The maître d'hôtel, smiled sweetly. A tall man in his mid-thirties took her hand. Slowly he brought the hand up to his lips as he formally bent forward. When she looked into the eyes turned up to hers, there was no sign of a predator. He was the most beautiful man she had ever seen.

Had she been looking out of the dining room window onto the courtyard she would have seen Jim Bowman walk across into the men's bar. He had stopped briefly, seeing what he saw before hurrying into the bar.

JENNY THOUGHT long afterwards how naïve she had been to accept Pierre Le Jeune's second invitation. But that was after she knew the habits of men better. The rich and the poor. At nineteen she had still thought everyone was nice, even her officer's wife had only been protecting a husband from temptation.

Pierre Le Jeune was not French as she had first thought. He was a Belgian. His father had been an impoverished aristocrat as Jenny learnt, so many of them, to be three generations down the line, had gone to the Congo for Leopold the Second, King of the Belgians and Soi-souverain of the Congo. Pierre told her there were many riches in the Congo and few Europeans prepared to risk their lives. The mosquitoes were the size of an English penny. The Congo River so wide it was more like a sea, even if it was thousands of miles from saltwater where it rose in the heart of darkest Africa. The tribal people looked at through European eyes, were savages in the true sense of the word. Instead of wasting their enemies they ate them. The parts they could not eat, like the head, they boiled and shrank in the sun, hanging them in their grass huts as a reminder to their victory.

Among the lakes and rivers, the mango swamps, the man-eating crocodiles and snakes that swallowed men whole, Pierre's father had made his fortune only sharing the wealth with the King himself. Even the British had failed to penetrate the heart of Africa, hard as they had tried.

It was in the Congo that Pierre had grown up in a great house built by his father on the banks of the great Congo River, a mile downriver from Leopoldville, named after the second King Leopold of the Belgians. A stream of tutors were brought from France and England to tutor the boy and his three brothers. The boys, born in the Congo, bitten by insects from an early age, survived. The tutors mostly died or ran away demented in the head.

Pierre had survived eleven tutors prior to being sent to Oxford to finish his education and then returned to Africa where he belonged. Speaking English as easily as French and Flemish, even with a continental accent, had made it easy for the Le Jeunes to move into the territories of Cecil John Rhodes. Northern Rhodesia having a common border with Katanga, the copper-rich southern province of Leopold's fiefdom.

The four brothers were all good businessmen. The father was still very much alive. The family's problem was finding new homes for the piles of cash generated by the family business. Pierre had proudly told Jenny it was said in the Congo, the old count would trade his grandmother for a profit, if he had had a grandmother to trade. Everything that came in and out of the Congo, a country nearly half the size of continental Europe, passed through the Le Jeunes's hands. The old count even admitted to his children he was not sure of the size of his wealth. Largely, the Le Jeunes only had one fault. They never knew when to stop accumulating wealth, to find time to enjoy it. The old count never forgetting his parlous state before his king sent him to the Congo with Pierre's mother as a young bride. Over the weeks Jenny had pieced together the family story from snatches of conversation.

Back at the beginning, Pierre Le Jeune wanted to show Jenny what he had done since arriving in Rhodesia. The lunch had gone far better than he thought it would. The girl he had seen three times without her knowing his presence was not just a pretty face. There was English north country savvy behind the eyes that savaged his sexual parts from the moment he looked up from kissing the back of the hand. Uneducated maybe but the girl had brains.

"We're going to Inyanga for a week," he had told her after lunch. "A house party. The Inyanga and my estate in the Eastern Highlands. Some of you English say it is like your Scotland. It is high, six thousand feet above sea level. Free of mosquitoes. The place to be at this time of year. You'll come with us, of course, Miss Jenny. Jenny is so much nicer than Jennifer. You could never be a Jennifer. Always Jenny. We can catch the trout. Fly my aeroplane which we have to do to get there."

"How big is the aeroplane to take all those people?"

"They will go by car. You will come with me, yes?"

"How many people fit in the plane?"

"You and me, Miss Jenny. Just you and me. We each have a cockpit."

"YOU know how to fly?"

"Of course. In the war, I kill Germans. One time I also kill Austrians though mostly they stay on Italian front. It is a British aeroplane. Made by your Mr de Havilland. In France she was a bomber though she never dropped the bombs. The war finished so I bought her cheap from the British government. Took it to pieces. Pieces in big boxes. Big boxes to Africa and I put her together. You'll be quite safe. There can be no hanky-panky in an aeroplane." Jenny remembered he had giggled like a small, endearing boy. She had accepted his invitation for the following week.

SOMEHOW THE OTHER guests never arrived. She was still in the Inyanga when Jim Bowman was offered his job on Elephant Walk which was why he had not seen her for sixteen days and why their love story, except in the papers, came to an abrupt end. In the time between the lunch and her first flight in an aeroplane, she went on seven dates.

JENNY NEVER KNEW that Pierre's mother was of peasant stock, the real glue that held the family together. The last thing Pierre wanted as a wife, was some social lady wanting to hide from the African sun. Pierre wanted to live out his life in Africa without having to traipse backwards and forwards to Europe. Society bored him. Long journeys cooped up on the same ship with the same people bored him. Maybe when aircraft flew regularly from Africa to Europe, he would not mind the journey so much.

When it suited him he was no more a gentleman than the rest of them. He was rich and bought what he wanted when he wanted. Which was why, he told himself, he had never married. He was thirty-five and every woman he met and liked he turned into a whore. The only woman he had ever respected. The only woman he had ever loved was his mother. No one had ever turned his mother into a whore and it was not what he would do to Jenny.

PIERRE KNEW the full story of Jim Bowman and Jenny Merryl from the newspapers. When he found out later his friend Harry Brigandshaw had employed Jim Bowman, he was not surprised. Salisbury. Rhodesia. All were small places for white men. The country, someone had said to him, was vast, the white population sparse.

Pierre Le Jeune and Harry Brigandshaw had both been in the Royal Flying Corps. They had both been at Oxford but though they were up at the same time they had never met at university. Oxford was a bigger place than Rhodesia. A bigger place than the RFC for that matter.

What had brought them together as friends on the Western Front was being African. It was when the air war was talked through in the wet days, when there was no flying, that Harry and Pierre found themselves lost in the general conversation. Most of which was social trivia that neither of them liked or had experienced.

They had been on a conversion course together, learning to fly the new Sopwith Camel. Among the terrible noise, the mud and slush, the quick death of the Western Front, the idea of the Inyanga farm had been born.

"We can't grow deciduous fruit," Harry had told him. "Apples, pears and plums. Elephant Walk is too hot. My grandfather is growing tobacco, believe it or not. The place to put a great orchard is in the Inyanga. The Eastern Highlands. If you can think of a way of packing, cooling and shipping to Europe when there isn't any fruit in the shops you will make a fortune. Rhodes had an estate in the Highlands which is still flourishing and he left the estate to the people of Rhodesia in his will as a national park. You buy yourself ten thousand acres up there, Pierre, and I'll visit you every summer to get away from the lowveld heat. The air is like champagne. Clean. Cool. Beautiful. You can stop sweating your life out in the Congo. When this course is over, keep in touch. You and I are the same. We're Africans. It's in our blood. Build yourself a beautiful home when the war is over and find yourself a wife who loves Africa. That bit's difficult, I know… Europe is too cramped with too many people and a man needs space. You can see forever from the Inyanga. Put some trout in the mountain rivers. Build some dams. In the Rhodesian winter you will need a big log fire up there. That's nice… Just don't get yourself killed in this damn war. What made you come and fight?"

"We drew straws. Father thought one of us should go when the Germans invaded Belgium. What about you?"

"My younger brother was killed. I wanted revenge."

"Did you get it?"

"Revenge is rarely what you think it will be. The other side is just the same as us. How men get to kill each other is built into us. We are born with a wish to have a good fight. Such a waste of time. Maybe none of us ever wanted to grow old. Elephant Walk, Rhodesia. A letter will get to me. I'm sure you can remember Elephant Walk. What made you join the RFC? The British?"

"The Belgians don't have an air force so to speak... How long before an apple tree bears fruit?"

"Fourth year. Peaks at seven or eight. You get a crop for twenty years if you prune the trees properly."

JENNY MERRYL STAYED with Pierre Le Jeune for a month. No one visited. The black staff ran the small house. The big house, he told her, was yet to be built. Never once did Pierre try to touch her.

"You are Royal Game, my dear. Untouchable as a guest under my roof."

"Have you never been with a woman?"

"Oh, don't be silly. I'm thirty-five. I won't ask you if you have been with a man as I don't wish to know the answer. Many things are best not spoken."

BACK IN SALISBURY after her second flight in the air, men kept knocking at the door of Jenny's small room. Her landlady was also from the northern part of England which was why she had taken the room. Her month away was not even questioned. Mrs Winterbottom was the height of discretion. Her only rule was no men in the room.

"I have my reputation, dearie. Can't have that kind of thing going on now can we? Enjoy yourself while you're young, I say. Be careful, Jenny. Careful. Don't let 'im touch you till ring on finger. The wedding ring, not the engagement ring. Men never want no second-hand goods neither. I know. Not for me to say. No it isn't. But I'm going to say none the less. That foreigner's too old for you. Nearly old enough to be your father."

"He's thirty-five, Mrs Winterbottom."

"That's what I say. Old enough to be your father. He ain't touched you, has he?"

"He's a perfect gentleman."

"There ain't no such bloody thing."

"I've got a job at the new hospital."

"You're not movin'?"

"Of course not. I love it here. I don't know what I would have done without you. I may have to go on night shift so don't get the wrong idea."

They both laughed.

Pierre had flown himself back to the Inyanga after only one night in Salisbury. With all the new men coming into her life she settled down to enjoy herself. She had a job as a nurse. She had a comfortable room. She was happy. Jim Bowman stayed further and further back in her mind. Jenny lived for the day and made herself look as pretty as possible. If Pierre came back, all well and good. If not, she told herself, there was more than one fish in the sea. Doors, she smiled, were opening for her all over the place. The sun was shining, and the sky was blue.

9

GAMES AND MORE GAMES, JUNE 1921

*T*ina Pringle found Barnaby St Clair's one weakness the moment his brother Merlin invited her out to lunch. He was jealous.

Through the English winter and spring Tina taunted him with a sweet smile before turning her back. They had met many times on the social circuit after the one and only time she had agreed to see Barnaby when he invited her to his brother's flat for dinner. Smithers had prepared a meal better than she had eaten in any of the expensive London restaurants. She had enjoyed herself. The suave Barnaby thought everything, including Tina, would fall at his feet. Whenever he tried to make the conversation intimate she turned the subject, usually back to Merlin who was grateful for every crumb of her attention while trying to tell them he knew she was Barnaby's friend, not his. The poor man was besotted with her right through dinner.

The next day Barnaby had called her room at the Savoy, trying to give her the impression nothing had changed from their halcyon days in Johannesburg. He had invited her to dinner, an invitation she refused. He had tried again three days later with the same result. Tina even told the girl on the telephone exchange at the hotel to not put calls from Barnaby St Clair through to her room. Only when she saw him from a distance during the social swirl of the tea dances, the American new fashion of stand-up cocktail parties, the groups that gathered at the nightclubs after the West End shows, did Tina give him a warm, sexy smile and lick her lips.

More than once he came across with the swagger of an old friend.

"Ah, you must be the Honourable Barnaby St Clair."

She would then turn back to her friends, leaving him standing. There was nothing more she enjoyed than ignoring Barnaby. The boy thought himself too popular. Expected her to jump back into his bed. Like the other men that flowed through her life she gave them just enough to send them crazy and then went cold. She wanted a husband. A rich one. She wanted Barnaby more than anything in the world. But not as his mistress. She was no longer the little girl from the railway cottage that had lugged jam jars back from the river that was more of a stream, jam jars full of tadpoles and once a baby stickleback. With Barnaby. Always with Barnaby. Always her carrying the jam jars.

She had sent her brother Albert copies of all her press cuttings knowing the mention of his name in the London social papers would stroke his vanity, even bringing him back to London for a visit. The one-time gentleman's gentleman to Jack Merryweather returned a rich man to the town where he had lived as another man's servant. She told him she had seen Barnaby. Had seen Merlin. That she was now socially their equal. She even told him in her letters how she snubbed Barnaby on more than one occasion. Only then had she asked her brother for an allowance that would give her time to land a rich husband, a prize close to the heart of Albert Pringle. It would be her brother's way of getting back at the English class system.

Just before her money ran out. Just before she would have had to run out of the Savoy Hotel with her tail between her legs a man at Lloyds bank rang to ask her to visit the bank to open her account. On her behalf, the bank was holding five thousand pounds. Miss Pringle, the man had said pompously, would need a chequebook. She only just refrained from telling the man at the other end of the telephone just how much Miss Pringle needed a chequebook.

She had cabled her brother her joy and gone out and found herself a small, well-furnished flat to rent in St John's Wood.

She had found the perfect address to further her campaign. She even employed a woman to come in and clean every day, Tina's first servant. The poor girl was almost destitute and glad of the job. Tina did not tell her how near she was to having more in common with the girl in the circumstances of their births. Servants talked. Among each other. No one was ever to know. So far as London was concerned she was South African. Sister of the rand baron, Albert Pringle.

EVEN AT A YOUNG age Tina had worked out the nonsense of life. That it was what you appeared to be that counted, not who you were. A man in a smart suit was a man in a smart suit. Nobody asked if he had paid his tailor. The Savoy. The rand baron. The flat in St John's Wood, the perfect elocution, compliments of Miss Pinforth. That was who she was. Her brother's money had made her a lady. To those who asked, she told them her parents were dead, rolling sad please ask no more questions eyes, making the conversation fall silent. Like in a church. Each time she denied her parents she mentally apologised to her mother and father.

Only Barnaby knew. She would have to be careful of Barnaby. She had watched him take the tadpoles from the water in the jars. One by one. Letting them squiggle out their short lives on dry land before squashing them under his feet. She knew him better than he knew himself. She loved even the evil hidden in his mind.

PLAYING Merlin as a pawn had not been her idea at first. Merlin presented the idea without her help. The two colour eyes gave her the shivers. The one eye almost black, peering at her through the monocle had the same effect on her as Merlin had on animals. Cats that arch their backs. Dogs that ran away. Where Barnaby's evil was hidden in a smile, Merlin's was visible in the turbulent stare of the one dark eye. Only this time Tina had no idea if the stare was false. The evil only in the pigment of the eye.

The brothers were still living together in the Park Lane flat when Merlin asked her out. She had been expecting something for weeks. Like Barnaby, they met on the social circuit. Always, Merlin was polite. Never once did he refer to the circumstances of her birth. Somehow he had even found out she was saying her parents had died when she and Albert were young. She even thought he knew the game she was playing.

They had found themselves in the same group of people at Epsom Downs that day they were running The Oaks, a minor classic of the English flat racing calendar. The group had hired an open-topped, double-decker bus that was parked at Tottenham Corner. Formally dressed waiters served ice-cold glasses of French champagne and smoked salmon sandwiches. The men wore morning dress; tall, dove-grey hats and dove-grey suits with tails. She had worn a large hat made of straw and covered in artificial flowers. Dressed in crimson, the material soft and clinging to her legs, she was visible from the stands on the opposite side of the racetrack. Merlin had sat himself next to her. Barnaby was nowhere to be seen. Merlin had a tall cane between his legs, the monocle dangling at the end of the cord on his chest. She was seated on his right, next to the one blue eye and felt more comfortable.

Without the two glasses of champagne that had gone straight to her head she would probably have refused his invitation.

"Have I ever said how beautiful you are?" he had said.

She was trapped in her seat on the side of the bus next to the track. Caught like a rabbit in a car's lights, she froze. Her hackles rose. She was sure there was a sword hidden inside the tall cane between his legs that would flash out and impale her. She had dared not look at him. Even her big hat had felt silly on her head.

"Why don't I call for you tomorrow? At twelve o'clock. You have not seen my new car, Miss Pringle. Tomorrow for lunch. Just the two of us."

"You don't know where I live."

"Oh, but I do. St John's Wood is such a good address. May I congratulate you? And upon your dress. Your hat... I shall call for you tomorrow."

Merlin had stood up and turned his full face to hers, the coal-black eye pinning her speechless to her seat. Then he had smiled. Excused himself to go and lay a bet with a bookmaker. Bookmakers lined the railings. She could see them down below.

Only when he had gone did she think of what to do. Instead of letting him call on her, she would call on him. Call on the both of them. At the Park Lane flat. They would all go out together. The three of them. Herself, Merlin and Barnaby.

WHEN SHE HAD REACHED home that night, having refused an invitation from the group to go on to dine in town, she had told Smithers, who answered the phone at Merlin's Park Lane flat of her change in plan.

"I have to be at my hairdresser in Oxford Street, Smithers. You understand?"

"Perfectly, Miss Pringle. Mr Merlin is to remain here."

"Silly for both of us to go to St John's Wood."

"Silly indeed, Miss Pringle. I will inform Mr Merlin... You did say Mr Merlin, Miss Pringle? I'm sure Mr Barnaby would be pleased to speak to you right now."

"I'm in a terrible rush, Smithers."

When she put down the phone, she swore out loud in a Dorset accent.

"Damn servants know more of what's going on than we do."

The irony of what she had said to the telephone back on its hook was lost on her. Only in the middle of the night did she wake and change her plan. Only then, in the dark of the summer night did she recognise the irony of her words. She even smiled before falling back to sleep.

BARNABY ANSWERED the door. The man downstairs at the reception desk had rung the flat. She was dressed perfectly, her close-cropped hair freshly cut, the small cloche hat perched skilfully in her soft brown hair with its tint of red. She smiled her sweetest smile at Barnaby, her new plan working right from the start.

"Is Merlin at home? He kindly invited me to lunch. So sweet of him. He has a new car." She giggled right in Barnaby's face, making him step back to reveal Merlin and behind Merlin, Smithers. At that moment she knew that Smithers knew exactly who she was. There was a familiar smirk on his face. A look of 'you and me, darling', not 'you and him'.

In a glance Tina knew the damn cook fancied her. She even gave him a second look which was probably a mistake. They were all playing games, anyway.

"You don't mind do you, Barnaby? We were childhood friends. All of us."

"You talk nonsense."

"Do I? I don't think so... Are you ready, Merlin? I've been so looking forward to our lunch... Where are we going?"

Again Tina giggled deep in her throat. For a moment she thought Barnaby was going to slam the flat door in her face, his own face had turned so livid. With another sweet smile at Barnaby she turned on her heels and waited for Merlin. After a long ten seconds she felt a hand take her elbow and walk her to the still open lift, the lift attendant having been told to wait for her. She was not sure until she turned whether it was Barnaby or Merlin. For the first time in her life she found the coal-black stare of the left eye reassuring. Then the wrought iron concertina door to the lift closed, and they were going down.

Tina had time to raise a quizzical eyebrow at Barnaby still standing in the doorway to the flat. "If looks could kill," she told herself.

THE THREE-LITRE Bentley was black. Only the chrome on the rounded top of the radiator shone in the brilliant sun.

Merlin had left his monocle in the flat. He was still asking himself why he had called Tina 'Miss Pringle' on the bus. No one else had been listening. Most of them were down on the track, laying their bets. The two o'clock was about to be off. Once the starting gate went up, the betting stopped. Still it had taken him months to find the courage to ask her out. The Honourable Merlin St Clair, once Captain B Company, Dorset Fusiliers, a regiment first called out by an ancestor more than two hundred years before he was born. A man so rich he would never again have to work in his life. Reduced to a suppliant by a girl not even in his class. A girl with no better birth than Esther who had gone off and married a corporal soon dead in the war. Esther, the mistress to whom he still paid a small allowance.

The power of the engine, the force of their speed, pinned them both back in the front seats of the car as Merlin hurled the new machine round the tight corners of the English country lanes, fighting his demon. Why did he always wish to seduce girls well below his class, he asked himself? Never once had a classy girl made him go weak at the knees. They left him cold. Trivial chatter. Their sole interest in themselves. Frivolity at its worst. Like being down with a sack of potatoes on a wet blanket… Oh, how he knew. How many times. Not one of them making him wish to go back again let alone to make one of them his wife.

Now he was old. Set in his ways. Too old to bring up children even with a house full of servants. The eligible girls in his age bracket loved horses and dogs more than men. Only wanted a husband to stable the horses, kennel the dogs for the hunt. For most of his adult life, Merlin was sure the girls he was introduced to by so many mothers with so many understanding looks mingled with fear were more satisfied by the rhythmic hump of the saddle than any man. They didn't want him. Any of them. Just a home. A large country home where they could wear their two-piece set of tweeds and hunt foxes in the winter. Watch chinless wonders play endless cricket in the summer.

Merlin pushed down again on the accelerator pedal. A small stretch of straight road. To his surprise, Tina seemed to be enjoying herself. Twice she had whooped as he brushed the hedgerow on the curves. She was alive. Her eyes sparkling. Her leg so close to his.

There was no chance of talk. No chance of questions. The top was down and the wind rushed over the windscreen. Tyres squealed on the newly tarred road. There had never been any doubt in his mind where he was going for lunch even if the end result had been so humiliating.

His mistress gone off from his house while he was fighting in the trenches. Gone off to marry her corporal because she knew he would never ask her to marry him. To have children. To have a real home of her own.

He had met Esther at the Running Horses in Mickelham. On a walking tour in the countryside before the war. Esther had been the barmaid. Young. Big-breasted. Full of life. None of it trivial... And he was going back. Hurtling down the lanes of Surrey back to the pre-war days with another girl that made his hormones scream for the joy of life. He was going to find the magic once again before he died. To hell with Barnaby. To hell with Smithers. To hell with all of them. He wanted to feel again. To want to live. He wanted Tina. Even as a wife. Merlin knew they were travelling much too fast as he shouted out his joy to the rushing air. He had admitted it. At last. He wanted her as a wife. To hell with all the family consequence. Skilfully his right foot brushed the brake before the onrushing hedgerow. Next to him on the seat was a small hand gripping the red leather with all its might. Taking one hand from the wheel he briefly covered the hand with his own. They were back down a straight. Faster than before.

By the time they reached the Running Horses, Tina was not sure if she was dead or alive. She had never been so frightened in her life. The journey blurred between tree and hedge, flashing past, hurling her sideways in the turns, the big engine throbbing power the full length of her body. Her knuckles gripping the red leather seat for dear life were white. She whooped and whooped to replace her fear.

When the car stopped on the gravel driveway, she was unable to get out of the car. Her small hands were still gripping the leather seat. Merlin was smiling at her, the engine turned off. The long black bonnet in front of her seemed ready to go again. Ready to fly. No wonder a thick leather strap bound down the rounded bonnet to keep the power of the engine deep inside. Again he covered her right hand, smiling at her, willing her to enjoy his fun.

For a moment Tina thought she was going to be sick. Her cloche hat had long gone with the rushing wind. Her new haircut was free of all restraint. Her hands stopped gripping the leather seat. She brought them together pertly on her lap.

Merlin got out of the car and walked round the front, touching the shiny chrome of the radiator top in passing. A lover's caress. Merlin licked the hand that had touched the chrome. It was hot, she thought.

He was smiling deep into her eyes. The dark eye and the blue eye working together. His hair too was ruffled by the wind. His left hand ran the full length of the car's bonnet towards her and opened the door.

The fear had gone, replaced by something more familiar. Sexual. It was as though she had never seen the man before. Seeing him in a different light compared with the well-dressed somewhat detached gentleman full of conceit. All appearance and little substance despite the frightening eye. A man made up of an eyeglass and a cane. Everything perfect. The flat. Smithers. The daily routine. The unspoken money.

"I'll buy you another one."

"Oh, the hat," she said after a moment.

"You weren't frightened of my driving?"

"Petrified."

"Don't be silly. Tina Pringle has never been frightened of anything in her life. I'm sorry. We would have been late for lunch. They stop serving lunch at two o'clock. Come on. We left Hyde Park at ten past twelve. It's a quarter to two. Not bad. One of those corners was a bit close but you sometimes have to take a chance in life. No point in driving all this way without getting lunch."

"You'll be slow on the way home?"

"Of course. Like a lamb. I never drive fast when I drink a bottle of wine."

"I need a stiff gin after that."

"I used to know the owner. We'll have a drink in the bar and order lunch. A gin first and then a bottle of wine. How does that sound?"

"Where'd you learn to drive that fast?"

"On a racetrack. I don't take up many hobbies but when I do I like to know what I'm doing. Cars can be dangerous if you don't know how to handle them."

"Isn't your eye out of focus?"

"Of course not. The monocle is for effect. Plain glass. Why I left it at home. You don't need a distraction when driving at speed. Believe me… Are your knees a bit weak, Tina?"

"They're rubber. You'll have to help me out of the car."

"It will be my pleasure."

"Do you ever get the feeling you have only just met a person you have known all your life?"

"No. I don't think so… It's not going to rain. We can leave down the top. What a beautiful day. There is nothing more beautiful than an English summer's day. You can leave your coat on the back seat of the car. No one steals anything in the country. Don't you miss Dorset?"

"And my mother, Merlin."

"I miss mine too. In a better world we could take a journey home together. Maybe we will. Who knows?"

"It would be a disaster."

"Probably."

THE BUILDING WAS very old. Someone had told Merlin there had been an alehouse on the same site during the Crusades. The man had not said which Crusade. The place had likely changed names a few times over the centuries. During the reign of King Richard the First, there were unlikely to have been running horses at nearby Epsom Downs.

The thatch was thick and black, patched many times over the years. The thatch stood out three feet from the walls, giving the small, low windows some protection from the rain and sun. The leaded windowpanes were small, the glass uneven, the old bubbles in the glass making the occasional magnifying glass into the dark interior.

Before the war Merlin had looked in through one of the bubbles in the glass. Everything inside was distorted. He was unable to make out anything real. The bulged figures moved around, he could see that. He had been looking into the low-ceilinged dining room. He had thought the moving gargoyles were waiters.

The wood slats on the side of the tumbling buildings were black with age. The buildings had been built onto each other when they were needed. Some of the joins were strange where the long-dead builders had made them fit together with great skill.

The then owner said the thatch leaked, and every summer had people on the roof putting on another layer of combed straw. Starlings nested in the thatch which Merlin had thought was probably the problem. In those days he had not made his money out of shares in Vickers Armstrong. He relied on his small wage from Cornell, Brooke and Bradley. Philip Spence had been his senior in those days. It had been Philip Spence who had first brought him to the Running Horses.

By the time he got a shaken Tina Pringle from the car, the owner was walking towards the car across the wide, gravel driveway. Merlin was surprised to see it was the same man from before the war. Most things he found changed in nine years. They might look the same but they weren't. The man had his hand out. Merlin had not visited the Running Horses since before the war. There was a girl of about seven standing in one of the side doors of an outbuilding looking at the car. The door was so low anyone over five-foot tall would have to bend their heads to go inside.

This same man walking towards him had told Merlin Englishmen were much shorter at the time of the Crusades. There was an old suit of armour at Purbeck Manor that had belonged to one of Merlin's ancestors which bore out the shortness of early Englishmen. The ancestor had had to be very small to get into the suit of armour. And very strong to carry the weight. Merlin had got into it as a small boy. The armour had fallen on its face, the part Merlin had squirmed into. His mother had found him an hour later still lying on the floor. He had never tried to get into the suit of armour again.

He gave the little girl a smile, but the girl turned quickly back through the open door and slammed it shut.

"I don't believe it," the man said, "the Honourable Merlin St Clair. What a pleasure. Just in time for lunch. Some salmon straight from the north of the Lyn River. Peas from the garden. Potatoes. Your favourite."

Surprised seeing the same man, Merlin fought to remember his name. Then he remembered.

"Stanton. Nice to see you again. This is Miss Pringle. Do you like my new car? Goes like the wind. Thought we would have a drink in the bar while you prepare our lunch... You do have a table?"

"Of course... Well, why not go straight to your table? The waiter can bring your cocktail. We do make cocktails now, you know. The building may be old but we're up with the times."

Merlin saw the man was suddenly flustered. The confident hand held out became a soft, brief handshake. The man would not look him in the eye. Merlin had forgotten how much darker the left eye had become. The man was frightened.

"Be warned not to travel in that car Mr Stanton," said Tina.

Merlin saw Tina had recovered her composure. Like all the men in her life, she quickly had the owner of the Running Horses under her

spell.

"We'll go to the bar, thanks."

"If you insist…"

"He's a good driver, I can tell you that," said Tina. "Just a tad too fast for my taste."

"It's a beauty of a car… What is it?"

"The latest three-litre from Bentley. I've had her on the track at Brooklands. Wonderful… What's the latest you serve lunch?"

"Whenever you wish. Many of my old customers died in the war. You and your lady are most welcome. Maybe you would like to come to my office for a pre-lunch drink?"

"The bar will do just fine."

The little girl did not appear again. There were three other cars on the driveway. Merlin could smell honeysuckle. The trees behind the building were tall, thick with large green leaves and white flowers. The flustered owner caught the direction of Merlin's look.

"The horse chestnuts are beautiful at this time of year… You know the way to the bar, Mr St Clair."

The man turned away from them and walked to the closed door through which the little girl had run. The man went inside, bending his head and closed the door.

"Strange. What's got into Stanton? I'd expected him to join us at the bar for a drink. Always did with Philip Spence in the past. Philip was my boss in those days."

WHEN THEY reached the bar, it was empty except for a good-looking girl behind the bar. Tina thought her breasts were too large but knew men would like what they saw. The girl was probably twenty-five and dressed like a barmaid. White frilly blouse cut low and a skirt that flowed from a tight waist over large hips. The girl had a big, luscious mouth, painted red. She wore large earrings but no rings other than a thin wedding band of gold. She looked weary to Tina as if life had already given her too much of a hard time.

Tina smiled at the girl and received a glare in return. No one had ever glared at her before without a reason. Merlin had stopped before reaching the bar. The girl was looking straight at Merlin. Merlin, when Tina turned to look at him, was as white as a sheet. When he saw her looking, he regained his smile, and the colour drained back into his face.

"What you goin' to 'ave, lovey?" asked the barmaid.

"Large gin. My escort drives a car like a lunatic."

"And you, sir?"

"I'll have the same, thank you."

They had each other fixed in a glare. Tina was sure of it. She looked from one to the other.

"You two know each other, don't you?"

There was silence. The small girl she had seen from the driveway rushed across the driveway and through the door into the bar. Tina began to laugh. The barmaid glared at her. The little girl looked so like Lucinda St Clair. Tina remembered Lucinda and briefly thought of Harry Brigandshaw. The story of Lucinda's murder had been all over the papers. Even if Tina's mother had not told her the story, she would have known of the tragedy. She remembered feeling annoyed for some reason. That Harry had married Lucinda. Married anyone.

"I'll leave you two alone. Get someone to bring me the gin to the dining room. I'll ask them to wait for lunch till you join me, Merlin... You had no idea did you?"

"No. No, I didn't."

Tina left them alone in the bar. The owner was hovering just inside the door that led to the dining room.

"How have you been, Esther?" she heard Merlin say before the owner ushered her through the door away from the embarrassment.

"You know Merlin well, don't you?" he said when the door to the bar was closed behind.

"We all grew up together. That's his daughter isn't it? Too like Lucinda and Lady St Clair not to be."

"Come and have a drink in my office. Had he ever mentioned Esther?"

"Oh, yes. She ran off and married a corporal during the early part of the war. The corporal was killed."

"He still gives Esther an allowance."

"Nice of him. Does he know about the little girl?"

"No. So far as the army is concerned the girl's father is the corporal. The only way Esther could be sure of anything was to marry Ray Owen. Merlin would never have married her. Even with the child. Esther was sure Merlin was going to be killed. Few of the junior officers came through more than a month. It was my advice to marry Owen. That way the British government would look after the child. Even if both of them were killed. Merlin St Clair and Ray Owen. She knew she was pregnant when she met Ray Owen."

"Why didn't she tell Merlin she was pregnant before she married the corporal?"

"Merlin was by then back in France. In the trenches."

"Did she love the corporal?"

"I don't know. They hadn't known each other long when they married. The boy was frightened. It was Esther's way of giving him something before he went to war. Ray Owen was only a kid. I don't think he had turned twenty. It was partly my fault. I told Esther to marry Ray Owen after he blurted out a proposal of marriage. He had worked here once. As a waiter. He was back on leave, his nerves shot to hell. I saw the marriage as Esther's last chance to secure a legal place for the child she was carrying. Ray Owen was besotted by Esther. She was even prettier at eighteen. I gave Ray a room for the last week of his leave. He didn't want to stay with his mother any longer in Wales. His mother was crying all the time. Ray Owen was the only male in her family still alive. Her husband and two other sons had been killed in a methane explosion down a coal mine in 1912. Owen knew he was going to die. They all did. It was just a case of Esther legalising the child. While she could... There were no widow pensions for unmarried mothers. How could the government help? How could anyone prove who the father was if the mother wasn't married? They were all doing it then. It was the war. Good girls giving the lads something the lads had never had. And most likely never got. It was the war... How was I to know Merlin St Clair would go through four years of trench warfare without a scratch?... I thought I was doing the best thing for Esther. For the child. We all do what we think is best at the time Miss?..." He had forgotten her name in his fluster.

"Pringle. My name is Tina Pringle."

"Trouble is, what's best at the time can be wrong later on. I knew Ray Owen was a good boy from the time he was working for me. I knew Esther was a good girl even if she did go off and live with Mr St Clair without being married... Maybe that's it, Miss Pringle. We pay for our sins. Poor Esther's paid for hers. That child will go on paying I suppose."

"Why didn't she tell Merlin about the child when it was born? Corporal Owen was dead by then, wasn't he?"

"Owen was dead three weeks after marrying Esther. I tried getting hold of Mr St Clair. Left messages. The only response was Esther's yearly allowance. His pride was hurt. He's a very proud man. Didn't take to his mistress running off and getting married."

"How did he know she had married the corporal?"

"Esther wrote and told him."

"Why?"

"She had her pride. She wanted to terminate the affair. She had sent the letter before Owen was killed. I think she liked the idea of thumbing her nose at the high and mighty, the Honourable Merlin St Clair."

"So she never loved Merlin?"

"Who knows whoever loves anyone? Mostly we do things for selfish reasons. Even getting married. No, always when we decide to get married. Getting married is the most selfish thing we do in our lives. We always think of ourselves. Especially when it's the rest of our lives we are thinking about. It's all about what the other person can do for us in life that counts. We are all selfish, mark my words."

"Are you married, Mr Stanton?"

"We won't go into my life… Yes, I'm married and it's hell on earth, if you really want to know."

"Where is she today?"

"With her mother. She spends a lot of time with her mother. She only married me because I own the place. Found that out after. From one of her so-called friends."

"Any children?"

"No, thank the Lord."

"What did Esther call the little girl?"

"Genevieve. She was going to call a boy Arthur. Romantic don't you think. Esther's way of saying who the father was… Merlin. Arthur. Genevieve. Camelot. From losing a father before she was born to being part of the mighty St Clairs. Going back all those years in history. I think Esther hoped the girl would want to go and find her real father. Her grandfather who was a lord. We all want to be more than we are. Why the exploits of our ancestors should make any difference to our own lives, I never worked out. The romantic in us, maybe… Well, now it has all come down to this. A confrontation in my bar. I never thought Mr St Clair would ever come here again in his life. I thought his pride would stop him. The memory of being jilted."

"I don't think he expected you to still own the place."

"Maybe not."

"Strange he wanted to come back here. With all those bad memories. I wonder why?"

FOR A LONG TIME they could find nothing to say to each other. Esther had thought she was seeing a ghost when Merlin walked into her bar. There had been so many of them since the beginning of the war. And after. Living and dead. Young men grown old frightened by a car backfiring out of the driveway. Old ghosts. New ghosts. Faces imprinted on her mind that had come and gone for whatever reason man had found to kill each other. Esther didn't know. She couldn't read properly. Not a book, anyway. But she could think. And remember. So many young men through the war looking for the familiar for the last time before hell.

"She's a nice girl. Common as dirt, of course," Esther said when they were alone. She had disliked Tina on sight.

"How do you know?" asked Merlin.

"It takes one to see one. I know you, Merlin. You like 'em so common... Genevieve please go to our room. Close the door, luv."

"Let her stay... Am I her father?"

"Genevieve! Out of the room. Now. This moment."

The door slammed shut. Merlin could see the girl walking across the gravel towards the same outbuilding.

"Why didn't you tell me?" he asked into the silence.

"I thought you were dead. Back in '14... You got my letter about Ray?"

"Thank you very much," said Merlin sarcastically.

"I'm goin' to have a bloody drink. 'Ow've you been? Long time no see." Esther tried to put on a good face. She had no wish to lose her job. The room outside was her home.

"Didn't you get the money?"

"Oh, that. Yes I did."

"Then how could I have been dead?"

"By then Ray was dead and Genevieve born. Didn't matter. Thought you left me a bit in your will. Bloody should 'ave done what I done for you. Best bleedin' years of my life."

"Who was Ray?"

"Corporal Owen. He never knew. 'Bout the kid. Poor sod was dead three weeks after getting back to France... Who's the fancy lady? The one trying to be all la-di-da?"

"Remember me talking about Barnaby's girlfriend, Tina?"

"What's she doin' with YOU then, Merlin?"

"Barnaby won't marry her."

"Neither will you. Don't make me laugh… How the bloody 'ell did you get right through the war?"

"The Germans couldn't shoot me. You want some money for the child?"

"Course I do… Are you happy, Merlin?"

"No. No I'm not. Not that it's any matter to you… I would have liked to have got to know her. Can't have everything. No, that wouldn't work. Money will help. Money always helps… At least I will know some part of me will go on living when I'm dead. Better to let her go on thinking Corporal Owen was her father. Make it easier to fit in. I won't come down here again unless you ask for me. Sometimes people need help… I feel as if someone has kicked me hard in the stomach. Goodbye, Esther."

TINA WAS NOT in the dining room. He found her in the manager's office.

"Ah, there you are. There's a place I know down the road at Headley. You understand, Stanton. If you want, I'll pay for the lunch."

"Don't be silly… I've been telling Miss Pringle what happened."

"It's none of your damn business."

"Unfortunately I thought it was at the time."

"What has Miss Pringle to do with anything you know about me? It's none of her business either."

"I think she will explain the truth better than me. I assure you, Mr St Clair, I thought I was doing the right thing at the time."

"I have no idea what you're talking about."

Tina told him what Stanton had said once back in the car.

There had been no sign of the child or Esther when they drove away. When she finished, Merlin stopped the car and turned it round by backing into a farmer's cart road. Then he drove back to London without saying a word.

Merlin drove well but not as fast. The top was still down. Tina even wondered if he had heard everything she said. She should have minded her own business. No one ever wanted to hear the truth in life.

Merlin dropped off Tina at her flat in St John's Wood. He had helped her out of the car. Walked her up to the front door of her small flat.

She was starving hungry. She was about to thank him for the lunch they had never had.

"Nice car," she said.

The dark eye burnt into her brain. Merlin bowed formally and left. She heard the car start up again as she slowly closed her door. Then she went to the small kitchen and opened herself a small can of baked beans. Her maid had come and gone. It was five o'clock in the afternoon.

HALF AN HOUR later the telephone rang. It was Merlin.

"I must apologise for my bad manners. Just to let you know Barnaby has moved out of my flat. He was gone when I returned. Smithers helped him pack."

"What would you two boys do without Smithers?"

"I'm sorry, Tina. I really am. Maybe that was meant to happen. You are Barnaby's girlfriend, not mine."

"For a moment back there I thought I knew you, Merlin. Really knew you. Keep in touch. Not everything works out the way we think."

"I hope you're not too hungry?"

"I just ate a tin of Heinz baked beans."

"Oh dear, I'm sorry."

The telephone line went dead as Merlin at the other end put his telephone back on the hook.

Ten minutes later the telephone rang again.

"It's me. Merlin gave me a ring at my club. Can we have supper?"

"Why not, Barnaby?"

"I don't want to hear anything about Merlin."

"You really are arrogant."

"Seven o'clock... You haven't ridden in my new car."

"Oh, not again."

"What do you mean?"

"Just come and pick me up at seven."

"Why don't you sound excited?"

"Because I'm not."

WHAT TINA wanted most was a meal. She also did not want to be alone. The day's events had upset her. From the terrifying car ride to the realisation that most people's lives were a mess. Stanton with a wife he disliked. Esther without husband. A father for Genevieve. The fate of life.

When Barnaby phoned, he caught her on the wrong foot. She accepted the invitation without thinking clearly. If nothing else she told herself as she had a bath and dressed for dinner she knew Barnaby St Clair inside out. He was a rotter. Quite selfish. Would probably come to a bad end. At least she knew what she was getting. They would laugh. Look into each other's eyes. Talk about the so many things they had in common. The so many things they had done together... Only this time he was not going to end up in her bed. She swore that one to herself. Twice.

THEY WENT to Simpsons on the Strand where they had been before. He obviously wanted to show her off. To tell the crowd, she was his girlfriend. The rich heiress. The noble son. He had even tipped off the *Tatler*.

They joined a party of his friends with hugs and smiles. Some of the people she knew herself. The dress she wore had never before been seen in public. It was a sensation. Red had always suited her. She had worn a feather band around her head. The same diamond and pearl earrings given to her by Albert for her twenty-first birthday.

Everyone talked at the same time. No one listened to a word. The band played, and she danced with Barnaby. She ate the first course of asparagus swimming in melted butter. The baked beans had done more for hunger. She was careful to only sip the wine. Tina knew all about drink on an empty stomach.

Barnaby danced with the girl on his right. The man on Tina's left asked her to dance. She danced. When she sat down the waiter put a small fowl in front of her. She told herself it was no wonder they were all so thin. The poor bird would have been better left wherever it was. Tina managed to get two small mouthfuls from the bird's breasts. The small, knuckle-ended legs looking up at her from the plate were quite pathetic. A small new potato rested in a pool of red wine gravy that had doused the bird. Tina ate the potato. The waiter whisked away her plate.

This time she danced with Barnaby who was full of robust noise and *joie de vivre*. They danced the Charleston and caused a sensation on the small dance floor. They had learnt the dance together in Johannesburg when the dance first arrived in South Africa from America. They were perfect together. Everyone clapped.

Afterwards, Barry Jones from the *Tatler* asked for a photograph of them both together. Everyone clapped again after the flash from the camera.

A piece of fish on a large white plate was put in front of her. There had been confusion among the guests getting up to dance then sitting down. The fish should have come before the bird. Tina ate the fish in two mouthfuls. Everything seemed to be in mouthfuls. The girl on Barnaby's right leaned towards her. Barnaby was now dancing with somebody else. Tina had seen the girl a few times but did not know her name. The girl was trying hard to impress Barnaby. Barnaby winked at Tina over the girl's shoulder.

"I couldn't help hearing Barry say you were from South Africa. My father was killed in South Africa." It was the girl sitting next to Barnaby talking. Tina tried to listen. "Right at the end of the Boer War. I never knew him. My name is Justine Voss. I've never met anyone before who lived in South Africa. Is it very nice? I'm going there one day to find my father's grave. I have to do that for him don't you think? I live in Chelsea. You can tell me where to look for my father's grave. I tried the War Graves Commission I think they call themselves. Absolutely no help at all. They don't even have a record of Father dying. Colonel Voss. He fought with General Gordon. Chinese Gordon. Gordon of Khartoum. You must have heard of him?"

"I've heard of General Gordon. Did he die at Khartoum?"

"I meant my father."

"I was only just born during the Anglo-Boer War. We call it the Anglo-Boer War in South Africa. The Boers prefer it that way. We all live together now."

"I'll remember that, Miss Pringle... I say, you do dance the Charleston well. You think that charming Mr St Clair will teach me?"

"I'm sure he will... I hope you find your father's grave. Nothing I can help with there I'm afraid. My brother Walter fought in the Anglo-Boer War. He was killed in France in 1914."

"I'm sorry."

"Billy died also. In France. They never found one piece of him. Blown to pieces. Probably why the army know nothing about your poor father." Tina was still watching Barnaby dancing with the girl.

"I never thought of that... Surely they would know if he was dead or alive."

Barnaby sat down at the end of the dance. The band were taking a break.

"Barnaby, Miss Voss wants you to teach her the Charleston."

"It'll be my pleasure."

"You two aren't together then?" said Justine Voss.

"Just old friends," said Tina.

The waiter had put a piece of steak in front of her that had some meat to it. She turned back to her new plate with relish.

By the end of the meal she was still hungry. Barnaby was trying to teach the girl how to Charleston. They were terrible together and sat down again. Tina was sick of the talk of war and avoided any further conversation with Justine Voss. She drank down the last of her glass of red wine. Barnaby gave her a look that made her thighs melt. She was going to have a difficult time saying 'no' to him but she was still going to say 'no'. She had sworn to herself in the bath.

As the red wine took hold of her, she decided she liked making him jealous. This time he was not going to get away with his nonsense. It was all or nothing. She was going to tell him so. In no uncertain words.

After Simpsons they went to a nightclub. The Voss girl had gone with them. She seemed to like Barnaby. There was another man. Tina flirted with the other man.

When Barnaby drove home, they were both drunk. The Voss girl had gone off with the other man whose name Tina could not remember. At her door Tina put a finger in Barnaby's chest.

"This is as far as you go my sweet," she said leering at him.

"Why?"

"Because I say so."

When she closed the door to her flat, she was proud of herself. Five minutes later she heard the car drive away down in the street.

When she fell asleep, she was still hungry. She dreamed of Africa. Being chased by lion. She woke up in the light of first dawn, just before the lion caught her. She had dreamed of Harry Brigandshaw and Elephant Walk for some reason... Then she remembered the girl whose father had died in the Anglo-Boer War. She thought that was why she had been dreaming of Harry Brigandshaw. He was chasing the lion that was chasing her in her dream. The lion was still vivid in her mind.

When Tina woke again the bedroom curtains were still drawn tight. The telephone was ringing. She let it ring. When the phone stopped ringing she got out of bed and made herself breakfast. The smell of frying bacon made her hunger come back.

"I never want to be really hungry in my life," she said to the kitchen table when she had finished her breakfast. It was ten o'clock in the morning by the kitchen clock. All through the day she wondered who had been on the phone. It never rang again. She was sure it was Barnaby. He was trying to play her game. She would play the game better than Barnaby.

She had an invitation that night to the theatre. When the young man arrived to pick her up, she was freshly groomed and ready to go. He smiled at her in appreciation. She hoped Barnaby would be at the theatre. He was not there though she did see the Voss girl again. They smiled at each other across the bar during the interval. Tina had no idea what the play was about. Her mind had been elsewhere.

When the second bell rang, they went back to their seat in the stalls. She managed not to fall asleep. They went on to supper. Barnaby was not there either.

When they reached Tina's flat in St John's Wood, the man she had been with said he wanted to see her again. Tina could not at first think of the reason why. They had talked very little all night. Tina had told him how much she had enjoyed the play. Which had probably prompted the idea for the man to make a second attempt. When he tried again, she would say no to him politely. She liked to keep all the men she had been out with as friends. She never wanted them saying nasty things about her behind her back. When she saw them again, she smiled just enough to make them think they still had a chance. The personal smile, between her and the man.

The women were bitches. Women were always bitches when it came to men. And not just the ones with the horsy faces... She often wondered why people so often looked like their pets, proving to herself once again that all women were indeed bitches when it came to men. Including herself. She rather liked the idea. It was fun. Making Barnaby jealous was fun. Being a little bitch was a lot of fun.

10

ENGLAND AND HARRY, APRIL 1922

The leaves were falling in Africa when Harry Brigandshaw found his way to his ancestral home at Hastings Court.

Elephant Walk was running smoothly. Emily, Harry's mother, said Jim Bowman was quick on the uptake. They were going to plant fifty acres of Virginia tobacco for the first time. The seedbed had been prepared and for three days brushwood burnt an intense heat into the heart of the beds to kill cutworms. This would ensure the seedlings grew to be ready to plant out into the lands when the rains broke in October.

Harry's grandfather had supervised the making of bricks in a hollowed out kiln that allowed trunks of trees to be burnt right through the kiln for weeks. By the time the bricks were baked the foundation had been dug for a new block of ten barns to cure the tobacco leaf. The three rows would stand parallel with each other.

Harry had brought back enough corrugated iron from Salisbury in the new five-ton truck they had imported from British Army surplus. At least some good had come out of the killing of Harry's pet giraffe. One of Harry's neighbours had gone to England to buy ten trucks similar to the one that had followed the touring cars into the bush loaded with the safari equipment. Lord James Worth had cut a path of destruction right to the banks of the Zambezi River. All they took were trophies. Tusks. Heads. Lion skins. The horns of rhinoceros. The carcasses were strewn through the bush left for the scavengers. A man in Salisbury had said to Harry in disgust he could see where His Lordship had been by looking up at the sky where the vultures circled in the wind, waiting their turn to join the carnage. Vultures flopped around the dead elephant day and night after reaching the ground, too full of meat to fly. Instead, the man said, they squabbled with each other like old women, the beauty of the earlier flight no longer imaginable.

"I was ashamed of being an Englishman, Harry. The smaller tusks were left on the carcasses. Most of the animal heads were still attached to the carcasses. Only when they had killed did they measure the tusks and heads, taking the biggest back to their dark dank mansions to collect dust. It was as if they liked killing for the sake of killing. Found joy in destroying God's creations. One of my friends wanted to shoot the bastard and send his head back to the ancestral home in England... What makes people like that?... Why do they do it?... I stopped my friend and now I wonder why."

THE FIRST THING Harry had done at Hastings Court was to remove the stags' heads that adorned the low walls of the great chamber where for centuries his family and retainers had eaten their food below the thirty-foot high vaulted roof of blackened timber, blackened by the open fires at each end of the dining chamber. The same chamber where the Pirate, Harry's paternal grandfather, had died alone of a heart attack.

Harry had put a ladder up to the ancient walls himself and taken down the heads. Some, the old ones from centuries past, fell apart as he pulled them from their plaques. Alone, in the semi-darkness, old portraits of his ancestors looked down on him, faintly smiling, their eyes following him wherever he walked in the chamber. Thankfully, none of them had gone to Africa. There were no lions. No elephant tusks. Not even a tiger's head from India. The dead stags had only roamed the hills of England and the Highlands of Scotland.

The house was greater than he remembered as a child. Mostly what he remembered had been told to him by his mother. He thought he was two or three when his father had come back from Africa and put a ladder up to his mother's bedroom window. There were distant shades of childish memory of the old house. The rest was what he heard growing up in the African bush.

Within a week, Harry wanted to go home to Elephant Walk. The place was too big. Twenty-seven rooms. Too dark. Musty, damp inside. Old. Smelling of mildew. Full of ancient ghosts. Dead people. Despite all the money spent restoring the old pile by his grandfather and Uncle James.

There was no pull. He thought there might have been by what his grandfather had said. There was nothing he wanted from Hastings Court. Not even its history. In the years during the war when in England on leave from the Western Front he had visited his friends the

St Clairs at Purbeck Manor in Dorset. Never Hastings Court where Uncle James lived in all his splendour. Even his Grandmother Brigandshaw had gone to live in a London flat. He had been to that flat but never to Hastings Court.

"Now the place is mine," he had said looking up at the house from the edge of the ornamental lake that spread to the woods and fields. "I don't want it. I'm an African. Africa runs in my blood. All the bird sounds are strange. Where are the animal calls other than the dog fox at night?" Even then he had had to ask one of the servants that ran the court.

"Must have been a dog fox, Sir Harry."

"I'm not Sir Harry. Plain mister."

"I'm sorry, Sir Harry."

Harry gave up. After cleaning the house of animal heads, Harry had instructed the chauffeur to drive him to Leatherhead railway station where he caught the eight ten to Waterloo and the next stage of his odyssey.

THE HEAD OFFICE of Colonial Shipping was in the City of London, in Billiter Street, close to Aldgate tube station. The showroom and booking hall for the Empire Castle Line was in Regent Street. There was more to Colonial Shipping than a company that owned passenger and cargo ships. There was much for Harry to learn, none of which he found of the slightest interest.

After a first day of obsequious hand-wringing by the staff and far too much bowing and scraping, he found a small bar near the office, bought a pint of beer and sat down alone to survey his lot. So far, he had told none of his friends he was in England. The two executive directors he had met that day in the office, he had given another story to free himself from their cringing company. He told them he had to go and see his grandmother, Granny Brigandshaw. Which he should do but wasn't yet ready. The call of duty would be put off for a little longer.

The small bar was half full of clerks having a drink before going home to the suburbs. Harry could hear them talking from his seat at a small table away from the bar. They sounded mostly joyless. The pint of beer the only bright points in a dull day between the drudgery of clerical work and the nagging words of their wives.

Outside it was getting dark. Twilight. Something Harry had never seen in Africa. In Africa it was daylight and ten minutes later pitch dark. With the sound of crickets singing in the long grass. Not the snarl of London traffic.

Harry felt sorry for them. For their dull lives. It made him more determined to fulfil his task. The sooner he sold the family business, created the family trust, ensconced Uncle Nat, the bishop, in Hastings Court, the sooner he could go home, his duty done.

"I don't even want any of the bloody money."

"What you say, mate?"

"Sorry. Talked my thoughts out loud."

"You can give me some."

The man at the next small table had not been put off by his colonial accent. Harry was dressed in a suit they had made for him in Salisbury. A light, tropical suit. Harry knew he looked out of place. He knew the English from the war. The bar he had chosen was a working man's bar. The cheapest beer. There was sawdust on the floor and the rich smell of long spilt beer. Harry knew for certain none of the managers at Colonial Shipping he had met during the day would so much as deign to put their feet inside such a bar. It was why he had picked this one for his private sanctuary.

"Where you from, mate?... You got a funny accent."

"Africa. Rhodesia. I'm a tobacco farmer from Rhodesia."

"And what the bloody 'ell you doin' here?"

"It's a long, long story... Where do you work?"

"Colonial Shipping... You 'eard of 'em?"

"Yes I have," said Harry, warily.

"Thirty-four years this year it'll be. Every day the same. Same train to work in the morning. Same train home at night. Flossie. That's my wife. Flossie knows I have two pints in the Lion and home on the ten past seven. Takes an hour to get home. Last bit I walk from the station. Sun, rain or snow. Ten minutes. In the dark when it's really raining seems longer. Much longer... Can't complain, can I? Got a job. Sixteen I was. Offices were right on the water then. The Captain didn't like being too far from his ships. Could see them in the estuary from his window.

"My first job was cleaning those windows. Showed me himself the first time. 'Samuel,' he said, and he always called me Samuel till the day he died, God bless his soul, 'if you clean the window proper, you do the rest proper.' Never left a speck on those windows, inside or out.

We were on the second floor. Had to put a ladder up to clean the outside. The Captain was a stickler for having everything clean. Came from his days at sea. Said a dirty boat was a killer boat. People died of disease on a dirty boat. No one died on our boats. Some that didn't like the Captain called him the Pirate. More like Robin Hood, I say. There was a story at the beginning. During the American Civil War. A Frenchman was trying to run guns to the South. The Yanks caught the Frog. Chased him onto some rocks. When the Yanks came back with a big enough boat to take on the Frenchman's cargo someone had cleaned it out. The Yanks had taken the crew off after putting the boat on the rocks. Kind of sailors' honour. They say the Captain had watched the action from the small island where the Frenchman went aground. By the time the Yanks came back, the Captain had taken the guns overland to his ship. The canon was quite a good job to shift, so they say. While the Yankee navy was busy looking for the guns, the Captain put up sail and took the ship into Mobile without a hitch. Sold the guns to the Confederacy. That's not piracy. Just good thinking… Not boring you am I, mate?"

"Not at all," said Harry.

"The French government told the British that the guns were stolen. The British told the French the guns were abandoned. Rightful salvage… After that, the Captain ran guns to the Confederacy for the rest of the war. Took cotton back to Liverpool. How he got rich, they say. You have to be lucky to get rich. Or make your luck, I say."

"Can I buy you a beer, Samuel?"

"Very kind of you. There's another train at seven forty. Sometimes I tell Flossie I had to work late… You know how it is… My name's Samuel Adams. What's yours?"

"Do you have any children Mr Samuel Adams?"

"A boy and a girl. Pigeon pair. The boy's a sailor. Empire Castle Line. Too young for the war. The girl married and went to Australia. When I retire, me and Flossie are going to Australia. For a holiday, mark you. None of this emigrating."

Harry went to the bar and came back with two beers. He was thinking how one man's conception was so different to another. For the first time in the day he was interested in Colonial Shipping.

"When do you retire, Mr Adams?"

"When I'm sixty. Ten years' time. And that's my worry. When the Captain died suddenly, he left the business to his eldest living son, Sir

James. James had been in the army. Regular soldier. A good man even if he did not know how to put up a sail. Or navigate a ship. Changed nothing. Always asked what the Captain would do. So we told him and everything ran smooth. You see, all of us what worked for the Captain, loved the Captain. If you was loyal to him and the company, he was loyal to you. Twice he helped me out. 'Cleaned my windows them years ago, Samuel,' he said to me, 'now it's my turn. You go home and nurse your Flossie till she gets better. Pneumonia needs good nursing. And love, Samuel. Come back to work when she is better. I'll get your pay packet to you. She'll be all right.' That's what he said to me. And he was right... Then I got sick. A few years later. Doctor said to Flossie I was going to die. The Captain came down to my little house in Fetcham. Brought his own doctor to have a look at me. When I came back to work, he never mentioned it to the day he died. Loyalty. Now Sir James is in his grave there's no loyalty at work. There's talk of floating the company on the London Stock Exchange. Making it a public company so all the managers get shares for very little and sell the lot. Not us workers, mark you. The clerks. Like me. I never got past desk clerk, first grade. No education, so to speak. Like the Captain. Taught himself to read on board ship. They said he was no gentleman but to me he was more of a gentleman than all of them toffs put together. If they sell the company, what's going to happen to me? Floss and I have a little saved but you can't save much on a clerk's salary, first grade... You got to have loyalty. The Captain had loyalty. Sir James had loyalty. A company owned by all of them people who buy shares on the stock exchange don't have no loyalty. They don't know Samuel Adams. I don't know them. I didn't clean their windows when I was a boy. Now did I? Dump me, they will. Early pension they call it. I'll get half for thirty-four years instead of all my pension in ten years' time. I asked the chief clerk if they could do that. He said they could. Daylight bloody robbery... Now that's piracy, I say. Things like that didn't happen when the Captain was alive. And some called him the Pirate... You think it's right they throw me out ten years short with half a pension for the rest of my life?"

"No it isn't, Samuel. And it isn't going to happen."

"How do you know? You live in the colonies. What do you know about the toffs in the City? They'd cut your throat to make a profit. Throw out any deal to push up the share. We need a union. A clerks' union. Look after our rights... What's it like where you come from?"

Samuel Adams drank down half his beer.

"It's very beautiful. The sun shines most of the time. Animals. Lots of wild animals. The bush has a smell of its own. There's a saying in my country, that if you drink the water of the Zambezi, Africa gets into your blood. That's my problem. We all have problems, Samuel. They are just different."

"What brings you to England, then?"

"I've come to sell a company. Give away a big house. Now you have made it much more difficult. My name is Harry Brigandshaw. I'm the Captain's grandson. I now own Colonial Shipping."

"WHAT on earth are you doing drinking here?"

"The same reason you are, I expect. Getting away from those managers at Colonial Shipping. I'm sure most of them are good men but I hate servility... I won't forget what you said. You won't go on half a pension... Remember me to Flossie when you get home... I think I'm going to walk the streets of London. At home when I want to think I walk the bush. With a gun. I hope I don't need a gun in London. Sounds like the predators here come in a different form. Then maybe some men are animals... It has been a pleasure meeting a friend of my grandfather. He never wanted to know me. Up until now I never wanted to know him for what he did to me, my father and my mother. You gave him a different light. Good day, Samuel."

"It's raining outside."

"I walked in the rain before... There was a time not so long ago on the banks of the Chobe River..."

"You don't have an umbrella."

"All I needed was my horses to get home."

The man Samuel was looking at him strangely. Harry smiled at him and picked up the empty beer mugs. On his way out of the Lion he put the mugs on the bar counter.

Outside the soft drizzle was pleasant on his face.

By the time he reached the Savoy Hotel he was soaked to the skin. The man at the reception desk was about to say something rude.

"My name is Harry Brigandshaw. You have a room for me."

"You don't have any luggage, sir?"

"No, I don't. I hope my staff sent my overnight bag ahead of me. You can send supper to my room. A bath and bed. By tomorrow my suit will be dry and someone can give it a press... Will that be too much trouble?" The man in the dove-grey jacket with black, pinstripe trousers checked his records.

"Of course, Mr Brigandshaw. Anything you wish Mr Brigandshaw. Colonial Shipping did indeed send us your suitcase. Welcome to the Savoy. Your uncle was a regular guest of ours. A very special guest."

Harry smiled sadly. The man had gone from hostility to servility in ten seconds.

Harry squelched across to the lift and went up to his room, the lift man giving his wet clothes a rueful smile.

"I'm from Africa," said Harry to the man as if that explained everything.

Inside his room he wondered why he had had to say anything. Why people always needed to explain.

His suitcase was sitting on a low stool ready for easy opening. His only change of clothes was his evening dress. Tails and white tie. In case he was forced to attend a formal function. He had never before worn tails. In the air force he had worn uniform. His number one uniform on formal occasions.

Changing his mind, Harry rang down to the reception desk.

"Brigandshaw... I've changed my mind, can you call me a taxi please? I will not be eating in my room." As he put down the telephone, there was a knock on his door. Harry sent the man away with a five-shilling tip. The Savoy was certainly efficient. The man had had the supper menu in his hand.

"Where to, guv'nor?"

"I'm thirty-five. A bachelor. Where'd you think I should go?"

"New to London, guv?"

"I was here a bit during the war."

"Where you're from, guv?"

"Rhodesia."

"Never 'eard of it. Try the Trocadero, seeing you is dressed like that."

"It's in Africa."

"Blimey. I thought the Trocadero was in London." Harry laughed as he was obliged to. "Is the Troc all right, guv?"

"Troc sound fine. Can a man dine on his own?"

"Don't see why not... You don't know nobody in London, guv?"

"Not a soul."

The taxi pulled up outside the ornate entrance to the supper club. Harry had heard of the place. Expensive. He hoped they would give him a table. Not sure of himself, he asked the cabbie to wait. After booking a table he went back and paid the man.

"You 'ave a good time, guv."

On his own, Harry was not so confident. Inside the lights were dim. Tables were set around the small dance floor. A band was playing ragtime. A waiter showed him a small table at the back, furthest away from the dance floor, each table had red shaded lamps in the middle. The waiter cleared away the excess cutlery leaving one place setting. Harry ordered a drink and sat back to survey the room from his place of obscurity.

It was ten o'clock. The theatres were yet to come out. The big room with its tables and alcoves was comparatively empty. Harry noted he was not out of place in evening dress. Would probably have not been allowed in dressed in a suit and tie.

The band was good. The whisky he had ordered came quickly. He made it a double, for a starter. He told the waiter to bring back the menu in half an hour. No one took any notice of him. They were all absorbed in themselves. Most of the people were young. Harry had heard of the flappers and thought he was looking at them. It was pleasant to observe without being observed.

A large party came in noisily. Harry finished his second drink. The dance band was taking a break. To Harry's surprise he recognised one of the crowd. He was almost sure it was Barnaby St Clair. For some reason he quickly remembered Barnaby owed Jim Bowman ten pounds. The girl with Barnaby was now also familiar. Three tables were being put together for the new party. Some of the party were already dancing on the dance floor, even without the band. They were well known to the staff. They were loud. Harry thought they had been drinking.

He distinctly heard the name St Clair being spoken. Harry had known Robert and Merlin better than Barnaby. Harry had met Barnaby at Purbeck Manor in 1916, he remembered. Barnaby had just been posted to Palestine and was on embarkation leave. Harry was on leave from his squadron in France. They had walked the small river together once. It was all Harry could remember.

The story of Jim Bowman's ten pounds was back in his mind… Then he remembered the girl with Barnaby. It was Tina Pringle. The girl who had visited Elephant Walk with a much older American. Harry remembered her brother had made himself rich in South Africa. Something to do with explosives and gold.

The whisky had gone to his head, making the stories cross over and swirl in his mind. It was bad of Barnaby to borrow ten pounds and not give it back.

The girl with Barnaby was looking across at his lonely table and then she was getting up and walking across the empty dance floor. The band was still on their break. The flappers had given up dancing without music.

"Aren't you Harry Brigandshaw? Someone said you were in England. Yes, it was Merlin. He read it in *The Times*. I once visited your farm in Rhodesia. Don't you remember me?... You did meet Barnaby St Clair? He's over there. Come and join us. Can't have you sitting in splendour all on your own. I'm afraid we've all been drinking so you'll have to excuse us. One of those dreadful cocktail parties that just went on and on. Why the Americans invented them I don't know. You have to stand up to drink, for goodness' sake. They probably think you'll go home early if you have to stand up. We were the last to leave. Come and meet everybody. I was terribly sorry to hear about your wife. Things like that always seem to happen to nice people. Nothing ever happens to people like Barnaby."

"Isn't he nice?"

"Of course he isn't. Everybody knows that. Charming. He's charming. But not very nice. You can take my word for it and I've known him all my life."

"I do know Barnaby St Clair. He owes a friend of mine ten pounds."

"Barnaby owes everyone ten pounds. Well, probably more than ten pounds. Even now he's rich he can't get out of the habit of borrowing money."

"How did he make his money? If I remember, he was going to be a soldier for life."

"Who knows? Who knows anything with Barnaby? Good. You've finished your drink. Come along. They are much better sober. Once you've had a few, you'll get in the swing. The band here is terrific. Can you do the Charleston? Well it doesn't matter. You can do some native dance for us when we're all drunk. Then it doesn't matter what you do. Look, here comes Barnaby."

"Harry Brigandshaw in the living flesh. Bless my soul. Harry, old boy. How are you? Tina recognised you. Quite a gal, our Tina. Come and meet the crowd. The bill will follow you, don't you worry. I've table-hopped six times and still been given the bill. For everyone. That was a hoot... Merlin said he read about you in *The Times*. So. You've come to live in England?"

"How are you Barnaby? How are your mother and father?"

"Why didn't you tell us? You are my brother-in-law you know. Lucinda was my favourite sister. She was everyone's favourite, dammit."

To Harry's surprise there were tears in Barnaby's eyes. Even with all the drink they surprised him. Taking a hold of himself, he only just managed to stop his own tears.

"I'm going down to Purbeck Manor next week," he said, keeping the choke out of his voice.

"I should think so."

Tina had Harry by the hand as they walked across the small square that made up the dance floor between the tables. The band was on a raised dais behind. The band were coming back again for another set. Some of them were picking up their instruments. The same waiter from his lonely table at the back was making a place for him at the three tables put together next to the dance floor. Harry thought the trick in keeping track of the money was not to change the waiter for the men. The men always paid. It was expected of them. Girls only brought enough money for the taxi fare back to their mothers. They all had very small handbags. Some of them exquisitely worked with needle and cotton. Harry thought there was a French word for it.

He was introduced to a flurry of excitement with his brother-in-law telling everyone he had just inherited Colonial Shipping and that Harry was his brother-in-law. Harry was not sure whether he liked Barnaby St Clair and suspected another motive other than boosting Harry's standing with the crowd. He watched the word begin to circulate about the death of his wife. In turn, as they heard from the whispers, they looked at him with drunken sympathy. The sympathy was quickly lost as the band struck up again. Tina made him dance, which was a mistake. He knew he was a terrible dancer. As it was required of him, he did his best. They had never taught dancing at Bishops in the Cape. Maybe they should have done, Harry thought ruefully.

The dance floor filled up quickly, everyone squashed onto the one small square between the tables. All Harry had to do was sway with the music. Tina was very close to him. She was brushing her thighs against his. He looked down into her eyes to make sure that her brushing against him was an accident. A necessity in the small space. It wasn't.

Harry's hands began to sweat where they held Tina's hands. The girl leaned into the crook of his arm. Harry was sure he could feel her breasts. No one seemed to notice. Or care. The music was slow and sultry. To protect himself from making a fool of himself, Harry thought of the reed hut he had built for himself on the banks of the Chobe River. The idea was good, but it did not help. Looking up at him, Tina licked her lips. She could feel what was happening to him. Before the music stopped, she thrust in her hips and gave him a turn. Then she smiled up sweetly.

"Let's sit down, Harry. You don't like dancing. You can take me to the theatre another night. I love the musicals. There's one I haven't seen."

"I thought you were with Barnaby?" His voice was husky. The girl was fully in control.

"Barnaby is just a friend… I remember you so well from Elephant Walk. Once, during the war, I saw your photograph in the *Rand Daily Mail*. In Johannesburg. I thought then I wanted to meet you again… You have to go on in life, Harry, you can't stay frozen in a tragedy. My number is Primrose 101. You can remember that, can't you Harry? You see, we are both Africans. I love Africa… You don't like the idea of running the shipping line. I could see that in your eyes when everyone was talking about how rich you were. You can take me back to Africa with you. On the same ship, I mean. I hate travelling alone. I want to spend my life in Africa. Not in England. All this is so trivial. After a few months it all becomes boring."

Harry could see Barnaby looking across to them still swaying to the music that had stopped. He had another girl in his arms. There was no longer good-hearted humour in his eyes. The condescension of having a rich brother-in-law. Instead there was hatred. The same hatred he had seen before in the eyes of Mervyn Braithwaite when he had killed Sara Wentworth. Barnaby St Clair was jealous. The girl was trouble. Harry could see that as plain as a pikestaff.

"We had better sit down, Tina."

Harry was back in control of his body. The palms of his hands were no longer sweating. The shot that had killed his wife had come out of the crowd on Salisbury railway station. Harry had not even seen Mervyn Braithwaite on the platform as he helped Lucinda down from the railway carriage. By the time he turned round at the sound of the shot, Tembo had wrestled Mervyn Braithwaite to the ground. Harry was sure he would have seen the hatred. The same jealous hatred. It made him go cold. His first instinct was to run away. To go straight back to the Savoy. Barnaby was his brother-in-law. Part of the family he loved as much as his own.

There was so much noise at the table, no one could see there was anything wrong. Tina sat down away from him. Barnaby had left the three joined tables to talk to a couple at another table. He could even hear him laughing over the rest of the noise. The girl Barnaby had been dancing with had sat down on her own. To recover his composure and not to have to talk to Tina Pringle, Harry went across and asked her to dance, confident he would only have to do the shuffle. It would give him time to think. To watch Barnaby. To avoid any embarrassment.

"Come on and dance," he said to her. She was young and pretty. "My name's Harry Brigandshaw. I didn't catch your name. Barnaby was too quick with introductions."

"I know who you are. You're from Africa. Did you know my father? Colonel Voss? My name is Justine Voss."

"I don't know your father well but the man who works for me does... They went together to the Valley of the Horses. Colonel Voss and Jim Bowman."

"You have the wrong man. My father died in the Anglo-Boer War. Tina told me to call it the Anglo-Boer War. Before it was the Boer War."

"Well, the man that fought at the battle of Omdurman and knew Chinese Gordon was very much alive at Christmas time."

The girl had gone white.

"Don't let's dance," she said. "Sit down next to me. Tell me everything you know about this Colonel Voss."

"Well, he can't be your father. That is for certain. The Colonel Voss I know is as poor as a church mouse. Lives off young immigrants by talking them into giving him a grubstake to look for gold. Or anything else you can think of."

Harry was glad to sit down away from the danger of Tina Pringle.

The girl was pretty. Well-spoken. From a rich family, he expected, or she would not be in a party that included Barnaby St Clair. Harry had no idea he was putting his foot into a place where it should not be.

"Old Voss caught Jim at Salisbury Station. The day Jim arrived in Rhodesia from England. Jim now works for me on Elephant Walk. That's my farm."

The waiter had followed Harry with another double Scotch. The girl had in front of her half a glass of white wine. She only sipped it once as he went on blindly with the story.

"Old Voss thinks the Arabs colonised Rhodesia many centuries before the British. The strange thing is he and Jim found a valley high up in the Chimanimani Mountains in eastern Rhodesia that was full of Arab horses. Jim Bowman swears they were Arab horses. No one believes them because there are no indigenous horses in Africa south of the Sahara. Well, certainly not in Central Africa. Voss talks about the Valley of the Horses. Swears the Arabs brought their civilisation to Africa long before the birth of Christ. Poor old chap. No one believes him."

"What about General Gordon? My father knew General Gordon. He was a lot older than my mother you see."

"That explains the coincidence between your father who died in the war and old Voss who now lives with Sir Robert. The dog is called King Richard the Lionheart. The horses Hamlet and Othello. You see what I mean. Colonel Voss is a storyteller. You never know what is true and what is false. Everyone in Salisbury thinks the chance of old Bob being a knight of the realm, are pretty slim. I think Jim Bowman gives old Voss a few shillings every month. Jim has a soft spot for him. Says he learnt more about the African bush from Voss in three months than he will for the rest of his life. On that he may be right. Voss must have heard of your late father. Taken on his name. Bits of your father's story. Maybe he was your father's batman. For goodness' sake, our old Voss is a confidence trickster who talks young men into paying for his stories. One of the stories says he knew Winston Churchill for goodness' sake, was with him at Omdurman."

"My father was at Omdurman with Churchill."

"That's exactly what I'm saying. Our Voss is an impostor. Mark you, I always thought our Voss was genuine. If you say your father was Colonel Voss, and he was killed in the Anglo-Boer War then it puts the lie to it. My word, what people do to get money. He even said he had a daughter in England about your age. I think he said her name was Justine. But he would if he was your father's batman. If he had taken on your father's name... He's a nice old bird. Normally I would confront someone with a lie. But he is old. Harmless. Jim says he got far more out of old Voss than he gave. The Chinese have an expression. Never break another man's rice bowl. His means of earning a living. There's always more to any story than meets the eye."

"Can you do something for me Mr Brigandshaw? Please give me your address in Africa? I want to find my father's grave. If this man knows all this about my father, including my name, he'll know where they buried my father."

"The Imperial War Graves Commission will tell you that."

"I've tried. They say they have no record of my father being killed. If this man was my father's batman as you say, he would know exactly where my father fell. He would have been with him. He would have seen the same action. I want to meet the man who was my father's batman. I don't even care if he took my father's name. I know nothing about my father and that just isn't fair."

"Why don't you ask your mother?"

"She won't talk about him. Just bursts into tears. She was only nineteen when I was born, I did work that one out. She loved him so much, you see. My poor mother. She never so much as looked at another man."

"How can your mother, a widow, let you dress so well?"

"Grandfather was rich. Barnaby says he was stinking rich," the girl giggled. "My mother inherited all his money. Granny was dead by then."

"And after your mother?"

"Oh, I'll be rich all right. Probably as rich as you Mr Brigandshaw if that isn't rude. I will write to you. You are going home? Or do you now have to stay in England? Now, can we dance? I usually find these parties such a bore."

"May I have my supper first? I'm starving hungry. Nothing since breakfast. I didn't want to favour anyone of them in the office so I went without lunch. Let me order some food first and while it's coming, we can dance. I must warn you I'm very bad. I am more at home in the African bush than in a London supper club. Drink without food is a killer. What you do, Miss Voss?"

"Please call me Justine. It turns out we have so much in common. I don't do very much. Nothing at all, really. Mother encourages me to go out. I'm looking for a husband, you see. All girls in my class and age are looking and when they find one they don't have to think any more… Oh dear, I'm sorry. Don't think I'm trying to make you into a husband. I just want to find out about my father."

Harry smiled. The waiter from his first table took his order.

"I want a steak an inch thick and a foot wide, red right through the middle. The rest on the plate doesn't matter."

"Where you're from, sir?" asked the waiter politely.

"Africa. Can you do that for me, Thomas?" The man wore his name on his jacket collar.

"I'll have a word myself with the chef."

The waiter went off on his personal errand.

"Now we can dance. Don't worry, Justine. I'm old. Much too old for you."

"But Father was a lot older than Mother!... Oh, there I go again. I'm always putting my foot in it."

They did not talk on the dance floor. Just swayed to the music. Harry watched for the waiter with the steak he wanted so badly. The rest of the party at the three joint tables were not eating. Drinking and dancing and hopping from table to table. Everyone it seemed to Harry knew each other. They were all trying so hard to have a good time.

Harry was glad to keep his mouth shut. He had invented the batman story off the top of his head. Over the years, Harry had met Colonel Voss on more than one occasion. If nothing else the man who called himself Colonel Voss was a gentleman. If he had taken on a dead man's identity he had not been his batman. Surreptitiously, Harry had a good look at the girl on the dance floor swaying in front of him to the music. He could see no resemblance to the old man. Harry did not think it surprising. The man who had found the Valley of the Horses was an old man. Weathered by too many years in the African bush. What he looked like as a young man had long left his face.

There were two things Harry decided before going back to eat his steak at the table. He was not going to phone Primrose 101. He was not going to write back to Justine Voss and introduce her to the 'batman'.

When Harry finished a very good steak with one small new potato on one side and a spoonful of peas on the other, Barnaby sat down next to him. There was an older man with him. Barnaby was exuding good humour. The hatred caused by jealousy had gone. Were it not for the family ties, Harry would have been less affable. He would just have to remember not to tread on Barnaby's toes again.

"I want you to meet an old friend of mine, Harry. C E Porter this is my brother-in-law, Group Captain Harry Brigandshaw. The air ace. C E is a chap to know in the City. If you need anyone to help you float

Colonial Shipping, C E's the man."

"How did you know I was thinking of taking the company public?" With less whisky fogging his mind, Harry would not have pursued the issue.

"It's the right thing to do," said C E Porter putting out his hand for Harry to shake. "Put in a professional manager. With respect, Mr Brigandshaw, never try to run a business you know nothing about. The business world is changing. Leave it to the professionals."

"You know about me?"

"It is my business to know about what is happening in the City. The internal politics at Colonial Shipping will run you ragged. Find a good, strong man from the outside. Give him a mandate. Then leave him in charge. If you wish to learn the business that is another story. But mark my words. It will take you five years. You can't start at the top of anything. However many shares you own. It simply doesn't work."

Barnaby was smirking at Harry like any good pimp with a really sexy woman. The world worked in strange ways. The man Porter was talking sense. More sense than he had heard all day. Harry was well aware that a man with money was always a target.

"Do you have a card, Mr Porter?"

"Of course, Mr Brigandshaw. I have to leave now. I like to wake fresh for business each morning. The City of London may look polite and gentlemanly at first. It is not. Keep a cool head, Mr Brigandshaw. And watch your back for a Brutus. Some of them would stab a brother to make more money."

Across the table, Tina was trying to catch his eye while licking her lips. Harry avoided eye contact. He was ready to go home. Some of the others had already left.

Harry called for his bill. When it came Barnaby was nowhere to be seen. The bill included everyone's drinks and cover charges. It was the largest single bill Harry had ever seen in a restaurant. Harry paid the bill with a sigh. He said goodbye to Justine Voss and left on his own.

At the exit door his waiter was waiting for him. The man had called him a taxi.

"Whose bill was it really?" asked Harry knowing perfectly well.

"Mr St Clair. He said you wouldn't mind. Didn't have the cash on him."

"I thought so."

Outside in the taxi, Harry laughed at himself.

"Teach you to dance close with another man's woman."

"What did you say, guv?"

"Nothing. The Savoy Hotel. What time is it?"

"Midnight."

"Feels like four in the morning," said Harry.

"One of those nights, guv... You a foreigner?"

"Yes I am. But I also know the shortest route to the Savoy."

"A man can only try."

The man was brazen. Harry liked it. When they reach the Savoy by the direct route Harry gave the man a pound note for a tip.

"Blimey! What's that for, guv?"

"Being honest."

What C E Porter was trying to tell him was right. A fool and his money are soon parted. When he drifted off to sleep, he thought of the free drink for Samuel Adams in the Lion was the best value for his money all day... First thing in the morning he was going to check up on C E Porter.

Then Harry fell into a dreamless sleep.

THE OFFICE of the managing director of Colonial Shipping was an unpretentious affair. Harry's grandfather had seen to that and Uncle James had carried on the tradition. The board table was in the same room. The board of directors met in the managing director's office. It made the point of who was in charge as well as saving space. Harry soon gathered his grandfather was not a man to fritter away his money showing off.

They showed him the books of accounts that might just as well have been in Greek. They showed him pictures of the ships. They gave him a list of subsidiary companies that was as long as his arm, with job descriptions that meant very little. There was a confirming house, whatever that was. A shipping and clearing company divorced from Empire Castle Line with subsidiaries with foreign sounding names. There was a freight company that Harry surmised rightly moved goods by truck from inland in Britain and Africa to the ports and the ships of Empire Castle, as well as a company previously owned by two companies merged by Colonial Shipping. There were storage companies right throughout Africa and at all the large British ports.

C E Porter was right. He had no idea what was going on. He knew how to fly an aeroplane. He knew how to explore for minerals and recognise a rough diamond from a piece of quartz. He knew how to grow maize and look after a herd of cattle. Thanks to his Grandfather Manderville he even knew how to grow and cure tobacco.

"Five years! I don't think so."

"What did you say, sir?"

"Nothing, Grainger. Well, not nothing. I just have no idea what this lot is all about."

"You'll get the gist of it soon enough."

"I had no idea the business was so spread. So diverse. So complicated... Just out of interest, do we have ships with cold rooms? Places where the temperature is kept to say five degrees on the centigrade scale." Harry was thinking of his friend Pierre Le Jeune and the acres and acres of new fruit trees growing in the Inyanga.

"I don't know, sir. Why would anyone want a commercial cool room on board a ship?"

"To carry fruit from Africa to England when the fruit season is over in Europe. An industrial-sized freezing compartment to carry my beef from Rhodesia to England."

"We have beef in England, sir." Now Grainger was buttering up.

"Thank you... We don't have such ships, do we?"

"No, sir."

"Ask around. Better still go to Birmingham, Mr Grainger. Go and see an engineer or two. The British are the most inventive nations on earth."

"The Americans?" Grainger was now being generous.

"Yes, well, maybe the Americans... Do you wish to go to America, Mr Grainger?"

"No, sir. Birmingham will be sufficient. We have clients in Birmingham who make heavy machinery. Bakers. Electric generators. We ship their goods out to all parts of Africa. They'll probably know what to do... Are there any fruit growers in Africa?"

"Maybe this business is not so difficult after all. If I'd studied economics at Oxford instead of geology, I'd know what all these books and papers were about."

"You went to Oxford, sir!"

"Even colonial hicks from Africa are sometimes allowed into Oxford, Grainger."

"I'm sure they are, sir... When would you like me to go to Birmingham, sir?"

Harry mentally gave up. Any minute he expected the shipping manager to put up his hand and ask permission to go to the small boy's room down the corridor.

"As soon as possible, Mr Grainger."

"Right you are, sir. Will that be all, sir? There's a woman outside said she wants to see you, sir. Mary at reception was going to come and tell you but I thought it was better for me to knock on your door, sir."

"Very kind of you, Grainger. Please ask the lady in question to come in... I met this man last night." Harry handed Grainger C E Porter's card. "I want him investigated."

"Has he done something wrong?"

"Bank report. Where he lives. Clubs. Friends. Business partners. Everything about the man. Can you do that for me, Grainger?"

"Before or after I go to Birmingham?"

Harry went back to reading the paper on his desk that he had been reading when the knock came at his door. He was just glad Grainger had not flown as his wingman during the war or else he would have been dead. He was reading and comprehending very little when Mary from reception showed Justine Voss's mother into his office. It was almost lunchtime.

"I think you and I should talk about this over lunch, Mrs Voss," he said gently after Mrs Voss introduced herself. "I presume Justine told you I know your husband?"

"Well, he wasn't exactly my husband, Mr Brigandshaw. Larry was married to another woman at the time. She's dead now. So is her son, Justine's half-brother. Walter Voss was killed in 1916. On the Somme."

MRS VOSS, as she liked to call herself, was a good-looking woman. Better looking than her daughter whose prettiness came from her youth. Mrs Voss had a mature good look that was rare in women. Harry guessed she was only a few years older than himself. He liked her directness. For not beating around the bush.

On the fifth floor of Colonial Shipping House there was a small private dining room. The managing director's private reserve. On the other side of the kitchen was a larger room for senior managers. The executive dining room. A similar room fed the rest of the staff. The canteen. The Captain liked his staff to eat properly. Said they worked better, so Harry been told. The real reason, Harry thought, was a half hour lunch break instead of an hour. The old Pirate had traded a free lunch for an extra half hour of their time. Harry thought the trade was worth it. The food was good and overabundant with fresh vegetables. Even on land Harry's grandfather had not forgotten the scourge of scurvy. A disease caused by not eating fresh fruit and vegetables.

The small dining room was only big enough for two people. The Captain did not entertain in the dining room. He either did business, one-to-one, or ate lunch on his own. For an employee to be invited to lunch by the Captain was usually an ordeal he remembered for the rest of his life. All the snippets of gossip were fitting together in Harry's mind. Already he knew he had missed something important in his life by not knowing his grandfather.

"I want you on my side, Mr Brigandshaw," Mrs Voss had said the moment they sat down at the table that was set for two people. Harry now had an excuse to eat in his own dining room without inviting one of his managers.

Once the food came, he decided in future to eat alone or with someone from outside the company. The food was as good as the food he ate at home on Elephant Walk.

"This had to come, of course," said Mrs Voss. "No one can live forever with a lie. If it gets out, Justine's chances of a good marriage will be over. Despite my father's money which will one day be hers." Mrs Voss had waited for the food before getting into the delicacy of her subject.

Harry was smiling broadly.

"Why are you smiling, Mr Brigandshaw?"

"Please go on, Mrs Voss. I assure you, I was not being rude."

"How is Larry?" the good-looking woman in front of Harry had a whimsical, faraway look.

"Last time I heard of him he was trying not to be stampeded by a herd of wild horses. Please, I don't know him well. He's more of a legend in a perverse kind of way. You know he does not have a penny?"

"He gave his wife and son his money before he disappeared. That is before Justine was born. Larry resigned his commission when he found out I was pregnant. Everyone knew of course. Among the families. It was agreed by everyone Larry would go to Africa and not come back... Have you ever been torn between duty to a son and duty to a child not born? To a woman on one side indifferent to anything but the social swirl. To a woman you loved more than life itself. Divorce was a rare thing in 1899 but it was possible if all the parties were to agree. Agnes, that was Larry's wife, would not agree, of course. In exchange for every penny of Larry's money she agreed to a compromise. She would tell the world she had divorced Larry. I would tell the world I had married Larry. Larry would never again see his son. Larry would later get it reported he had been killed in the war in South Africa that had just started... He would never set eyes on the child that was growing in my womb... I don't think she cared a fig about Larry. Or Walter for that matter. She was only concerned with herself. How she appeared in society. She was quite frivolous, Mr Brigandshaw. My parents agreed to the compromise. So did her parents. What else could they do? I went away for two years to Greece. And came back as Mrs Voss. The irony of the whole thing was Agnes was by then dead. I don't even know what she died from."

"Why didn't Colonel Voss come back to England?"

"He had no money. My father would not allow it. And anyway, how did one live with a dead man?"

"You could have gone to Rhodesia."

"And been penniless. For me, that would have been perfect. But not for Justine. The evil tongues had stopped wagging, Mr Brigandshaw. Whichever way, people might have found out. I had sinned in the face of God. I had fallen in love with a married man. I did not want Justine to bear the burden of my sin... Mr Brigandshaw. Please. This is no laughing matter."

"I only found out properly quite recently that my mother was married to my uncle when I was born."

"I don't understand."

"I am also a bastard, Mrs Voss. So is my sister, Madge. So was my brother, George. And it doesn't make the slightest difference to who I am... But I promise you in the name of God, no one will ever hear from me what I know about you and your family... How was your lunch?"

"Fabulous, Mr Brigandshaw."

"I thought so too, Mrs Voss... Why don't you both come out and visit me in Rhodesia?"

"Why would I do that, Mr Brigandshaw?"

"To meet Larry Voss again. He's old, yes. Not the darling soldier. Somehow I don't think you'll mind... As I have pointed out, things are different in Rhodesia. There are more important things than social protocol."

"We would never get away with it."

"You would if you never came back to England again. As I heard it, you now own your family money."

"Justine would never want to leave London."

"She would for her father. A child only has one father, remember."

"She'd never find a husband in Africa."

"You'd be surprised. Good-looking young girls are scarce in Rhodesia. Rich, or poor. Rhodesia attracts real men like Larry Voss. Men who want to do something for themselves. Not fit into dead men's shoes like they want me to do here. You'd be surprised how many men of good family are looking for wives in Rhodesia."

"Are you looking for a wife, Mr Brigandshaw?"

"Not any more, Mrs Voss. My wife was killed by a madman. She was pregnant at the time."

"How terrible."

"Life rarely turns out how it is meant to. How we think it was meant to. Lucinda was Barnaby St Clair's sister. I met your daughter with Barnaby at the Trocadero. She may not have known he was my brother-in-law... There is just one thing I don't understand. How does Colonel Voss know the name of his daughter?"

"I wrote and told him. I wrote three times. The second to say Agnes was dead. The third to say Walter had been killed in action. He never replied. I myself began to believe he had died in the Boer War."

TO HARRY'S SURPRISE, Grainger was a good report writer. Both reports were concise, well-written and well-researched. They had taken a week to reach his desk by which time he had visited his grandmother and twice postponed his trip to Dorset and Purbeck Manor. Having found a considerable respect for his grandfather he had hoped to find out more about the man.

The flat was looked after by a paid companion. Outwardly, his grandmother looked perfectly well. Glad to see a visitor, offering him tea and cake. She smiled and smiled. An old, bent woman with white hair and hands gnarled with arthritis but otherwise well and happy with the world.

At first, Harry thought his visit was difficult for his grandmother. That she had no wish to confront the history that had left Harry growing up in a remote part of Africa. Slowly it dawned on him. His grandmother had no clue as to who he was. Inside her head her mind had gone. When she gave the paid companion a third name in ten minutes Harry knew his grandmother was suffering from total loss of memory. Even that part of his grandfather that had been in her mind was lost to Harry forever.

He finished his tea. Said he had to go and left, his duty done.

Outside the block of flats, Harry found himself crying. Without the old, bent lady upstairs, he would have had no life. The coming and going of life seemed so pointless. Even more, he wanted to go home before all the ghosts of England sucked the life out of him. The cry for his grandmother was silent on the street, only the tears were wet and salty. There and then he decided to write to his Uncle Nat to give him Hastings Court. It would be easier written down. More final. If the Bishop did not want the family home that had caused Harry's parents so much pain he would sell it. Get rid of it. Be done with the whole damn thing.

HARRY TOOK a taxi back to the Savoy Hotel and had the desk put a phone call through to his old friend Robert St Clair.

"I'm driving down now, Robert. Will it be all right? Your mother, I mean."

"You are family, Harry… I want you to read my new book."

Harry smiled. Happy in himself again. There was always something Robert wanted him to do.

"It's been a long time," said Harry. "Too long. Did I tell you I even have a chauffeur?"

"You did. Hoot when you get to the main gate. I'm still working on the book."

HARRY READ Grainger's report again while seated in the comfort of the back of the car. By the time Pierre Le Jeune's apples and pears were growing on his trees, there would be cold rooms on the ships. Grainger had even done a costing. He asked Fortnum and Mason what they would pay for fresh fruit during the months of the English winter. Pierre would be pleased. He would make a fortune.

Instead of reading again the report on C E Porter, Harry sat back in the comfort of the car. At the least, Porter was devious in his business dealings. At the worst he was a thief. The kind of man to know a thief when he saw one. Dangerous as an enemy. The man, of course, would be able to run Colonial Shipping standing on his head. Whether the shareholders would profit was altogether another thing.

"It's all too damn complicated," Harry said out loud.

The uniformed driver was unable to hear. Someone had built a glass barrier between the servant and the master. Harry would have much preferred to sit in the front seat and chat the miles away while they drove down to Dorset. Better still, he would like to have driven the car himself.

11

HASTINGS COURT AND COLONIAL SHIPPING, APRIL TO MAY 1922

*B*arend Oosthuizen had gone back to his old haunts and old habits. Madge's husband and the father of their three children was a mean drunk. He enjoyed inflicting pain. In the years since he had parted company with Harry Brigandshaw on the Skeleton Coast of South West Africa he had put on weight and muscle. He had two uses for the money he earned a mile down the bowels of the earth. Hard liquor and the bodies of cheap women. No one loved him. No one liked him. Down the gold mine where he dug rock from the face of the seam of gold, sweating in the damp heat, shirtless, covered in dust and dirt, they kept their distance as they tried to do in the bars he trawled, looking for the fights that gave his violent aggression the pleasure he craved, the exquisite pleasure of inflicting pain on other people. He neither liked the world nor its people, especially the English people who had killed his father. His father, a Boer general, hanged by the neck by the victors of a war to show the world what would happen to them for daring to defend their land and farms from the greatest empire on earth.

Barend had done it before as a younger man. Had even then forsworn his hatred of the British. Married a British girl. Now, happy again. Wallowing in his self-pity, he fought his way through the bars of Jeppestown hoping that one day he would get himself killed.

The small room he slept in contained a bed and dirty blankets, the cheapest rent he could find. Every night he returned home drunk, a great bulk of a man swearing to himself, often bloodied, mostly with the blood of his victims. When the drink had been enough, he picked a fight. When his lust was satisfied, he hit the whore. Always he paid. Always they forgot and let him back again. He never broke anything other than his victims' bodies.

In the mining camp that was Johannesburg, below the surface of the new wealth wrenched from the bowels of Mother Earth, Barend was at home. This time he was the bully. No one knew his name. No one knew his background. The wise never even met the mean stare in his eyes. Only the very large or very drunk stood their ground and paid the price.

In the weeks and months of his nightly destruction he never found out the name of the woman to whom he paid the rent. She never once asked his name. Never wanted to know. The old hag had seen many men like Barend come and go through her life. She only had one rule. They must pay. What they did with their lives after that was their own damn business. She knew better than any of them. There was nothing soft below the surface of Johannesburg. Life was hard. Mostly short. Always painful.

IN THE MORNING, Barend's hangover woke him feeling depressed. The day was torment, hitting the rock face with a pickaxe, the dregs of the alcohol fighting to sweat itself out of the pores of his skin. Barend ate a mean lunch of bread and cheese he took down the shaft at the start of the day he did not want. By the time he came out of the ground his body was screaming for alcohol. The shower and change of clothes made no difference to his feeling. The first three beers only quenched his thirst. Then the brandy began to answer the screaming. Helped for a while. For an hour, sometimes two, Barend was content. Until the brandy brought out the aggression.

What Barend wanted more than life was to get his own back on a world that made him go on living. He hated them all.

ON THE NORTH side of a larger world, while Barend Oosthuizen was self-destructing, unbeknown, Harry Brigandshaw was fighting his own demon.

Most people would have been content to inherit a fortune. To take the title and benefits of being managing director of a large, successful company. Harry even understood the ungratefulness of what he was trying to do.

The responsibility was not the problem. Learning the job was not the problem though he could still not understand in his mind why any man would wish to earn more money than he could possibly ever spend. Or gain satisfaction from the applause of other people impressed by the simple fact of wealth.

What he did not like was living in a city. Concrete and tarmac under his feet. The noise of man to pleasure his ears. Getting up in the dark, going to work in the dark, working under electric light in a concrete building all day and going home in the dark. Never the trees, the grass, the sound of birds. The blue sky and cotton wool clouds. A distant bark. The smell of earth. Insects singing in the grass.

The months of the English winter gone were heavy on his mind. There was now a spring, but it was far away from London. Even giving away Hastings Court had proved a problem, a mountain of a problem.

Uncle Nat, the Bishop of Westchester, had prospered in the church. The zealous missionary had gone. Harry even thought God had gone having proved his worth in his uncle's pursuit of a successful career in the Church of England.

"Oh, goodness me, Nephew. For what do I want Hastings Court? That was my father's goal in life. When I'm Archbishop of Canterbury, I will live at Lambeth Palace. Surely you can't compare Hastings Court to Lambeth Palace. Ridiculous. You'd better go, Harry. Kiss my ring."

Harry had kissed the bishop's ring on the bishop's hand and gone. His uncle, he rather thought, had become a pompous ass. For the first time in seeing him his uncle had not asked Harry when last he had been to church. The man had bigger things on his mind. Goals more lofty than one stray sinner.

A week later, Harry had offered the house of the Mandervilles to the National Trust, promising to endow a rehabilitation centre for wounded soldiers from the war. At least the home of his ancestors would again have a purpose. Men blasted in the hell of war could sit among the green land of England and try to repair their souls.

Harry was asked by the man from the National Trust to put the proposition in writing. The prim voice had sounded no more interested in Hastings Court than the Right Reverend the Lord Bishop of Westchester, the one time Uncle Nat and African missionary in the diocese of Mashonaland. Harry shook his head and wrote a plea from his heart for the men who had suffered in the war.

Having then had no reply to his letter, Harry telephoned the man.

"Oh, no, we don't want any more houses, Mr Brigandshaw. People are trying to get rid of the big houses these days. Giving them to us to maintain and still go on living in a small part of the premises. The war was most unkind to the landed gentry. You must know that. Sometimes two generations killed within months of each other. Two lots of death duty, you see. They're broke. We are the last resort to save the old piles, you see. We have enough, Mr Brigandshaw. Quite enough, in fact. You can try to sell the place to a developer if you are near enough to London. Or just watch it crumble. There are ruins all over England. One more won't make any difference."

"I am prepared to endow the property, you remember?"

"What do I remember, Mr Brigandshaw?"

"I wish to turn Hastings Court into a rehabilitation centre for wounded soldiers, sailors and airmen."

"Then why don't you, Mr Brigandshaw?" The man was now irritated.

"I want you to own and administer the property. I wish to go home to Africa. I'm an African. I have a farm in Rhodesia."

"I don't see what that has to do with us, Mr Brigandshaw. It is Mr Brigandshaw?"

"You haven't read my letter, have you?"

"I told you, we don't want any more properties, Mr Brigandshaw."

That weekend Harry had gone down to Hastings Court to have a quiet word with the portraits of his ancestors that hung on the walls above the great staircase that led up from the hall. It was a cold wet day in November. The light was dim. The features of his ancestors, other than their eyes, dim. All of them, including the women seemed to give him a rueful smile.

"They know. They jolly well know. They probably tried to get out of their own responsibility."

"I'm sorry, sir," said a voice from the stairwell. It was Uncle James's butler. Harry had kept all the staff though he lived in a small flat in London.

"I was just talking to my ancestors, Crosswell."

"Very good, sir."

Harry chuckled. Talking to dead ancestors was more common than he thought. It seemed the house and Harry were bound together whether he liked it or not.

He wrote a long letter to his Grandfather Manderville explaining his dilemma. Suggesting his grandfather come to live at Hastings Court where he was born and lived the most part of his life. Harry thought his reasons persuasive. There was now money to live in the style the house suggested. Harry would pay for everything.

A letter came back in six weeks.

"Elephant Walk suits me well, Harry. There's the tobacco, though Jim Bowman is learning fast. The girl from the newspaper article came for a visit. Jenny, somebody. Nice girl. Jim's going to be a competent farmer but I hope he will always need my guidance. Emily doesn't want to live in England. Madge is still hoping Barend will come home but we haven't heard a word. You seem to have forgotten my great-grandchildren. Paula is now six. Tinus is five. Doris four. They spend a lot of time with me. Emily says it is my job to give them an education which I've started with Paula. She is more interested when we go out looking for butterflies so I have shown her butterfly books. We are using them to teach her how to read or I won't tell her the names of the butterflies… All you find in England are cabbage whites in profusion. The other day Paula was surrounded by at least a hundred butterflies. Big and small. She was so excited. A small girl in a small dress with butterflies flying all around her. I'll take that beautiful memory to my grave. I'm not going back to England, Harry. Have the ancestors been talking to you or something? And on the subject of grandchildren, when are you going to marry again? Lucinda died three years ago. She would not want you to live out your life alone, Harry. You need children of your own. I thank God I had your mother before my dear wife died."

Harry had smiled at his grandfather's double standards. The man had been a widower most of his life. It was quite clear. No one was going to help his problem other than himself. He owned Hastings Court, and that was that.

BY THE TIME spring came Harry understood most of what was going on at Colonial Shipping. What had once seemed Greek was now plain English. Harry's experience of life helped. Commanding the squadron during the war. Managing Elephant Walk after his father was killed by the Great Elephant. It was mostly running people. The actual business, whatever it was, had the same end product. The making of money.

Through the English winter, Harry had never worked harder in his life.

HARRY THOUGHT the last thing in the mind of Brett Kentrich was having babies. All her thoughts were carnal. On and off the stage. Whether eating oysters or ravaging Harry in her four-poster bed she slyly claimed had once belonged to Anna Lightfoot, the mistress of

George the Third.

They had met through Merlin St Clair who was so besotted with Tina Pringle he no longer pursued the actress in the West End. The spat with his brother Barnaby was the talk of London town. Two brothers chasing the same girl. Once the *Tatler* had managed to take a photograph of Tina Pringle, the sister of the South African rand baron, and the brothers St Clair. In the photograph Barnaby was glaring at Merlin which Harry learnt had pleased Tina no end. The girl was a terrible tease and though it seemed through the winter to Harry that Tina was everywhere to be found, he made it his business to avoid the 'come on' looks and the winks. It was as if they had some big secret together which from Harry's perspective they did not. Unless it was to make Barnaby so jealous he would overcome his class snobbery and make her his wife. It was no doubt even to Harry, Tina Pringle was the one girl all the men wanted to wine, dine and bed. Even himself. She oozed sex appeal. Her body. Her eyes. Her mouth. Only the danger lurking at the back of Barnaby's eyes kept him from inviting her out. He owed that much to Lucinda. Not to make her brother Barnaby do something the whole family would regret.

Miss Kentrich was playing the second lead in a musical at Drury Lane that had lasted a fortnight. She was out of work though not out of money for the moment. She said she was twenty-five which Harry thought a lie to get her work. Most drama companies favoured girls with long experience. The young, very pretty ones too often forgot their lines or were more interested in catching a husband, using the stage as their net. She had all the looks and use of Tina Pringle without the power to control a man. She was far too nice. She liked to give. She liked to make people around her happy, especially the men. The demands of her own body were insatiable. When she had satiated herself on her man, the man was drained to the last drop. He had had all he wanted. The mystery, the tease that kept women in control of their men was spent. Brett, like the men she satiated, wanted something new. For Harry, she was the perfect foil to Tina Pringle.

"Why don't you come and see me more often, Harry?"

"Because I have to work harder than anyone in the office to understand what is going on. But if I did, you would get bored. You are far younger than you say and you love men, Brett darling. As many men as possible."

"Do you mind if I am naughty when you don't come? Your 'Penny' needs to be comforted in bed. Now I am resting from the stage I need comforting more than ever... It's that Tina Pringle, isn't it? She's rich and she wants you, Harry. That's it. You don't love Brett. I hate her. Next time I'm going to scratch out her eyes."

"Please don't. And be warned. She is not what she seems. She is not rich. Her brother's rich and sends her an allowance from South Africa. If I told you the truth, you would not be jealous."

"Then why don't you come to me more often?"

"Why do we always want what we can't have and ignore what we can?"

"What do you mean?" the girl was pouting.

"Never mind, Brett."

Harry smiled, quite happy with the relationship he knew was only part-time for Brett. It usually was, anyway.

Unbeknown to Harry Brigandshaw he was getting into the groove. Adjusting to his new home. Enjoying a girl who only wanted fun. Who thought marriage and babies drudgery of the worst kind. Thought living with one man for the rest of her life a perfect waste of her charms.

"Dear old Harry. You can be a fossil. Share the happiness. Before you know what, a girl isn't wanted. By men. If you have married, all you have then is a boring old goat and a clutch of screaming, snotty-nosed children who all want their own way. I just got out of one of those families and don't want to go back. I'm free. I want to enjoy my freedom. Who knows, I could be run over by a bus and then what good would I be? No, Harry darling. We only have one life. More certainly we only have one youth. Oscar Wilde said 'youth was wasted on the young'. Well not your Brett. I'm going to suck life dry to the last drop so when I'm old I never look back and regret what I could have done when I had the looks. I want the memories, Harry. Good memories. Not a house full of children that wants to suck my blood. Just the noise from ten children was enough to put me off. Now, let's go to a supper club and dance all night. I love music. Dancing. Being full of joy. Why are you so old today?"

THE NIGHTMARE began again for Harry on the steps leading up to the Aldgate tube station. During the war, the soldiers said they never wanted to put their heads above the parapet. Only shells lobbed by the Hun could then find them in their trenches. Provided a man kept his head below the parapet he had a good chance of surviving another day. Harry, by having his name in the financial newspapers had metaphorically put his head above the parapet. He was visible. The articles announcing Colonial Shipping was going public in May made Harry glaringly visible.

Harry felt the stare before seeing Fishy Braithwaite, his one-time commanding officer in the Royal Flying Corps. The murderer of Sara Wentworth and Harry's bride Lucinda, the daughter of Lord St Clair. Harry expected to see a gun and was ready to throw himself along the concrete step when Fishy Braithwaite smiled at him from thirty yards and wagged his finger. Then he carried on with the flow of the home-going crowd.

Harry was told the man would stay in a mental institution for the rest of his life. They said he was mad. Harry thought otherwise.

The next day, Fishy Braithwaite appeared out of the crowd in front of the office building. The rush hour crowds were going to work. Again the smirk and the wagging finger.

The man at the police station said it had nothing to do with them. If the man was Braithwaite, he had done nothing wrong.

"He murdered my wife."

"You say the man is in an institution, sir. You had better ask them."

"But won't you find out?"

"No, sir, we won't. With due respect there has not been a crime."

"And if he shoots me?"

"We will investigate, sir."

The mental institution at Banstead, not more than four miles from Hastings Court, said Colonel Braithwaite had been released on orders from the Home Office.

"But he's mad. He killed my wife. You can't let the man roam around again. The first time he escaped after shooting his fiancée Sara Wentworth. He then travelled all the way to Africa and killed my wife. I was just a friend of Sara's brother, Jared. The bloody man was mad jealous."

"Please don't swear at me, sir. I'm a very religious man."

"I'm sorry."

"Good day to you."

First, no one at the Home Office would take his call. After seeing Fishy Braithwaite again on the tube from Aldgate he demanded to see the Home Secretary. With no avail, he then chased down his MP, though Harry had never voted in England, or anywhere else for that matter, in his life. Rhodesia was still run by the British South Africa Company. The MP owed his seat in Parliament to Sir James Brigandshaw, Harry's late uncle. After the one interview at the Houses of Parliament Harry thought the man was a bigger ass than the Bishop of Westchester. The British establishment was littered with fools.

"There were many men traumatised during the war, Brigandshaw. The doctors are calling it shell shock. A wound like losing a leg, only shell shock can often be cured. The man becomes normal and leads a normal life, the horror of the war put behind him. You must remember that prior to the unfortunate incidents. I believe you witnessed both of them. Before then, Colonel Braithwaite was a hero of the Empire. An ace. Shooting down over forty enemy aircraft… Now I have been told on good authority that a panel of expert doctors found Colonel Braithwaite to no longer be suffering from his war wound. His shell shock. He has therefore been sent home to enjoy the fruits of our winning the war. He is an Englishman. Under repatriation, the Germans are being made to suffer considerably. The Treaty of Versailles was quite specific. The Germans started the war and must pay for the damages."

"What the hell's that to do with a murderer let loose to kill again?"

"Please, Brigandshaw! You must remember this is the Houses of Parliament. Hallowed ground. For centuries. We don't swear at people in the British Houses of Parliament whatever they do in Africa."

"So you'll only do something if he kills me. Something I know he has wanted to do since I joined the squadron as a novice pilot."

"My dear Brigandshaw. How could that be? You were pilots fighting a common enemy. Comrades in arms."

"He thought his fiancée had a romantic interest in me."

"Well, Brigandshaw, that just isn't cricket. Looking at another man's fiancée! That's as bad as looking at another man's wife."

"But I wasn't. Her brother, you see…"

"You don't have to explain. I do not wish to hear the sordid details…"

"He's a convicted murderer…"

"Suffering from a terrible war wound. He is now well. The Home Secretary has personally assured me. Colonel Braithwaite is now well."

"I never said he wasn't," said Harry clenching his teeth.

"Then you have nothing to worry about."

THE IDEA OF confronting his old CO came to mind. The idea of going straight back to Africa came to mind stronger. Once the public offering was complete, Harry was going to go home where he could wear a gun. If Braithwaite came after him he would shoot the bastard. If they then sent him to jail for killing his wife's killer it did not matter. There was justice and revenge. If they did not want to give him justice in England, he would take his revenge in Africa.

Three days later, Harry saw Fishy Braithwaite at the tube station before Braithwaite saw him. Harry got right up behind the man so he could whisper in his ear.

"If you come out to Africa again, I'll kill you myself."

When Braithwaite turned round to look at him it was the first time Harry had seen fear in the man's eyes. They locked eyes for a long moment. Then Braithwaite broke and disappeared into the morning crowd. The man did not appear again outside the office or at the tube station. Harry hoped he had seen the last of him.

THE FOLLOWING DAY in Pall Mall, the manager of Cox's and King's was having lunch at the invitation of C E Porter, something that had never happened before. On occasion he was able to persuade his important clients to have lunch with him at the bank's expense to discuss their affairs. Never before had a client of such wealth invited him to lunch. He was duly flattered as he was meant to be.

C E Porter and his partner Max had suspected Barnaby St Clair of trading on his own account with the information gleaned from their instructions. Without instructions, Barnaby would never have made a profit as he would not have known which company to enquire about or how to use the information. Whether to buy the shares of the company or do the opposite and sell them short.

They wanted to teach Barnaby a lesson, but they first wished to be sure he was using his bank as a nominee to hide the purchase of his shares. The share offering of Colonial Shipping was too important to them.

Max and C E knew Barnaby had become astute and would have some idea if the shares of Colonial Shipping were being offered to the public at a fair price. A fair price that would maximise the worth of thirty per cent shareholding being sold by Harry Brigandshaw. Not only would C E Porter and Max make a pile of cash as the sponsoring stockbroker, they would make another pile out of the profit on the shares in Colonial Shipping they bought for their own account if they could keep the offer price as low as possible without Barnaby telling his brother-in-law the true value of the shares.

C E Porter winkled the fact of Barnaby's nominee account out of the bank manager before the desert. He was charm personified, stroking the man like a faithful dog.

"I shouldn't tell you of course," said the bank manager purring. "It's Lord St Clair, Mr Barnaby St Clair's father, he is concerned about. Does not wish his father to know he is in trade. Silly, in this day and age but you know those old families. So old-fashioned. I just need your word, Mr Porter, that you will never tell Lord St Clair his youngest son is now in trade. Apparently it will cause him to cut off Mr St Clair without a penny… This luncheon has been such an honour. You are such a gentleman, Mr Porter."

If the manager had later overheard C E Porter telling Max the story, he would have thought of him as anything but a gentleman.

"Barnaby even convinced the bank manager Lord St Clair is still worth a fortune."

"How do we lay the trap for Barnaby?"

"We're going to tell him to sell short Colonial Shipping to keep him from the truth. We'll tell him that in our desire to maximise his brother-in-law's cash for the thirty per cent of the company we are selling for him we have overpriced the share. We tell Barnaby that when the share lists it will drop twenty per cent. He'll probably not tell Harry. I mean you don't short a family share. It will be delicious. We make a fortune and Barnaby loses his shirt."

"Will we tell him after the event?"

"Of course. From then on he pays us half his share trading profits."

"Is that greedy C E?"

"We made him rich. I want half."

"It won't upset the offering of Colonial Shipping?"

"How can it? All that happens is the shares go up twenty per cent when they list, Barnaby has to buy his short shares at a hefty premium and goes bust and serves him right."

"But if he's broke, he won't be able to work for us."

"We'll bail him out for the shortfall. Really have him by the balls. He can pay us back later. He's been getting too big for his boots of late. Anyway, when he has no money, I'll be able to take out his girlfriend. All she wants is money. I just can't wait. Tina Pringle. Really has me going."

"You're a dirty old fox."

"Thank you, Max. Life really is a lot of fun. Once Brigandshaw has gone out to Africa, we will be able to rip the share price up and down and always know where it is going. And no risk. He said he's going to make us his nominee on the board of Colonial Shipping. To vote and oversee the remaining seventy per cent of the shareholding."

"Isn't that illegal? You will know what's happening before the public."

"It damn well should be. One day I'm sure it will. For now we get rich. One jump ahead, Max. One jump ahead."

"She'll never go out with you."

"The biggest aphrodisiac for that kind of woman is money. You mark my words. Money and power. Though they really are the same thing."

"Do you want to marry her?"

"Oh don't be damn silly. In ten years' time she won't be worth a look let alone the price of a wife. Wives keep you paying for what you already had. Now that's plain silly, Max my boy. Always pay cash. Never owe anyone anything. The most expensive whore of this world is a wife. You mark my words."

"What about children?"

"Who on earth wants children to spend your money?"

"Don't you want a family?"

"Not if I can help it."

"You'll die a lonely old man."

"It will be a pleasure. Far better than dying with a nagging wife at your bedside. Or a brood of children whose only interest in you is how much money they are going to get. Life is all about money, Max. Anything else they tell you is a pack of lies. To get at your money. The church wants ten per cent of your income in exchange for external life so the clergy can live well in this one. God never asked for money. Why does the church want money? To give away to the poor? More likely to give them power over the poor. They make it look right for the wrong reason. The same applies to marriage. They say we should marry for love. A man marries for lust. You mark my words."

"I don't understand you sometimes, C E. You frighten me."

"Never mind. Being honest in life is usually painful. The truth hurts. If we all know the truth about life, we'd kill ourselves. If we were poor that is. If you're rich, you can buy anything you want. Including Tina

Pringle."

A WEEK BEFORE the shares of Colonial Shipping were to be listed on the London Stock Exchange by C E Porter, Harry set off with Merlin St Clair to drive to Hastings Court. He found it more pleasant to have friends in the house. The gardens and surrounding fields were beautiful. The twenty-seven rooms in the house gave him the creeps. In Africa, Tembo was a friend as well as an employee. Harry had known Tembo most of his life. The thought of Crosswell ever becoming a friend was absurd. The man was always around hovering. Being deferential with such civility Harry knew it had to be false. The man just wasn't human.

They had taken the black, three-litre Bentley on condition Harry drove down to Surrey. Brett was excited as it was her first visit to an English country house and Harry had no wish to have the poor girl frightened to death by Merlin's Brooklands driving. Tina Pringle had warned him.

"He drives like a lunatic, Harry. Get yourself behind the wheel. Can I come if you drive?"

"I'm taking Brett."

"I don't like Brett."

Tina always seemed to find him. Brett liked to be seen at the supper clubs. The brief conversation had taken place in the Savoy Grill after a show. Harry only went out on Saturday nights. The rest of the week he concentrated on the business.

"Would you mind if we went through Mickelham?" said Merlin before they got into the car outside Merlin's flat in Park Lane. Harry had had the chauffeur pick up Brett and come back for him to the office. Harry worked until noon on a Saturday. They were all going to spend the night at Hastings Court. Harry thought he had a buyer for the house which was why he was going down into the country.

"It's on the way," Harry said to Merlin.

"We can have lunch at the Running Horses."

"How do you know the Running Horses? My grandfather talks about it. One of the oldest pubs in England."

"It's a long story, Harry."

"They usually are."

"Why didn't you let Tina come with us? I know she asked."

"Brett wants to scratch her eyes out."

"Don't be silly. Brett would never do anything like that."

"Oh yes I would. She's always making eyes at Harry. I'm jealous."

"She always makes eyes at everybody," said Merlin miserably. "Except me."

They drove the rest of the journey in silence. The top was down and the wind picked the words out of their mouths. Harry drove fast, twice brushing the hedgerows. Merlin smiled next to him complacently. Harry could not see Brett in the back. She was hiding under the cover that fitted over the back seat at chest height to keep the rain out. When it rained the slipstream kept the rain even off the front seats. Both Merlin and Harry in the front were wearing goggles and leather caps. That evening, Brett said it was easier to die lying down on the back seat. She said she had been petrified; it was the first time she had driven in a sports car.

Merlin directed him to the Running Horses. Harry was not sure why. They were too late for lunch by the time they drove into Mickelham.

They stopped on a wide gravel driveway between the outhouses and the old thatched public house. There were no other cars in the driveway. Early, Harry thought, May was either too early for the day trippers or they had had their lunch and gone. When they stopped, Brett came up for air from behind, pushing over the cover to one side. Only the side where she was meant to sit had been unclipped. She looked around nervously.

"Is that Hastings Court?" she asked in disgust. "Why's it got a sign hanging outside? It's small, Harry."

"It's a public house. Merlin wants to pay the place a visit."

"We can go and have a drink in the bar," said Merlin.

"That's the only good idea today… I want a large one. My nerves."

"Were you frightened?" asked Harry. He was holding her hand as they crossed the few yards of gravel to a small, low door that led into the building.

"Yes, I was."

"Then you don't wish to go up in an aeroplane?"

"No, I don't."

Harry thought she was looking particularly pretty. Her hair was ruffled. Her big summer hat was in her free hand with her shoes. Brett very often took off her shoes. Harry wondered why the gravel did not hurt her feet, though as he watched her she picked her spots carefully.

The door led straight into the bar. There was nobody in the bar. The whole place was silent. A man came into the bar and greeted Merlin. Harry thought they seemed to know each other. A girl, probably the barmaid, had followed the man into the bar that smelled deliciously of ancient beer spilled into the woodwork of the bar over the centuries. Harry wondered how many of his ancestors and relations had taken drinks in the bar. They were four miles from Hastings Court. He liked the feel of the place. It was friendly. Like home.

Outside a small girl was crossing the gravel. She stopped and looked at the car. The small girl ran towards the open door into the bar and burst into the room.

"Genevieve, this is your father," said the barmaid.

"Is he really my daddy?" the girl asked looking up at Merlin with big eyes.

"Yes I am," said Merlin. "Did you get my presents?"

"Why don't you come visit?" The girl pronounced her words in a broad vernacular.

"I'm here now," Merlin answered.

Harry looked from the girl to the barmaid and understood.

"You must be Esther," said Harry putting out his hand to the girl, all the pieces falling together. "I'm Harry Brigandshaw. I was over here during the war. Merlin talked about you more than once. You have a very pretty daughter."

"Am I pretty?" said the small girl.

"Very pretty." Harry had got down on his haunches to look into the girl's eyes. They were familiar from long ago when he had first met Lucinda when she was only fifteen. "I am your Uncle Harry. I was married to your Aunt Lucinda."

"Are you Aunt Lucinda?" the girl asked Brett.

"No. She lives a long way away. Your Uncle Harry is just visiting. My name is Brett. What's yours?" Brett was being diplomatic. She had not wished to tell the small girl her aunt was dead. Harry smiled, liking Brett even more.

"Genevieve. My mummy calls me Genevieve. I like Gen."

The man had gone leaving them alone in the bar. They all had one drink and went on their way.

The buyer was due at Hastings Court at four o'clock. Brett had the small girl in the back of the car, seated on her knee. She still had her shoes off and wriggled her toes in her stockings. The idea of taking the girl had been Brett's. Esther had to work. They were to have her back after tea. When the pieces fell together Harry had remembered Merlin's mistress before the war had been the barmaid at the Running Horses at Mickelham. He had even remembered her name. Esther. It was an uncommon name.

HASTINGS COURT had undergone great change since Harry's Grandfather Manderville had left the home for Italy and Africa. The roof had been sealed. The crumbling stone was repaired and the red clay pots replaced on top of the clusters of Queen Anne chimneys that dominated the skyline of the old house.

There were no longer weeds in the front driveway. The hedges were cut. The lawns were cut. The trees trim. The acres lost by the Mandervilles had been bought again and added to the estate. The flowerbeds from which Harry's father had placed a ladder to his mother's bedroom window were full of daffodils and tulips, the weeds long gone. All over the twenty acres of garden, gardeners toiled.

The fields beyond were full of cows and sheep. From the woods came the loud call of the mating pheasants. Peacock strutted paths between the rows of flowerbeds. Lily ponds were full of fat coloured carp.

From the outside everything looked perfect. Even Crosswell was standing at the top of the steps that lead through the double front doors, the oak doors studded with small iron crosses dating back to the eleventh century. Above, the old battlements had been replaced with ornamental battlements that would no longer withstand a siege.

Harry looked up at his ancestral home for a long moment before getting out of the car he had parked in the driveway below the wide steps that led up to the house. Servants were coming out behind Crosswell, ready to add their obedient greetings to that of the butler's. The Lord of the Manor was home. Harry shook his head in disbelief. It was all too mediaeval.

"It's marvellous," burst out Brett. "You can't sell this. Never. Just look at it. Just look at all that history. I can't wait to go inside."

One of the peacocks let out a terrible sound. Harry had suggested getting rid of the peacocks. They even screamed at night from where they roosted up in the trees. For Harry, the peacock had the only bird sound that jarred. That and the hadeda ibis when the birds slowly flew in flocks to roost.

"Welcome home, Sir Harry," said Crosswell, coming down the steps and walking to the car where he opened the door for Brett. Harry had given up explaining to his newly inherited butler he was not a knight of the realm.

"A man called, Sir Harry. The American will not be coming at four o'clock."

"Will he be coming later?" said Harry in alarm.

"The man did not say, Sir Harry."

Harry shook his head again. He was stuck with the place. An ancestral conspiracy.

The small girl had run down to the first pond to look at the fish. She looked more at home than Harry. The girl looked back to see if her new-found father was watching her.

"Welcome to Hastings Court," said Harry wearily to his guests.

The butler was already directing two young men in uniform to take the bags from the back of the Bentley. Crosswell had taken the keys from Harry. The butler even knew how to open the boot of the car. There had obviously been more guests at Hastings Court when Harry's uncle was alive.

There was a rich smell of perfume coming from somewhere. Harry was not sure of the scents of the English flowers. He looked around but could not pinpoint where the lovely smell was coming from.

There were no dogs to greet him. Only the servants. Not even a pair of tame Egyptian geese. Not even a cat sleeping on a windowsill. The thing that worried him most was the pure waste of money he was forced to spend maintaining the place. It was pure ostentation. A rude show of wealth.

Silently, as he walked across to his home, he cursed the American for not taking the white elephant off his hands. Why people wanted to show off their wealth, Harry would never understand.

"It's older than Purbeck Manor," said Merlin looking up at the house.

"Parts are about the same time as your Corfe Castle. The keep to the right was built first and rebuilt. That's where they started. Soon after the family came over with William the Conqueror from France."

Merlin was shaking his head, "I agree with Brett. You can't sell this place, Harry. You have a duty to all those people who came before."

"You sound like my grandfather."

Genevieve came racing back from the fish pond. Nearer to Merlin she was not so sure of herself.

The small girl ate a crumpet dripping in butter and strawberry jam in front of a big log fire in the one small room Harry found he could enjoy. The rest of the rooms were too big. The ceilings too high. He had long concluded his ancestors were a hardy lot. Even in May the old house was as cold as charity.

Each of them had been allocated a room. Harry was given the master bedroom. The right cases were left in each room. Brett was furious. Her room was half a corridor from the master's bedroom, almost fifty yards of a cold night.

A fire had been lit in each bedroom as soon as they had arrived. The place had a smell about it Harry had found no place else in his life. Then he had the answer while sitting round the fire in the small, inner room.

"Age. The place smells of old age. Old people smell of old age. This house smells of old age. It seeps out at you." Harry was twitching his nose.

"It would have been different had you grown up in the house," said Merlin complacently. "We all like what we find when we come into this world. It's what we find later we don't like. It's better with lots of family in these big houses. In the old days everyone had a dozen children. The grandparents stayed where they were. Maiden aunts never left the family house. Poor cousins came to live. The only way to entertain was to have people to stay. In those days you couldn't drive down from London for a night like we've done. The servants were family too. The old bird dusting the grand piano was probably the woman who gave you your first bath. It's quite different once they've seen you naked in the bath. You remember Aunt Nut and Granny Forrester, Harry? And old Potts? They made Purbeck Manor what it is. A family home. You need to find a wife and breed lots of children, Harry. Bring your mother home. Your grandfather. Your sister is on her own. Then the place will feel like a home."

"They won't come. I see your point. Elephant Walk is our home. Why I want to go home so badly."

"What about poor Brett?" she was pouting again, both hands firmly on a large glass of gin that she drank with very little tonic water.

"You'd love Africa," said Harry wistfully thinking of Africa.

"ARE you taking me to Africa? Oh, I couldn't do that Harry. What about my brilliant career in the theatre? Even if I have been resting rather a long time. I like this place. Though I wouldn't want loads of children, oh no. What's wrong with Hastings Court?"

AFTER TEA THEY took Genevieve back to her mother at the Running Horses. Brett had stayed at Hastings Court next to the bottle of gin.

"What are you going to do with her?" asked Harry, referring to Merlin's daughter. They were driving back with Harry at the wheel of the Bentley. He was driving slowly through the English lanes, freshly green with spring.

"I have no idea. I'll be damned if I do and damned if I don't. Her mother and I come from different worlds. Which one should Genevieve belong to? What did they do in the old days?"

"They did not recognise their illegitimate children. Paid for their other family and kept quiet."

"I can't just leave her. Anyway, she is the only child I've got. And I can forget about Tina Pringle. You see, Tina now speaks properly. Knows how to behave. Did she ever tell you about Miss Pinforth? She did all that away from her own parents as she was living with her brother in Johannesburg. That makes a difference. What is it about Tina Pringle that makes me want her so much? The others I could take or leave. Like Esther. I was jealous of the corporal but now when I look at her there is nothing."

"Tina's dangerous, Merlin. She's using you to get at Barnaby."

"It's the way she looks at me."

"I know. She does it to me. Not many women have that power in a look. History is dotted with a few of them. Bonaparte's Josephine. Helen of Troy. Some of the new film stars. It's something about being unobtainable. Stay away, Merlin. She's trouble. A very nice girl and I like her very much. But dangerous. Whichever man she gets she will destroy. She probably doesn't even know she's doing it. Girls like Brett are much easier.

"You'd better drive, Merlin. If we stay away too long Brett will finish that bottle of gin and then she won't be to walk round the estate… I want a walk tonight. I miss my dogs. I need to stretch my legs. London is so confined."

Harry stopped the car so they could change drivers.

In the end, Harry walked on his own leaving Merlin with Brett talking round the fire. The spring evening was cold. Fresh air filled his lungs bringing him alive.

Harry walked fast round the ornamental lake that unbeknown to him had once been his Grandmother Brigandshaw's haven from the world. Then he walked into his fields among the cows and sheep, having a good look at them. There were no wet brown blotches from blowfly on the sheep. No sign of ticks on the cows.

"They probably have different problems in England."

The small rabbits looking at him from a hill to his left said not a word in reply. Harry waved, and the rabbits disappeared. Harry knew he was at a crossroads in his life. He knew which fork to take. Which fork he wanted. He was not so sure if it was the right fork for the other people who depended upon him. Even now, after so few months as a businessman, he was sure he was well capable of running a shipping line... Africa was wild and dangerous. The black people would not accept the English complacently forever. Unless the English gave them a far better life. The idea of a school on Elephant Walk passed through his mind. If the black people were to compete in the modern world, they had to be educated in modern ways. The idea to Harry was good and bad. Often at home he thought the black people would have been better off without the English. The trappings of wealth looked attractive. Alluring to some. For Harry, a thatched hut next to an African river was far more alluring.

"There must be something wrong with me," he said again out loud. "Or is there?"

He stopped to pick wild flowers for Brett and ask her the names. Merlin would know. They were pretty. Some even similar to the ones he found in the African bush after the rain. Flowers came and went in Africa according to the patterns of the rain. Harry liked that.

12

MANIPULATIONS, MAY 1922

"*Y*ou can come but you can't stay. Why are you here, Barnaby?"

It was six o'clock in the evening at Tina Pringle's front door in St John's Wood. The May evening was still full of sunlight.

"Max and C E Porter think I'm a fool. They are trying to tell me to sell Harry Brigandshaw's company short."

"I have no idea what you are talking about," said Tina. "Did you know Merlin had a daughter?"

"He's a bachelor and will remain one for the rest of his life… They are trying to tell me they have overvalued the shares. That when the shares are listed on Monday, they will sink well below the asking price. It's rubbish. I know the offer is oversubscribed. That bank manager of mine couldn't get me more than one thousand shares. I'll have to go and see Harry and buy the shares openly in my own name. He's my brother-in-law. He can allocate the new shares or at least tell C E Porter I'm to have some. Word I heard is, it's oversubscribed five times. It'll go up terrifically."

"You're being boring, Barnaby… Her name is Genevieve, and she's seven years old."

"What are you talking about?"

"Merlin's daughter. You remember Esther?"

"She married a corporal. Made a perfect fool of Merlin. He was paying for her flat. Everything. What comes of sleeping with low-class sluts. What else can you expect?"

"Esther has a daughter." Tina Pringle was enjoying herself. It was not often she knew about something before Barnaby. Something with so much juice in it.

"Then the child is the corporal's."

"She was born six months after they married."

"That doesn't mean anything. Makes it worse. While Merlin was away fighting the war, his mistress was having an affair. Worse than her getting married behind Merlin's back. Merlin would never have married her of course. She was so common. A barmaid. Merlin had no sense of decorum. Picked her up at a country pub and brought up to London. It was a nice flat. I remember Esther."

"Were you also her lover, Barnaby?"

"She was Merlin's mistress! Merlin is my brother."

"That wouldn't stop you if you wanted her."

"Well I didn't."

"Why did you go around?"

"I was with Merlin."

"You're a liar. Merlin would never have introduced you to a mistress. You St Clairs are far too snobby."

"I was with Merlin. Before he went to war. He was going to Purbeck Manor. It was my last hols from school. We had to go and see Esther for some reason. Before we took the train to Corfe Castle. The flat was on the way."

"You are digging a hole. Really. Sixteen and giving one to your brother's mistress. You never fail to amaze me, Barnaby. Just how low you can go to get what you want."

"Can I have a drink? It's six o'clock. We can go to a show. Why don't you answer your phone?"

"I knew it was you and I didn't want to talk to you. You can have one whisky and then you can go."

"What is it you want, Tina? We don't have sex. You don't answer your telephone. When I do come round to your flat we fight. Share dealing for me is important. How I get rich. Though not as rich as I want to be."

Tina stared at him silently for a long time.

"I'm not going to get married if that's what you want," said Barnaby defiantly. "If I did want to, I'd marry a rich girl."

"And keep me as your mistress."

"That would be nice. I can afford the allowance your brother pays. I just need Harry to let me have a good block of Colonial Shipping shares. We'd have the best of both worlds."

"No. You'd have the best of both worlds."

Tina stared at him again. She felt like hitting him hard across the face. Or better still, she thought, with something hard over the head.

"The girl has different coloured eyes. Like Merlin's. They must have recognised each other. Brett says Merlin has no idea what to do."

"You hate Brett."

"I hate you more."

"Give me a whisky and shut up."

"Don't you want to make love, Barnaby?"

"Of course I do."

"Come on then. Just a quick one. Then you must go."

"Why must I go?"

"Harry Brigandshaw is coming round at eight," lied Tina, leading him into her bedroom before closing the door and lifting up her dress. Underneath, she was wearing nothing.

Lying back on her bed, Tina waited for him with her legs open, smiling all the time.

"Why Harry?" managed Barnaby. His erection was so strong he was having trouble taking off his pants.

"I want to live in Africa. Come on. You're wasting time." Intentionally, she had made her voice sound husky.

HARRY BRIGANDSHAW was well aware the shares of Colonial Shipping were undervalued. That whoever received an allocation and sold them after the listing would make a handsome profit. It had been his intention. Why all the staff were offered shares to be paid for out of their salaries and wages over five years. Harry hoped the staff would hold onto their shares and watch their value grow, giving them an incentive to make the company even more profitable. To make the staff part of the family. He was also aware C E Porter through bank nominees had allocated himself a hundred thousand shares.

Grainger's investigation had been thorough and accurate. Well before Harry appointed C E Porter the sole sponsoring stockbroker. As had been the report on building a cold storage facility into two of their ships.

Harry and Grainger had spoken in April, soon after Grainger came back from Birmingham.

"He's sharp, Mr Brigandshaw. But not dishonest. So far as the law goes he is always within the law. Every company he has taken public has been a success. When he goes through the accounts and doesn't like what he sees he tells the client to look for another stockbroker. When the shares eventually list through another sponsoring broker, he sells the shares short and from what I hear almost always makes a killing."

"So he knows how to value a company."

"And knows what the market wants. What the market will pay for a share. The future value of the company... There are five banks. All listed in my report. If all five banks apply for our shares, their applications will stick out like a sore thumb. Porter doesn't think anyone knows about his nominee buying. Buys the same number of shares through each bank. So if all five banks ask for say twenty thousand shares we'll know it's Porter."

"Not if the bank is asked to buy our shares by other clients?"

"I think we will see a pattern."

"Do you recommend we use Porter?"

"Yes. He will make the flotation a success if he takes it on."

"And make himself a fortune."

"It is the way of business in the City, Mr Brigandshaw. If I may say so they are mostly only gentleman on the surface. An Englishman's word as his bond can mean many things... Once I know a man's modus operandi I can do business. The man who says he has never stolen a penny in his life is the one to watch. A man who says that in the City is a liar. In the City of London there are more ways to steal than you can possibly imagine. Why we are the centre of world finance and at the heart of the largest empire on God's earth... We need a sharp stockbroker to stop the rest of them in the City doing us harm. You set a crook to stop a crook, Mr Brigandshaw. Never be fooled by a man's public school accent."

"You think Porter a crook?"

"He will always be just within the law."

"Then some of the laws need changing."

"That they do. Business evolution. Each side looking to get ahead, with the government of the day claiming they are legislating fair play. And that one is usually a lie. Governments are run by vested interests."

"You are saying the City of London is a house of dishonesty."

"Not at all. What I am saying is if you don't know the rules and the ways round the rules you will never become rich in the City of London."

"Then we will have to use the services of Mr Porter."

"I am glad you agree, Mr Brigandshaw. Better the devil we have found out about than the devil we don't know."

"How many shares are you going for yourself?"

"As many as you will offer me."

"Thank you, Grainger. That is the best reason so far for using Porter. I was not sure at first. Now I know we are going to get on. I will, of course, make sure you are not working for Mr Porter before we go ahead."

"You have learnt fast, Mr Brigandshaw."

"We also have predators in Africa, Grainger... Will you have lunch with me today in my dining room?"

"It will be an honour."

"Did my grandfather ever entertain you in the managing director's private dining room?"

"No, sir. I was never given that honour. Only the ships' captains ate with the Captain."

By the time Tina Pringle was lying to Barnaby St Clair about Harry going round to visit her flat in St John's Wood at eight o'clock in the evening, Harry knew that institutions and the public had asked to be allocated five and a half times more shares in Colonial Shipping than were on offer. He was also considering Percy Grainger for the job of managing director when he finally went home to Africa and Elephant Walk. Though C E Porter had given him a list from outside the company, Harry's instinct was to promote from within. Grainger would watch Porter who would have Harry's proxy at directors' meetings and be able to vote Harry's share at the annual shareholders meetings. Porter would watch Grainger. There would be a balance of power.

Harry was going to introduce a third safety precaution and the one he considered most important. When the ships of the company arrived in Beira on their round trips of Africa, Harry would fly himself down to the Mozambique port from Elephant Walk. He was going to build himself a grass airstrip on his farm. He was going to buy a twin aircraft in England and send it to Cape Town on one of his ships in crates. Harry would take the train to Cape Town and fly the aircraft to Rhodesia.

A system with the Rhodesian post office would be put in place to get cables to Elephant Walk within three hours of their arrival at the Salisbury post office. Harry was determined to have the best of both worlds. He was going to live where he wanted and still keep his finger on the pulse.

When aeroplanes grew bigger with a longer range, he would introduce a commercial airline to fly from Cape Town and Johannesburg direct to London with fuel stops on the way. He had begun talks with the Sunderland aircraft company to build an amphibious passenger plane that could land on the great lakes and rivers of Africa so he could hop his passengers up and down Africa. They had looked at him amazed but said they would see what could be done. Even in 1922, four years after the end of the war against Germany, Harry was still respected in aviation circles. Harry had smiled to himself. It was the only time he could remember when he had used his fame from the war to get himself something that he wanted.

Flying boats. They were going to build him flying boats.

Straight after the first lunch with Percy Grainger in the managing director's private dining room, at which they had talked more than eaten, Harry found a use for the chauffeur that drove the managing director's Rolls-Royce. For weeks the man had had nothing to do. Harry had bought himself a 350 cc BSA motorcycle and some old flying clothes. The one-bedroom flat off Regent Street was used during the week. During the weekends, Harry rode the bike into the countryside to get away from the noise and other people. The driver had sat twiddling his thumbs. Now each time an Empire Castle ship arrived at Southampton, the driver was sent with the car to bring the ships' captains to London for lunch in the managing director's private dining room, a tradition started by Harry's grandfather that Harry reintroduced. The navy and the air force had a lot in common. Most of the time they liked each other and Harry found out what he wanted to know about the business he had inherited from his Uncle James.

The private, one-to-one lunches had triggered his idea to buy himself an aircraft. To talk to Sunderland. To think ahead to the new world of travel he was certain would come whether the people of the world liked it or not. The world was going to shrink, and he was going to help it to shrink. For moments, Harry even found he was enjoying himself being in business. There were now so many new things, he could do.

AT NINE O'CLOCK that night Harry drove his motorcycle to the small flat he rented off Regent Street in Regent Mews. The Mews had not so long ago stabled horses. Harry had rented his flat over one of the stables and Harry parked his motorcycle in it. Even in May he needed the long leather flying jacket to keep out the cold. Even the slightest cold penetrated Harry's thin blood. It was an ongoing story in his head with himself to explain his dislike for the English weather.

He wanted an early night. Harry found mental exercise more tiring than walking the bush all day with a rifle over his shoulder and the dogs at his heels. Harry stopped. When he thought of the dogs, he could still feel the loss of Fletcher, killed defending his Grandfather Manderville from an old lion. Even after five years... Harry could still remember every dog he had ever owned.

"Evening, Harry. Thought you were going to visit Tina tonight?"

"What are you doing here, Barnaby? Why would I want to visit Tina tonight? Where did you get that idea?"

"Straight from the horse's mouth. Tina Pringle."

"She wants to make you jealous. You have my word I have no interest in your girlfriend other than as a casual friend I meet on the social rounds of London. A round frankly I could do without but Brett insists. She has a new part by the way. Some play by Somerset Maugham they are putting on at the Adelphi. Quite a good part. Seeing you are here, you'd better come in for one drink. Then I'm going to bed. I'm dog-tired... What do you want?"

"How do you know I want something?"

"Either you were spying on me to see if I was visiting Tina which makes no sense or you would be outside her flat in St John's Wood. Or you want something."

"You know me too well, brother-in-law."

"Yes I do," said Harry wearily. They had climbed the outside stairs to his Mews flat and Harry was putting the key into the door.

"You can afford something better than this, Harry. Why the motorcycle?"

"Come in, Barnaby. Pour yourself a drink. The drinks are in the sideboard. How'd you find my flat? People don't come here often."

"Brett told me."

"Did she? I must tell Brett not to broadcast my hideaway. Now, what do you want?"

"An allocation of Colonial Shipping shares before Monday."

"You have one thousand already allocated."

"How do you know that? The allocation is in the name of my bankers."

"Who are Cox's and King's? Why does the whole of the City imagine we colonials are all fools? That only someone born to it can know what's going on here. We help fight your wars and you still look at us down your noses. Irritating, Barnaby."

"A thousand isn't nearly enough."

"Why? The shares can list below the offer price and then you lose money. We'll all only know that on Monday."

"They'll go up in the first hour of trading."

Harry watched Barnaby pour himself a whisky from the decanter he had found in the sideboard before turning to offer Harry the decanter.

"Not for me. I'm not going to eat."

Barnaby turned back to his drink and with his finger stirred the water he had poured into his whisky. It looked to Harry as if he was thinking as fast as his brain could think. Then he turned round with his best smile spread gently over his handsome face. As usual when Barnaby wanted something he was trying to turn all his charm on Harry. Harry smiled back.

"My father is not wealthy, Harry. It worries me. Even with Merlin buying him that pedigree herd of cows he still doesn't have any real money. I want to use the money I have made since coming back from Africa to help my father and mother. I thought you might want to help. I'm prepared to risk my money to buy Lord St Clair as many shares as you're able to offer him."

"You want the shares in your father's name," said Harry in surprise.

"No. He wouldn't understand that. And if they went down, he would think he owed me the money. The shortfall. No. Better the shares are allocated to me and I give my father the profit when I sell."

"All the profit, Barnaby? This is Harry you are talking to."

"Shall we say half the profits?"

"I want that in writing from you, Barnaby. Now."

"You don't trust me?"

"You still owe Jim Bowman ten pounds. You conned him out of lunch and ten pounds. You also stole from the officers' mess fund in Cairo which was why you were not asked to stay on in the army after the war. The British Army rightly forgave you after you put back the money. You were brave during the war blowing up Turkish trains. Getting off was your reward instead of a medal. You are also known to wear an old Harrovian tie to which you perfectly well know you are not entitled as you did not attend Harrow School."

"Is this a lecture?" The blue eyes had gone cold. Dangerous.

"Sort of. You are my brother-in-law. You are much younger than me.

If you want me to make you some more easy money, I want you to know the truth. Not everyone is fooled by the charm of the Honourable Barnaby St Clair. We are not all fools. Fact is, I like your idea. I would very much like to give your mother and father some money in a way they will accept. They gave me Lucinda, and I lost them Lucinda when she was in my charge. When I was meant to be looking after her with my life... I will allocate to you one hundred thousand shares in your own name. If your bankers will not extend to you an overdraft to cover the purchase for the short while before you sell the shares at a profit, I will guarantee your overdraft at Cox's and King's. For making the trade, you will receive ten per cent of the profit. The balance will be deposited to your father's bank account. If it is not within seven days of receiving your profit cheque from your stockbroker, I will run you out of London. Run you out of England. The financial world will be told who you really are."

"You're a bastard, Harry."

"On that one you are perfectly right. Do we agree on the details?"

"Every one of them. Ten per cent is better than nothing. How long can I wait? Before I sell?"

"A month. One month from Monday. There's a writing desk over there. Go and write down what we have agreed."

"May I tell Mother and Father how it was?"

"No. They think you are wonderful. You may take the credit."

"What will the one pound shares go to, Harry?"

"Our last guess is twenty-five shillings. Now, sign right now and I'll have one drink with you and pretend the ugly part of this conversation never took place. I am not your enemy Barnaby. I'm still your friend. Try to remember that."

ON SATURDAY morning at first light, Harry wheeled the heavy motorcycle out of the stable under his flat and kick-started the engine. He was wearing his long leather flying jacket. Large goggles hid most of his face. On his hands were gloves that came halfway up to his elbows. Birds were singing in the plane trees that had attracted Harry to the flat in the Mews. He was whistling to himself. Everything had gone as well as he hoped. On Monday they would find out the price the market would pay for his shares. All the allocations were in place. The unsuccessful had been sent back their money in the post. The day the morning after Barnaby's petulant visit to his flat, had been most satisfactory. It was the first time Harry had seen C E Porter's face drop. The first time the smooth confidence had vanished for a moment, replaced by a fear Harry recognised in his eyes.

"I'm sorry, Harry, but Barnaby can't be given one hundred thousand shares."

"Why not, C E?"

Harry had taken the time to go to the offices of C E Porter. He wanted to look at the man so they would understand each other in the future, not just talk to him over the phone.

"The institutions have been told their allotments by telephone. The return cheques are in the envelopes and will be posted tonight. We are oversubscribed five point seven times. There are no more shares we can allocate."

"Institutions. The banks, for instance. They can be phoned again. The transactions will only be finalised once the shares are listed by you on Monday morning."

"But everything is finalised, Harry."

"Maybe not, C E. The banks buying shares for their clients as nominees will only inform their clients when they receive the share certificate in two weeks' time. It doesn't really matter to the banks which of their clients are lucky. They applied for shares on behalf of their clients to hide their clients' names from our share register. So we as Colonial Shipping don't actually know the names of some of our shareholders. Personally, I think that is a practice that should be changed. It has an air of dishonesty even if it is perfectly legal. You kindly gave me a list of allocations where the number of shares was over ten thousand shares, other than staff shares, where the list covered everyone. I was pleased you remembered my request to treble the allocation of one Samuel Adams... Now I have my own small list of allocated shares that we will change. There are five of them. Each twenty thousand shares. Barnaby St Clair will receive their allocations instead of the banks. We don't even know the real buyers so it doesn't matter to us."

Harry handed C E Porter the list and watched him carefully as he read the names of the five London banks. Harry watched the colour drain from C E Porter's face. The man had gone white. Then he had looked up at Harry. They finally understood each other.

"Of course, any bank nominee shares will do, C E," Harry said sweetly. "These just add up so nicely to one hundred thousand shares."

"You know these are for me, don't you Harry?"

"Yes I do."

"How did you find out? It's quite legal, you know."

"I think a big, personal investment, out in the open, of my sponsoring broker would have been nice. But you have your reasons. Better let the banks have those shares then and find a hundred thousand somewhere else. Here is Barnaby's application form and his cheque. Just to put your mind at rest, I had him ask Cox's and King's to guarantee the cheque. The bank has agreed on the back of the cheque."

"I'm glad I did not fly in combat against you, Harry."

"Now that everything is finalised, I would like to thank you for a splendid job well done. Which is why I'm here in your office. I will be at the London Stock Exchange on Monday morning when they ring the bell. Keep your fingers crossed for a good opening price. I want my staff to see an immediate profit... Did anyone sell short as far as you know?" Harry was at the door of C E Porter's office when he turned back to smile. Barnaby had told him C E Porter's scheme to make Barnaby broke. Again C E Porter went white.

"Not so far as I know, Harry."

"Good."

BY THE TIME Harry was out of the London traffic and had opened the throttle of his bike he was smiling again at the recollection. And he had finally made up his mind to make Percy Grainger the managing director of Colonial Shipping, the holding company for Empire Castle Line.

Instead of taking the high road, he wound the motorcycle along the path that followed the river. It was the same path he had taken with Robert St Clair so long ago when they came down from Oxford in 1907. They had walked from Corfe Castle railway station to Purbeck Manor along the river. That was the day he first saw Lucinda when she was fifteen years old. He could still see her standing at the end of the pathway.

When Harry saw the chimney pots of the old house over the trees, he could hear Lucinda calling in his head.

'Come on, Harry. We're home,' she said. 'We're home.'

Which made him cry.

ROBERT ST CLAIR heard the motorcycle when it was three miles away and cocked his ear. Walking on a peg foot was painful after a mile. He had stopped under an oak tree with a twenty-foot girth. Under the great spreading oak Robert had constructed a wooden bench with its back to the gnarled trunk of the old tree. Last year's acorns were strewn on the moss and further away among the new grass of spring, too many for the squirrels.

On the bench and three others in a two-mile radius of Purbeck Manor was where he sat of a day thinking through the plot of his book before going back to the house to write down what he had seen and heard in his mind.

The army rehabilitation people had twice given him prosthetic feet in exchange for the one he had lost in France during the war. Twice he had gone back to his peg foot. The look of two shoes at the end of his trousers was not worth the jerk and click of the artificial limb that made his walks in the woods a stumbling pain.

The sound of the motorcycle drew nearer. Robert thought the man must be following the course of the river that was really a stream. The pictures in his head were shattered by the loud, intensive noise of the bike's motor. Robert gave up. Once the pictures left his head, it was a long process to get them back again.

The path along the river was visible from under the oak. Robert waited silently. A traveller was lost, if he kept quiet the man would find the path ended in the private garden of the manor, turn round and go back the way he came. With the return of a birdsong to his ears, the pictures would slowly come back again. His characters would again start talking in his head.

He knew the intruder was a man. Women, so far as Robert knew, didn't ride motorcycles. The motorcycle came into view. The big machine coughing smells and ugly sound drew level and stopped. The rider was fifty yards down the slope from Robert sitting silently on his bench. Robert had not moved an inch.

The engine was turned off bringing back the silence of the woods. The man had big goggles over half his face. Robert recognised the long leather coat that stopped at the thighs. He had seen them during the war, worn by pilots from the Royal Flying Corps.

Robert could hear birds again, calling from far away. A breeze moved the thin strands of new green grass that only grew away from the shade of the oak. Under his foot was green moss. Earlier, Robert had removed the peg and put it on the bench. He liked to massage the stump. He could not run away if he wanted.

The man was getting off the bike and hooking out the stand with his foot. The man in the goggles waved. Robert ignored the wave. The man began to walk towards him. The bike was standing at a slight slant against its metal stand, the machine leaning away from Robert. He imagined the stand or the motorcycle would have fallen over on its side. The man stopped short and put his hands on his hips.

"Fine way to greet your brother-in-law."

"I say. It's Harry. Well I never. I thought you were lost. Don't have many visitors. You'll have to hang on while I put on my peg. Well I never. Why didn't you phone? Mother will be pleased."

"How's the book going?"

"All right until that damn machine shattered my concentration. There are fresh scones for tea and raspberry jam from last year. We can get the cook to make a big supper now you are here. The cook sometimes needs motivation. Harry, take off those goggles!"

"Good to see you, you old bastard."

"None of that, Harry. You're the bastard, don't forget. Why is this only your third visit since you came to live in England?"

"Not to live. I'm going home at the end of the English summer in time for the seedbeds. The seedbeds go in in September. We plant out the tobacco seedlings in the lands at the start of the rains."

"I have no idea what you are talking about."

"You want a lift to the house?"

"Don't be silly. Wouldn't get on that thing if you paid me... Where is the Rolls-Royce? The chauffeur?"

"This is more fun. I'll go on up. Is your mother in the house?"

"You'll find her in the herb garden. Father went out to check the cows. Best thing Merlin ever did was buy Father the pedigree herd. Joy of his life. With the pigs of course. Ah, the pigs!"

"You don't have to hurry."

"I'm hungry."

"You are always hungry, Robert. You have worms. You have always had worms."

"No I don't."

"Then why aren't you fat?"

"I burn up the fat with mental energy... I really am glad to see you."

"So am I to see you, old friend. It's nearly twenty years since we first met at Oxford."

"Eighteen to be exact. Yes, it's eighteen years. Can you tell Mother to tell the cook about supper? You know where the herb garden is? Behind the kitchen. Remember the herbs hanging in Mrs Pringle's kitchen? They came from our herb garden."

"Yes, I do, come to think of it. Glorious smell, wasn't it?"

"It certainly was. Memories! Life is all about memories, Harry. Fact is, that's all life is about."

"When I saw the chimney pots back there, I saw her again when she was fifteen. We were together, you and I. When I first set eyes on Lucinda."

"Are the memories all right?"

"They are getting better. The bad are fading. The good becoming more vivid."

"She fell in love with you that day. She told me. All the girls fell in love with you that day. My mystery man from Africa… You go on. I don't like people to watch me put on my foot. It's the only thing I don't like apart from not having a foot. Private Lane doesn't have anything except his soul. Just one wayward British shell ending in the wrong trench. Quite ironic. There was Albert Pringle in Africa making shells for the army. They mustn't have loaded the damn thing correctly. Or whatever you do to make a dud shell. You think Albert from the cottage down the river blew off my foot?"

"I doubt it. I'll ask Cook to put the scones in the oven. Can I call you peg leg?"

"You call me what you like. I just called you a bastard."

THEY WERE all pleased to see Harry. No one mentioned Lucinda using words. The cook's eyes spoke volumes as did the bluster of Lord St Clair. Harry was first taken to see the pigs. The bull and the cows came next. They were Sussex-Brown with soft brown eyes.

The rest of Saturday was spent in comfortable small talk. The kind of talk among old friends who did not have to say very much to each other. There was no need for any explaining.

There were more dogs and cats around the old house than Harry's first visit back in '07. The dogs sprawled comfortably in front of a log fire. Even in May the house was cold. They ate roast pork with an apple sauce that the cook had bottled in the autumn. There was a row of apple sauce in Kilner jars in the pantry. For some reason they ate in the grand hall with the vaulted ceiling. They all sat at one end of the long table. Only one of the fires had been lit. Harry thought eating in the hall was for him. There were just the four of them as one of the sisters who had lost a husband in the war lived with her mother-in-law in Norfolk. The other sister, Annabel, lived in Manchester, happily married to Geoffrey who had been a sergeant during the war. Harry remembered the man had won the Military Medal and was now a painter. Geoffrey had painted the covers for Robert St Clair's novels. The covers were very good.

Politely, neither Lord nor Lady St Clair mentioned the motorcycle.

THE NEXT DAY, Harry and Robert found their way back to the bench under the oak. They wanted to talk. The weather had held. Robert had insisted on bringing with them a large packet of chicken sandwiches. The sandwiches were wrapped in greaseproof paper. Harry had seen some of the chickens pecking around in the garden. The cook had put in a thermos of tea and two slices of plum cake. Harry carried the basket. They had only just finished a large breakfast.

"Don't like to be too far from the house without food," Robert explained.

"I see," said Harry. His friend was stumping along quite well next to him. The dogs had all been told to stay behind. Robert had used many strong words before the dogs did what they were told.

Harry breathed good clean air with satisfaction. The tension from the office and the share listing was leaving him. To have an old friend, he knew, was one of the joys of life. To never have to be on the defensive.

"How's the new book going, Robert?" he knew Robert liked to talk to him about his books.

"I'm back in the twelfth century again. It's not a sequel to *Keeper of the Legend*. England before the Norman invasion. By the way, I had a letter from the American Glenn Hamilton last week. He wants to know when he can read the manuscript of the new book. No title yet. Usually I get the title somewhere through writing the book. It'll come. Glenn has been so good to me after finding me my publisher for *Keeper of the Legend*. I think he really likes my books but you never know. I can never judge my own works so I don't know what the fuss is all about. Living here is cheap so I don't worry about the new advance. Well, maybe I do a little. Father is always short of money."

"Well he won't be soon if all goes well on Monday."

Harry told Robert what Barnaby had done. Leaving Barnaby as the only benefactor to his family. Harry told Robert he thought Lord St Clair would get a tax-free cheque for as much as twenty thousand pounds from Barnaby.

"It wasn't his idea was it, Harry?"

"It was, matter of fact. I just set the rules. It's how Barnaby makes a living."

"How did he get allocated so many shares?"

"How'd you know about these things? You don't know a thing about finance."

"Nonsense. Long ago a teacher told me to read the whole newspaper including the letters to the editor. Not just the sport or the stage reviews. Or the court circular. He said if I wanted to write fiction I would have to know everything about life. You'd be surprised how much useless information resides in this head of mine. Among the rubbish are treasures I hope. How many people other than Barnaby received a one hundred thousand share allocation?"

"The sponsoring broker. He hid it in nominees if you know much about the stock market."

"Then you are giving Father the money, Harry."

"He won't look further than Barnaby. Lead your mother off the subject if she starts asking questions. You're very good at leading people off the subject, Robert."

"Would you like a sandwich?"

"I have only just finished a very large breakfast."

"Have a mug of tea. There are two mugs so we don't have to use the top of the flask. The cake is very good. Rich well-dried fruit. Why do plums become prunes when they dry up? Why can't they just stay as dried-up plums?"

"You love words, don't you?"

"Yes I do. They are such fun. I love writing as I can go anywhere I want, whenever I want in any century. The leg becomes irrelevant. Sometimes I am so much there in the story it is more real than sitting at my desk. As if that old ancestor has gone into my body and taken me back to his life. It's so vivid, Harry. I am there in every way. Mentally and physically. I become each one of my characters in turn. Or more exactly each character takes over my body and lives through me."

They sat down on the bank of the stream to drink their steaming hot mugs of tea. Neither of them put sugar in their tea. The fresh milk from one of the cows was in a screw-top bottle in a napkin. The cook was from an old school who believed in doing it the right way or not at all.

The morning clouds were upside down in the floating stream. A frog watched them from a perch on a stick in the water. The stream flowed over the frog's feet.

After ten minutes they got up and walked the rest of the way to the oak tree and looked at the bench Robert had made for himself. They had not said another word.

"I always wonder how many St Clairs have sat under this tree. Do you think any of them made love to their ladies? That somehow I started under this tree? Conical hats with long hanging silk thrown urgently on the moss of summer. I don't think they would have done it in the winter do you?... Horses jangling at the bits. Armour propped against the far side of the tree with a great sword hilt ready for strong hands. Great big swords with Christian crosses for handles. Long white smocks with the red cross of St George emblazoned on the back and front. Thrown away on the ground, oblivious to love. Chain armour. The fading smell of the Holy Land. A manservant discreetly keeping guard with his back to the naked lovers. Right there, Harry. Where I put the bench. Where I sit on the moss when I lie down to sleep, dappled by the sun through the leaves of summer... Love among the sweet smell of vanilla from the wild flowers of England. The coo of doves. Happy. Just happy. How it was. How it should be. And isn't... Now can I have a chicken sandwich? I always eat the sandwiches before I eat the cake. Otherwise it would not be right... I'm a romantic old fool."

"Better more of us should be. In London they only think about making money and spending it and they waste most of it. While poor people go hungry."

"That is too serious for my mood. Too sad. Questions like that lead us to feeling miserable... Did I tell you Merlin came down last week? With a girl. Not for himself. For me. She had read my book and made Merlin drive her down in that car of his. I won't get in the thing. Poor girl was exhausted with fear. What's wrong with Merlin? Something's up. The girl knew you. I like her. She likes my books. We talked about my books all day while Merlin moped around all day. Do you know what's going on?"

"Yes I do but it's up to Merlin to tell his family."

"Is it serious?"

"Oh, not in that way. He hasn't gone broke. He's in love with the wrong girl. That I can tell you."

"Who is she?"

"That I can't."

"Do you know anything about the Voss girl, Harry?"

"Yes, I do."

"Well go on."

"I can't. I know her mother. You'll like her mother. Are you in love, Robert?"

"I don't know. She didn't mind my foot a bit. Said I was so brave. I didn't want to say there was nothing brave about standing in a trench when a British shell lands next to you. Her father was killed in the Anglo-Boer War. When are you getting married again?"

"I would like some children. Elephant Walk needs lots of children."

"You'd better hurry up."

"So had you."

"Now, have a chicken sandwich. The cook has put pickles in with the sandwiches. Like Mrs Pringle. Albert's mother. She always gave us pickled onions with our doorstop sandwiches on our way to and from school. Old man Pringle was the station porter. Barnaby still sees Tina?"

"Yes."

"Are they lovers?"

"Why don't you ask him? She's a very nice girl. She wants to marry Barnaby."

"Oh, he'll never do that. Barnaby is far too much of a snob. He wouldn't have a railway station porter as the grandfather of his children. Gracious me, no. Doesn't matter to me. Probably doesn't matter to my father and mother. It matters to Barnaby. Tell Tina from me to marry someone else. If she waits for Barnaby, she'll be an old maid when she dies. Anyway, we have an heir to the title in Frederick's son, Richard. Do you know Penelope never married again after Fred was killed in the war? So many of them were killed. So many nice girls are withering away without husbands or children. At least Pen has young Richard and Gwen. He's five years old. They never visit. They've gone back to India. Her grandfather is a merchant prince in India. Along the lines of Clive and the East India company. Her mother and father are both dead. I think Mother would like the children to live at Purbeck Manor... There are no fish in the river to speak of. You know that. Sticklebacks. How is your mother? That grandfather of yours is quite potty. I'll visit you again one day. Even on a peg leg. I can ride a horse. Please come down again before you go home? I get lonely."

Harry had to turn away. So much had happened to both of them since Oxford. The innocence had gone in the war. Blown to pieces. Robert had told Harry he was talking to Lane when the shell arrived. That Lane never answered. There was no Lane. The man had vanished in front of him. The eyes, the mouth, the voice. Had gone. He had not even registered his shattered leg in that appalling moment. Instead of fading into old age, the boy had gone with no recognisable trace. Blown out of the world.

Harry knew he was getting old thinking such thoughts. At Oxford they had only thought of the future. Talked of the future. Of how wonderful and exciting it was to be alive. They never even guessed at the reality. The horror of war. The drudgery of making a living. The sadness of seeing people for what they really were and not what they wanted to be seen to be. Even the questioning of faith and the avalanche of science. Man's evolution from the apes. All the old skulls and bones of not so long ago. Evolution showing the progress of life from the primal swamps up into the trees and down again. From four legs up onto two. The growing size of the craniums as ape became man and the process of thought became what it was.

Harry was glad in his mind to be going back to Africa where life was less complicated. Where money wasn't made by some alchemy on the stock exchange where man had finally found out how to turn lead into gold. A gold that could equally quickly vanish before the eyes because it was not real. Just a number on a cheque that foolish men exchanged for the real gold of life. Land. And what was on it. Only land to Harry could produce real gold.

When he looked, Robert was far away in space. Gone on his travels. Harry smiled, envying his friend. He hoped the false gold of the stock exchange would be quickly invested in the ancient land of the St Clairs. Harry liked the idea of keeping them where they were for more generations. Continuity. He hoped Africa and Rhodesia would provide his own family with so long a destiny. Then he smiled at his own irony. If his mother had first married his father and not his uncle, his destiny would have been with Hastings Court.

"A man can't have two destinies, Robert."

"Of course he can't."

Harry laughed. To Robert it was just a silly question, worth no further pursuit… He had needed the company of his old friend more than he had thought.

13

PAPER MONEY, PAPER DREAMS, MAY TO AUGUST 1922

*T*he share went straight to twenty-seven shillings and Barnaby began to unload. It was not his money with which to gamble. That much he understood. To his father, the money would solve all his financial problems. Purbeck Manor would be safe for another generation. He, the seventeenth Baron St Clair of Purbeck in the County of Dorset would have fulfilled his obligation to the family, to his ancestors. Barnaby was clear in his mind when it came to that kind of obligation.

He was going to sell his shares in Colonial Shipping slowly, not to frighten the market. The City of London was fully aware of his relationship to Harry Brigandshaw. Slowly. That was what he was going to do.

In the end, and most importantly, he was going to make a great display of his magnanimity. He was going to make more for himself than the measly ten per cent forced on him by Harry Brigandshaw. He was going to make himself into a jolly good chap and trade on it for the rest of his life.

He could hear them now. 'Good old Barnaby. He would never cheat you out of a penny. Remember when he gave all that money to his father. And the shares were definitely registered in his name. Barnaby St Clair is sound. You can rest assured on that one.'

When the time was ripe, he was going to leak the story to the newspapers. Have them hunt down the truth while he dined out on being more than a good son to his father. 'Impecunious baron made financially safe by his younger son, the famous Captain Barnaby St Clair who blew up Turkish supply trains with Lawrence of Arabia.'

When he sold the shares no one would ever again dare to question his integrity. The whisperers would be silenced.

Puffed up with his own vanity, Barnaby went to see Tina Pringle in St John's Wood soon after the day's trading came to a close on the London Stock Exchange. The flotation of Colonial Shipping into a public company had been a great success. He wanted Tina to know. He wanted to tell her his plan. She would understand the scheme of things. The irony of being forced to give away a fortune.

"You know something, Barnaby. You are worse than I could ever have thought. Bad enough borrowing money from your inferiors with no intention of giving it back. Now you want to build your name for a really big fraud. You are evil. Plain evil. Just be careful you don't find fleecing people more enjoyable than making money. How is it you manage to turn everything to your advantage? If you insist, you can take me out to dinner. We shall celebrate. Why don't you ask Harry? And Merlin. Give C E Porter a ring so he can give me the creeps. That man positively leers at me thinking he's laying on the charm. He is physically quite revolting. He's so smooth you can almost see the oil dripping down his back..."

"You look very desirable. Whenever I've made a deal, I want to make love."

"Did I tell you I have a new boyfriend? He's rich and besotted with me."

"Why don't you marry him?"

"I think I will."

"What's his name?"

"I forget... Go home and get dressed properly. I want to dance all night. Let's make a splash. Oh, I do enjoy life in London so much... Your father will be surprised."

LADY FREDERICK was playing to full houses at the Shaftesbury Theatre. Only the Saturday matinees were half full. Children's plays and matinees were full on Saturdays. The critics said Somerset Maugham's play would have another long run. Brett knew that was not everything to go by. She had a small, good part which she milked for all it was worth. She had slept with the leading man so she was confident. He was better at acting than making love. He was married which Brett thought might have had something to do with it.

For Brett it was business. Plain business. She was pretty, sexy, a passable if not brilliant actress and nineteen years old. Men had the decisions. Word spread in the theatre. Brett had made up her mind to get a lead in a West End production by one means or the other. The trick, she told herself, was to use her attributes and there was no doubt in Brett's mind which of her attributes was the best. She had 'it'. She knew she had 'it'. Every male who ever looked at her saw 'it'. Best of all 'it' oozed over the footlights into the male section of the audience.

She was going to be a star. People came to look at her not to hear what she said. If she had to sleep with people what did it matter? Most times it was just good fun.

The play itself was trivial. Comfortable to watch. Good dialogue which surprised Brett until she found out the playwright was a queer. Most male writers had no idea what women really thought. What they said was only part of it. The hidden meaning had the power. Only a man with female instincts could have written the words she was asked to say... She had her man on the stage and the men in the audience right in the palm of her hand.

What she was not aware of, what had in fact got her the part, was her boyfriend. Unbeknown to Brett the backer of the play, Oscar Fleming, was always looking for new angels, the theatre-struck fools who poured good money into doubtful plays with the wish to be part of the theatre, the smell of the grease paint, the fame of finding a success, mingling with the stars. They were prepared to invest in the glamour they did not find in their day-to-day boring lives of making money they would ever know how to spend.

BRETT KENTRICH was the hook Oscar Fleming, the backer, wished to put into Harry Brigandshaw. With an angel that rich, Oscar Fleming could put on any old play and make money for himself. Brett had been surprised Oscar never responded to her advances. Oscar Fleming smiled to himself at so much innocence. For him, girls were two a penny. Rich men like Harry Brigandshaw were much more difficult to come by. Oscar Fleming knew dozens of girls just as able to act the part. Some even much better. But none had a man behind them who owned the controlling interest in Colonial Shipping whose shares had gone to thirty shillings by the end of the second week of its public listing.

BRETT WAS ECSTATIC. She received an invitation to every theatre function in London. She was meeting play producers she had only read about in the newspapers. Everyone told her how good she was. She was on her way. Her life was a constant excitement. She was at the centre of the world of theatre. In her young mind, Brett told herself she had arrived. She was going to dazzle the world.

"Why is life so good?" she said to Harry.

"Because you are young."

Harry loved to watch her. Loved to see her joy. Loved to hear for her sake what he felt might well be fake praise. He wanted her to live as long as possible without realising the realities of life. Harry loved her innocence and wanted Brett to have it for as long as possible. He even played along with Oscar Fleming. The man was so transparent Harry wanted to laugh in the man's face.

THE NIGHT OSCAR FLEMING finally propositioned him to finance a new play, Harry was ready to laugh.

"You may be a cynical old bastard," he told himself, "but once again you were right. It's not your bright eyes they are after, Harry, or Brett's. They just plain want your money."

"It's a lovely opportunity, Oscar. Let me think about it," he said with a quizzical smile.

"You'll have to hurry."

"I'm sure I will."

"They all want a piece of this action."

"I'm sure they do… Do you have a part for Brett?"

"Of course we do, old boy."

"Glad to hear that, old chap."

"Can I expect your phone call?"

"Of course you can… You don't want me to read the script, I hope."

At that moment in his life, Harry would have given anything to ride a horse into the African bush and divorce himself from the whole human race.

But he knew he owed something more to Brett. He had eventually found out what he had suspected, and that was she was nineteen years old having told him at the start she was twenty-five. At the time Harry had not even bothered to question the lie. Now he felt guilty. He was burning up the best months of the girl's life. From what Harry had seen a girl had to find her husband while she had the power of youth. Before it was all too late.

They were probably both using each other, but it added up to the same thing. Harry knew what was happening. Brett did not.

"CAN YOU SING?" he asked.

"Of course I can. Everyone can sing."

They were sitting on the small veranda of Harry's flat in Regents Mews. It was Sunday night. The veranda was a wooden projection above the stables at the back of the Mews. Pigeons were cooing from the rooftops of the houses. The noise of London's traffic was muted by the many buildings. Hops grew over the veranda. The big green leaves made the small sitting place a pleasure. There were tight little clusters of hops growing on the vines.

"Then sing me something."

"What do you want to hear?"

"*Greensleeves.* There is a story it was written by King Henry the Eighth. I like to believe the story. My grandfather says we are related somehow to two of his wives. He never said which ones. If you listen to my Grandfather Manderville, the whole of England is related. Maybe we are... Do you know the tune, Brett?"

"I need a lyre or whatever they had in those days... I'll try on my own."

In the soft summer evening, the words so pure lifted gently to the air with a tune so beautiful it made Harry wish to cry for all the loves so lost. Gently, softly, Brett sang the old song to its end. Even the pigeons had stopped their cooing but none had flown away. Neither of them spoke for a long time. Both had felt the magic. Both had felt something more than human life.

"I want you to take singing lessons," Harry said into the perfect silence.

"But I can sing."

"I know you can."

MRS SCHNEIDER WAS an opera singer long before the war. She was at the height of her fame when Bismarck brought the states of Germany together and made Berlin their capital. To Harry, looking at the frail old lady with the snow-white hair, it was difficult to imagine her as the toast of Berlin during the Franco-Prussian War.

Mrs Schneider had lived in London for thirty years giving singing lessons. Berlin had long ago turned its back on her. Only the eyes that looked at Harry with approval were still young. The rest of the old lady was shrivelled and gnarled. They had just finished listening to Brett sing a melange of songs.

"Oh, thank you, Herr Brigandshaw. You bring an old lady much happiness. A voice so pure is rare in heaven. Here on earth I never hear it before. Maybe, yes, I exaggerate. But not too much, no. Not too much. What is your first name, young lady?"

"Brett."

"Then I will call you Brett. To act and sing. Oh, such joy in heaven. How did you find me, Herr Brigandshaw?"

"I have a man named Grainger. He is good at finding the best."

"Then treasure your man you call Grainger. Often the best is never found. What you want, Brett? To sing opera? To sing musical?"

"You really think I have a good voice?"

"Not at the present. But you will. Breathing. Control. Phrasing. There is so much to learn on the road to perfection."

They all looked at each other. Conspirators.

"You'd better get me to the theatre, Harry, or I'll be late. I still have to earn a living."

"Three times a week," said Mrs Schneider as she saw them to the studio door.

By the time Brett had received her tenth singing lesson from Mrs Schneider, the story of Barnaby St Clair's generosity broke in the *Daily Mail*, the *Daily Telegraph* and the *Evening Standard*. After deducting his ten per cent, Barnaby had given his father a cheque for forty-one thousand pounds. To Barnaby's surprise the giving of the money had given him pleasure. He told Tina when he arrived back from Purbeck Manor that the smile on his father's face was so bright they could have seen in the dark.

With the cheque in his father's hand, Barnaby had been taken to look at the calf born the previous day.

"First Merlin and now you, Barnaby. I'm a lucky father. You have saved the family line."

His mother had not been so gullible when Barnaby came back alone from the ten-acre field.

"Where did you get the money, Barnaby?"

"Harry, Mother," said Robert interrupting. "I'll explain later."

"Then he didn't steal it?"

"No, Mother."

"Thank God for that."

Lady St Clair looking from one son to the other, sat down heavily on the bench outside the dining room. The French windows from the great dining room were open to the summer day.

"Then it is something to do with Colonial Shipping going public?" she said looking from one to the other.

"Yes, Mother," said Robert.

"Poor Lucinda. She would have been happy in Africa... I think I will go to my room. I like to think about these things on my own... The Lord works in strange ways."

TINA PRINGLE KNEW she was running out of time. Barnaby was so self-centred nothing had worked. All her well-planned ways to make him marry her had come to nothing.

"I will not be his damn mistress," she said to her empty flat. "Who the hell does he think he is? I am the only person who understands his bloody nonsense and still wants him for the rest of his life. With or without any damn money."

The kitten Barnaby had given her that was almost a cat did not even bother to get off the kitchen chair. Tina picked up the tabby cat and gave it a hard squeeze. The cat clawed her hand and was flung on the kitchen floor. The cat got back on the chair and went to sleep.

"Damn you, Pickles. Why don't you listen to me?" There was blood dripping from the back of her right hand. Tina sucked the wound and tasted blood. Frustration made her kick the wall which hurt her toes. She was wearing slippers.

Barnaby had left ten minutes ago. Tina was furious with herself for sleeping with the man. He had left to go to C E Porter's offices with a big smirk on his face. He would not now come back for a few days. Until the pressure again mounted in his loins.

The damn man had not even given her a lift down to Corfe Castle to visit her parents. At first she had thought he was taking someone else. She even hoped he was. The truth that he did not wish to be seen with her in Dorset was worse.

For a brief moment, she thought of going back to Johannesburg. Until her obsession surged. The jealousy came back screaming through every fibre of her body.

She kicked the wall again with the other foot to see how much it hurt.

JUSTINE VOSS WAS DREAMING of the family she was going to have. There were five boys and five girls evenly spaced. Boy, girl. Boy, girl.

There was a big house with many rooms. Servants were ready to look after her perfectly brought up children. The elder boys had tutors. They learnt Latin and French. Mathematics and the arts of science. The elder girls had tutors. They read good books. Learnt needlepoint. How to play the piano. How to listen to a man… Everything in Justine's mind was definite except for the whereabouts of the great house and the name of the man who was to be the father of her ten well-behaved children… It was all she wanted. All she had ever wanted. A family. With her family surrounding her she would be happy for the rest of her life.

Justine fantasised for large parts of her day. Always the same fantasy. What she had not had in her past she was going to have in her future. Her family would be a shrine to her poor father killed by the Boers in the Anglo-Boer War. To Justine, the Boers were more wicked than the devil.

MRS VOSS WATCHED her daughter dream away the summer day. Justine was to turn twenty-three in thirteen days' time.

Mrs Voss could remember the day her child was born as clearly as yesterday. The loneliness of the nursing home in Athens. Not one familiar face. Not even sympathy for her pain. No one from England had come to help. Not even a word.

They had said for a first child the birth was easy. Only the matron had spoken a little English. For twenty-three years she had not been alone. Now it was coming back again. The loneliness. The sense of permanent loss.

The angelic look on Justine's face had been on hers.

Justine was alone in the small arbour that overlooked the sea. A small parasol kept the eleven o'clock sun from the unblemished white of her face. Mrs Voss was standing in the bay window of her bedroom two stories above the slope that dropped all the way down to the ring of beach. They were both looking out to sea, a calm blue sea, sparkling in the morning sun.

Because of the curve of Hope Cove she could see her daughter's face. Justine was yards away and down to her right. The girl had walked and sat. Walked and sat. Ever since breakfast.

There was a small boat in the cove with a red sail. A man was casting a line from the grassy slope of the cove, not far from the water's edge. Mrs Voss stood back from the window, not to be seen. The picture was framed by the large sash window. She had raised the bottom half as far as it would go. Quietly, very quietly. The cup of tea on her chest of drawers had gone cold. She caught the smell of flowers wafting up from her garden. She could hear the gardener working at the back of the house. The sea in front of her was the English Channel. The village of Salcombe was near to them, a little way to the east along the coast.

The house at Hope Cove in Devonshire had been in her family for three generations. It was the place they came to for eight weeks every summer. Never at any other time. During the rest of the year, the servants had the house to themselves.

As a girl of six, Felicity Voss remembered wanting to be a servant so she would not have to go back to Surrey and the house in Epsom at the end of the summer holiday. Always she went. Always they came back as a family the next summer.

One day Felicity hoped the house would go to Justine. She knew the girl loved their summer house. It would all depend who she married. The girl was in love, she thought. The look she saw down below spoke of love. Twice Justine had mentioned Harry Brigandshaw. The girl was agitated. The thought of Harry Brigandshaw taking her daughter to Rhodesia made Felicity's heart stop. Her mouth went dry. She drew back from the open window.

Her daughter got up and began to walk round the garden. The gardener came into the frame made by the window. The small boat with the red sail had moved out of sight. The fisherman had a fish on the end of his line. Consumed by fear, she remembered Justine's words each time they spoke of Harry Brigandshaw.

"HE'S GOING home in September. To Africa. Wonderful Africa. He's so wonderful, Mummy. He tells me his farm is beautiful. Thousands of acres. A river down the garden from the houses. He once had a pet giraffe, but it was killed by an Englishman for its head. It was terrible. I want to go to Africa."

"Has he asked you?" she had said.

"Oh, no. We don't even go out. He has a girlfriend called Brett. She is on the stage. Do you know, Brett's younger than me? She says she's twenty-five, but she's not. I caught her out on the year she was born. I asked her if she was born before the Boer War and she said she wasn't. Three years after the end. I think she told Harry she was twenty-five. So it's not my age. He likes young girls. His wife was killed by a madman. Poor Harry. I wish he would ask me out. He's so handsome."

"You think he might?"

"Oh, no. He loves Brett... All the others want to take me out. Never Harry. I see him lots with Brett... What was it like to be in love?"

Felicity had the idea of staying in Devonshire until the end of September. When Harry went home and was no longer a threat to her peace of mind.

"When are we going back to London, Mummy?"

"Next week, darling. On Tuesday."

DOWN BELOW THE fisherman was casting his line. Justine had walked out of sight. A ship that had been on the horizon caught Felicity's eye. The smoke was trailing the ship from the one funnel. Seagulls mocked her. Lonely in their cries. Mournful.

At that moment Felicity had no idea what she was going to do with the rest of her life.

"I'm too young for it all to be over."

Down below, her gardener looked up to see who had spoken.

"Morning, ma'am. Lovely day."

"Beautiful, Frank," she called down.

She loved the spoken accent of Devonshire. He had been working in the garden all his life. He had a small cottage for life in the village. Felicity's grandfather had bought the cottage. Frank was about her own age. One of his sons was now the garden boy. Learning to be a gardener. The house was practical as well as beautiful. All their fruit and vegetables came from their own garden. The fish came from the sea. The garden boy's most important job at morning rise was to take out the rowing boat and catch fish. Fresh mackerel straight from the sea. He usually went out with his friends when the sea was kind. In the winter the skiffs stayed in the small boat shed at the bottom of the garden.

Justine had picked an armful of flowers and was coming back into the house.

When Felicity went downstairs, the flowers were beautifully arranged in a silver vase on the dining room table. The butterfly, a small cabbage white, flew from the vase of flowers and through the open window, out into the summer day.

Felicity walked from the house and down to the tiny beach before her daughter could see the tears in her eyes. The girl had looked so happy.

ON THE MONDAY before Felicity Voss was to take her daughter back to London with what she feared would bring the inevitable consequence of losing her, Len Merryl, Jenny Merryl's brother, returned to England from his travels around the world, eighteen months older and wiser.

He had signed off the *SS Runnymede* at Liverpool at the end of its journey from Singapore. The name of the ship was grander than the old rust bucket that had brought them safely home. Only the captain knew how he had brought the four thousand-ton, thirty-year-old ship round the Cape of Good Hope. They had anchored off Cape Town for three days in a raging southeaster, finally protected by the mass of Table Mountain from the hurricane force wind gusting at eighty miles an hour.

On the fourth day the waters of Table Bay were as calm as a millpond, the wind having lashed itself to a standstill during the night. Had Len known his sister was living in Rhodesia sixteen hundred miles to the north he would have considered breaking the contract with his ship. Instead they had rested three days in Cape Town harbour before sailing on the last leg of their journey to Liverpool. They carried a cargo of raw rubber from the rubber plantations of Malaya.

"NO WONDER they call this place the Cape of Storms," Ben Willard had said when they got off the ship in Cape Town. "Without the old mountain the *Runnymede* would have been a goner. All of us down in Davy Jones's locker. Be sure, Len, you have a good captain before signing on for a voyage... You want to go find a whore?"

Len had said no thank you, the memories of Cousin Mildred still vivid in his mind.

"I wonder if she's all right?" he had said.

"Who, mate?"

"My cousin Mildred. Had a kid by a bloke killed in the war."

"You in the war, Len? Never talked none on the ship."

"Tail end. Never saw no action."

"Merchant navy kept me out of the army. Sometimes in the North Atlantic with all them Jerry submarines we all wished we were in France. Oil tankers. I was on oil tankers. One torpedo up your arse and you all go to heaven on a fireball... Mind you, better than jumpin'. Then you just freeze to death in the bleedin' water. If we don't go for whores can we get drunk? Know a place in Long Street with a pretty barmaid, dark but who cares. Said her people were brought over by the Dutch from Malaya in the last century. Or the one before. Hope she still there. Real nice. Wish I could remember her name?... Girl in every port... Come on, Len. This bar's only full of drunks."

Three weeks later the two had parted company on the docks of Liverpool with little chance of meeting again. Len remembered. And her name. Teresa. She was Cape Malayan. A Christian or she couldn't work with alcohol she said. Muslims didn't drink. Len had asked why and received a shrug for an answer. Teresa was quite beautiful. She had smiled at Len every time he bought a round of drinks.

Len had not remembered leaving her bar or how he got back to his ship. They had sailed the next day. Len still carried a picture of her face in his mind.

He was not looking forward to seeing his mother or his two brothers. If he had had somewhere else to go in Liverpool, he would not have gone home. After signing off the *Runnymede* he had seven pounds and change in his pocket. Along with his money went the sad thought he had no idea what to do next. Other than being a shrimp fisherman like his brothers on ten per cent of the catch.

With his ship's duffel bag over his shoulder caught in his right hand by the rope, he boarded the local train that went through the Mersey Tunnel, down the Wirral of Cheshire and dropped him off at Neston. It was still early on the Monday morning. Washday.

When Len reached the row of ten semi-detached houses where he was born the washing lines were all billowing wet washing. There was a good wind from the sea whipping up the white sheets pegged to the washing lines. Only Mrs Trollope had not put out the weekly washing. From Mrs Bowman to Mrs Green, Mrs Snell to his mother, all Len could see of the backyard gardens was washing. When he reached his mother's back door by ducking under the washing line, he could smell the soap on the washing.

"Blimey, it's Len. What you doin' here?" said his mother.

With an inward sigh, Len realised he was home.

"Hello, Mum. How you been?"

"Lousy, no thanks to you." His mother always complained. Jenny had said it was the only thing their mother enjoyed. Complaining. Being miserable. Probably making everyone around her miserable. It had been just the same before their father had been killed in the war. Their mother liked to wallow in self-pity. The deaths of two sons and a husband in the army had given her a lifelong licence to wallow in her own misery.

Len wanted to escape. His old pair of boots was still in the room he had once shared with two of his brothers. Only Jenny among the children had had a room to herself. To Len's surprise his room did not look lived in. The window had not been opened for some time. There was a pervading smell of mould. The beds were made but, when he put his hand inside, the sheets felt damp. He had pulled the sheets from one bed and hung them over the window which opened inwards stopping them from blowing off. In winter, gales from the sea lashed the houses. The boots were still covered in the grease that kept them waterproof and stopped them cracking. He put them on.

With his old catapult in his pocket Len went downstairs and said he was going for a walk. The shrimp boats were out and his mother was still washing some of the vicar's clothes. The ones on the line belonged to his brothers. Neither had found a wife while he was away. Everything in the house was much the same. Except his mother's hair. Her arms, dipping into the washtub and running the clothes over the washboard were still the size of hams. Her face was still blotched red from the salt wind from the sea. Her fingers were red from chilblains that would swell and hurt her in the winter. It was the hair that shocked Len. In the time he had been away her hair had gone white. It made his mother look ten years older. He wondered if there was anything in her life that gave her real pleasure.

He had never thought of his mother before. Only himself.

There was a lunch box on the scrubbed white kitchen table. Between the washing while he was upstairs his mother had taken the time to make him lunch. He wished he could love her.

"Thanks, Mum… Where are they?"

"Fishin'."

"You all right, Mum?"

"Do I look all right?"

Len did not reply. With the lunch box under his arm and the sun shining, he went out the back of the house and ducked under the washing line.

"Morning, Mrs Snell. Not going to rain?" The woman was leaning over the short fence.

"That you, Len? Filled out, you 'ave."

"Thank you, Mrs Snell."

Outside the garden gate Len stopped to look across the mudflats. The tide was out. The hills of Wales on either side of the flats made by the River Dee looked nearer than he remembered.

He walked down the leafy lane and began to enjoy his first day back in England. He had missed the smells and sounds of the English countryside. They were friendly. Never threatening.

An hour later, well away from the village of Neston, Len climbed over a farmer's gate and walked across his field. The cows took no notice of him.

Under a tall oak on the cropped grass, Len sat and opened his lunch box. Inside were slices of buttered bread and a large chunk of Cheshire cheese. In the corner was a pot of fresh shrimps. He was starving hungry and chewed off the cheese and bread separately. He was so hungry he even ate the shrimps in their shells. They tasted good, salty, cooked as he knew in seawater. Around him the insects droned through the summer day.

The bull from across the field came and had a look at him. Len lay where he was with his back to the oak tree. The bull went off again. A fine bull with black testicles ranging through the top of the grass where it had not yet been eaten down. Len closed his eyes and fell asleep without a worry in the world.

WHEN HE WOKE, Len felt the instant joy at being alone. On the *Runnymede* they were always on top of each other. Growing up, there had been too many of them in a small house. As a boy he had got away into the fields to avoid the constant sibling bickering. They had all kept on picking at each other. Fraying his nerves. Len needed peace in his life and a place he could think on his own.

The afternoon sun had now moved, peering at him under the tree. The warmth of the sun had brought him awake. He never wore a watch. By the angle of the sun it was six o'clock. He had slept in peace a long time.

The cows and the bull had gone from the field. Len wondered if the farmer had seen him asleep under the tree and let him be. The gate to the field must have been opened and shut to let the animals out. Len liked the idea of being looked at in his sleep and left alone. You could do things like that in England he told himself.

If he had something to do and somewhere to stay he would like to live in England. Not in London. Never again in London. Len liked the fields and the smell of the sea.

He hoped when his brothers came home they would not argue with him. Tim and John had always been close. It was lucky neither of them had been killed in the war. They had both been too young. Which was why they were not yet married. Lying on his back looking at a grey squirrel looking at him from the tree above Len wondered why people always argued with each other. The squirrel was flicking its tail with anger at the danger. Not sure what to do. All around Len, birds were calling from the trees and woods.

There was a good thick wood on one side of the field that Len remembered. Len thought of firing his catapult at the squirrel and then asked himself why he wanted to hurt the poor thing. He concluded that down inside he was as nasty as the rest of them. Which made him think of Cousin Mildred but he didn't know why. He made a mental note to ask his mother if she knew what had happened to Cousin Mildred and her little boy.

Instead of shooting at the squirrel with his catapult Len got up and began shooting last year's acorns out into the field. He knew that if the cows had still been there, he would have aimed at them. The farmer would have chased him away. He was as nasty as the rest of them.

He walked across to the woods but was unable to go far inside. The brambles were thick. There were nettles on the edge of the wood that stung his right hand. He found a dock leaf and rubbed it into the nettle sting. Len thought it made a difference.

If he had had a shotgun, he would have killed the rabbit that sat in the field just outside the line of nettles. The rabbit lifted its tail to him and hopped away. Len liked rabbit stew. It was one of his favourites.

He went back to the oak tree and picked up the empty lunch box. To have left it behind would have caused an argument at the time. He owed his mother more than an argument for his lunch.

It was past seven o'clock by the sun and Len began to wend his way home. He was not in a hurry despite being hungry.

He wondered what Ben Willard was now doing with himself. Which made him think of Teresa, the Cape Malay in the bar in Long Street. Cape Town felt a long, long, way away. Teresa was still very pretty in his mind. He thought she was the prettiest girl he had ever seen. He wished he could remember leaving her bar. He hoped he had said something nice to her.

Drinking was silly. It was nice at the time but he could never remember what happened after the fifth drink. Once in Colombo, he and Ben got into a fight with the crew of another ship. The ship was French. He remembered that. The fight had sobered him up. They were all too drunk to do any real damage to each other. In the end they were arm in arm and getting drunk again.

He had liked that evening and the bar. The next day the *Runnymede* had sailed away from the island of Ceylon and all he could remember of the place was a fight in a bar.

He had done better in Singapore while looking for a ship. But not a great deal. Most of his money from signing off the *Matilda*, his previous ship from Hong Kong, had been spent in the Singapore bars by the time he signed on with the *Runnymede*.

The original idea had been to learn something from his travels. He had lost his virginity in Singapore to a Chinese girl he could not remember. Afterwards he was glad she had been clean.

THE SHRIMP BOATS were coming up the River Dee like swans with their wings behind them when they came into land on the water. He had seen the swans on the River Thames when he lived in Lambeth with the Italian. The wings were the shrimp nets held back on long arms that were as long as the shrimp boats. The nets pointed back and one of them had a big hole in the middle that would need mending. He could clearly see the hole, even at the distance of half a mile.

The boats were fitted with outboard motors and Len could smell the petrol fumes coming in on the wind. From where he was far away he could not recognise his brothers. He hoped there were lots of shrimp on board. The more shrimp the less the Merryl family argued with each other.

They would not be home for another hour as they had to unload the catch which went to the factory for shelling and putting in the pots to be sealed by boiled butterfat and sent down to London to market.

To Len it had always seemed in England as if everyone was doing something for somebody else. Like bringing in the raw rubber on the *Runnymede*. In the very old days, people ate what they grew. They hunted for their meat. Caught fish for themselves. Picked the blackberries and mushrooms from the fields. Len thought there would have been more satisfaction in that kind of life. Fewer arguments. People would not have been able to cheat each other so easily.

He would have preferred to see the shrimp boats come in under sail as they had once done when he was a small boy. Or had his father told him about the sails? He had not thought about his father for a long time. He wondered why Germans had killed his father and why his father had gone out to kill Germans. He was sure none of the soldiers had anything personal against each other. Not at the beginning. Before they started shooting others dead.

For five minutes he looked for a round flat stone to bounce over the water of the river. Finally he gave up. Stones were rare in the black mud at the edge of the water. One of his brothers had said there were more stones in the Welsh bank of the river. He could not remember which brother. None of them had ever been to Wales in their lives.

It was time to go home.

NO ONE WAS interested in where he had been. Tim and John were home. Len had dawdled as long as he could before letting himself in the back gate. The washing had gone but the wooden pegs were still on the line.

"The water was too cold. Shrimps don't like cold water." He had not seen Tim for two years and this was his greeting.

"That's bad luck. How are you?"

"Bloody fishin' don't pay. No room on boat for you, Len. Don't think of trying to come with us." John the elder of the two had a shifty look. His right eye wandered off which made him look shifty.

"Thanks for the lunch, Mum." He gave her back the empty box.

"You all want to go down pub?" he asked them all, remembering his seven pounds.

"Closes in an hour," said Tim.

"Get down a couple."

No one seemed interested. Tim and John were wearing long trousers attached to thick braces that ran up over their shoulders. Neither of them had on a shirt. They had washed off the saltwater and put on trousers. Neither wore shoes. They were like ugly strangers to him.

"You're too late for supper," said his mother.

"Anyone hear from our Jenny?" It was the only thing in common he could think of on the spur of the moment. Strange the boys did not want a drink.

"She's in Rhodesia. Nursin'." His mother had spoken.

"Does she write?"

"Not much point when I can't read. That no-good Cousin Mildred gone too so they say. With 'er bastard. Good riddance to bad rubbish, I say."

With a deep shock, Len remembered holding Cousin Mildred naked in the bed that was soaked with her fever sweat. He remembered the doctor who had made her well. The doctor had been old and kind. The little boy's name was Johnny. After Johnny Lake who had died in the war before his son was born.

"Excuse me," he said to them all.

Upstairs in his room, he packed everything back into his duffel bag. He was crying again for Mildred. And for himself. He kept the boots on and went downstairs. Nobody noticed the duffel bag over his shoulder. He kissed his mother on her red-blotched face. He had wiped the tears from his eyes before coming downstairs.

"I'll get something to eat in the pub," he said to them. No one even looked at him as he went out of the front door.

THE NEXT DAY he went back to the docks to look for a ship that was going to Africa. He had not gone home. He had not gone to the pub. He had walked back to the field where the cows were still gone and laid himself down under the oak. By the time he fell asleep, plans for his future were formulating.

When the sun had come up Len was full of hope. He had made up his mind to go to Africa while sitting under the oak. The squirrel had gone.

He was hungry and very happy. As if his life had just begun.

HE SOON FOUND out Liverpool was not the port to look for a ship that would take him to Africa. That the *Runnymede* rounding the Cape with a cargo of raw rubber was an exception. They told him to go down south. To Southampton.

With the strength of his mind he wanted to see Cousin Mildred again. He had saved her life. She had not died of pneumonia. There was a bond.

Instead of wasting money on a train ticket he made for the road and hitched a ride in a truck. He could smell the fish in the truck. The fish were packed in ice.

IT TOOK LEN four days to get to Southampton. Always he slept under a hedge. It had not rained in the night and during his journey.

Len found a cheap room. Every day he went down to the port looking for a berth. In his pocket he carried the discharge papers signed by the captains of the *Runnymede* and the *Matilda*. With them were certificates of character. Both captains had said his character was good. It was just a matter of time before he found himself a ship.

His family had made him turn his back. It was not his fault. He would have liked to say more to his mother. With a sharp pang in his heart he knew he would never see her again. All that pain she had been through for him and he would never see her again. He was not sure what was worse. Being a bad mother. Or being a bad son. Then he had remembered the lunch box on the scrubbed white kitchen table and felt even more terrible. He wanted more from life than pain and feeling terrible. He wanted to be happy. His family in Neston were not happy. He sadly wondered to himself if they ever would be happy. Whether they would ever see the point of life.

The days dragged into weeks and still Len Merryl could not find a berth on a ship that would take him to Africa. They all wanted crew for round trips or discharge in the Far East. He thought of buying himself a passage but was jealous of his seven pounds.

The money began to dwindle as July came and went. He was strangely content.

MERLIN ST CLAIR felt comfortable. He had never felt so comfortable. Esther had left Mickelham at the end of August and came up to London. Merlin had taken a thirty-year lease on a small flat for them and given Esther a housekeeping allowance. It was like a marriage though they were not married and Merlin did not spend every night in the small flat. He had allowed Esther to choose her own furniture and curtains and though much of it was not to his taste, it made Esther happy. When Esther was happy all three of them were happy which was all the time. The strangest thing to him was Genevieve loved her father. Merlin had never been loved by anyone before. Never been told before.

She sat at his feet or on the side of the bed he shared with her mother and looked at him with the same strange eyes that looked back at her. It was as if they both knew what was going on inside the other one. The child liked to listen to what he had to say. Merlin liked a good listener. Merlin was willingly taken in by his daughter.

ESTHER, aware of the alternatives in her life, was happy to play second fiddle to an eight-year-old. She liked the flat in Chelsea. She liked the River Thames flowing down below at fifty yards from her bedroom window. She liked being lazy. She liked not having to think what was going to happen to them.

At twenty-six she was too fat for some men. Her large breasts hung lower. Her face was red, the cheeks more pronounced. She did not have the energy to make herself attractive to men as she had done in her teens when it was all new. The arrangement suited her, especially the days when Merlin stayed at his Park Lane flat and she could be alone without having to smile and pretend all the time. She had not been to the Park Lane flat and did not wish to go there. Any more than she wished to mingle with his upper-class friends. Not that his friends would have talked to her. She even giggled at the thought. They were bigger snobs than Merlin.

"This is my friend Esther. The mother of my child. She was the barmaid at the Running Horses at Mickelham. During the war she married a corporal..." All said with his eyeglass screwed into his one dark eye and staring at them, daring them to say anything. Every time, the thought made Esther go into giggles or peals of laughter.

They lived a quiet life, and that was fine by Esther. When he visited, she had the supper ready. She never complained. He could do what he liked. He paid the rent and gave her enough money to buy their food and clothes and once in a while go to a musical on her own. The flat was quite safe for Genevieve for a few hours the child was left alone.

What Merlin did not know and would never be told by Esther was the act put on by their daughter was more monumental than her own. They both liked being kept. They acted their parts. They paid for their supper. Or as she told her one friend Joan who visited from Lambeth in the East End each time they were alone.

"It's a job, ducks. A job. Better than a whore. Better than a wife. Needs doing well. Let him feel he is the most important sod on earth and he'll do what you want. Sick I was of the drunks in the Running Horses' bar. Tell you, Joan, every man's a pain in the arse drunk. Pain in the arse when they're not drunk but that's another story. Fact is, Merlin is not unkind. Never raises his voice. Never hits me. Likes to cuddle with the lights out more than fuck."

"You going to 'ave another kid by 'im?"

"Not bloody likely. That Genevieve is more trouble than a pack of monkeys. You know what she did last week? Brought 'ome a cat. In comes Father. Cat sees Father and jumps out the bloody window. Now you 'ave a look, Joan. It's two stories up. Never seen the cat again. Hit the lawn down there runnin' it did. Animals don't like Merlin. Only owls, he says. Only owls."

"It's that funny eye of his."

"You can say that again."

"Gives me the creeps."

"Wasn't so bad when I first met 'im."

"Should think not."

"Want another gin?"

"Never say no to someone else's gin… Where is Genevieve?"

"Down by the river. Likes feeding them ducks. Got 'er father around her little finger, she 'as."

"Maybe she loves 'im."

"You think so?"

"If she don't, she's a bloody good actress."

"She says to me it's a game."

"Pullin' both your legs, I'd think… Just look at 'em together. Peas in a pod. Not even the devil would say they weren't father and daughter. I felt a bit jealous, Esther. No one loved me like that before."

"Well I never. Life really is a strange thing."

"You never know what's in another person's head. Even a kid's head."

GENEVIEVE SAW life at the level of her mother's belly button. Which was once a week when the tub in what was called the bathroom was filled with hot water from the kitchen. They both took a bath in the same water. The water was heated on the kitchen stove. The flat they lived in was old. The even older flats, her mother had told her, had a tin tub they put in the middle of the kitchen floor to have a bath. Genevieve thought the older flats were more sensible. Not so far to hump the hot water. Her father told her his other flat had running hot water whatever that was. The idea of hot water running around the house gave Genevieve an even weirder view of her father. When she looked at the top of his trousers she wondered if her father even had a navel. She thought of asking her mother. The idea of asking her father never crossed her mind.

Her view of life had really started at Mickelham. The Running Horses was a small hotel and once she had heard a child tell her father that she loved him. The result had astonished Genevieve, the father who the night before had hit the mother hard across the face and told her she was something called a bitch, dropped down on one knee and gazed into the girl's face. The big, nasty man was crying he was so happy. Or so it seemed to Genevieve.

"Can I have a tricycle?" the little girl had asked looking lovingly into the horrible face with the big whiskers and the tears.

"Of course you can, my darling."

And so it was. The next day to Genevieve's astonishment the little girl was riding round the parking lot on a bright red tricycle. It was all so wonderfully easy. The little girl was six years old.

When Genevieve was told she had a father who wasn't dead, all she could see was that tricycle. At first she had been shy with the man with the round piece of glass stuck over his eye. Tentatively, she had use the magic word 'Daddy' even before they went to live in London. She didn't mind London as the river was nice to look at. There was a path along the side of the river that was flat. Just right for a tricycle. With excitement building up to burst she bided her time.

She was alone by the river with the man who liked to hold her hand while they both stared at the river. He was not wearing the piece of glass in his eye. The piece of glass when it was in his eye was the size of a penny. Her mother was nowhere to be seen. If it went all wrong, it would not matter.

"I love you, Daddy," she said in her smallest voice, fluttering her eyes down to look at his big hand holding hers.

To Genevieve's surprise and joy it worked. The man she called Daddy went down on one knee and looked adoringly into her face. With great effort, mental and physical, she managed to squeeze out a tear. Which made it happen. The man now at her head level was crying. Big tears were going down between the dark brown side whiskers that came to the line of his jaw. Almost holding her breath she went on with her plan.

"Can I have a tricycle?"

"Of course you can, darling. What colour would you like it to be?"

"Red, Daddy." Then she flung herself at her father's chest so he would not see the triumph in her eyes.

After that it was the easiest game of her life. She followed him wherever he went when he came to the flat. Only the idea of finding a cat had been wrong. Even if she had taken the cat from a house down the river. After the cat jumped out of the window, she just fluttered her eyes at him and called him Daddy.

After the first time she was careful not to tell him again that she loved him. Once was enough. Whatever she asked for she was given. She did not have to use the magic words again.

Life for Genevieve had never been more beautiful. What she liked most about the new game in her life was not having to do anything in return. Just make him feel she loved him whenever he came for a visit.

For a while she wanted to ask her mother what the word 'love' meant. It was a very powerful word whatever it was so she kept it to herself. The red tricycle was perfect. So were the little red dresses he gave her that went with the red tricycle.

When she heard Aunty Joan ask her mother about another child, she went quite cold. Looking up from the lawn at the open window she made up her mind. If another child came into her life, she would kill it. No one else was going to call her daddy, daddy. To make her point clear, she got off her red tricycle and stamped her foot hard on the lawn. She had not even listened to the bit about the cat.

Getting back on the tricycle, she pointed it through the towpath and rode as fast as it would go across the lawn. A family of ducks jumped into the river as she passed. He was hers to get what she wanted. No one was going to interfere.

14

JOURNEY HOME, SEPTEMBER 1922

By the end of September the swallows were lining up along the telephone lines. Len Merryl had watched them from his rooftop room in Southampton while he waited for a ship to Beira. For days the small birds had been sweeping around the evening sky chasing the late summer insects.

The day Len signed up on the *SS Corfe Castle* the birds were twittering in a long line, their tails dipping up and down to keep their balance on the wire. The next day there was not a swallow in the English sky. Len sat in the window on his last night in England, lonely for the birds, wondering what had become of them.

"Gone to Africa, Len," said his landlady in the morning when he made his goodbyes. She had been kind to him in the weeks of his waiting. "They'll be in the Cape before you reach Beira. Most of them. The strong. By February they'll be winging back to England. Now make sure you send me a postcard when you reach Salisbury safe and sound."

"How do you know all these things Mrs Steadham?"

"I'm an old woman, Len Merryl. Since Frank died my company has been my tenants, young men like you. With dreams. Going out to the Empire. They talked to a lonely old widow. One of them knew all about the swallows... All that way on a wing. Stuck in my mind. When they come back in the spring, I asked them how they'd been. Even when I'm sick in the cold winters, I think of the birds coming home. Gives me a purpose to live... Frank and I never had children we didn't. No, we never had no children... Now, you have a good life Len Merryl. You go with my blessing. Don't forget that. I'll think of you on your journey as I think of them swallows. God bless you."

AT ELEVEN O'CLOCK that morning the *SS Corfe Castle* was due to sail.

From Len's vantage point on the upper deck he could see it all. Late provisions were still coming up the lower gangplank, the porters hurrying up into the ship, pushing past other porters coming down. The gangplank to the first-class deck was still open. The brass band had been playing a medley of old tunes for half an hour. For some reason the captain and officers were lined up at the entrance from the first-class gangplank looking down on the deck side. The hawsers fore and aft were still holding the ship to shore. Both funnels were making smoke. Len could smell the sulphur. They would need to swab the deck again at first light. The new worsted of his seaman's sweater made his skin itch. He had forgotten to wash the new sweater before wearing it. To the passengers Len leaning on his broom was invisible. The passengers saw passengers, never the crew. One of the prettiest girls Len had ever seen was standing at the rail ten yards away looking down at the last-minute commotion on the dockside. A part of the customs shed was wide open. A last pile of luggage came out on a trolley and was rushed to the lower gangplank. A man and two women came out of the shed and walked to the bottom of the first-class gangplank. The man let the older woman go first. Then the younger. Len guessed they were mother and daughter. Both had looked up to see where they were going and shown Len their faces. The man who was too young to be the father came up last. He was the last passenger to board the ship. He did not look up as if he knew where he was going.

The pretty girl at the rail leaned over to look down. She had brown hair with a suggestion of red. Len was staring at her. As if she felt his stare she turned and looked at him. The girl had large brown, bedroom eyes that gave him a flash. Under the taut dress Len thought there were large breasts. When she looked down again at the shore, she looked angry. Not at Len. At something she saw down below.

A girl had appeared from the customs shed to watch the ship sail. She stood behind the crowd. Len could see the girl was just as pretty as the angry girl who had now turned her back on the docks. Len speculated there was a connection between the two of them. The one on the dockside, even at a distance, was strangely familiar to Len. He had seen her before. It was the way she walked. Theatrical. Every movement a gesture.

The girl with the brown eyes flashed another look at Len which told him to mind his own business. How had she known what he was thinking?

At the top of the gangplank, the captain was shaking the hand of the last passenger. The first-class gangplank came away from the ship. When Len looked down to his right, the service gangplank had gone. The hawsers were being removed from the bollards at both ends of the ship. The band was playing *Land of Hope and Glory*. The ship's horn let out three deafening blasts. The passengers were all at the rails, some holding paper chains that ran down the side of the ship to friends below.

The third-class passengers were shouting obscenities to their friends onshore. The girl at the back of the crowd had gone. Len looked for her. The pretty girl near to him had also gone.

A gap appeared between ship and shore. Len saw clear water looking down. The band played *God Save the King*. Everyone on the ship and shore came to attention.

By the time he reached the seamen's quarters in the bowels of the ship they were at sea.

"Len Merryl. I'll be damned."

It was Ben Willard. From the *Runnymede*. Len had never expected to see him again. They shook hands. At least they both had one friend on a strange ship. It was a good feeling for both of them.

"I want to see Teresa again. Remember the girl in Cape Town? Ancestors came from Java. Slaves of the Dutch. Don't you remember her, Len?"

"I don't think so," lied Len. He was jealous. He thought she had only smiled at him.

"You said you were staying in England. *Runnymede* was your last voyage."

"My sister's in Rhodesia. I'm going to join her. And Mildred."

"Who's Mildred?"

"She's my cousin."

"How was home?"

"Terrible, Ben. They didn't even know I was there."

"Didn't ask you nothin' where you'd been?"

"Not a word."

"Not good. We have two days in Cape Town. The ship's half cargo and half passengers. Takes two days to unload cargo for Cape Town and take on new. Did you know we've got the owner on board?"

"So that was it. Saw him come on board. Why captain was waiting at the top of the gangplank. Who is he?"

"Grandson of the Pirate, they called him. Some did, anyway. The grandson has a farm in Rhodesia where he wants to live. Inherited all that money and not wanted. No telling people. Shot down twenty-three Germans in the war. Came over to fight for us. Came back when he inherited the shipping line. Now he's going back home. They say there's something about Africa that makes you go back again."

"I hope so."

"You plannin' staying in Africa?"

"That's my plan. I signed on as far as Beira. Lucky, I was. A bloke of another Empire Castle ship fell sick in Beira. Yellow fever. Put 'im ashore. Now he's okay. He'll take my place back 'ome through the Suez Canal. Lucky, I was. I get paid for going where I want to go. Just pay for the train trip from Beira to Salisbury."

FROM THE THIRD-CLASS rail, standing back from the paper chain throwers, Mervyn Braithwaite had also watched Harry Brigandshaw come on board. Then he had gone down to the cabin he shared with seven other men. Not even his mother would have recognised him. The face that some said looked like a codfish was covered in facial hair. Ever since Harry had threatened to kill him if he went to Africa he had stopped shaving. The beard had not even been trimmed. For the record of Empire Castle, he was John Perry, emigrating to South Africa to work on the mines in Johannesburg. He had even lied on the forms about having a job with the Serendipity Mining and Explosives Company. The forgery had been simple. He had got the company letterhead printed and written himself a job offer. The South Africans wanted white people on the mines even if the miners were threatening to go on strike. The forged passport and birth certificate were only a little more difficult. Money could buy anything.

No one had even bothered to check his luggage. He was going out of England not coming in. His Webley service revolver was safe in the battered suitcase he had bought in London on the Portobello Road.

This time he swore to himself he was going to kill Harry Brigandshaw and make no mistake. The two women he had seen on the gangplank would also have to die. The thought made him powerful. He wanted to stare into their eyes. Before he shot them. It did not matter he did not know their names. They were with Brigandshaw. When they caught him, he would go back into the Banstead asylum. They would never hang him. The British never made a bad fuss about their war heroes.

Later, when it all quietened down, they would let him out again.

The suitcase with the gun was safely under the bottom bunk he had quickly claimed as his own. No one would ever call him Fishy Braithwaite again. Not even in their minds.

He lay back on his bunk of happiness.

SHORTLY AFTER A PASSENGER came into the cabin with hand luggage.

"Hello? I'm John Perry. They called me Johnny in the army. You in the war, cock?"

The man looked at him in amazement. The first part had been spoken with a posh accent. The second in cockney. The man backed out of the door taking his luggage. He was shivering. He had looked into Fishy Braithwaite's eyes and seen the madness.

The man found the second purser on the lower deck and changed his cabin.

"There's a bloke down there who's bloody nuts."

The purser, used to complaints, gave the man another berth. So far as the purser was concerned, anyone travelling in an eight-berth cabin was nuts. He thought no more about the incident. The man who wanted his berth changed was lucky. There were only a few left.

BRETT KENTRICH WAS FEELING miserable when she caught the train that would take her back to London alone, not sure if she had made the biggest mistake of her short life. Now he had gone he was far more important to her. Everything was suddenly nothing. Hollow. Mrs Schneider's training, and the musical were just what they were. Not the great desire they had been yesterday. A West End star in waiting could still be unhappy.

"Aren't you Brett Kentrich?" a well-dressed woman was smiling at her from the seat opposite. They were both travelling first class. "I saw you in that Somerset Maugham play. You are very good."

Brett felt instantly better from being recognised. She smiled deferentially at the woman as she was meant to do. The train began talking to her through the rails. Taking her back. She was going to be famous. Really famous. The rhythm of the train repeated and repeated itself. She was numb. She hoped it mattered more than being happy on a farm in Rhodesia. She could feel the ship sailing away from her. Brett forced herself not to cry. She knew she would never sing again on a top-covered veranda to Harry Brigandshaw however famous she became.

In her mind she saw Tina Pringle leaning over the rail looking down at her. If she had known that bitch was on the boat she would have changed her mind. The bitch was after Harry. Why else would she be on the boat. Justine Voss was no kind of competition. Tina Pringle had power over men.

"BRETT YOU CAN STILL COME."

They had been inside the customs shed.

"I don't have a ticket."

"You do have your passport? You just got one."

"I'm not sure, Harry. I want to be in the show. Oscar Fleming says I'll be a sensation."

"I'm sure you will, Brett."

"You put up so much money for the show."

"My present to you, Brett. Well, not really. It'll run for a year and treble my money. You know that better than me."

"It is good. Thank you, Harry. Have a wonderful trip. I'll write. I promise you. Tell me how big the baby giraffes are grown. I love you, Harry."

"You're far too young to love anyone but yourself. I mean that in the nicest way, Brett. At your age, love the world. Not the hope of one man who is too old for you. Have a good life, Brett. And thank you."

"ARE YOU ALL RIGHT, Miss Kentrich?" It was the woman in the carriage.

"I'm a damn fool."

"Darling, we all are."

THE THEATRICAL PAGES of the London newspapers had been full of *The Golden Moth*. The star of the musical was splashed across the pages. Everyone in London knew Harry Brigandshaw had put up the money to make Brett a leading lady on the West End stage... The war hero and the showgirl. Love had returned after the tragedy of his wife's death. The resurrection. The great wealth of Colonial Shipping. Not wanting the job or the wealth. Going home to the heart of Africa. A new, shining Africa where Englishmen were going to remove the darkness first told by Joseph Conrad... It was a publicist's dream and it worked. Even before the opening night the Drury Lane theatre was booked solid for weeks. The fact Harry Brigandshaw was going home before the opening night made the drama of love that much more poignant. The voice would sing to him across the water, all the way to the heart of darkest Africa. It had made Oscar Fleming tremble with the pleasure of greed.

TINA PRINGLE, reading it all had been jealous of Brett's success far more than Brett's relationship with Harry Brigandshaw. With all her social success, with all the photographs of her in the social press, Tina knew her world would never shine so bright as Brett Kentrich. Even for a moment.

Barnaby had been his usual selfish self. The papers had gushed at his magnanimity towards his father. Everyone she knew toasted his generosity. Even C E Porter gave lip service to the lie. Barnaby had bought himself a small town house in Mayfair. They said one day soon he would be a millionaire with the stock markets of the world rising every week. He was above her. He ignored her in public.

"I'M GOING HOME."

"To Dorset?"

"Don't be a fool. Africa. Johannesburg is my home."

"Don't be a fool, Tina. Corfe Castle and that little railway cottage along the river. That is your home."

"You really are a snob, Barnaby. A fraud and a snob. You'll come a cropper one day."

"You wish, Tina. People never come a cropper when they are rich. Father's story in the papers has put me beyond reproach."

"One day you'll crawl back to me."

"You go on off to Africa. Why don't you go back on the *SS Corfe Castle*? Did you know Harry named the new ship after my family's first home? The one Cromwell tore down. To remember Lucinda. I thought it rather a nice touch. Has its maiden voyage at the end of the month. Harry will be sailing. Rumour has it that rather plain Justine Voss and her mother are taking the same trip. To look for her father's gravestone or something. What on earth is she going to do with a gravestone even if she finds it?"

"You really are very nasty, Barnaby."

"We're exactly the same, Tina. Never forget that. Have a good trip. You will excuse me now, won't you? I want to talk to that man over there about his company. His accounts are due out next month. I want to know whether to buy or sell his company shares. Now be a good girl and run along... How's your mother?"

They had stood and glared at each other for a good ten seconds.

TINA HAD TAKEN an outer cabin in first class without even telling Harry Brigandshaw. It was going to be her surprise. Early in the morning, turning her back on Brett Kentrich from on board the ship had given her pleasure. Seeing the girl had made her angry. The pleasure had come a moment later from Brett seeing her up on deck. Even from the distance across the deck side she was well aware Brett Kentrich would have liked to scratch out her eyes. She doubted Brett had known she was travelling on the same boat as her darling Harry... Being a bitch was such a pleasure.

She was going to wait until evening before coming out of the cabin. Then she would make the grand entrance into the dining room in her new evening dress that would stop them all dead in their tracks. She liked making a room full of women jealous... She was going to have one more go at bowling over Harry Brigandshaw. The very idea made her want to have sex.

AFTER THAT SPAT with Barnaby and when she dressed for dinner, she had worked it all out in her mind. They would live in England. There was no point in being rich in Rhodesia. Nobody would see her. Nobody would envy what she had. They would live in a fine house in Mayfair. Regularly go to the theatre to be seen. Especially by Brett Kentrich from the stage. They would eat supper in the right restaurants. At weekends they would host wealthy friends at Hastings Court where all the rooms would again be in use. They would buy a villa in the South of France. Once every now and again she would allow Harry to take the Prince of Wales and his friends on safari to Africa while she would stay at home and have some fun behind his back. The thought of her infidelities made her quite dizzy... Never even once would Barnaby St Clair ever forget who she was, the lady of the manor.

Dorset and Purbeck Manor were backwaters. Hastings Court was only twenty miles south of London. Later, much later, she would have two children. To bind her marriage for later in life when her power of sex over men had left her.

She had it all worked out. To hell with Brett Kentrich and *The Golden*

Moth. Long after the theatre had forgotten Brett she would be rich and famous. A hostess to whom everyone in London deferred. Later manipulating grande dame.

She looked at the diamond watch she had bought for herself. She was nicely ten minutes late for the captain's cocktail party that preceded the opening ball in the first-class lounge.

In her mind's ear she could actually hear the music.

THE DRESS CAUSED an audible gasp as she stepped forward to shake the captain's hand. She was no longer a flapper. Gone was the bodice that strapped her together to look like a boy. Gone was the pencil dress that illuminated her curves. If she had jumped down from the roof from the chandelier it would have caused no less of a sensation.

The man in Paris had smiled his approval but not at Tina's body that spoke sex louder than words. The dress designer was queer; preferred young boys. His smile had only been for the red dress he had made from silk that flowed from the sumptuous breasts he was going to show to the world. There were no shoulder straps to see. Flawless skin all the way up from the bosom that pushed from the top of the dress. The dress was showing off the body, not the other way round. He had dressed Tina Pringle in the antithesis of the current London fashion.

Even the captain was unable to avert his eyes from the largest breasts in the room, abundant, glorious and both on full display in front of his popping eyes.

"Madam will you join me at my table for dinner?" said the captain leaning forward to kiss her hand and to get a better look down her dress.

Inside her head, Tina was screaming with laughter at the dirty old man. He was sixty to a day. White beard, white, mutton-chop whiskers. And a belly the size of a large wobbly balloon.

"Captain, it will be my pleasure," she said giving him a smile she knew would go straight to his genitals.

"Till later, Miss Pringle. Welcome on board for the maiden voyage of *SS Corfe Castle*. I trust you will have a pleasant journey on the great high seas… You are alone, Madam?"

"I'm afraid so, Captain." This time her smile was sweet and innocent.

All the time she was giving her performance, Tina was looking for Harry Brigandshaw who was nowhere to be seen. Within seconds she was surrounded by the ship's officers trying their luck. She went on smiling at them all. Enjoying herself. A place at the captain's table would give her a position of strength for the rest of the voyage. Even Harry would be her captive audience at mealtimes. Smugly, she flirted with each of the officers in turn knowing that in her cabin were different dresses for every night of the voyage, all as provocative as the one on display.

As luck would have it, the Bay of Biscay was as calm as a millpond though Tina was unaware of the luck. The orchestra was good. The ship full of admiring men. For the first time in her life she was the total and absolute centre of everyone's attention.

LEN MERRYL had been sent to first class now all the passengers were congregated at the captain's cocktail party. The rich, Len found, were mostly contemptuous and trod out their cigarettes on the deck. Only a few used the sand-filled ashtrays at intervals around the deck, the deck where the rich old farts, as Len thought of them, took their constitutional before going off to drink themselves silly and stuff themselves with the rich food that in Lambeth would feed a whole family for a month. The orchestra was playing medleys from the West End shows, invisible men in evening dress pulling their bows and playing the trumpet as much ignored as Len outside on the deck pushing his broom. Len could watch through the windows from the deck. The windows followed the first-class lounge and dining room round the ship that was ploughing its way through the sea, the bows making waves down the side of the ship.

There was no one else on deck and Len stopped his work to look down over the rail at the black sea. He stood with his back to a cupboard that housed the fire hoses and the deckchairs he had begun to put away for the night. Len was melancholy. Sad for leaving England. Apprehensive for what he would find.

There was little light on the deck where he stood and the stars above in the great night sky were beautiful. There was a half-moon threaded over by wisps of white cloud. Behind the few stars and the moon was a black void that warned him, like the black sea flowing past the ship down below. Both were telling Len that nothing was ever what he saw.

He thought of the lunch box on his mother's kitchen table and

wondered if any of his family would even remember he had come home and gone. Whether they spoke of him even once. If he had any part of their lives… Would any of them see each other again? Len wondered whether it mattered to any of them.

Pushing the broom to give him the excuse he walked to the bows of the ship while the music faded behind him replaced by the throb of the ship's engines that were conquering the sea. He was still alone and cherished the feeling. The crew's quarters were stuffy, full of sweating, unwashed men half clothed lying in their hammocks.

An officer came to the rail high above him on the bridge and looked down. Len walked over quickly towards the music and the sound of party voices mingling in an angry chorus as if they really did not like each other despite all the outward appearance of civilisation that dressed them to look as they were.

For the first time Len looked into the room of standing groups of people, drinks in hand, waiters invisible again, offering the canapés. Strangely, he had no wish to be where they were. No envy.

He had enjoyed his moments of solitude with a deep, inner pleasure, hugging his personal loneliness. He stopped in the shadow to have a look at them. The rich. The privileged. The ones he was supposed to envy.

For no reason Ben Willard come up the deck looking for him.

"Poor sods," Len said. "They're all putting on an act. Especially that girl in the red dress with the big tits."

"Blimey, they are big. Never seen knockers on display like that before. Except the barmaid. Wouldn't mind fuckin' her, Len. What you say?… 'Ave a fag. No one is worried about us just now. There's one in third class with big tits but she don't look like that one."

"It's the girl by the rail. She gave me a filthy look this morning… You really goin' to see Teresa in Cape Town, Ben?"

"If you're a good boy, I'll take you along."

"Don't put your fag out on deck or I'll get it in the neck."

"You worry too much. Never worry, never hurry, just keep your bowels open. What my grandfather said to me. Good advice."

"You're full of shit, Ben Willard."

They finished their cigarettes in comfortable silence, put them out in the sand-filled ashtrays attached to the inner wall below the window line and walked off down the side of the ship to the steps that would take them back to their quarters. Neither of them spoke.

HARRY BRIGANDSHAW WATCHED Len Merryl and Ben Willard pass his cabin window. He found it strange to know the two men worked for him but he did not know their names. On Elephant Walk he knew everyone's names and most of their family and tribal history. His cabin was the largest on the ship, boasting a small double bed instead of bunks. Felicity and her daughter Justine were in a two-berth at the other end of the passage, comfortable but bunk berths just the same. He still hoped Felicity Voss was right to confront her past. He had agreed to take them to Elephant Walk, an invitation he had extended more than a year ago.

"HE'S AN OLD MAN, Mrs Voss. Not what you remember. He's been living in the bush for all these years. You remember a soldier. I know an old man conning young immigrants out of a grubstake… Have you told Justine the truth yet?"

"He will still be the same man underneath. We all get old."

"He looks rough. Very rough. Last I heard he was living with his horses with a friend rougher than himself. You can't imagine what years of living under the stars can do for a man. Physically and mentally. It can make them mean."

"I envy him. All the comforts don't make you happy."

"When are you going to tell her?"

"When we set sail. When we are on the water."

"So she can't run away?"

"So she will have time to realise she has a living father. All he has to be is kind to her."

"She still thinks she's looking for his grave. A soldier killed in battle. Not a broken down old man. I think you're wrong, Mrs Voss."

"It will put everything finally to rest. I also want to see him again. You won't say anything?"

"Of course not," Harry had lied.

Telling the old man what was coming was the least he could do. After telling himself more than once to mind his own business he had written Jim Bowman, to visit Colonel Voss and warn the poor old man of the ghosts coming from his past to blow away his life. Harry rather hoped Voss would get the hell out of the way and save everyone pain. 'Tell him to vanish into the bush for six months. He is good at that,' he had told Jim Bowman in the letter.

HARRY POURED himself a whisky from the bottle he took from a small cocktail cabinet, sat down on the side of his bed and drank it slowly with pleasure. He hated cocktail parties. Hated, for the journey, being the owner of the ship. He sighed inwardly. It was what the captain expected. Sometimes Harry found in life it was better to comply with the rules no matter what.

Emptying the crystal glass of whisky, Harry got up off the side of the bed and prepared himself to join the captain's cocktail party. Even if the party was halfway through... There would be plenty of time for solitude when he got home.

The thought of the African bush made him smile. He was going to see his dogs again soon. His family. He wondered how much Madge's children had grown while he was away.

Harry took one look out of the open cabin window before latching it shut. The deckhands had gone. The outside decks of his ship were empty of people. With a wry smile he noticed the fag ends had gone from the deck. People!

With a second sigh, this time audible, Harry opened the cabin door and went on his way.

AS AGREED, Harry called at the Voss cabin to take his guests to the cocktail party. Later, they were all to sit at the captain's table for dinner.

When the door of the cabin opened to a beaming Justine Voss, it was clear to Harry her mother had told her nothing about her father. For all of them, Harry held his breath. He could hear the distant thunder. Why people did not live their lives as they found them he never knew. Justine looked so happy.

Thinking of how much nicer the voyage would have been to have Lucinda by his side, he led the way. For Harry, there was a sense of vulnerability without his wife. For the first time in weeks, as if someone had walked over his grave, he thought of Mervyn Braithwaite. He was glad to be out of England. Away from it. Africa was so much less complicated. So fewer people.

There were many young officers on board. He would ask them to pay special attention to Justine Voss.

He hoped Brett would enjoy the present he had left for her in London. A small red car outside his flat in Regent Mews. Where she was to live for as long as she wished. With his love and memories, the flat was only a short walk from Drury Lane. By now even she would have found herself a new boyfriend. Feeling a twinge of regret, Harry

walked into the first-class lounge behind Mrs Voss and her daughter to
come face-to-face with Tina Pringle.

"Where's Barnaby?" he gasped in surprise.

"In London, I expect."

"What are you doing here, Tina?"

"I bought a ticket. You may remember my real home is in
Johannesburg. Can't you look a little pleased to see me, Harry? How do
you like my dress? Straight from Paris. Only the French know how to
dress a woman."

"Sensational, Tina." Harry hoped he had recovered himself.

"See you at dinner. The captain asked me to join his table."

Brazenly and to Harry's amusement, Tina turned her back on him.
Even the back of the dress was sensual. The voyage was going to be
better than he thought. They were both now single...

"Why is she on board?" asked Justine Voss at his side.

"I'm really not sure."

"Wow. What a dress."

"Yes, it does do something for her don't you think? I'll bet not a man
in the room is unaware of Tina. Poor old Barnaby. How true it is that
the best things in our lives are under our noses and we do nothing
about them."

"You think so?... Mother told me, Harry. I'm so excited."

"Oh, my God," Harry had spoken soundlessly, under his breath.
They were all going to perdition.

THE CAPTAIN of the ship saved any further embarrassing conversation,
doing an exhibition in servility to the owner of the shipping line that
made Harry cringe. He leaned forward close to the captain's ear, still
holding the hand that had tried to pump off his arm.

"I'm a farmer, Thom. You're the boss here, not me."

Harry stood back and smiled at the now flustered captain and
retrieved his hand from the man's gnarled grip. Harry introduced Mrs
Voss and her daughter. The captain recovered his authority though his
eyes were still bewildered. To the captain there was a chain of
command. It was how it worked. How everything worked.

Harry found a drink in his hand, took a sip and smiled, it was the
same brand of whisky from his cabin. The same brand he had drunk
since his days at Oxford long ago. The captain was watching his face.
The captain grinned at him. He wondered how the captain had found

out about his whisky. Harry grinned back. At that moment they both knew they liked each other.

Harry began to circulate. There was not a person in first class, it seemed, who was not aware of his controlling interest in Colonial Shipping. Quite a few owned new shares. All were happy with their acquisition.

The chatter of trivia went on until they filed into the elaborate dining room for dinner.

The dining room was splendid. Harry made a mental note to write to the interior decorator. There was one thing Harry had learnt in his short stint at running a shipping line. It was all in the detail. If each small part was perfect, the whole became very profitable. Everyone in the company had their part in the success or failure. Harry hoped Percy Grainger, now ensconced in the managing director's office, would remember the little bits that meant so much. Praise was as important to any person for a job well done wherever they stood in the company hierarchy.

Keeping the smile on his face, Harry went on talking to the passengers until he reached his seat at the captain's table.

"May I introduce to you, Mr Brigandshaw, the delightful Tina Pringle who has so graciously agreed to sit at our table."

"You may, Captain. Though it is not necessary. Tina Pringle and I are old friends. There is hope one day she will marry my brother-in-law, the Honourable Barnaby St Clair and live happily ever after. There is nothing more beautiful than a couple who have been friends since childhood, becoming one under God and growing old together in a loving home surrounded by the same loving happy children." The sarcasm he hoped, was only understood by Tina. The two of them understood each other far too well.

"That's so beautiful," burst out Justine Voss. "I'm so happy for you, Tina, to love forever. It is my dream. One, big, happy family. You are the luckiest girl alive. Please come and sit next to me. The grown-ups can sit at the top of the table."

"Aren't we grown up, Justine?" said Tina, acidly all the time thinking what she was going to do to Harry.

"Oh, you know what I mean. Harry is an absolute darling, but he's old enough to be your father. At that age they talk about boring things. Ask my mother… We girls like to talk about clothes. Now, where please, just where did you get that dress?"

Harry, wincing at the innocent jibe at his age, realised Justine thought he was after her mother. That the idea of the voyage was as much to set him up with the mother, something that had never even crossed Harry's mind. To add to his consternation, Tina looked at him with a long, sympathetic smile before slowly pushing the tip of her tongue along the lower lip of her mouth. Then Tina gave him a barely recognisable wink.

Harry shook his head while looking at his soup. Now the father was alive, he wondered what the daughter would think of him as her mother's potential beau. Maybe mother telling daughter had been a blessing after all.

"Do you believe in fate, Captain?" asked Harry.

"Always, Mr Brigandshaw. What shall be shall be. There's nothing we can do about it."

The captain stood up and raised his right hand. The dining room fell silent. The captain picked up his glass.

"I ask you all to rise… To the good ship *SS Corfe Castle* and all who sail in her. God Save the King."

"GOD SAVE THE KING!"

LATE NEXT MORNING the ship was alone on a vast ocean with nothing in sight. They had passed the Spanish coast in the night and were headed for the Portuguese island of Madeira where they were to spend a few hours picking up tropical fruit and a few passengers who would be ferried out to the ship in the same lighter that brought the hands of bananas. Anyone who wished would be allowed to go ashore. There was a tangible excitement at three o'clock when the high cliffs of the island were first sighted.

FOR JUSTINE it would be her first step ashore that was not on the land of England. She had slept not a wink all night thinking of her father and all the wonderful days they were going to spend together while she told him everything that had been in her life while they were separated. How a man who had died in the Anglo-Boer War had suddenly come alive she was yet to question. In that new morning she could only feel the joy, not the strange reality of a man coming back from the dead.

Standing on deck alone looking at the slowly looming island coming out of the ocean sea she felt the first small bell of alarm. Of danger. Of something most terribly wrong. She felt a cold shiver despite the warm summer air from the African desert far lost over the sun-soaked sea to the east.

HER MOTHER HAD GIVEN her the night to think, overjoyed by her daughter's first burst of excitement in their cabin the previous night.

Now she watched her daughter standing alone by the rail. Mrs Voss was seated in a deckchair that let her see without being noticed. She had watched for some time.

Felicity saw the girl's shudder and got to her feet. Still not sure, she walked halfway across the deck and stopped. Most of the passengers were down below getting themselves ready for the trip ashore. For some reason Harry Brigandshaw was standing next to the funnel. She had not seen him from her deckchair. She thought he could also see Justine without being noticed. He waved forward. They both had seen the girl's shoulders convulse in sharp violent shudders.

The girl turned on her. "If he's alive why do I only find out now, Mother? Why didn't he come to us long ago?"

"He was married to another woman."

"But then how did he come to be my father if he was already married?"

"Because we made love. With passion, love and no care for the consequence. The only time in my life I have been happy with a man. Do you grudge me a few weeks of happiness?... That dreadful marriage of his! Married to a woman for the sake of convenience is no way to spend a life. I didn't want the same with another man. I needed something to remember. A girl has to have something to remember for the rest of her dreary life."

"Have I been dreary for you, Mother?"

"No, of course not."

"Then what do you mean?"

"You will go soon. Find a man and go and just maybe look back on your dear old mother once in a while. When your life is full with your own family, your mother won't matter very much."

"I would never discard you."

"You wouldn't even know you'd done it. I had a mother too. Yes, I think of her sometimes."

"So would this father of mine have made so much difference?"

"Probably not... We are going to find out... Memories live better than life."

"Then I'm a bastard," Justine spat at her mother.

"So am I, Justine," said Harry coming out from the shadow of the forward funnel where he had been waiting. "Luck was my mother ran away from her husband with my father and went to Africa where my grandfather who started this shipping line could not find them. Not at first, anyway. He was so concerned about himself he had my father arrested in Cape Town. The police were going to bring my father back to England to face the charge of abduction. My grandfather hated his younger son that much for destroying his dream of pushing the family up a social class or two!"

"Are you part of all this, Harry? It's a charade, isn't it? It can't be real. Are you part of it, then?"

"Reluctantly."

"SO, you do know who my real father is?"

"Not well. He's an old man. Much older than your mother. There are many more years between your father and mother than you and me, Justine. And I'm not quite old enough to be your father or Tina's."

"I'm sorry."

"It was said without malice."

"Does he know I'm coming?"

"He will by the time we arrive."

"Harry! You said you wouldn't," said Mrs Voss.

"Larry has the right to make up his mind."

"So I'm not Justine Voss, legally. Who am I then?"

"I suppose you should carry my maiden name. I brought back a forged birth certificate from Greece where you were born."

"So I'm a Greek!"

"No, darling. I had your birth registered at the British Embassy."

"My word, that really is something. I'm going to the cabin. Please leave me alone. Both of you. I shall not be going ashore. The father I didn't have yesterday doesn't know I'm even alive."

"Oh, he does. I wrote him. Told him your name."

"Then why by the name of God didn't he come to me?"

"Why don't you ask him when you meet?"

"MEET him? I wish he were dead."

They watched her go.

"You still think I'm wrong, Harry? She'll think through all this and want to see him."

"I told Jim Bowman to tell Larry to do one of his bush trips. Where no one can find him."

"Maybe he'll spruce himself up and not run away. All men are vain... Thanks for the bastard bit, Harry. She won't believe it, of course. Life really isn't what it was made out to be... The bar is open. Will you buy me a drink?"

"Sure... She'll be all right."

"She's young, yes. At that age they are mostly resilient. I remember trying to be damn resilient... You'd better watch that Tina Pringle. She wants to eat you alive."

"There are times I wouldn't mind... I told myself for days to mind my own business. And still I thought I knew better. I'm sorry, Felicity."

Harry put both hands on the ship's rail and took a deep breath of the salt air. They were at the back of the first-class deck which looked down over to third class. A man with a full face of facial hair was looking up at them from the lower deck. The man raised a hand to them, almost ironically. Harry waved back thinking he had been recognised as the owner of the ship, even at a distance. The man was still staring at them when Harry turned his back. The man had paid his passage and had every right to wave. Harry was glad he had waved back.

A few steps away from the rail on their way to the first-class bar Harry looked back. The man was still staring. The man waved again. This time Harry did not wave back.

When they reached the small bar under an awning next to the swimming pool, Tina Pringle was already seated at the bar.

"Come and join me, Harry. Hello Mrs Voss. Madeira is a bit of a bore. You can see most of it from the ship, anyway. From right here at the bar."

Tina Pringle was wearing a flowered sundress that took in all her curves. Felicity Voss thought Tina Pringle might as well have been wearing nothing at all. After one drink she left them at the bar.

"You silly old bitch," Mrs Voss told herself. "You're jealous."

When she reached her cabin, Justine had locked the door. She could hear her daughter's sobbing. She shook the handle to no avail.

"This is going to be quite some voyage."

Back on deck she found herself a deckchair and got herself down. Lying almost horizontally to the wooden deck she fell asleep. She dreamed of a man with a full beard who waved at her time and time again.

When she woke, the ship was still anchored off the island of Madeira. Boats, some being rowed, were going to and from the shore.

When she went down to the cabin, there was a note on her bed.

"Sorry. Gone ashore. Maybe with my feet on land everything will be real again."

Felicity Voss sat on her bunk and had a good cry. Later she felt better. She changed for dinner. By now she thought all the passengers would be back on the ship. Among the last was Justine.

WITH JUSTINE LOOKING all the world the same as she always had been they joined the ship's captain for dinner. They could feel the throb of the ship's engine, coming up through the floor. The ship was under way.

When they went up on deck after dinner, all they could see of Madeira were the distant lights of the houses climbing up the hills. Neither of them spoke of Larry Voss. Or Tina Pringle and Harry Brigandshaw.

They were comfortable with each other again.

A sharp breeze came up from the south-east. They went down to the cabin to read their books.

When Felicity slept that night she again dreamed of a man with a beard.

"PENNY FOR YOUR THOUGHTS?"

Harry had been watching the sea go by for half an hour standing next to one of the lifeboats. There was little room on a ship. Unless he stayed in his cabin his company was anyone's for the asking. Part of the shipboard romance.

"Brett Kentrich," he said without looking round at Tina. There was no mistaking her voice.

"Do you love her?"

"No. I've never loved anyone in the way I think you ask. All-consuming. I never have. Anyone."

"Not even your wife?"

"Lucinda and I grew comfortable with each other. I love them all, the St Clairs. Even Barnaby as a child. Madge and I were a family but not in the St Clair way. She wanted to be my wife. Since she was fifteen when we met. I wanted a family just like hers. Robert was like a brother to me. It was so terrible taking Lucinda so far away to Africa. Marriage was what she wanted. Often we do things for people because they want them so much. It's said you can grow to love people. That slow burning love lasts longer. More satisfying. We all confuse sex with the love. When we first look at someone, sex is the motivation. The clash of eyes is sexual, not that instant love people like to talk about. Primal. Nature wanting to renew itself... We would have been happy. Even a devoted couple. We'll never know. Only when we all get to the end of our lives, can we look back and say what happened. Why old people don't smile so much. That's from my Grandfather Manderville. He says all young people smile but they don't know what they are smiling about."

"I never talked to your grandfather that one trip with Benny Lightfoot. He was that American I brought to Elephant Walk. Or maybe he brought me."

"I remember your visit to Elephant Walk."

"During the war I saw your picture in the paper. They said you were a war hero. I said to the photograph I wanted you. There was something about your look. Do you want me, Harry?"

"There are many ways to want someone."

"Carnally, you idiot. In the biblical sense. What else is there?"

"Do you love Barnaby?"

"I want him. Oh yes. He is so bloody evil. He'll come a mighty cropper one day. You can't think only of yourself all your life and get away with it. The effect of charm will wear off with age. Then I will feel sorry for him. I'm looking forward to it."

"Would you marry him?"

"At the drop of a hat and live in hell."

"Why would you live in hell?"

"Because he's evil, Harry. His name should have been Merlin. They got it wrong. God disguises evil with charm and perfect looks. Merlin is a softy and frightens the wits out of everyone with that one dark eye. Dogs and cats bolt from him. Barnaby, they purr and brush up against his legs. They don't know Barnaby would break their necks if there was something in it for him... You haven't answered my question. Do you want to take me to bed? Just for carnal pleasure. We're stuck on this boat for weeks. Have fun when you can. Death hangs over all of us, even the young."

"There's something bad about a girl being so blunt."

"There's something good in it too. Mark my words, Harry Brigandshaw. We're going to do it. It would be such a waste. My father says the worst thing in life is to look back with regrets. Not what you did. He says it's far worse to regret what you didn't do. Come on, Harry. Let's be honest. We growl at each other every time we meet."

"You're dangerous for men, Tina."

"Isn't that the fun of it? If you get snared, that's your problem. All I want is some fun. I found out the owner's cabin has a double bed. Now isn't that just great."

"He's not evil. Greedy. Insensitive. Not evil."

"He's evil, Harry. Like something from the past. The long ago past carried down the generations. How do you think the St Clairs got where they are today? Rape and pillage. They did the rape and pillage. The likes of us Pringles were what they raped however charming their manners are. Now Barnaby's just perfected the art of hiding treachery. Of making people believe he thinks them wonderful when they have something he wants while all the time despises them. Anyway, I want a drink without people. I hate all the people staring at me in public. You must have a cocktail cabinet in that plush cabin of yours... Do you?"

"I do... I think you're lying about the stares. Every woman likes being stared at. Even lusted after. Gives them their power in life."

"Then what are we waiting for?"

"It's only ten o'clock in the morning."

"Harry, darling, I finished drinking at eleven o'clock last night. That's eleven hours ago. We're on holiday. Cooped up on a ship. Ten o'clock doesn't make an excuse. Anyway a ten o'clock drink in the owner's cabin is the best drink of the day."

THE THIRD-CLASS passenger deputation to the second purser's office took place while Tina Pringle was telling Harry Brigandshaw the edited version of her life. Instinctively she knew what she hoped looked like honesty was her best weapon. Having gained access to the owner's cabin she was no longer in a hurry. The poor man couldn't exactly run away from a ship on the high seas. Or take leave of the ship at the wrong port. With Harry as her captive audience she was going to make the best of him. Test her skill. Anyway she rationalised the whisky was good. Tina never considered a hangover from a good cause a waste.

"NONE OF US is goin' to stay in that cabin with 'im. He's got a gun in 'is case under 'is bed. Willie 'ere had a look. One minute he's playing cockney then 'e's a toff. Worse than mad, officer. Gives us the creeps. Always staring at you. Once he yelled at me 'e wasn't a wet fish. Who is 'e anyway?"

"John Perry. A miner. Going out to a job on a gold mine. Has a job offer from Serendipity Mining and Explosives Company."

"Never used a pick in 'is life, you ask me. Hands as soft as a woman. You know what he said yesterday, 'Can you fly an aeroplane? I can. Shot down thirty bloody Germans, I like killing'… Gives me the creeps. I'll sleep on deck but not down there with 'im."

"I'll look into it."

"You'd better."

"You're not the first to complain."

"Now you tell us. You go to the captain and 'ave him lock 'im up, I say. Put 'im ashore at Cape Town and warn the police. What's 'e doing with a bloody gun under his bed? Willie says it's a service revolver. For officers. Now where'd a miner get that legal like? We want him and 'is gun out of our cabin. Now. Before 'e kills someone."

"Has he actually threatened anyone?"

"Not that I know."

"We get all sorts going to the colonies."

"We done our bit, officer. Now you do yours. Bloke's bloody mad, you ask me."

THE PURSER was more interested in the logistics of the fancy dress ball that was taking place in the first-class lounge the next day than listening to the second purser.

"The captain can't do anything, Findley, you know that. How about locking up everyone someone doesn't like? They buy a cheap ticket and bear the consequence. I don't want you worrying the captain. This Perry hasn't done anything except try on a gentleman's accent so far as I see. That's no crime. The way some people mince the English language maybe there should be a law. The law to make people speak properly."

"What about the gun?"

"All we know is a second-hand report. Goodness, Findley, we can't go rummaging in passengers' suitcases. There's a law against that."

"But the gun, sir. I'm sure it's there."

"It probably is. There's no maritime law against carrying a gun. Good

Lord, we're sailing to Africa. Everyone going on safari has an armoury on board, I'll bet... This John Perry has to threaten someone with the gun or better still shoot at someone before I can do anything. If they want to sleep on deck so be it. Done plenty of times myself in the tropics when I was young. In a lifeboat. With a girl. Why do you think I joined the merchant navy?... We don't have enough Admiral Nelson outfits this trip. For some reason half the male passengers want to run around with a sleeve hanging loose and a patch over one eye. Last trip I was on they wanted to be Arab sheiks. It's these newfangled American moving pictures. Can you believe it? Some idiot made a bad film of the Battle of Trafalgar. You could see all the boats they filmed were miniatures wallowing in a fish tank of water... What you should do is get this Perry with his gun to shoot the man who made that film, ha, ha... It's a joke, Findley. Push off and do something important."

FISHY BRAITHWAITE HAD SEEN Tina Pringle going to Harry Brigandshaw's cabin at ten fifteen that morning. A rage of jealousy surged through his body. The door had closed. Only Fishy Braithwaite's imagination was left to torment him. The girl was even prettier than his fiancée, Sara Wentworth. Watching the closed door of the owner's cabin from his vantage point the man who now said he was John Perry smiled. At least Sara could not torment his imagination any more. She was dead. Harry had stolen her. She had been standing next to Harry when he shot her with a similar gun to the one that lay hidden in his suitcase under his bunk.

From more than seventy yards he had been able to devour every detail of the girl's body as she stood waiting for Harry to open the door to the cabin. For a moment he thought she had seen him. His eyes were by far better than most people's. Pilot's eyes. What had made him a great killer in the air... Saliva drooled at the thought of death. He had liked it best when they went down in flames screaming all the way to the ground. Now he was going to kill another girl. He stood riveted to his small part of the deck wishing the cabin door to open. He hoped she would look satiated. Dishevelled. It would make his rage scream harder at his torment. A satiating rage.

LEN MERRYL PASSED twice in the course of his duties and both times acknowledged the bearded man standing on the same spot on the third-class deck. The man did not seem to see him. On the third time just before noon the man was still staring at the same spot ahead. Len stood ten yards behind the man and followed the fixed gaze. The line of sight was directly at the owner's cabin door.

Everyone on board knew Harry Brigandshaw by sight. He was a man who found time to talk to everyone in the company. He had not spoken to Len Merryl but Ben Willard had had a brief conversation. About the fag ends passengers left on the deck instead of the ashtrays. It had surprised both of them that the owner had taken any notice of cigarettes thrown on the ship's deck. Len had seen Harry once while sweeping the deck the first night out. The owner had closed his own cabin window onto the deck and the sea. It was one of the few cabin windows. The rest were portholes with only the top line of portholes able to open onto the sea. Len had ducked out of sight the moment he recognised Harry Brigandshaw. He did not think the man had seen him. The man was something of a legend to the crew.

Len shook his head. It was none of his business. Anyone could look where they wanted.

On his fourth time round the deck to pick up empty glasses the passengers left beside their deckchairs, Len subconsciously looked at the owner's cabin. A steward was standing outside with a trolley. The owner himself opened the cabin door. The lunch trolley was wheeled inside. Instinctively, Len looked from the cabin door to the spot on the deck where he had seen the bearded man staring. The man was still there. Rooted to the spot. Staring at the man in the doorway with rabid hatred. To Len's understanding there was no way the man did not know Harry Brigandshaw. The man was drooling down both sides of his beard. Such venom came from personal animosity.

"Excuse me? Do you know Mr Brigandshaw?"

"Mind your own damn business and get on with your work."

"Who the hell do think you're talking to?"

"You."

The eyes that turned on him cut through him. Full of contempt. Full of superiority. Disdain.

"What's your problem, mate?" said Len, bridling.

"You at the moment… How dare you speak to an officer like that. You are dismissed."

"If I ever see you onshore, you won't speak to me like that."

"If I ever see you onshore, I'll shoot you like the rest. Now bugger off."

Len stood back and deliberately and silently counted to ten, not taking his eyes off the scruffy individual daring him to take a swing. There were times in life he told himself where saving pride was a waste of time. He did not even know the man. With the small pay from the half voyage to Beira and after paying the train fare to Salisbury he would arrive on his sister's doorstep with close to the seven pounds with which he had signed off the *Runnymede*. Mrs Steadham had not been expensive. For a moment he heard her voice in his mind. He knew she was thinking of him like she thought of the swallows.

Looking to make sure he was not going to be attacked when his back was turned, Len went on with his duties, looking for hidden glasses on the deck. There were more important things in his life than a passenger who made no sense.

Far enough away to be safe, Len shrugged his shoulders. He had enough worries of his own not to take on other people's. If the owner did not know how to look after himself with a boatload of employees what was a temporary deckhand to do. The master of arms would throw any third-class passenger off first class.

Len began talking to himself. "Your trouble, Len Merryl, is too vivid an imagination. If you hadn't opened your stupid mouth none of that would have happened. Am I not always telling you to stay out of trouble? Even a toff with a fancy accent could fall on hard times. Why the man is going out to the colonies."

He was still mumbling to himself as he bent down and picked up a tray full of empty glasses. When he stood up a steward was watching him at work.

"Isn't this your job, mate?" he said with a smile.

"Thanks, Len… Did you see that freak with a beard? Been standing there all morning. Told me to bugger off when I asked him if he wanted a drink. Las Palmas tomorrow. Never been to Canary Islands before."

"Join the navy and see the world… Let's hope he gets off in Cape Town."

WILLIE HAD BEEN watching John Perry for most of the morning. If the shipping line were going to do nothing he was going to do something himself. There were seven of them in the cabin. Enough for one man in a small space. Only the gun came between them.

The sun was due to go down at seven fifteen. He had watched the confrontation with Len Merryl and heard what was said. Without a word to anyone he went downstairs to the eight-berth cabin they shared with John Perry.

Removing a piece of board from his bunk, he propped one end under the door handle and the other he pressed down against the bunk bed nearest to the door. The door would not lock from the inside for some reason. Quickly from under the bottom bunk he pulled out the suitcase. This time it was locked. Willie began to sweat. Using his penknife, he forced the lock and found inside the black heavy Webley service revolver. He had hoped to wait till dark. The threat to the deckhand had changed his mind. The gun was too big to hide in his pocket in daylight.

Willie put the gun under the bedclothes in his bed and left the cabin. In his pockets were the bullets.

Up on deck John Perry was still staring at the first-class section of the boat. Willie followed his gaze. A pretty girl was coming out of one of the cabins. He could see she was drunk. The man with her was laughing. Willie thought it early to be drunk so soon after lunch. The rich, he told himself, had their own rules.

The moment the man and girl were out of sight, John Perry left his post and walked towards the gangway that would take him down to the inside berth.

Willie followed John Perry down into the ship. When Willie opened their cabin door, John Perry was on his knees rummaging in the suitcase.

"Looking for something, my china?"

John Perry looked up and understood. Willie was grinning at him, showing his bad teeth. Willie looked across at his own bunk, at the hump made by the gun. John Perry was fast across the small cabin.

"I'm not a wet fish and you're dead," screamed John Perry pulling the trigger repeatedly.

As a cabin steward pushed open the door, the gun was pointed at him. The gun did not fire. Willie still had a smile on his face. Then he moved slowly and hit John Perry across the head with a board from the bunk bed.

"Is that a gun?" screamed the steward.

"Fuck off!" said Willie.

Willie picked up the gun from the floor and hid it under his shirt. The steward had run out of the cabin. John Perry was trying to get up.

Willie kicked him in the head and left the cabin.

Up the stairway he took the corridor that took him to a door on the side of the ship. The water was rushing by the ship twenty feet down below. Willie dropped the gun and the ammunition over the side.

If anyone asked he would deny the whole thing. He had been in the army during the war. Any enquiry had a life of its own. All he wished to do was reach South Africa and go on his way.

Feeling not a little pleased with himself Willie went to the third-class bar. The one thing he had found out through his thirty short years was other people never solved his problems for him. The rest of the voyage he was going to sleep with a knife in his hand.

When he went back to his bunk, he was drunk. John Perry was already in his bunk.

"If that sod puts a foot out of bed, yell," he said to the others showing them the knife. "Sleep tight, everyone. And fuck the navy. From now on we sleep with the lights on." By the time he began to snore, the knife had fallen from his hand.

Willie woke in the morning with a hangover. John Perry was staring at him. There was a smirk on John Perry's face. Willie smiled back.

"Did someone smack your face, my china? You should be more careful. Fact is, everyone in this cabin would like to smack your face. Hard. Take that grin off your face. Little men without guns are little men. You behave for the rest of the voyage and we'll all go our separate ways. I don't give a fuck who you are. Where you came from. Where you're going. None of us do. Don't try no messing, see."

John Perry was still smiling at them when they left for breakfast. Over breakfast, Willie told them what he had done. As they were finishing their food, John Perry came into the third-class dining room. He was still smiling. He sat down away from them at a small table on his own where he ate meals. No one else on the ship wanted to eat with him.

He was still staring at Willie when they got up to leave.

FELICITY VOSS'S IDEA of Justine's disappointment at meeting her father being tempered by a brilliant marriage to Harry Brigandshaw came to nothing at dinner time.

They were lovers. Even an insensitive fool could have seen the change in Tina Pringle and Harry Brigandshaw, she told herself. Not just the way they slipped looks at each other. Not even the look of satisfaction in both of their faces. They were different people.

With a shock of familiar recognition, Felicity wondered if the girl would now fall pregnant. God has strange ways of anointing his people. Momentarily it hurt her feelings which she recognised as jealousy. It made her feel old. It made her think her life was over. Which it was for all practical purposes. Apart from eating and sleeping, what had she to offer life? Or anyone else that came in contact with her life. She was on a fool's errand going to Rhodesia. Only a fool looked to resurrect a life that was already dead. Only God could do that.

The waiter put a small piece of fish on a large plate in front of her. She looked at the fish with a sprig of parsley. At the two small new potatoes. And wanted to cry... Then she sighed at the irony of so much sadness inside of her while she was surrounded by so much material wealth.

For the rest of the evening she knew she would be unable to look at Tina Pringle.

The next day was to be the fancy dress ball. She was going as a witch with a tall black hat. Justine was to be a Vestal Virgin dressed all in white. Before the ball, the ship would visit Las Palmas in the morning, then came the Ascension Islands followed by the island of St Helena. Mentally, Felicity ticked off all the ports of call. Everything punctuated by meals. By dressing up and going in to meals.

The captain was saying something to her. She turned to him with a smile. Determined to enjoy herself. What was the point of going anywhere if she was not going to enjoy herself? Very slightly, the ship took on a roll.

By the time coffee was being served, the ship was rolling and pitching in slow rhythm. Justine had gone as white as a sheet. They were in for some heavy weather.

The captain excused himself from the table.

A HOWLING gale hit the SS *Corfe Castle* in sight of Las Palmas. The fancy dress ball was cancelled. The captain made a new course to avoid the Canary Islands. Most of the passengers stayed in their cabins. Some in the clutch of seasickness even wished they were dead.

IN THE EIGHT-berth cabin, the only passenger to thrive was John Perry. He seemed to be enjoying himself.

FOR A NIGHT and a day, Tina and Harry holed up in the owner's cabin making love. By the time the wind abated they were both satiated for the first time in their lives. No one had taken any notice of them. Neither of them suffered from seasickness. Mostly they had made love on the floor, rolling around the cabin in search of each other, later laughing till the tears poured down their faces.

All Tina's preconceived calculations had been thrown to the wind.

"I never knew the meaning of carnal lust before this," said Harry.

"Neither did I," said Tina. "Do you know we haven't eaten a damn thing for nearly two days and I'm starving? Wow, am I hungry. I'd better go to my own cabin and get dressed. See you at dinner, Harry."

"It'll be my pleasure... There's just one thing before you go."

"Oh, all right. Just please don't hurry."

WHEN THEY sat down to dinner looking prim and proper the ship was back on an even keel. The captain sat down with them to dinner. Tina and Harry ate ravenously. Only once did Tina let out a giggle. In what seemed to be the first time in her life she had not given Barnaby a thought.

15

SEA VOYAGE AROUND AFRICA, OCTOBER 1922

*T*en days later the *SS Corfe Castle* was standing off Table Bay to the west of Robben Island waiting for the dawn. The ship's screws were turning slowly, holding her position. Harry could see the phosphorescence in the churned sea trailing back into the paling night.

They were holding hands outside his cabin leaning over the ship's rail. The rest of the passengers were still sleeping. The lights of Cape Town were away to the east in the dark shadow of Table Mountain. Harry was waiting for the sun to rise from behind the flat table of the mountain. It was always his welcome home. To Africa. Where he belonged and loved and cherished with all his heart… When God's rays rose behind the mountain at the foot of Africa he would know he was home. That Elephant Walk was just a while to the north. The animals. The smell of the bush. The great flowing rivers that swept down from the heart of Africa to the plains and the ocean sea.

EARLIER the change in the engine had brought him awake. He had woken her gently.

"We're here. Cape Town. Get up. The African dawn. Homecoming is complete for me when the rays of the sun come up from behind the mountain. From the Twelve Apostles. Did I tell you I went to school in Cape Town? During the Anglo-Boer War there were times I could not go home for holidays… Get up, Tina, or we'll miss it."

"I'm asleep."

"No, you are not. I just woke you… If you don't want to be tickled to death get up and put on some clothes. Even owners can't let their ladies stand naked at the rail."

"Am I your lady, Harry? What about Brett?"

"You are sharp so early in the morning. Brett wishes to be a great actress. Whether she will be only God knows. How can you think of

Brett?"

"Or Barnaby?"

"Tina, we are alone together. Let it be. The ghosts will find us without bringing them awake. Life has to be enjoyed at the moment. Not in the past or the future. Now is what it is all about. And now is watching the sun rise over Table Mountain with the sexiest girl in the world."

"Am I sexy, Harry?"

"You have my word for it. Come on. The sun won't wait."

"What are we going to do today?"

"That's better. Get up, lazy head."

Harry could see the shape of her in the light of the dawn. Pale. Ethereal. Wanton. Was landfall in Cape Town the beginning or the end? He could not remember when he had ever been so happy.

STANDING BY THE RAIL, Harry pointed. Rays of light were fingering the sky. They could make out the flat top of the mountain. As the sun rose the lights of Cape Town began to fade. The new day had begun. The throb of the engines increased. The ship headed for port as two tugs came out to meet them.

"Why am I so happy, Harry?"

Secretly, Tina wondered if she was pregnant. Neither had taken precautions. It had not seemed necessary at the time.

THE MOMENT the third-class gangplank was in place Len Merryl watched the man with the full beard disembark, glad to see the back of him.

A group of third-class passengers were watching him go. One was waving ironically. Someone called the man waving Willie, and he turned, showing Len his face. The man was happy with something. The man with the full beard Len had found out was John Perry, passenger from Southampton to Cape Town. Len watched him carry down onto the docks an old suitcase. There was something wrong with the lock. A piece of rope was holding the case together. The man stood on the dock for a moment looking up at the first-class section of the ship. Then he turned and waved at the group of passengers surrounding the big man one of them had just called Willie.

"That was the bugger who pointed a gun at me," said the man next to Len. Len did not know his name. He knew the man was crew.

"Pointed a gun!"

"Told the second purser. That big bloke over there said I was seeing things. That there wasn't a gun. Hit him with a plank across the face hard and kicked him when he was on the ground."

"Well, he's gone. All's well that ends well."

"Two days onshore… You're going ashore?"

"Tonight. Me and Ben Willard. There's a bar in Long Street. Hope she's still there. You ever see a woman and want to see her again?"

"All the time, mate."

"Her name's Teresa."

"Good luck… You mind if I come? Name's Alan. Alan Adair. The wags call me Robin Hood."

"Can't think why… Better I give you the address of the bar."

Len gave the man the address on a piece of paper he found in his pocket. The man had found a stub of pencil too.

"See you later," Len said.

"Is she that good-looking?"

"Believe me… What a beautiful day. They say it's spring this end of the world… Now, just look at that. See that telephone line going into the warehouse? Those birds are swallows."

"Even I know that."

"What you don't know is they flew all the way from England."

"You're just kidding."

"Gospel truth. My old landlady thinks of them swallows all the way to the Cape. Waits for them to come back for the summer. It's called migration."

When Len looked round the man was walking away shaking his head.

SHOWING OTHER people what he most loved was one of life's joys for Harry Brigandshaw. At ten o'clock they went ashore. A car from Colonial Shipping was waiting on the dock. Tina was disembarking at Cape Town. She was taking the six o'clock train to Johannesburg.

IN TWO DAYS Tina knew she would be back in her brother's house not knowing what to do with the rest of her life. Like so many other things, the shipboard romance with Harry Brigandshaw had come to an end at the dock. She was standing at the top of the first-class gangplank waiting to go down. Big, black-backed gulls mocked her from the top of the bollards that lined the dock. She could see an old tower with four faces of the time, all looking different ways. All telling the world it was ten o'clock.

The porters had taken her cases onshore. Customs and immigration had come on board soon after the ship docked to process the passengers, so she was now free to go. There was only the trip to see the wild flowers still in her life... But shared with the Voss family who were to be Harry's guests on his farm in Rhodesia.

Silently Tina damned the Voss family as she followed an officer down the gangplank right down onto the docks. The dockside was hard and ugly... A breeze had come up and made her hold on to her hat with one hand.

They all sat in the back of the large chauffeur-driven car. Harry was not even holding her hand. They drove for what seemed like hours in silence, everyone looking out of the window for something to see. There were flowers everywhere across the fields. Daisies. She was ending her affair surrounded by daisies. White daisies most of them. There were always white flowers at funerals. She had gone to her grandfather's funeral.

At the picnic lunch with the daisies they talked trivia. No one seemed to notice her tension. Even Harry. Tina wanted to give Justine a good slap across the face, always talking about the father she had never met. Was her life forever to be just bits and pieces?

They drove back a different way. It all looked the same to Tina... It had just been an affair. A shipboard romance.

HARRY SPENT HALF an hour in the office. He said another car had taken her luggage to the train. They were all behaving the way they had behaved with each other when they first went on board the boat... Did nothing in her life ever stay together?

The Voss family were taken back to the ship. Harry came out. He was flustered. Other things on his mind. She had been sat in reception to wait for him.

"One of the packing cases was dropped. I don't even know which part of the aeroplane. How the hell can they do something like that? Incompetent. Bloody incompetent."

"What are you talking about, Harry? You haven't said anything to me all day."

"The Handley Page. An adaption with long-range tanks. They're going to put it together in Cape Town. Take them months. Then I'm coming down to fly it to Elephant Walk. Pierre Le Jeune is helping Jim Bowman to build an airstrip on the farm. During the latter part of the war, Handley Page built bombers for the air force. This one will take six passengers instead of bombs... WHY the hell did they drop it? Tina, you'll have to see yourself off at the station. If I don't watch everything myself, this is what happens."

"Do you fly the plane via Johannesburg?" said Tina sweetly.

"What's that got to do with it?"

"We can see each other again."

"Of course we're going to see each other again. Just at the moment I'm busy. You said you have to see your brother. Go and see him. You may not want to stay... Damn that crane driver. Why couldn't he have looked at what he was doing? I try to do the right thing by everybody and end up in a mess."

"Are you going to do the right thing by me?"

"What does that mean?... Yes, course. But it's not my decision."

"Then whose is it?"

"Barnaby. He'll know about us by the next mail. Someone will write and tell him. People like to tell tales. It's one of the problems of being well known. There were three or four couples on board who know Barnaby. What do you think he will do?"

"Nothing."

"Don't you believe it, Tina. That man gets jealous. He thinks he owns you."

"Well, he doesn't... Go and sort out your aeroplane, Harry. I can look after myself. I've just been a fool. With Barnaby, I'm always a fool. Now you... Go on. Push off. You've more important things to do in your life than see me onto a train."

"I'm sorry, Tina."

"So am I."

Harry gave her a quick kiss and went back into the inner office. Tina hoped he would come out again.

An hour later the driver took her to the railway station where she boarded the train for Kimberley and Johannesburg. Her luggage was already in her compartment. Somebody had put it there. There was no one else in her carriage. When the train puffed its way belligerently out of the station, she was softly crying to herself.

"I'm twenty-four next month," she told the end of the platform as it slid away. "My life is over." She was wondering if Barnaby had even given her a thought since she left England. She hoped someone had dropped the rest of the damned aeroplane into the sea. Harry had not even said goodbye to her.

BY NINE THIRTY that night Forty Winks was asleep with his face resting sideways on the bar counter. Teresa let him alone. He had tried to go home once already. He even managed to get on his motorcycle outside the front door of the hotel and kick-start the engine. The clutch went out, the bike moved forward up the road towards the mountain with Forty Winks leaning to his right. He had wanted to turn the bike round in the road and go home. With Teresa and some of the regulars watching, the bike had kept going round in a full circle bringing Forty back to the spot by the kerb where he had parked the bike in the first place. Carefully putting the bike up on its rest he had gone back into Teresa's bar without saying a word.

There were travellers off the liner from the harbour and some of the same ship's crew in the bar. None had taken any notice. Two of the crew said they knew Teresa from a previous trip. She had smiled in fake recognition. All the sailors remembered her when they came ashore. She was the reason the bar made a profit for the Van Riebeeck Hotel.

There had been three Van Riebeeck hotels over the years. The first it was said had fallen down, the woodwork eaten away by borer beetles. The second had burnt down. The third was comprised of Teresa's bar, a dining room and ten rooms upstairs. The bar was a working man's bar. The rooms were cheap. Teresa was coloured like some of the customers from District Six a few streets up the hill from the road outside. Mostly the customers were men. Cosmopolitan. All colours and creeds. No one cared. Like Forty Winks, most were happy drunks trying to forget their miserable lives in a haze of alcohol.

Teresa poured a fresh tot of brandy into a small glass and put the small glass close to his nose. He had been asleep long enough. Forty Winks opened his eyes and lifted his head, his hand coming up for the glass from where it had hung down the side of the bar. Teresa and the regulars smiled and said nothing.

She went across to the window that opened onto the road, passing through the group of tourists who parted to let her through. Everyone was smoking. The air was thick. Even though it was still early October, she opened the windows wide. They opened outwards from each other.

She smiled again at the customers on her way back. One was called Willie. He was a big man and drunk but happy. All of them looked down the front of her dress as she passed. It is why she wore a low-cut blouse. Five per cent of the bar profit was hers. She had once covered up her large bosom and cut the day's profit in half. The men all drank to look at her. To receive her smile. It was better than going home to their nagging wives. Sometimes the nagging wives came into the bar. When they came she kept her smiles to herself. It was only business, which the wives would not understand. She never spoke to the wives who placed themselves between the husbands and where she served at the bar.

There were six sets of square high tables and high stools away from the bar. The man Willie and his two friends were seated nearest the open window. None of them complained at the cold fresh air sucking at the smoke, clearing the air in the room. The two who had been in her bar on a previous voyage were seated up at the bar with a third member of the same crew. The ship was the *SS Corfe Castle* on its maiden voyage. They had told her that when they ordered their first drink and asked if she remembered them.

"Come by St Helena?" she had asked. "Did you see the ladder up the side of the cliff? They call it Jacob's Ladder. My last name's Jacobs. Great-grandad came from St Helena. Grandma too. Most from St Helena are called Jacobs. Only a few related. Story has it our name comes from that ladder. You ever heard anything like that before?... You want the same again?" It was just something to say to them drinking at the bar.

Back at the bar, between the bar and the bottles on the rows of shelves, she smiled at the three men. Two of them were young. The two that could not take their eyes away. Teresa bent down for no reason other than to give them a better look. Men were so stupid when they drank. Mostly harmless. She gave them another smile as she poured them another drink. Men without women on ships were her best customers after Forty Winks. Forty was in love with her. He was older than her and spent all of his money in her bar. He said he had never been married, but she never knew with men. They all lied when it suited them.

"Why would your great-grandfather change his name to Jacobs?" the youngest one asked.

"He was a slave. From West Africa. Brought by the Royal Navy to run the harbour at St Helena."

"But you don't look West African."

"Products of the Royal Navy. Not all the slaves were men. Brought to South Africa by the Royal Navy after a generation or two in St Helena. Who knows? Some Jacobs say they are Malay. Brought by the Dutch from Java. Never went near St Helena. Part of the melting pot, I say. A right good old mix... That'll be one shilling and a penny... You never know. Most likely you and me are related."

"We're all related if you go back far enough," said Len Merryl. "The whole world."

"Now that is philosophical, Len," said Ben Willard. "Cheers. To the world and everyone in it, God bless them... The brandy in the Cape is the best in the world. If we need, Teresa, can we get a taxi back to our ship?" Ben liked to use her name.

"Just ask me when you want one. Better than walking. You can drop Forty Winks home on your way to the docks."

"Who's Forty Winks?"

"The bloke that was taking his nap at the bar. Does it regular. Why we call him Forty Winks. A ten-minute nap and he's up again right as rain... You don't mind the window then? Why I don't smoke myself. Even then I cough in the morning." She was smiling at another customer as she told them.

THE IDEA OF so young a girl having to cough in the morning made Len Merryl look away from the bar to the open window. There was a man's face half framed in the window. The people at the table between Len and the window were moving around. One of them was plainly drunk but happy with his friends. Len had seen the man on board the SS *Corfe Castle*. The man looking through the window had a full beard. It was the same man who had watched the owner's cabin door for so long and told Len to mind his own business. Len remembered the man had threatened him. Threatened to shoot him like the rest.

"Shit!" said the steward who had joined Ben and Len from the ship. He was the same man who still had Len's piece of paper in his pocket with the address of the bar written in pencil.

Len saw a hand come through the window holding a large black revolver. The gun fired twice. A man at the nearest table to the window staggered backwards across the floor and crashed against the bar splattering Teresa's open bosom with blood. Everyone in the bar was looking at the man shot through the head. It was the same man Len had seen on the ship.

Len ran for the door and out into the street. By the time he reached the street there was nobody there. There were no street lights. Len ran a few yards and came up short not knowing what to do. His adrenaline from primal fear was pumping. He went back.

The man on the bar floor was dead. Teresa was screaming. Forty Winks was asleep again with his face on the bar, the brandy glass empty in front of him.

The man in the window had shouted as he had fired. They had all heard at the bar.

"What was he shouting?" asked Alan Adair, the man with the pencilled address in his pocket.

"'I'm not a wet fish and you're dead'," said Len. "Each time he fired. He was one of our passengers. The one who pointed a gun at you in the cabin. We saw him go down the gangplank with the broken suitcase."

"The dead man was one of our passengers," said Ben Willard. "His name was Willie."

"Better wait for the police," said Len. "Then we go to the captain."

The other passengers who had been at the table nearest the window were staring at the dead body. None of them had seen the man at the window. They were all facing the bar looking at Teresa at the time the gun came through the window.

When the police arrived, Forty Winks was still asleep at the bar.

After giving his name along with the rest, Len and the other two walked out into the night. There were no taxis to be had. They walked back to the ship more sober than when they had walked into the bar at five o'clock that afternoon. All Len could see in his mind's eye was thick blood on Teresa's chest. He knew he was going to remember Teresa for the rest of his life for the wrong reason.

THE NEXT DAY everyone in third class was talking about the dead passenger. Everyone was animated, old and young alike. Everyone said they had seen Willie or knew Willie. They all felt part of the drama. More important than the day before. Not every day in a life was a fellow passenger shot through the head.

Everyone said the shooter fired at random through the window into the bar. The passenger shot dead was due to disembark in Port

Elizabeth. The word of mouth had soon told everyone Willie had never been to Cape Town before. No one even gave a thought to the possibility the killer was a passenger from the ship. Everyone on board the ship was British. The British did not shoot their fellow passengers. The killer was a thug or worse. A Boer still fighting the Anglo-Boer War more than twenty years after it had come to an end.

Len expected the Cape Town police to come on board. To take a statement. He had given his full name and the name of the ship. He had told the flustered policeman he had seen what had happened. In the panic and hurry to get Willie to hospital the policeman had taken little notice of Len.

By ten o'clock in the morning, Len asked an officer to see the captain.

"What about, son?"

"The shooting in the bar. I saw what happened."

"Did you tell the police, lad?"

"They weren't interested."

"Then why should the captain be interested? The passenger died onshore. The captain only has jurisdiction on board ship under maritime law."

"Willie McNam was a passenger. So was the shooter. He had a beard. There was a man on board acting funny who had a beard."

"Then point him out. I can check if he went ashore."

"The man with the beard disembarked at Cape Town."

"Then he's nought to do with us, son... You told the South African police you saw what happened. Everyone in that bar saw what happened. The whole ship's talking about it. More than one saw a black revolver pushed through the window which was open. If the police had wanted your statement as well they would have come back on board. The ship sails in six hours. All crew are required on board now. You can't go ashore."

"Why I want to see the captain. I recognised the man at the window."

"What was his name?"

"I don't know. He had a full beard."

"And he's gone. Do you know how many people in Cape Town have full beards? Why the police took no notice. You had a shock, lad, seeing a man get killed. Everyone in third class is in on the act. Just get on with your work."

"Don't you want to take my name?"

"What for? The captain has enough problems sailing the ship without taking on everyone's problems onshore. Leave it to the police. They know what they are doing."

"Can't you give the police a list of passengers who disembarked at Cape Town?"

"Just because you saw a man in the dark you say was wearing a beard, you say was a passenger without a name doesn't give the shipping line a right to suggest a fare-paying passenger is a criminal. Even if we did know his or her name which we don't. Now please. Or I'll take down your name for another reason. Which you won't like."

AT THE SAME time the *SS Corfe Castle* was sailing out of Table Bay a clean-shaven man in a new suit with a soft-spoken British upper-class accent was booking into the Mount Nelson Hotel that had once been Lord Milner's headquarters at the end of the Anglo-Boer War. The man who gave his name as the Honourable Peyton Fitzgerald to the clerk, looked pleased with himself. When the clerk took his name and looked for the best room in the hotel, the man looked back from reception at the revolving door in the front of the hotel and the row of palm trees in the driveway outside. Anyone in the know would have said he had the faraway look of an aviator. The thousand-yard stare of a hunter. The look of a man who had been in battle.

When the clerk coughed, and the man turned back to him the clerk involuntarily stared at the man's left side of his face where it was turning black and blue. The clerk quickly looked down at the register, turning the large red book round to face the man with the bruise on his face.

"Twenty-three, sir. Best room we have in the hotel. Please fill in the register Mr Fitzgerald and welcome to the Mount Nelson Hotel. How long will you be staying with us, sir?"

"I thought a week."

The clerk was again staring at the left side of the man's face. The man smiled. The clerk smiled back.

"Horse bolted. One of those newfangled cars backfired and she bolted. I was going to ride her up into the wine lands."

"You arrived on the *SS Corfe Castle*?"

"Been here a while, old chap. Staying with friends. They are sailing through Suez back to England. My ship doesn't sail for America for another week."

"Very painful."

"Yes it was, very. Hurts the old pride more than the face… I'll go to my room. No, I'll take that small case. The porter can bring the other one. Rather thought I'd take a bath before having a drink. The room does have a bath?"

"Of course, sir. Your key, sir. Have a pleasant stay, sir. The dining room opens at seven o'clock and stays open until nine. We do have a deposit rule or we hold a passport."

"Of course… My passport. If you so wish, the manager can ask the Standard Bank. I had money sent to them for my stay in South Africa."

"Just rules, sir."

"There must always be rules, my man. Where would we be without rules?"

Upstairs in room twenty-three, the man waited for the second case before locking the door from the inside. Then he opened the small case and took out a German Mauser pistol, the same type of pistol the German pilots had flown with during the war in France in case they were shot down by the British or the French. The man had taken the pistol from a well-worn leather case. The case was embossed with a set of initials. In the case was a pull-through which the man used carefully to clean the barrel of the gun. In the case in its proper place was a box of shells. The box had been opened. The box was short of two shells. Feeling the side of his face, the man looked down at the clean gun now resting in the open case with satisfaction.

At eight o'clock that morning a scruffy man with a full beard had entered a barber's shop in Loop Street. To the barber's surprise the man spoke with a soft upper-class British accent. He asked for the full treatment and offered the barber a ten-shilling note before sitting down in the chair.

"Bundu-bashing. Just arrived on the train. Can you believe it, someone stole my luggage. Where can I buy a good leather case and a suit off the peg? Jolly good trip. Bagged three lions up at Kuruman. Where Moffat had his church. Where Livingston met Moffat's daughter. Or was it his sister? A good wash all round the face first and then cut it off. No civilised man should ever be forced to wear a beard."

"The king wears a beard, sir."

"Naval type."

"And you, sir?"

"Royal Flying Corps. Shot down twenty-seven Huns."

"You must be famous, sir."

"Just did my duty. Honour. Duty. Country... Then you can't go wrong."

"Stuttafords should see you right, sir. In Adderley Street. The case and the suit of clothes."

Ten minutes later the barber had uncovered the bruise on the man's face.

"That looks nasty."

"You ever been in a bar fight?"

"Twice."

"You should see the other chap." They both winked at each other, fellow travellers through the vagaries of life.

At ten o'clock, after telling Stuttafords to alter the length of the arms on the suit jacket and the blazer, with two new leather cases ready to be filled with his purchases, the man now smiling to himself had walked to the foreshore. The *SS Corfe Castle*, way over to his right, was still in harbour.

Early the previous night the man had put the small gun case that he had purchased the previous day from a gun shop in Strand Street in a flood drain that in bad weather took water from the mountain down to the sea without flooding the streets of Cape Town. The man retrieved the gun case that had a dead pilot's initials engraved on the outside. The man had then walked back to Stuttafords and claimed his purchases. It was then two o'clock in the afternoon. With the gun case now inside the small leather case he had purchased at Stuttafords the man had hired a taxi to the Standard Bank. The small bank was a little further down Adderley Street. He told the man to wait. With the passport in the name of Fitzgerald that had been forged for him along with the passport for John Perry, he checked that the money he had transferred into the Fitzgerald bank account, before leaving England, was in the bank. The assistant bank manager gave him a South African chequebook which he put in his pocket having identified himself with the forged passport. Only then had the waiting driver driven him to the Mount Nelson Hotel where he was going to stay before taking the train to Rhodesia.

As the taxi took him up the hill towards the hotel, he looked back over the harbour. The *SS Corfe Castle* was sailing out into the bay. The man smiled pleasantly at the taxi driver who was watching him in the rear-view mirror.

Five minutes later the taxi was driving slowly through the opulent entrance of the driveway that led up to the hotel.

Alone in room twenty-three in the bath, the man soaked leisurely in the hot water. His watch by the side of the bath said the time was four thirty in the afternoon.

"People are fools," he said to himself.

He had never felt happier in his life.

AT EIGHT THIRTY that night in London, nine thirty South African time, when the steamship *SS Corfe Castle* had rounded the Cape, the curtain rose for the first time on *The Golden Moth*. Every box and seat in Drury Lane was full. Outside the theatre, high above the entrance, in lights that stood six feet tall as they ran up and down the letters, were the names of the stars of the show.

Inside the theatre in the front row of the stalls Mrs Schneider was holding her fingers and thumbs. In a box up to the left Oscar Fleming was tense. The overture faded as the curtain rose to the lavish stage. The show began.

Brett, as the heroine, made her entrance right of stage singing as she came. No one in the audience made a sound. The song rose and fell. The spotlight now on Brett as she moved forward to centre stage. When the curtain fell on act one, the audience sat in total silence as the lights in the auditorium came up. Only then did the chatter break.

Mrs Schneider unhooked her fingers and thumbs.

"I like to be alone so if the show sinks I can slink off on my own. It's your box Mr Fleming. I'm just a singing teacher. There is nothing more I can do but pray."

"She'll be all right."

"I hope so. Mostly all an old woman can do so late in her life. What a shame Mr Brigandshaw is so far away. She misses him, did you know that? She told me she never thought she would. That the stage was bigger than her own life. Well it isn't. Nothing is bigger than a person's life. Even when they are only twenty years old. Youth is not wasted on the young, despite the glib words of Mr Oscar Wilde. The only part that is important in life is being in love. And that is always for the young, I remember. It is what keeps me alive. The memory of love."

"You are a romantic, Mrs Schneider."

"Is there anything wrong with that, Mr Fleming?"

THE BUTTERFLIES had flown out of Brett's stomach the moment she began to sing. By the time the spotlight picked her out coming from the wings the only world was the stage and the song. The show moved smoothly on, automatically, rehearsed so well there was no thought to her moves, no waiting for cues, just a smooth flow of song and dance and brief sweet lines of dialogue. She was in her dream, consumed by the never real. She was nothing but her part as the show went from scene to scene, act to act until the last curtain fell and the noise began from the other side of the fireproof heavy curtain... The sound of thunder.

"What's that?" she said in alarm at the crashing noise.

"The audience, darling," said her leading man. "They love us. Quick, back into the centre stage, you and I. Bow low my Brett. You deserve the applause. Superb. Magnificent. You are a star, my dear... Come on. Smile. Here they come."

At first they were alone on the stage. Hand in hand. Then the cast came on. Twenty-three curtain calls. One with Brett alone. Most with the whole excited cast. Flowers thrown upon the stage. Showering her. Petals and perfume. Everyone loved her. Oscar Fleming smiled like a man smiling at his prize pig. Why a pig she had no idea. A prize pig with bows and ribbons, perfectly round... She smiled back at him standing in the wings, at last down from his box high above her stage.

THEN THEY were gone. The curtains came up again. The theatre was empty of people. The let-down began. The fear of the morning newspapers. Someone gave her a drink. Mrs Schneider was giving her a hug. The wine went straight to her head. The footlights dimmed.

The party moved to a private room of the Savoy. It was a Saturday night, with no show on the Sunday. They drank and talked, chattering about anything but the show.

When the first newspaper came into the room, silence came down like a fog. Fleming had the newspaper in his hands. Began to shake. Began to read. Began to laugh... Another London newspaper was thrust into his hands. Three more newspapers.

"We'll run for a year," shouted Oscar Fleming. "Not one dud. I give you a toast. To *The Golden Moth* and all who play in her."

"*The Golden Moth!*"

Only when Brett reached the flat in Regent Mews, did she cry. She had stopped anyone coming up into Harry Brigandshaw's flat with her.

She wanted to be alone... To think of him. To feel completely and totally miserable. Never so lonely in her life.

Only much later did she sleep. Exhausted with the night and all that had come and gone, not sure if it was the end or the beginning of her life. Brett Kentrich. Star of the musical stage. With her name in lights and her heart quite broken.

BY LUNCHTIME, with more flowers arriving at the flat for Brett every ten minutes, the SS *Corfe Castle* was fighting a second storm still three days from Port Elizabeth, the captain having turned the ship to sail into the twenty feet high swells to give the passengers some comfort. The ship was still pitching but no longer pitching and rolling like a corkscrew.

Nine hundred miles due north of the battened down ship, Barend Oosthuizen, Madge's husband and brother-in-law of Harry Brigandshaw, heard the first deep rumble in the earth from where he was working a mile below the surface. He had gone down in the cage with the morning shift at shaft number two as usual and as usual he was unable to remember what had happened in the bar the previous night.

He was eating the bread and cheese his landlady had left at his door in a tin box. Long ago they had stopped talking to each other. He had stopped bringing the whores back to his room, stopped crashing the doors when he came home drunk to fall asleep fully clothed on top of his bed. Mostly the bread and cheese was all he ate all day. He was gaunt and thin, his slate green eyes sunk deep in his bearded face, the blonde beard the colour of dirty straw. He looked at thirty-two an old man. His right hand was bleeding with a deep gash between the knuckles that had cut to the bone.

All morning he had ignored the pain in his hand, wielding the pickaxe at the gold seam with the full force of hatred. Five miners were feeding the baskets of one pony that trotted back and forth to the rail cart in the dark bowels of the earth, never again to see the light of day. As the weight in the baskets slung over the animal increased, the animal

sagged, pain showing in its eyes.

The pony, eating the fodder that kept it alive, was watching Barend with large brown eyes that reflected the candlelight inside the lamp attached to Barend's head. He was slumped against the end of the tunnel, against the same seam of gold he had been hacking out for months. The pony was looking for living comfort but found nothing in the slate green eyes staring back. For a moment to Barend it seemed the pony was feeling sorry for him.

His whole body was covered in a grey dust and his right hand was still bleeding from what he assumed was a fight the previous night. Had his hand not hurt he would have got up and slapped the pony or punched the animal in the mouth. Unlike the other four miners he had never found out the pony's name. Never fed it titbits. Never stroked the poor animal's muzzle. He even hated the pony along with the rest of his life and everything in it. One day he hoped when his body was too thin to take the punishment in the bars they would kill him and let him out of his miserable world.

The second rumble in the earth made the pony whinny. Barend stopped chewing the stale bread that foolishly kept him alive. Then the roof in front of him collapsed, and the pony was gone, no longer there, no longer looking at him. All he saw was a solid face of jagged rock six feet from his nose… Only then did Barend Oosthuizen smile, knowing at last he was going to die.

THREE DAYS LATER down by the sea so many miles away, the storm had exhausted its rage and the *SS Corfe Castle* was sailing into Port Elizabeth harbour looking none the worse for wear. Some of the passengers were wondering why they had ever left the safety of the shore to venture on the sea. A brass band was playing on the dock a day later than expected. Even Harry Brigandshaw was happy to go ashore.

The Colonial Shipping manager was waiting for him with a car and drove him to the office. On the way, Harry stopped the car and bought a copy of the *Daily Dispatch*. He turned to the financial page and found what he was looking for. Colonial Shipping shares were steady on the London Stock Exchange. He put the newspaper in his briefcase to read at his leisure.

There were two wires for him from his London office. None important. He had hoped for one from Oscar Fleming and felt the pit of his stomach sink. Not for himself. Gambling in the West End theatre was no different to backing a horse at the Epsom races. The odds the same. Some long. Some short. He had obviously lost his money. The opening of *The Golden Moth* had been a flop, panned by the critics. So be it, he said to himself. He had salved his conscience. A man nearly twice her age.

At four o'clock the post office delivered a third telegram to Colonial Shipping addressed to Harry Brigandshaw. Harry opened the cable.

GOLDEN MOTH SMASH HIT. I LOVE YOU HARRY. MISS YOU HARRY. PLEASE COME HOME HARRY. YOUR BRETT.

The guilt from his affair with Tina surfaced before he put the cable in his pocket and asked the manager to drive him back to the ship.

By the time they reached the docks, Harry had told himself he had the morals of an alley cat. He was a louse. The poor girl loved him and he was a louse.

There was a bar near the dock where the *SS Corfe Castle* was moored.

"Drop me here, please. And thank you." He had forgotten the man's name.

The ship was due to sail the following afternoon. Feeling sad, he went into the men's bar and put his briefcase on the bar counter. Poor Brett. It was the excitement of the show. She was a star. The love was meant like love from Brett at the end of the letter he thought one day she was going to write to thank him for her big chance in the theatre.

"She's a child. Children love differently."

"You want a drink?"

"Thank you."

They were the only two in the bar and they talked to each other. About nothing. The pleasant nothing of conversation that had no consequence.

"No one out so far. Three days it's been."

"Sorry. Came in on the *SS Corfe Castle*. Delayed by a day by the storms. We left Cape Town three days ago. What's happened?" Harry was just being polite. Not really interested. Playing the game he had played with so many barman in his life.

"Mine disaster on the Rand. Some say more than a hundred dead. One of the Boer generals' sons is down there with them. They'll be dead by now. The thirst gets them, the ones who are trapped. What a terrible way to die in the dark."

"What was the general's name?" Harry's whole body had gone cold.

"Oosthuizen. General Martinus Oosthuizen. The British hanged him for going out with G J Scheepers… The police were waiting for him. He killed a man in a bar brawl the night before his last shift. Luckily he never came up. They'd have hanged him like his father… You haven't paid! Isn't this briefcase yours? WHAT'S up with you?"

"Barend Oosthuizen was married to my sister."

The barman watched him go and then began cleaning the bar counter with a dirty rag. Then he looked again at the pound note the stranger had left and back at the now closed door to his bar. He could still see the man who had claimed kinship to the underground rockfall and shook his head. Then he rang up the cost of the drinks and put the change from the pound note in his pocket, shrugging his old shoulders.

He had been serving drunks for over forty years. They all had a story with themselves as the heroes. Bloke must have read the paper before coming into the bar and made himself a part of the current disaster to gain sympathy or just have something to say. Most of their lives were simply boring, going through the process of getting up, going to work, arguing with their wives, getting drunk and telling tall stories. Only when they were drunk, could they become more than themselves. Only when they were drunk, could they imagine themselves in a life that never happened, telling it time and again until they believed that themselves. Only that way could they ever have a life other than the dreary.

Sometimes he felt sorry for them. Always he listened to their stories. They could buy a bottle of brandy from the bottle store cheaper and take it home except they needed a listener. Someone to drink with. He was the listener. How he made his wages. He was just the listener. The only way the stories could be real even for a moment. It was what they paid him for.

He even knew how to change his opinion in mid-sentence to let the drunks hear what they wanted to hear so they liked old Jack and came back and back again. A poor way of making a living but a living like all the rest.

"I should write a book," he said to no one. The bar was still empty.

With nothing to do he dug the *Daily Dispatch* out from under the bar, spread it out on the counter and began to read. His trick each day was to take as long as possible to read the paper. He sometimes spent hours on his own waiting for a customer.

On the fourth page was a picture of Harry Brigandshaw. It was next to an article about the arrival in port of the *SS Corfe Castle* on its maiden voyage.

"Well, I'll be buggered," said the barman as he looked up at the empty street outside. "No wonder the bugger could afford to give me the change from a quid."

LEN MERRYL SAW Harry Brigandshaw down on the dock and wondered why the owner of the ship was alone and on foot. The man was carrying a small black case and was headed briskly for the first-class gangplank that would bring him up on board the ship. Apart from the duty officer, at the top of the gangplank there was nobody to be seen. The passengers were in their cabins or onshore.

Len had done his duty round of the first-class deck and picked up anything out of place. He had done an earlier round in the morning at first light before the ship docked. There had been little for him to do on his second round. He was off duty in half an hour when the sun would go down but had no wish to go ashore. Even the idea of drinking in a bar made him feel sick. The blood splattered over Teresa's bosom still vivid in his mind. What with the storm at sea and the passage of time the subject of Willie McNam had been dropped. The passengers' moment of excitement had been washed away by the storm.

Len leaned over the rail and watched the owner come up the gangway. The duty officer had seen who it was and for some reason stood back. Len was alone at the gate in the rail with his bucket and broom. The ship was quiet except for the forward hatch which was open and discharging cargo for Port Elizabeth. The one big crane that rode the dockside rail was swinging a crate held in a sling to the stevedores on the dock, the lone crane driver operating his levers perfectly so the crate came down on the dockside as light as a feather.

Harry Brigandshaw had stopped halfway up the plank to watch, smiling grimly at the crane driver. Then the owner went back to his preoccupation and strode up the last part of the gangway where he stopped and again glared at the crane driver.

"Why couldn't you have done that in Cape Town," he called to the man who was unable to hear. The crane driver ignored him, dangling his line and hook back into the gaping hole for another crate. He had not even seen Harry Brigandshaw at the rail of the ship.

On an impulse, Len stepped forward, the broom in one hand. The bucket in the other as Harry Brigandshaw finally stepped on board.

"Excuse me, sir. Could I have a word?"

"I'm far too busy. Damn all crane drivers. If it isn't one damn thing it's another. I need my aeroplane."

Len had no idea what the man was talking about but held his ground.

"I saw the man shot in the Cape Town bar."

"So did half the ship by all reports."

"No, sir. I saw the shooter. I think he knew you."

"I have enough problems for one day. My brother-in-law is a mile under the surface and probably dead. I hope so. To be trapped is worse. They haven't got anyone out, do you know that? Not in today's paper which I read standing up… I must make a phone call. Is the shore line attached?"

"I believe it is so… The man had a full beard and watched the door to your cabin for hours. I asked him if he knew you. Said he'd kill me too. I'm sure it was the same man who shot Willie McNam. The man who shot him was one of our passengers."

"Why didn't you tell the police?"

"I did."

"Describe the man."

Len did his best. The duty officer was hovering behind Harry Brigandshaw about to intervene. Len saw he now had the owner's full attention. He went on quickly.

"When he fired twice at McNam through the open window into the bar, I heard him shout."

"Can you remember what he said?" Harry had gone stone cold for the second time in one day.

"Something about a wet fish."

"What's your name?"

"Len Merryl."

"You'll be hearing from me."

"I'm only temporary. Getting off in Beira. I'm emigrating to Rhodesia."

The last part Len had said to a receding back.

Then the duty officer intervened and told him to go back to work. He knew he had been right. The man in the full beard and the owner of the ship knew each other. Having got it off his chest, Len felt better knowing he had done the right thing. It was now out of his hands.

LIKE ALL BAD days for Harry it came to an end. When he fell asleep that night it was from mental exhaustion imagining Barend trapped down in the dark a mile below the surface of the earth. Cursed with a good imagination Harry could see what was happening, feel the dread of lonely death. As if a conscious line joined him and his childhood friend, he knew his friend Barend was alive and suffering. All thoughts of Fishy Braithwaite were drowned in the horror he knew was tormenting his lifelong friend. Until he finally fell asleep, there was nothing he had been able to do but pray to God. And weep for Barend and somehow a little for himself and everyone else on earth.

The dreams jumbled all night. He was flying an aeroplane of a type he had never seen before. He shot down a German to find the dead pilot was Tina Pringle, her body mangled. Only her face looking at him with hate… He was in a dark hole and screamed himself awake. There was a tap on his door in the night. He shouted them to go away in his dream and the sky was blue. Too blue. All the time watching for a plane to kill him. All night long he tossed and turned. All night long the crane driver pulled cargo from the hold, arc light flooding the front of the ship. All night Harry abused the crane driver. How much was dream and real, he never knew.

In the morning, Harry was more tired than when he went to sleep. Still just as impotent. There was nothing more he could do for Brett. Nothing he could do for Barend. If Mervyn Braithwaite came anywhere near him, he was going to kill him even if it meant looking over his shoulder and waiting for the man to come after him for the rest of his life.

WITH THE HATCHES shut down, the cabin on top of the tall crane empty of the driver, the *SS Corfe Castle* sailed out to sea at five o'clock that afternoon. Harry had told no one onshore. Every time he had gone to the authorities nothing had been done.

"He got off in Cape Town, you fool," he had said to himself. "He'll go up to Rhodesia on the train."

As expected, there was no Braithwaite in the list of passengers. When he asked the master of arms to look for a man with a full black beard in third class, he was told there was no such man on board.

What had stopped Harry recognising the man who had been his commanding officer in France, was the colour of the man's hair and beard. In France and when he saw him last in London, Fishy Braithwaite had had blonde hair. Something in a bottle of dye had obviously changed. Harry could still see in his mind's eye the third-class passenger with a full black beard waving at him. He had even waved back.

TINA PRINGLE HAD been replaced at the captain's table by a man. Philip Neville was long in pedigree and short in income. Among his ancestors were dukes and earls. Some said the course of English history would have been different without the Nevilles. They had wielded power for centuries. None of which helped Philip whose private income was exactly one thousand pounds a year, adjusted for inflation, a figure that had been written into the will of an indulgent great-aunt just before she died. It was just enough to stop him having to take a job in the City. Not enough to attract the right kind of wife.

Philip had come on board in Port Elizabeth. He had travelled up the west coast of South Africa in an ex-army truck fitted out so he and his guide could sleep in the truck. They had driven as far as the Skeleton Coast and watched the colonies of seals. Unlike Harry Brigandshaw and Barend Oosthuizen he had not been looking for diamonds.

With the income for life from his great-aunt's estate he had gone up to Oxford and happily read English literature, a degree he knew would have little commercial value outside of his quest. He was rootless with no ambition and no real idea of what to do with his life.

The aunt had very kindly written a clause into his legacy that increased his allowance if the purchasing value of the pound went down. This calculation each year was made by the executors of her estate, a well-known firm of London solicitors. All they had to do was find out the cost of a single pint of best bitter in each of five public houses nearest their offices. If the average price had gone up, so up went Philip's annual legacy. What his Great-Aunt Constance knew about best bitter and English pubs was a mystery to Philip, but for ten years the calculation had kept him in exactly the same financial position. Not rich. Not poor. Enough money to go through university and travel.

All the aunt had asked in the will was for Philip to read literature at Oxford and write a good book which is what he had been trying to do with no avail since coming down from Oxford. It was, of course, his own fault like everything else in his life when it went wrong which it did more times than he could count.

Six months before Great-Aunt Constance died at the age of eighty-nine, Philip had made his weekly visit. He was then seventeen years old and still at Harrow School. His visits were not duty visits. His school was close to the London flat where Great-Aunt Constance lived with a paid companion and a pug dog that rarely left her lap, yapping at visitors as well as Philip from the safety of the old woman's skirts.

"He always barks, Philip, so don't look like that. Now come and sit next to me and tell me what you have been doing all week."

"Won't you tell me about India and Burma?"

"Later, Philip. First you. I want to know what you have been up to. You do remember I pay your school fees ever since your dear father died."

As usual, Philip gave his aunt a litany of his poor life. She seemed to take comfort from the day-to-day doings of a schoolboy, as if it kept her in touch with a life from which she was slipping away. His aunt fascinated Philip and not for her money. She had done so much and been to so many places always meeting people with something to say. The people who ran and made the greatest empire the world had ever seen as she told him every time Philip paid her a visit.

His mother had told him there had been so many suitors Great-Aunt Constance could never make up her mind. She had never married. Had never needed a husband to keep her and leave her money. Philip thought looking back on the so many conversations that his aunt had had no wish to domesticate herself with a large house and a brood of indulgent children. She was far too intelligent. Far too interested in life. She had inherited half a large industrial fortune from her father. Philip's grandmother had married a Neville who had gambled away the other half of the fortune. Nevilles had never been good at holding on to money.

He went to see her every week not for her cake and tea but her stories. Great-Aunt Constance was the best storyteller that Philip had ever heard. Every one of them true. Of that Philip was sure. They were far too vivid to have come out of the old woman's mind.

"What is the one thing you want to do most in your life, Philip?"

"I want to write a good book, Auntie," he had said off the top of his head.

"Then you shall; fiction or fact?"

"Does it matter?"

"Probably not. Someone said, I'm not sure which wise man, that history is fiction dressed up as fact. That if you want to know the real truth, read the fiction of the time… So you want to be a writer, Great-nephew?"

"Yes, Aunt Constance."

"Good."

That was all she had said. 'Good,' Philip had thought of it only again when the will had been read out in the dark, dingy offices of Simons, Tilby and Rockerman.

"Write me a good book, Philip. One good book." The words were cast in stone.

At first, Philip had thought the task quite simple. Armed with an Oxford degree in English literature he would write one good book and have an income forever. Trouble was for the last five years he had found the task not so simple. Writing the first paragraph was simple. Writing the rest was not.

By the time Philip sat down at the captain's table opposite Justine Voss he had stared at more blank pages than any man alive. Even travelling had done nothing to open the floodgate of his creativity. If only he had not promised his aunt. If only his income did not depend on it. If by the age of thirty he had not published a book, he was done. And here again with Great-Aunt Constance's usual thoroughness she had listed in her will the only publishers who would count. If there was not one good book by his thirtieth birthday, his income would stop. And then what was he going to do for a living he asked himself, fear rising from the pit of his stomach every time? What was a gentleman without money?

The day he sat down at the table, having boarded the ship at Port Elizabeth after roaming South Africa fruitlessly looking for a good story, he turned twenty-seven. It was his birthday. Until the third course of the meal he avoided all conversation. The man next to him had also not said a word. Twice he had caught the young girl opposite smiling at him and avoided contact with her eyes.

"Just three years to go," he said to the leg of roast chicken on his plate. He sounded totally miserable, even to himself.

"What happens then?" said Harry next to him.

They had been introduced at the start of the meal.

"If I haven't written a good book my income stops."

"That's a hard one. You want to tell me why?"

Harry needed something, anything, to take his mind from Barend who he was sure was buried alive.

"How far are you going?" asked the man next to him. Harry had already forgotten his name.

"Beira," said Harry, his mind drifting away again.

"That should be enough time. You don't know the Zambezi Valley by any chance? I'm looking for a story to write. A good story."

Justine Voss was looking across at him with big eyes. She was listening to his every word. "You should talk to my father," she said entering the conversation uninvited.

Wearily, with the weight of the world on his shoulders, Philip looked up and into the large, open innocent eyes of Justine Voss. Immediately, he knew he shouldn't have looked into those eyes. It was another one of his mistakes. If the girl in front of him, drowning in his eyes with himself drowning in hers, was seated at the captain's table she had to be rich. In exactly three years' time he was not going to have a bean. He was going to be poorer than a church mouse.

Harry looked from one to the other, his mind at last off of Barend. He had seen the deep exchange of looks. Which made him think of Brett and Tina bringing back another flood of personal guilt.

"I know the Zambezi Valley better than any man alive," he said to them both. "My father was Sebastian Brigandshaw. The big-game hunter. There was Selous, Hartley, Brigandshaw and Oosthuizen. The greatest hunters of their time. All of them hunted the Zambezi Valley. Why don't you tell Justine your story and we can all hear. I love a good story. You have been introduced to Miss Voss. And her mother, Mrs Voss. Miss Voss's father is Colonel Voss who fought with Chinese Gordon. Gordon of Khartoum."

At the end of the meal, Philip had finished the story of Great-Aunt Constance. The whole table had been enthralled.

"Come to Rhodesia, Philip Neville," said Harry having discreetly called for the passenger list from a steward. "We'll give you a story. What you must do is start the book with the story of your great-aunt and then tell your story."

"What a marvellous idea," said Justine. "We can all help."

"Or better still, tell her story. It's what she wanted, I think. What she prepared you to do by sending you to Oxford to read literature, what she's still paying for you to do. What do you all think?" Harry said to the table at large.

Instead of saying a word, everyone at the table politely clapped including the captain of the ship.

"There you have it then. Your book. All you need is a quiet place to write. Why not come to Elephant Walk?"

Harry was thinking of Justine. His own life was quite complicated enough as it was.

"Do you really mean that?"

For the first time that day the fear left the pit of Philip Neville's stomach. It was there right in front of him. As it had been all along.

"Mrs Voss and her daughter will also be staying with me at Elephant Walk."

Justine gave him the perfect look of thanks without saying a word. Harry smiled. Then he went back to worrying about Barend.

ON THE THIRD day of his entombment, Barend Oosthuizen had seen the pits of hell, the screams of the dead and it was far worse than anything that had happened in his sordid life. Hell was all-consuming and forever. By the time the SS *Corfe Castle* was steaming into the river port of East London for a one-day stop to discharge cargo which was the day after Philip Neville found his creativity and accepted the invitation to write his one good book at Elephant Walk, Barend was cowering away from the wrath of his God. For five days, while he went on living in the gap between the rockfall in the tunnel and the seam of gold at his back, every bad deed he had done in his life played through his mind time and time again. He knew he was in hell even before the everlasting torment began. With all his heart and soul he wanted to repent. To be forgiven. To start again. To make amends for the horror and filth he had made of his life as he fought to revenge the British hanging his patriot father by the neck. For all the years of his life until God found him in his living tomb, he had railed against the world. Tearing at it with his bare hands. Cursing its existence. Cursing his own life. Wishing to die. To be free of torment. Free of life's great injustice that had taken from him his father for a reason so wrong he had screamed inside every day of his life since it happened.

After the first hope of death had passed, and he found himself alive he had the time alone to revisit his life. To see himself as he was to other people. To see what he had done to Madge and his three children. The family he had abandoned, deserted, run away from to nurse his personal hate. The mother he had ignored.

On the fourth day he had shouted to his children. 'You don't deserve it. Why must you lose a father because I lost mine?' In his head, God had answered. 'Evil brings more evil. Stop the hate. Atone. Atone. Atone.'

Crouched on the ground he had seen his past and heard the wrath of God.

With the long metal spike he had once used to make holes in the face of the rock to insert sticks of explosives he banged on the tin box that had held his lunch. There was still light in his tomb from the box of candles he had carried in his pack. Only the day before that long ago morning when the tunnel caved in, the shift boss had inspected his pack.

"You're a bloody fool, Oosthuizen. So you hit your helmet a couple of times and walk back up the tunnel a mile for more candles at my expense. Time at the rock face is money. I told you more than once to take down a full box of candles… And where's your first aid kit? Follow the bloody rules or you go."

Barend had wanted to hit the man. Instead he had done as he was told and replenished his pack before going down in the cage for the last shift.

He had used the candles to give him light when the fear of the dark and his wrathful God had had him fumbling for matches in the dark. For some reason the air was still sweet, a quirk of the rockfall that had buried his way but left a small tunnel to bring him air and keep him alive.

It had taken Barend three days to finish his bottles of cold tea he took down each shift to quench his thirst as he hacked at the seam of gold-bearing rock.

He could now smell the pony buried in front of him. With his new will to live, came the revelation of food and liquid in front of him, sending him scrambling to unearth enough of the poor pony to give him food and blood. Only after he had cut the raw meat from the carcass and thrust it into his mouth had he laughed at God's irony.

God was keeping him alive to punish him. To show him there was no road other than to perdition unless he atoned for his terrible sins. He had to get out or face eternal hell.

In his cold fear he cleaned the cut on his right hand where human teeth had cut to the bone. The iodine stung. The dark came back. He was still alive and no longer wishing he were dead, fearing the hell God had promised more than death itself. Barend began to scream until his throat no longer let out a sound. Then he whimpered in the dark, fumbling for the matches to light a candle to take him out of the dark. Then his bowels opened, emptying the contents down his legs, oozing onto the rock floor of his tomb. The stench made him sick, heaving up undigested horsemeat from his stomach. The horsemeat tasted rotten, Barend began to cry as he sat down on the floor in his own shit.

There was no hope. There had never had been any hope in his life.

HARRY BRIGANDSHAW BOUGHT a two-day-old copy of the *Rand Daily Mail* the morning the ship docked in East London. He had made an arrangement with Justine and her mother to go up the Buffalo River to look at the game from a boat. Philip Neville had been invited along with two other passengers that had never been to Africa before. While Harry felt melancholy, the rest were excited at the thought of going into the bush, even if it was from the luxury of a boat powered by a petrol engine that would likely scare the game long before it came into view round the bends in the river.

The headline was simple. 'Survivors!' There was a picture of families at the pithead and a group of dirty men emerging from an iron cage.

Harry found a seat in reception and read the two-day-old story from the Witwatersrand. The Colonial Shipping receptionist watched him curiously. More worried about Barend than interested in his ships, he had not introduced himself. A quiet place to read came first.

Barend was not among the rescued. The paper told Harry to go to page three for more on the disaster. On page three there was a whole article devoted to the son of General Oosthuizen. There was a good human story to be had.

The man in the bar fight with Barend that had taken place the night before the rockfall had died soon after choking on one of his own teeth as blood gushed back from his lacerated mouth down his throat. The man had been drunk from a long day of drinking. The police had taken the man to hospital where a doctor pronounced the man dead. Only then did the police begin to enquire how the man had died. By the time they wanted to talk to Barend Oosthuizen he was down the mine. The police had told the mine manager not to let Barend off the mine premises when he came off shift and inform the police the moment he came above ground.

Before the police could do anything more than say a murder docket had been opened, the tunnels had collapsed. The *Rand Daily Mail*, sensing a good story, had talked to everyone who had seen the fight in the bar and came out strongly in defence of the Boer general's son. Harry sensed reading the article that had Barend been above ground in the hands of the police the newspaper story would have been different. People were more inclined to feel sorry for a dead man no longer able to defend himself.

The only sign of life reported by the paper on the third day after the rockfall was the distant sound of someone beating a tin can with a piece of metal followed soon after by terrible screams followed by silence. The rescue teams were digging out a tunnel that had collapsed during the underground earth tremor. The newspaper was doubtful there would be any more survivors, not wishing to create false hope among the families at the pithead. After more than three days anyone not killed by the rockfall would have died of suffocation, according to an expert quoted by the newspaper.

There was a long paragraph that talked about the injustice of hanging a prisoner of war who just happened to be a British subject as well as an Afrikaner. It was clear where the journalist stood on General Oosthuizen. The man wrote in English under the byline of Viljoen. The Viljoens were Afrikaners.

Harry smiled bitterly where he sat on the bench. At least Tinus Oosthuizen was no longer referred to as a traitor by an English newspaper. There was nothing else to read of the mine disaster after Harry read the editorial that called for more stringent safety regulations. Harry smiled again. Newspapers always called for regulations after the event, not before.

"Is the manager in his office?" he said getting up, leaving the paper on the bench.

"I'll have to see," said the receptionist snootily.

"Tell him Harry Brigandshaw would like a moment of his time."

The middle-aged woman shot out from behind the reception desk and ran towards the office marked 'Manager'.

"There's no hurry," said Harry to her back.

He felt weary. His friend was dead. He wondered if his sister Madge on Elephant Walk knew anything about the mine disaster. Whether the mine management even knew Barend had a wife and three children.

The manager came out of his office looking like he was prepared to be more deferential than at any time before in his life. Inwardly Harry sighed at the man's behaviour. There was nothing he could do to change it.

Harry saw he was a bald man of fifty with a moon face and rimless glasses. There were only four staff in the East London office of Colonial Shipping. More for processing cargo than passengers. Harry had not found time to ask the captain the man's name. He doubted if the captain of the *SS Corfe Castle* would have even known the man's name. The manager's office was a cubicle in the one small open-plan office.

"Have there been any more survivors?"

"No. Not that we've heard of. Terrible. Nearly one hundred men buried alive. Better the perils of the sea than the depth of the mineshaft."

"You were at sea?"

"Before I was sent ashore. I have served your family for over thirty years."

"I'm afraid I don't know your name."

"Barrow. Harold Barrow. My grandfather arrived in the Eastern Cape with the 1820 settlers. It is a great honour to meet you, sir. I have a cable addressed to you personally. I was about to send it on board. We all knew you were sailing with us. Just not that you would pay us a visit. A great honour indeed. May I present my staff?"

With great formality the man introduced his staff to Harry one at a time. The receptionist gave Harry a curtsy which Harry thought was taking it all too far. The manager Barrow beamed at the woman. Harry tried to shake her hand but was unable to attract the woman's eyes which were downcast in the direction of the floor.

"You have the cable for me?" Harry said to the manager.

The cable from the post office in a brown envelope had not been opened. Harry read the content and put it in his pocket. Then he smiled at them all and left. He had done his duty. In the strange manifestation of human nature Harry knew they would cherish his visit. People liked to know the human face of the company.

The cable from Brett was simple.

FLOWERS FROM EVERYONE BUT HARRY. YOUR DARLING BRETT.

Harry knew he was not going to reply. There was nothing to say. They had both come to the same decision. Brett wanted to be an actress. Harry wished to live in Africa. There never could be a compromise between the two of them. Soon she would start another affair. It was the nature of Brett. They both understood each other. The cables were part of Brett's thirst for drama. The reason why she had gone on the stage. Where everything changed and changed constantly. Great big statements one after the other.

He had time for a long walk on his own. Then they would go up the Buffalo River to look for the buffalo or anything else beside the river.

"Go well, Barend," he said out loud. Rarely did they find anyone alive after so long. The torment for his brother-in-law was over. Hopefully, he thought, he was killed when the rocks fell down with no time to contemplate his life.

As Harry walked away from the docks, deep in his own thoughts, he wondered if in the end he would die a rich, lonely man. He was thirty-five years old. Halfway through his allotted threescore years and ten. It had just been an affair. An affair he would remember for the rest of his life. In his memory, best of all, Brett would never grow old. Never fall out with him over the trivial hurdles of life. They would never be bored with each other. What they had would live forever without being destroyed by the human nature which Harry suspected had a tendency to destroy all good things in the end.

WHEN HE RETURNED to the ship, they were already waiting for him to take them on the trip up river. Justine Voss and Philip Neville looked most happy standing next to each other.

"You lot ready to go?" said Harry cheerfully. There was no point in spreading his melancholy to anyone else. Underneath the outward façade, he knew they all had their own problems. He hoped Brett's problems with him would soon be over, swept aside by something far more exciting. The new affair.

They had three more ports of call after East London. Durban,

Lourenço Marques and Beira. Then the train would climb up from the coast to the highveld and home. Rhodesia. The place where he really belonged on a farm. By now the baby giraffes would be tall with small knobbly horns. The first time since knowing about the mine disaster, Harry felt excitement.

THEY SAILED UP the Wild Coast in sight of land all the next day to dock in Durban in the evening.

No one else had been found alive. The proto-team still said they heard the sound of the tin can being faintly beaten in the one tunnel and were making progress moving forward. None of their shouts were answered. The proto-team were going to go to the end of the tunnel, pulling out the rockfall, rock by rock, and only then give up the search for anyone alive. The gruesome business of digging out the dead bodies would take weeks. Some of the men would most likely never be found and be left in the bowels of the earth.

IN JOHANNESBURG, Tina Pringle was lying naked in a hot tub with her knees up and her legs open. The half empty gin bottle was standing on a stool next to the bath. The water was as hot as she could bear and had been since she started drinking the gin straight out of the bottle. She was overdue and frightened out of her wits. The storm in the South Atlantic had come in the middle of her cycle. It was a storm that knocked the sense out of her head. The storm and Harry Brigandshaw.

As she lay in the bath half drunk she had no idea what she was going to do. In London she might have found a doctor to give her an abortion. In Johannesburg she had no idea which way to turn. Her brother Albert was now quite the rand baron. Far too aware of his position in society. Sallie, her sister-in-law, was remote. Why she had moved into the cottage in the garden that had been built for Miss Pinforth her tutor so long ago. But Miss Pinforth was now dead. She had nowhere to turn. If word got out she was pregnant and unmarried, her brother would kick her out of his house. Self-made men were like that it seemed to Tina. Bigger snobs than the rest of them put together.

She took a long swig out of the neck of the bottle and began to cry. She was finished. It was over. Finally she was finished once and for all. Little bastards were not welcome anywhere in the world. Africa or England.

WHEN THEY finally got Barend Oosthuizen to the surface eight days after he was buried alive, the police arrested him for the murder of Johan Potgieter. The press were at the top of the mineshaft. Dozens of them. Every newspaper in the region, including the *Rhodesia Herald*, had a reporter on hand.

The filth and exhaustion of the man was photographed by nine newspaper cameras. Solly Goldman of the *Rhodesia Herald* had travelled down in the train with Simon Haller four days earlier.

"Do you have anything to say?" shouted Simon Haller to the newly made prisoner.

"It is the will of God. Everything is the will of God. Sinners repent. I am a sinner. Repent all ye sinners or you shall go to hell. To eternal damnation. The road to perdition awaits all those sinners who do not repent. I go with God on my side. In the bowels of the earth I found God. God saved me. Whatever the police wish to do cannot change the will of God. I repent my sins. God forgive me... All of you go with God."

To Simon Haller's astonishment the man managed to break free from the police, standing his ground and delivered the same sermon in Afrikaans.

The Ministry of Barend Oosthuizen had begun.

"Isn't he related to Harry Brigandshaw of Elephant Walk?" asked Solly who was the only one of the two who had understood the Afrikaans.

"It's his brother-in-law. What a story," said Simon Haller.

"Will they hang him like his father?"

"You assume he's guilty?"

"Potgieter is dead."

"So will Oosthuizen be soon. Did you see the colour of his right hand? It was black. Gangrene. If they don't cut it off now, he'll be dead in the morning, all God's effort gone to waste."

"What gave him gangrene?"

"A man's teeth. The most poisonous thing on earth. He used his right hand to kill Potgieter. Now Potgieter's going to kill him... Quick, Solly, get a close-up shot of the killer's hand. What a story. This one will syndicate. Mark my words. Better than the girl finding her war hero. Did you ever hear again from Jim Bowman or Jenny Merryl?"

"Your imagination will be the end of you Simon."

"Do as you are told! Get the photograph. Now!"

"Yes, sir."

The prisoner stood with his back to the van that was standing ready to take him away.

"ATONE. ATONE. ATONE," shouted Barend Oosthuizen over the heads of the crowd.

His right hand, black to the wrist was held high. The man stank of excrement. He was smiling. His eyes full of hope. Alive. Joyous.

"He's nuts," said Solly.

"I don't think so... We're going to hear a lot from that man in the future."

"If they don't hang him first."

"Not this time. He has the press on his side. And God... That man has seen the light. Look at him. He's come out of hell and he's radiant. May God be praised. Can you imagine being alone in a hole for a week in your own shit? God truly does have strange ways. Don't you feel the presence of God looking at the man? I'm going to make this the biggest story of my life. I'm going to make that man famous."

"You'd better get a doctor to him or the story will be dead before it starts."

"You are cynical, Solly."

"You're a predator, Simon."

HARRY BRIGANDSHAW GAVE the Durban branch manager a cable to send to his mother on Elephant Walk telling her not to meet the boat train in Salisbury. Tembo was to bring the car on his own. There was not going to be a second chance for Mervyn Braithwaite to kill a member of his family.

In a moment of loneliness he had written a short letter to Tina Pringle at her brother's address in Parktown, Johannesburg. It was the least he could do for the girl to restore her sense of pride. Harry was sure she would go back to Barnaby St Clair. He and Tina had done what man and woman had done since the start of time even if the Bible and society forbade fornication.

He gave the branch manager the letter to be posted with the rest of the mail from the office at the end of the day. She was Barnaby's girl. Harry just hoped Barnaby would not find out. When it came to jealous men in his life, Mervyn Braithwaite was quite enough. Mervyn, unlike Barnaby, had no reason for his jealousy. Maybe the girl had used him. To get back at Barnaby for not marrying her. It had happened before.

As an afterthought at the end of the letter, Harry had suggested Tina come up to Elephant Walk for a holiday. It was a gesture of goodwill. A thank you. An invitation he was sure would not be accepted. Like Brett in London, Tina by now would have better fish to fry in Johannesburg. Like Brett, he was too old for her. The trouble for Harry with women was his age. The women he liked of his own age were married. And unmarried girls of thirty-five mostly had a problem with men. A widow was the only chance left, and they found it difficult to fall in love all over again. All the widows Harry knew had lost their husbands in the war. Trying to compete for love with a dead man was impossible. Anything they did not like was compared to the dead man who was now perfect.

Harry had done the usual rounds of the office. Shaking everyone's hands. The billboard on West Street outside the office had been short. 'NO SURVIVORS'. This time Harry had not bought the newspaper to read. The ship was spending the night and following day in the harbour and Harry had agreed to take the Voss family and Philip Neville to dinner at the Durban Club. The club was famous for the best Indian curry in Africa. The Salisbury Club in Rhodesia gave him reciprocity to the Durban Club. It was something to do. With Brett in London and Tina in Johannesburg, Harry felt at a loose end. There was no one else on the ship that had caught his eye. He was ready for a life of celibacy on the farm. There were said to be six eligible men in Rhodesia for every eligible girl. And he was too old. That part of life had finally passed on by. The bush and the animals would make up for his loss. He hoped. You couldn't have everything in life.

Harry was in the throes of leaving the office when a cable was delivered to the manager from the post office.

"They found one alive," shouted the manager waving the cable from the Johannesburg office of Colonial Shipping.

"Who?" said Harry walking back into the office.

"The general's son."

"Barend Oosthuizen?"

"The police have arrested him for murder though they don't think he'll live. His right hand has gangrene. The doctors have had to cut it off." The cable had run to three sheets.

Harry was grinning all over his face. He went out the office without saying a word and walked down West Street smiling at everyone. At last he had a real use for his money. He would buy Barend Oosthuizen the best lawyer in Johannesburg. Bar brawls could go any which way. Potgieter could have killed Barend. They were in a fight. There would be witnesses to mutual abuse. Bar fights in the mining camp that was Johannesburg were the way men without woman let off their frustration. Whores and fights went together. Barend had told him that while they rode the Skeleton Coast looking for the pipe of diamonds that both of them were certain was somewhere to be found. The original seven diamonds on the seashore had had to come from somewhere. There had to be a mother lode. Harry could hear Barend's voice in his mind.

'ON THE MINES, Harry, you work up a thirst, go to a bar, look for a whore and if you can't find one look for a fight. It's the only entertainment. What else does a man do on his own? If the one I fight is English, the pleasure of hurting him is all the more.'

'Why have you never tried a fight with me, Barend? I'm English.'

'I don't want to hurt you, Harry. Never have. Growing up with you much older, you are like a God to me… Those were good times on the farm before my father was murdered.'

HARRY STOPPED in his tracks in the street. The man behind bumped into him. Harry had gone back the same way before the man could apologise.

Back in the office of Colonial Shipping, Harry gave his instructions.

"You get this wrong and you never work for me again," he said to the manager only half threatening in his excitement.

"I don't understand, sir."

"Barend Oosthuizen is my brother-in-law. The father of my nieces and nephew. I want the best doctor. The best lawyer. We are going to bring him home… Were it not for my guests on the *SS Corfe Castle* I would go to Johannesburg myself… Get on with it man! Get on with it!"

"Right away, sir."

"Now we are getting somewhere."

Harry was still grinning with relief when he left the office to go back to the ship.

THE PRESS CORPS was camped in the Johannesburg hospital. Every reporter wanted to interview Barend Oosthuizen. Eyewitnesses to the bar fight in Jeppestown could be found for the price of a drink. The stories of ones who said Potgieter had started the fight were printed. The combination of the Boer general who had been hanged by the British and the son who had found God in the bowels of the earth resonated around the country. They wanted the son to be a hero. They wanted God to forgive him his sins. The loss of the right hand was God's punishment. The police ran into an orchestrated campaign and gave up. The policeman at the door to Barend's hospital room was withdrawn. The police withdrew the murder charge. The public shouted their approval. The newspapers trumpeted the news. Potgieter's wife was a lone voice of dissent. She had three children. The papers mentioned none of them.

By the time Harry Brigandshaw's lawyer and doctor were ready to move it was all over. Along with the rest of them, Simon Haller was allowed into the patient's room. It was a circus with Barend Oosthuizen lying back on the pillows at the centre of everyone's attention. Flashbulbs exploded. They all shouted questions, shorthand notebooks at the ready.

The nurses had cleaned him up. The bandaged stump of the arm was lying on top of pure white sheets. The long, blonde hair was washed and lay on the pillow down both sides of the man's head. The full beard had been washed and combed onto the man's chest. At the centre, slate green eyes stared straight ahead looking at something none of them could see. Everything about the man lying on the bed was calm in complete contrast to the rest of them.

When Barend Oosthuizen raised his one good hand, he was asking for silence. As if to each one of them he smiled. Then Barend began to speak. Quietly, gently and only about God.

At the end of the sermon, Simon Haller crossed himself before leaving the hospital room.

NEITHER OF them had said a word to each other until they reached their taxi in the hospital driveway.

"Do you think he believes what he says?" asked Solly Goldman.

"Oh, he believes what he says," said Simon Haller.

"Do you believe what he says?"

"That's a question man has been asking himself since he came out of the primal swamp and had the ability to think. I'd like to believe, Solly. You have no idea how much I would like to believe. Without faith in God there is no point to anything. Why we also desperately want to believe in a religion."

"But do you believe in God?"

"I don't know, Solly. Like all the rest of us deep down in what the priests would like to call our souls. I just don't know. Mostly when you want something really badly you don't get it. To some, faith is easier.

All they have to do is believe. We only find out the truth when we die. Whether there was any point to life at all. When we die."

"He's got you."

"Oh, yes. He's got me thinking all right."

"Don't you think he might be a fraud? All this to wash away the charge of murder."

"We are all frauds, Solly. Especially newspapermen. We'll say anything to sell a newspaper. The 'all good' fourth estate. I doubt it… Power. It's all about power. All the estates of man. From the King to the priests to Parliament. Everyone is trying to control our minds and bodies. It's the way things are and always will be. You can't have people running round the world doing what they want. That's anarchy. No one wants to live in a state of anarchy. Why we have a king or whatever we call the man at the top."

"Isn't God at the top?"

"There you go again, Solly. That question."

"All you have to do is believe."

Simon was shaking his head. There were tears in his eyes.

SEVEN HUNDRED and twenty miles to the north while Simon Haller was trying to find God, the Honourable Peyton Fitzgerald was well satisfied with the information gleaned on his own quarry. He had made a friend of the tall, big-bellied Zulu on the main door of Meikles Hotel where Peyton Fitzgerald had been staying for a week in room seventeen. The black man was a mine of information for ten shillings, the single note having exchanged hands the second day after Peyton Fitzgerald arrived in Salisbury.

"I'M WRITING A BOOK, you see. About the big-game hunters of Africa. Have you ever heard of Sebastian Brigandshaw? He died in a hunting accident but his family live somewhere hereabouts."

"Elephant Walk. Twenty miles from here on the Mazoe River," said the Zulu doorman. He was holding his shield and spear, monkey tails hanging from his waist, a leopard skin slung over his broad shoulders.

He looked, as he was meant to look, the picture of a Zulu warrior.

"Splendid. So you know what I'm writing about. Tell me about Elephant Walk."

"Talk is a man from the Belgian Congo has built a piece of ground for big, big birds to land down on. Very big birds."

"Aeroplanes? My goodness. Do they have aeroplanes in Africa?"

"I don't know."

"Who lives at this Elephant Walk? What is it?"

"A farm. Very big, big farm with water going from river onto ground. Tobacco. Maize. Much cattle... Very rich."

"And who lives there?"

"The baas is in England. Son of a hunter. Madam still there. Wife of hunter. Old man, father of wife. Daughter and children I think. People who work too. Many people."

"Big fence round the house?"

"Not no more. During Chimurenga big fence. Old man take it down they say. You go out on Mazoe Road. You go they give you lunch. Any white man go Elephant Walk gets lunch. Black men too if they travelling around country. Black men get lunch in compound."

"Does not the daughter have a husband?"

"He very bad man. Gone away. Beat up his black men with sjambok. His workers. Big whip. Very big man. Very nasty, they say... Excuse me, baas."

The Zulu had majestically walked to a new car that pulled up at the entrance to the hotel and opened the back door for an important-looking passenger. Smiling with satisfaction, the man who now called himself Fitzgerald walked away.

EACH TIME PEYTON Fitzgerald left the hotel he engaged the Zulu in conversation. Had it not been for the greater excitement of Harry Brigandshaw watching, he would have hired a car, driven to Elephant Walk and killed Harry's mother. Instead he was waiting for the boat train from Beira to arrive at Salisbury Station. Then he was going to do the same thing as last time. Only instead of the wife he was going to kill the mother and Harry Brigandshaw.

He had sent a messenger from the hotel to the offices of Colonial Shipping in Salisbury to find out the exact time of the train's arrival, a day later than scheduled due to the ship going through bad weather.

The pleasure of waiting for Harry Brigandshaw was exquisite. The

dead German pilot's gun was safely in its case in room seventeen.

While Simon Haller was trying to find a way to interview Barend Oosthuizen alone in an exclusive for the *Rhodesia Herald*, the two of them both being born Rhodesians, Peyton Fitzgerald was standing in room seventeen looking down on Cecil Square dripping spittle from both sides of his mouth. His day of atonement was nigh.

THE ROW BETWEEN Tina Pringle and her brother Albert started in Parktown as the *SS Corfe Castle* was sailing into the port of Lourenço Marques in the Portuguese colony of Mozambique.

"You're pregnant aren't you, Tina? That's it. It's that Barnaby St Clair. I can't have a scandal. I have a position to maintain."

"To answer your first assumption, you are probably right. I'm late and though I am not, I feel sick in the morning. Your second assumption is wrong. The father is not Barnaby St Clair."

"You're a slut."

"That's pretty good coming from a man who ran a knocking shop."

"It was not."

"What were all the rooms for over the bars and restaurants? It was a whorehouse. You want a real scandal then. I'll ask your old boss and mentor to open her mouth. Where is the esteemed Lilly White these days?... Sit down and shut up, Bert. The whole bloody town knows your fortune started in a brothel. They are proud of you. Johannesburg is a mining camp. You're part of its growth."

"Then who's the father? Sallie will want to hear about this."

"Your wife knows. When I told her she became human. I'd forgotten how nice she can be."

"Then who was it?"

"He's alive, Bert. Or he was when I got off the boat in Cape Town."

"What are you going to do?"

"You sound as if I'm the first woman to fall pregnant without a ring on her finger. You really can be a sanctimonious hypocrite. Sallie told me she was pregnant when she married you. It was why she married you. You were way beneath her class."

"I'll make him marry you."

"There you go again, Bert."

"Who is he? Some stoker off the ship?"

"I was travelling first class, remember. You should know as you paid for the ticket."

"Some junior officer?"

"If you must know it was the owner of the ship."

"Don't be silly. The *SS Corfe Castle* is part of the shipping line. They have dozens of boats."

"Exactly."

"Blimey. It's Harry Brigandshaw."

"Exactly. The fighter ace and grandson of the Pirate who started much the same way you did, Bert."

"How did he seduce you?"

"He didn't. I seduced him."

"Then you are a slut."

"Bert! You're getting boring."

"What are you going to do, Tina?"

"I have no idea. Are you going to kick me out of your house? If you do I shall go back to Mum and Dad... Can you imagine Barnaby's face when he hears? I hate him. He is so full of his own importance he doesn't have time to even be a sanctimonious hypocrite."

"We'll have to find someone to marry you fast... A month isn't too long. Thirty-six-week-old babies are barely considered premature."

"You should know, Brother dear."

"Do the servants know?"

"Oh shut up, Bert. It's me, Tina. We were born in a railway cottage. Our parents are as common as dirt and still the most wonderful people I know in the world. Thank you, Bert. You've made up my mind. I'm going to have my baby. I'm going back to my roots. I'm going home. Mum always wanted a grandchild to hold."

"What you mean by that?"

"You've never been home, Bert. Never taken your kid. Your wife. You've got too big for your boots. Don't you love Mum and Dad?"

"Of course I do."

"Then show it."

"They won't take money."

"They don't want money. They want you and Julia. Their own blood. And Sallie. They are nothing to be ashamed of just because they don't have an education. They are good people and that is worth more than all the money in the world."

"When are you going back?"

"I haven't decided yet. I want to be quite sure I'm pregnant. I'm going to wait another week and see a doctor."

"You said you were sick in the mornings."

"I said I thought I was. It was in my head. When you think you are pregnant, you have morning sickness. There's a lovely word for that which Miss Pinforth taught me. Psychosomatic. What the mind thinks the body confirms."

"Then you are pregnant. I'll go and see Brigandshaw. Where is he?"

"In Rhodesia by now."

"Then we'll go to Elephant Walk."

"Did you like Harry, Bert?" Tina said sweetly. "When you met him that one time, I was with Benny Lightfoot. The American. You were my chaperone."

"I didn't expect him to do this to my sister. Men are pigs."

"Oh, Bert. Get off that high horse of yours and pour me a drink."

"It's ten o'clock in the morning... Do you like Miss Pinforth's cottage?"

"That's better. Why don't you go and ask Sallie to join us? Celebrate. A new life is with us."

"Then you are pregnant?"

"Yes, Bert, I'm pregnant."

LATER THAT DAY, when Tina's brother and sister-in-law were comfortable with her pregnancy, Philip Neville was standing in front of a large church. The building was beautiful. A beacon of Christianity on the wild shores of Africa. They were all standing together looking up in awe at the spire rising up into the powder-blue sky in the centre of Lourenço Marques.

They had come ashore to look at the sights. To taste the strange continental smell of the Portuguese colony's capital. There was a rich, musty smell that reminded Philip of incense and God and ancient mysteries. The size of the church reminded him how small he was in the progression of life. For a long moment the great book he was about to write was insignificant.

He had mapped out the first three paragraphs in his mind. Word for word. Each carefully remembered to begin the triumph that would change his life and secure his income. Though once the book came out, he would no longer need his great-aunt's money. The book was going to make him rich and famous. Once he had one bestseller to his name, his confidence would rise. All the other stories he wanted to write would come flooding into his head. He would be part of the London literary set. He would join the Garrick Club. He would allow himself to be invited to the important soirées thrown by influential old ladies with too much money and too much time on their hands who sat to patronise the writers of the day.

Harry and the rest of the crowd from the boat had walked off down the wide street and left him alone staring with deep satisfaction into the brilliance of his future. The church right in front of him was no longer in his mind.

"Aren't you coming, Philip?" called Justine Voss. "It's a beautiful church but you can't stare at it forever."

BY THE TIME Philip was back walking by her side, the butterflies were back in Justine's stomach, fluttering with intense excitement. It was only days now she told herself before she met her father for the first time.

They all walked on down the street, the men on the side nearer the cars and horse-drawn carts, protecting the woman from road splash like all good English gentleman. The fact there had been no rain in the colony for weeks made no difference. It was the place gentlemen walked on the streets on the rare occasion a walk was necessary. The etiquette made Justine feel safe.

MRS VOSS, thinking to herself, about the soon to be faced confrontation with Colonel Voss, the man she was once meant to have married so long ago, had the same butterflies in the stomach, brought out not by excitement but by fear. She had no idea what she was going to say to him. What he would look like after so many years of deprivation? Would she cry or laugh or simply wish to run away when she saw the horror in her daughter's eyes at the oh so final reality instead of the dreams?

She had started the journey. Now she would have to make it come to an end and go back to her lonely life in England with death to comfort her at the end of a useless life.

Her daughter was giggling to Philip Neville. Somehow it made her irritated.

"It will be all right," said Harry next to her.

"Can you read minds?"

"Yours just then. Life is never as bad as we think. There's always hope."

"Do you really believe that?"

"No. But it's important to think so. And sometimes we get such wonderful surprises."

16

ELEPHANT WALK, NOVEMBER 1922

At Elephant Walk the dogs had sensed there was something going on. The two dogs were chasing the bitch around the msasa trees, trampling the round flowerbeds that marked the trees among the well-kept lawn. They were Rhodesian ridgeback dogs trained to track lions. Emily Brigandshaw, Harry Brigandshaw's mother, screamed at the dogs to get out of her flowers as the red and yellow cannas flew apart with the charge of the dogs in full cry. Then the bitch turned in her tracks around a tree trunk and came out charging the dogs. The dogs turned tail, yelping with excitement. The ginger cat asleep on the windowsill of the kitchen in front of Emily stayed fast asleep with his eyes wide open. The Egyptian geese, long tame around the sprawling homestead of what was now five houses, had taken off honking loudly for the safety of the nearby Mazoe River when the dogs first raced out onto the lawn.

The fifth small house had been built under the supervision of Sir Henry Manderville, Harry's maternal grandfather to give Jim Bowman the privacy of his own home. There was the main house now lived in by Emily and her daughter Madge, the wife of Barend Oosthuizen. With them in a permanent state of excitement lived the three children. Paula was going on seven, Tinus junior going on six and Doris going on five. They had all been born a year apart in the month of February during the three good years of Madge's marriage to Barend. The dilapidated old house once lived in by Alison and Tinus Oosthuizen was empty. All day long, until they fell asleep from exhaustion, the children yelled at each other to see who could make the most noise. They were wild, untamed without a modicum of education.

Sir Henry, their great-grandfather, had learnt to stuff cotton wool in his ears when he wanted some peace. He claimed he could hear the children from two miles away when he went out collecting his butterflies, many of which had ended up in the British Natural History Museum in London, all in perfectly handmade wooden boxes with glass tops and the names of the butterflies in English, Latin and the local Shona language. Sir Henry's only claim to fame was in the wooden boxes that were now sent to England in large straw-filled wooden crates once a year on the same day in January.

The fourth home in the family compound, which had been built for Peregrine the Ninth in 1915, during the war in France, was now occupied by a rebellious Colonel Voss. Othello and Hamlet, the horses that had transported Jim Bowman and Colonel Voss to the Valley of the Horses had been retired to a large field close to the Brigandshaw family compound. The big wagon with the canvas top was stored in a new shed built by Jim Bowman with the help of the same two African builders who had come to Elephant Walk to build Tinus's house. Despite all the scrubbing, haircuts, beard cuts and new clothes, Colonel Voss still looked like a man who had lived outside most of his life: a homeless vagabond who now hated living in his new house where he had been ever since Jim Bowman collected him from the canvas-topped wagon outside the dilapidated home of the man Jim only knew as Sir Robert. King Richard the Lionheart had refused to change his home, the dog preferring to stay with Sir Robert on his run-down yard outside the Rhodesian capital of Salisbury. The colonel had not wanted to go on one his bush trips as suggested by Harry Brigandshaw but was coerced to coming to Elephant Walk by Jim Bowman.

For many weeks, Colonel Voss had been in a deep sulk. He had been told so many stories in his long life and told quite a few himself that he believed none of them to be true. The very idea of Felicity travelling all the way to Africa after so many years seemed absurd. As for a well-brought-up English girl like Justine finding out her reprobate father was alive, let alone wishing to see him, sent him into fits of uncontrollable laughter. It was all a set-up like the rest of his life. It was clear to Colonel Voss that young Jim Bowman got himself a proper job and felt sorry for him. Felt it his duty to dig him out of a perfectly comfortable billet with his old friend Robert to be subjected to hot baths and haircuts and regular food.

It had all happened in a matter of weeks. First, they had put him in a vehicle that did not require a horse to make a journey. Then they had bought him a wardrobe of new clothes, burning everything else except his new boots. They had subjected him to a barber and a bath in one of the back rooms at Meikles Hotel Jim Bowman had rented for a day. Then driven him to Elephant Walk and his new home that had once belonged to his old friend Peregrine the Ninth before the old boy died. He was sure Peregrine was turning in his grave. He only wished he was doing the same. He had lived too long. The very thought of all that past catching up with him was appalling. He had made up his mind to sulk for the rest of his life or until they took him back to live in his wagon in Sir Robert's yard where he was perfectly comfortable and quite content.

"Why couldn't you have left me alone?"

"Oh, I do so wish I could," Jim Bowman had sighed.

THE SENSE OF something going to happen had started early that morning when Tembo brought the car round to the main house. Tembo had spent two hours washing and cleaning the big Austin saloon that Harry had sent out from England for his mother. It had taken Emily a month to pluck up enough courage to get in the thing let alone learn how to drive what she saw as a metal monster.

A man from the new garage in Salisbury had come out to Elephant Walk for a weekend and taught Tembo how to drive. He had taken to the task like a duck to water. To all four of his wives he had admitted the shiny black car was the most exciting thing that had happened in his life. So far the longest journey had been to Salisbury and back to Elephant Walk. Now the baas was due from England on the boat train that afternoon, Tembo imagined journeys of vast dimensions. Suddenly, his horizon had no limits.

As instructed none of the family were to ride to Salisbury to meet the baas off the train and Tembo started the engine and made it roar like a lion. Everything stopped in its tracks. The bitch even stood on three legs to listen to the new sound. After a moment's pause, the three children rushed at the car to get in. Colonel Voss looked out of his prison window to have a look. Madge rushed out of the main house to try to grab the children.

Tembo, knowing the problem, had locked all the doors from the inside. Making sure there were no children in front or under the car he let out the clutch and began the twenty-mile journey to the station. His control of clutch and brake was perfect. The car moved forward smoothly and down the drive towards the curing barns and the farm buildings.

The two old horses in the field to the right had trotted over to have a look for themselves. The two tame giraffes, almost as tall as they would grow, turned inquisitive heads but did not move. The giraffes shared the field with the horses.

In the rear-view mirror Tembo saw the children had stopped running after the car. The dogs were again chasing the bitch for all they were worth. Tembo felt very important in his chauffeur's uniform with the large peaked hat perched cheekily on his head. Most of all he was looking forward to seeing Harry Brigandshaw. They had known each other for most of their lives. Tembo was thinking what the baas would say about his new uniform.

Looking up at the sky through the windscreen by leaning forward in the driver's seat, Tembo thought it was going to rain later in the afternoon. The rains were late. The bush on both sides of the track, tinder dry. The smallest spark would cause a raging bush fire.

As Tembo drove the car up the winding path through the low hills, he could see herds of wild animals to his left down on the plain, on either side of the Mazoe River. The view was very beautiful and gave him comfort. He was at home in his own country and though he had been to nowhere else, he knew what he drove through was the most beautiful country in the world.

TEMBO REACHED Salisbury railway station two hours before the train from Beira was due to arrive. No one ever knew if the train would arrive on time. To Tembo an early train was as likely as a late train. He parked away from the long building and walked inside.

No one knew the time the train would arrive. There were people already waiting. People coming from England made the Rhodesians feel less isolated. The boat train was a big event.

A man standing at the end of the building in the shade looked familiar. Tembo walked cautiously down the platform to have a better look. The man turned his back when he saw Tembo and walked away. Out in the sun, Tembo saw the man had black hair. It was not the same man. Tembo thought the railway station had made him think of the man who had shot Lucinda Brigandshaw in front of him. Tembo had tackled the man to the ground to stop him firing the gun again. The man who had killed the baas's new wife was blonde.

Tembo walked back to the car. It was too hot to sit in the car. There was no shade in which to park the car.

More cars and people began to arrive. The car park filled up with all kinds of transport. There was a strong smell of horse dung. The horses stood in the sun without seeming to mind. One of the means of transport was an ox wagon. The black driver was sitting up on the box behind the span of oxen. There were six oxen in the span. Tembo thought the wagon must have come a long way to meet the train. He greeted the man up on the box. The round hood of the wagon gave the man shade from the sun.

Far away, Tembo heard the thunder and smelled the lightning. It was going to be a wet, muddy ride back to the farm. If the skies opened to start the rains they could stay in the hotel. The spruits that had been dry on his way in would be raging rivers. Once they had stayed in Salisbury for a week before going home.

A PRETTY GIRL in a nurse's uniform stood next to him while he waited in the shade of the platform half an hour later. The girl had long, blonde hair. She had big hips like an African woman; the young girl would have many children. The girl's brown eyes smiled at Tembo and he smiled back. Waiting with her was another girl of the same age. The other girl seemed agitated. Next to her clutching her long skirt was a small boy. The girl was frail with a thin, pinched face. She avoided Tembo's eyes. In a strange way for two so different girls they had a similar look. The way they spoke English was the same way the piccaninny baas spoke, the man they called Jim Bowman. Then he remembered why the blonde girl had smiled at him. He had seen her before on Elephant Walk. She had come to visit Jim Bowman.

The platform had filled up with people. The man with the black hair Tembo thought he had seen before was standing at the back of the crowd. Tembo tried to catch his eye without success. People were beginning to push from the back of the crowd making the ones in front close to the railway line uncomfortable. The small boy was crying. The frail woman picked him up, and the boy stopped crying. There was no sign of the boy's father.

From far away, Tembo heard a whistle. It was the train from Beira. Tembo stood up to his full height and waited for the steam train to come into view. Again they all heard the whistle from far away. Everyone smiled. The frail girl put the small boy up on to her shoulders to see over the crowd. The boy was holding on to his mother's hand for dear life.

"Be careful, Johnny," said the blonde girl. She looked excited to Tembo. The frail girl with the boy on her shoulders was getting more agitated now they could hear the powerful puffing sound made by the train as it slowly made its majestic way into the railway station. Everyone was craning their necks to have a better look. Tembo began looking for Harry Brigandshaw. Most of the passengers were leaning out of the windows of the train.

There were many shouts and greetings. Tembo craned his neck and stood on tiptoe like the rest of them. Passengers were recognising friends on the platform. People went off down to the guard's van to collect their heavy luggage. Porters with two-wheeled trolleys that worked like barrows followed the passengers. People went off to the car park with their luggage stacked up to the arms of the barrows. The crowd thinned out. Still there was no sign of Harry Brigandshaw.

The blonde girl greeted a man off the train. Tembo gathered it was her brother. Tembo gave her a last smile of recognition as the four of them went off.

The man with the black hair was still on the station. He had his right hand inside his coat. No one else was wearing a coat in the heat. Tembo looked hard at the man and was sure. Their eyes locked. The man abruptly turned and quickly pushed his way into the back of the crowd and was swallowed up before Tembo could thrust his way through and give chase.

When Tembo looked back the platform was empty of passengers.

"Over here, Tembo," came a familiar voice.

Tembo's smile lit up all over his face. With the baas was a young girl, a woman and a young man. As the two men smiled at each other with mutual pleasure, the rain began in earnest.

"Nice uniform… Come on or we'll all get wet. Better take us all to Meikles till we see what the rain does. How's the farm, Tembo?"

"Everything is good."

Only when they were near the car did Tembo mention the man with the black hair.

"Why we got off last. Why I wrote my mother to send you alone. Did you bring the gun as I asked?"

"Yes, baas. It's in the boot of the car."

"Get it, please."

"What's going on, Harry?" asked Felicity Voss.

"Wild animals on the road," lied Harry. "In the African bush I always like to carry a gun. Now just look at that. It's raining cats and dogs."

Tembo got back in the driver's seat, rain pouring from his peaked hat. His new uniform was wet through and began to steam. Even with the rain it was still hot.

Harry kept the Webley pistol on his lap as they drove slowly into the town. He was looking out the window for a man with black hair and a familiar face. The rain was too hard to see more than twenty yards.

The big Zulu was waiting in the rain under a large umbrella when they drove up to the entrance of Meikles Hotel. Harry greeted the big man with the monkey tail shirt and leopard skin over his shoulder in Zulu. Harry only knew a few words in Zulu which he kept for such occasions. The man's spear and black hide shield had been left just inside the main entrance to the big hotel out of the rain.

Everyone got out of the car and went inside. The Zulu kept the umbrella over their heads in turn. They were all laughing when they got together inside.

Tembo took the car round the back of the hotel to the servants' quarters where he had friends. It was still raining hard. They would not go to the farm that night. Even for a few days. Tembo was happy. There would be much time to drink beer with his friends, the thick white beer made from fermented maize in the way his people had been brewing beer for centuries. It was always better to drink beer a long way from his wives. All his wives complained together when he got drunk.

He was laughing after he parked the car and went looking for his friends. It was what friends were for. Drinking beer. One of the best pleasures he knew to be taken from life was drinking beer with old friends.

He had forgotten his uniform was wet. He had forgotten the man with the black hair.

FIVE DAYS LATER when the rivers had gone down and Harry made the last leg of his journey home, Tina Pringle received his letter. She read it three times still not sure how to take the words. Was Harry just being polite or did he want to see her again? Well-bred men were difficult to understand. What she might think was the truth was to them good manners. They wrote polite little letters when they had spent a night with friends as guests in their homes. Even if they hated the time spent.

The day spent out of duty. The right thing to do… Was Harry doing the right thing after bedding her solidly for days or did he mean what he said at the end of the letter? The letter ended 'Love from Harry'. 'Yours sincerely' would have been plain rude. Was the invitation to visit Elephant Walk again a way of atoning for the sin of fornication? To make her feel better with herself? Not meant to be accepted. Polite words of 'thank you' for mutual satisfaction in bed.

"To hell with it," she said to herself. "If I don't go, I'll never know. If I don't go, he'll never know he's going to be a father."

Excited at the prospect Tina walked up to the main house from the cottage to tell her brother. The thought of making love to Harry again in a few days' time made her knees feel weak. She knew she was wet without having had a pee. The morning sickness in her stomach left along with the butterflies. Tina smiled to herself. It was all in the mind.

THREE HOURS LATER she was being driven to the Johannesburg railway station by Bill Hardcastle, her brother's man. Bill and his wife Molly had worked first for Sallie when she was Sallie Barker before she became Tina's sister-in-law. Tina had never felt so happy in her life. It would take two days in the train to get to Salisbury via Mafeking and the railway line through Bechuanaland. She had sent Harry a cable she was arriving but not the reason why. Harry had once said cables were delivered to Elephant Walk by the Salisbury post office. There was no telephone yet on the farm. Tina hoped someone would be at the station to meet her and take her to Elephant Walk. If not she would stay in Meikles Hotel. Her brother had been so happy at the prospect of Harry Brigandshaw becoming his brother-in-law he had given her five hundred pounds for the journey which was far too much. If nothing else the trip to see Harry had given her the money to go home to Dorset. If Harry laughed in her face. The butterflies in her stomach were back again. Tina was a realist. Men were mostly bastards in every sense of the word. She only had to think of Barnaby St Clair. She just hoped Barnaby had heard of her affair with Harry by now. She hoped the jealousy cut his stomach in half. He deserved any pain she could inflict on him. If Barnaby had behaved as he should have behaved those years ago none of her present dilemma would have happened. Inwardly she cursed Barnaby as Bill Hardcastle drove the Rolls-Royce Phantom that belonged to Serendipity Mining into Johannesburg railway station. Serendipity Mining and Explosives Company belonged to Albert and Sallie. Both her brother and sister-in-law were at the office. Nothing ever came in the way of their work.

TO TINA'S SURPRISE there was a crowd on platform three. People everywhere. Men with large cameras and flashguns held above the heads of the crowd. Her sleeping compartment had been booked earlier by Bill Hardcastle. They pushed their way through to the train with Bill Hardcastle carrying her one small case. She did not want Harry to get a first wrong impression. That she had come to marry him, hell or high water. He had to want her and the baby or she would go right back to England and make the best of the rest of her life.

On the platform surrounded by the crowd and the newspapermen was a big, blonde man with long hair down to his shoulders and a full beard. He was the centre of everyone's attention, dressed in a long white robe that came down to his ankles. He was talking in a British accent to the crowd. He was talking about God and redemption.

How God had saved him from the pit of hell to do His work. The man had slate green eyes that seemed to look into another world as he spoke. The man had Tina stopping to listen. She was following Bill Hardcastle and her suitcases up into the train. The man was mesmerising. He reminded her of Jesus Christ as she had been taught he looked like in Sunday school at Corfe Castle church, the church where so many of the St Clairs had been buried so long ago in history.

She found her compartment with Bill Hardcastle's help and leaned out of the window to listen to the man. Bill Hardcastle said goodbye and got off the train. The man in the long white robe got onto the train and turned back to the crowd. He stood in the door looking down on the people from his new height. The man blessed the crowd three times. He had hanging from his neck the biggest iron cross Tina had ever seen. It was on a long chain. The man held up the cross in his left hand when he blessed them. The man's right hand was missing.

Someone blew a whistle, and the train began to move. There was a big engine at the front of the train puffing up white smoke. Tina put her head back into the compartment and closed the window. Acrid smoke from the engine was blowing down over the length of the train.

The people on the platform began to blur as the train puffed up speed. Houses appeared outside the window. Tina hoped some of the man's blessing had fallen upon her, her baby and Harry Brigandshaw.

She had a bar of chocolate in her handbag which she ate. She had a craving for anything sweet. The butterflies were back in her stomach with a vengeance.

THREE CARRIAGES AWAY, Simon Haller was reading back the notes he had made in his bad shorthand. Solly Goldman was putting away his camera equipment.

"I think there's a book in it," said Simon.

"You're not serious?"

"Don't you think so?"

"He's just so wonderful," said a woman who was sitting in the corner with a faraway smile on her face.

They were all travelling second class, eight to a compartment. The newspaper did not go to first-class travel for reporters and photographers. Their compartment was full of fellow passengers. The luggage racks above them were also crowded full.

"Is there a dining car?" asked a man.

"You have to pay," said another woman.

"No," said Solly Goldman, "the ticket says free lunch, dinner and supper. Mine does anyway. The food will be lousy. Get something to eat in Mafeking when we stop for half an hour."

"What do we do after that?" said the woman.

"Eat lousy food... Is the Preacher travelling second class?"

"No," said Simon. "Our charming editor gave him a first-class ticket."

"That's not fair on us... Are you going to interview him on the train?"

"I'm going to try. This time he can't run away. Captive audience. That's my big idea."

"Then why aren't we travelling first class?"

"Solly, you know the editor. Anyway, what's a walk down the corridor? Stretch my legs... You think he'll talk to me?"

"He would in the first-class dining car but they won't let you in."

"Not if I pay?"

"Not even if you pay. It's part of the snobbery. Part of the class system."

"You talk rubbish."

"I got some good photographs of Mr Barend Oosthuizen."

"The Preacher. From now on he is only called the Preacher. He is famous already."

"He's wonderful," said the woman in the corner with a faraway smile on her face.

It was going to be the biggest story in Simon Haller's life. Bigger than the story of the war hero and the nurse that syndicated round the world under Simon Haller's byline. He was sure he could find a publisher for the book on the Preacher. The people in England and America now knew his name. It was all about being known, getting published. Just as important as writing a good book. Anyone famous could find a publisher. He owed that much to the story of Jim Bowman and Jenny Merryl.

"Do you think they will get married?" he said.

"Now what are you talking about Simon?"

"Jim Bowman and the nurse. Jenny Merryl. She was pretty. I asked her out once and she said no. She said she was seeing Jim Bowman again. That would be a nice ending to the story."

"Didn't your last story say they were getting married?"

"It didn't say they were married... No, you're right. That story is dead. The war's been over four years today. It's Armistice Day. 11th of November. On the eleventh day of the eleventh month on the eleventh hour... People have lost interest in the war. They forget so quickly. Just as well. Anyway, the Preacher's a much better story... I'm going to write a book about him. People like to read about religion."

Solly Goldman was looking out of the window. The train was through the built-up area of Johannesburg. There were big mine dumps rising from the veld. The wind was blowing yellow dust everywhere. Eyesores.

The mine dumps gave way to the open veld that had once been fought over by the British and the Boers.

"What was his father like?" asked Solly. "The Boer general. Imagine being hanged for fighting for your own people. That wasn't right, Simon."

"Life isn't right, Solly... I'm going to write that book."

Solly ignored him. His friend had a one-track mind. Outside the window Solly could see a small herd of zebras. They were running away from the train. Running away from man... It was one thing to write a newspaper article. Quite another to write a full-length book. So many journalists try. Very few finished. Solly sighed. Zebras were now running away at full tilt.

"At least they have some sense," he said to no one in particular.

The rhythmic call of the wheels on the metal rails made his eyes close. He was fast asleep before Simon Haller had finished checking his notes on Barend Oosthuizen, the Preacher. Solly dreamed of a man and woman at their wedding. The wedding was in heaven. Among the white clouds.

AT THE DESTINATION of Barend Oosthuizen's journey from hell the sun was shining. The rain had stopped the day before though there was still no sign of Harry Brigandshaw and Tembo on Elephant Walk. Emily, Harry's mother, was trying not to worry. And yet, she found it difficult to contain her excitement. He would be staying in Meikles Hotel with his friends from the boat. She hoped this time he would stay. There had been too many years when he was away. At school in the Cape. At university in Oxford. Fighting the war in France. Too many years for a lonely mother with nothing else to think of but her children. Without Madge she had no idea what she would do.

Losing a husband to an elephant and her younger son to the war had been too horrible. Life had been cruel. Even her father living with them on the farm could only be so much comfort. What poor Alison was doing on her own at New Kleinfontein was beyond Emily's understanding. Every week she travelled on a horse to the other side of what had once been all of Elephant Walk to visit the woman who had been Harry's nurse back so long ago when both of them were young. Both their husbands were dead. Alison's hanged as a traitor at the end of the Boer War by the British. Alison who was English. There had been a recent rumour about Barend, Alison's son and Madge's husband. Emily had not mentioned the rumour on her last visit to see Alison. The rumour was too appalling. Barend had been buried in a rockfall a mile down at the bottom of a gold mine in Johannesburg. Madge was still beside herself with worry. Everyone had kept the news from the three children. Why Alison had not gone to live with her daughter Katinka in the Cape was another thing in life Emily did not understand.

When Jim Bowman had asked to use the old house on the family compound that had been derelict for years she had agreed. The boy had friends arriving from his old home in England. The friends had arrived on Elephant Walk in a horse and trap just before the rivers had become impassable. The horse had been able to drag the trap through the rising water of the spruits where a car would have bogged down. Harry would have known that. She knew she shouldn't worry. If he was caught between two rivers, he would survive. Harry knew too much about the bush. Where to find food. He had the Webley pistol he had asked for in his letter. The thought of her son lying dead shot by his old CO in the Royal Flying Corps set her off worrying. Harry would come before the sun went down she kept repeating to herself. All through their lives, Emily had never stopped worrying about her children. Life for Emily was one big worry. Then there was the old man in the rondavel. A woman who carried his name but had never been his wife was about to arrive with a daughter the old man had never seen. What that was all about she had no idea. The poor man had been scrubbed and brushed but still looked like a wild animal.

A Belgian had come all the way from the Inyanga to build an airstrip on the farm and gone off again. There was no aeroplane. Just an airstrip. She had no idea what that was all about either. They told her all these things but never explained anything. She had put new mosquito nets in the old house for the young people, that much she had remembered to do. During the rains the mosquitoes were ferocious. There was so much malaria around. At least the old roof was sound and kept out the rain. The broken windows had been quickly repaired. The guests would have to bathe in Jim Bowman's new house as the water pipes were broken in the old house built by Tinus Oosthuizen. It just never stopped. Finding enough linen for all the beds had been another problem. She just hoped Harry had not brought anyone else he had not told her about. Anyone else would have to stay with her father. It just never stopped. The men never even thought about the extra food. They just expected everything to work like clockwork. It was all too much. There was more to running all the people than running the farm... Where was Harry?

Emily Brigandshaw was quite beside herself.

NOT FOUR MILES away Harry had stopped the car where the pass through the hills came out to look down on the Mazoe Valley, where Sebastian Brigandshaw, Harry's father, had first seen the migration heading north. Fifty thousand elephants, one after the other, the small ones hooking their mothers' tails not to get lost in the swirling red dust made by so many slow-moving elephant. The sight seen only decades apart inspired Sebastian to call his African farm Elephant Walk.

'Miles of them, Harry. You should have seen them. The power of nature. Nothing would have turned them from their ancestral path. One day you'll see it. Every twenty years or so they migrate to the Congo from the Okavango swamps, skirting south of the Zambezi River until they swim across at Tete, the old Portuguese post in Mozambique. Then the migration path cuts back through to the Congo basin. There are Portuguese records of the migration going back centuries. One of the greatest sights of the world.'

Harry could hear his father's voice in his head as he looked far over the valley to his home. The days of rain had washed the air clean. Pockets of mist hung above the receding rivers, the water sucked up by the heat of the sun.

He had told his passengers about the elephants in the car to distract Felicity and Justine. They had both gone quiet. Deathly quiet. Ever since the car had finally left behind Meikles Hotel on the last leg of the journey from England. Philip Neville, seeing the turmoil in Justine's mind, had rattled on about the book he was going to write about his great-aunt. The girl had stayed silent, not even looking out of the car window.

Harry cursed his own stupidity. He should never have invited them to the farm. A dead father, now they were so close to Colonel Voss, was better than what she was going to find on Elephant Walk. The big Zulu doorman had told him the old man was living in Peregrine the Ninth's rondavel. That the new clothes and haircuts had made no difference. The Zulu had been proud of it.

"You can't change an old lion," he had said, clutching happily at the thought. The old Zulu and Colonel Voss had known each other for many years.

Now the moment had come. There was nothing Harry could do to stop the disaster.

Far over behind Elephant Walk he could see a small herd of elephants moving through the sparse flat-topped msasa trees still in the glory of their spring colours of red and russet brown. Harry could see ten miles without the Zeiss field glasses he had taken from the German pilot killed in combat, the leather case marked so eerily with his own initials. He put the field glasses to his eyes and focused on the big animals. They were browsing the trees, eating the fresh leaves, some of which were already turning green. He offered the glass at first to

Felicity and then to Justine. Neither took the proffered glasses.

The girl had a right to meet her father whatever his condition. A girl only ever had one father... Harry was trying to convince himself without success.

LATER THEY all got back into the black Austin. Tembo cranked the engine at the front with the long, probing crank handle. The car began to wind slowly down into the valley towards the distant elephants. Harry sent a short prayer to God to look after his friends.

HALF AN HOUR later they drove through the avenue of jacaranda trees, passing the curing barn for the tobacco, the grading shed and the workshop. They headed towards the cluster of houses on the slope that led down through the msasa trees and the well-cut lawns to the Mazoe River.

As Harry got out of his car, the dogs jumped all over him while the children screamed with excitement. Emily ran into her son's open arms, crying uncontrollably. Harry and his grandfather shook hands formally. Madge took her turn with a big kiss on her brother's cheek.

"He's all right," he said to her, "Barend's all right. Lost his right hand to gangrene, but he's all right. The papers are full of him."

They were both trying not to cry.

"When is he coming home?"

"The *Rhodesia Herald* has a special reporter in Johannesburg who says he's on his way home now."

"Oh, thank God... Children! Come here. Stop screaming. Daddy's coming home."

The dogs having been sidelined by the family were chasing each other through the flowerbeds.

"Someone get those dogs out of my flowerbeds," shouted Emily.

TEMBO TOOK the car round in a circle to put it in the shed next to the workshop. He had put all the luggage on the lawn. Two servants in long white shorts and white jackets were waiting barefoot to be told where to take the suitcases. Everyone was smiling except Felicity Voss and her daughter.

A wizened old man was standing in the doorway of a round hut watching everything. Harry did not see him in the turmoil. Jim Bowman had come out of his new house. Behind him were a man and two young women. Somehow the man's face was familiar to Harry. A small boy he had never seen before was screaming his lungs out trying to compete with Madge's three children. His home was happy bedlam.

"I don't believe it," said Harry looking across at his mother's house. "That damn ginger cat is fast asleep with his eyes open."

"May I introduce myself," said a voice through the throng. Harry went cold. "I'm Colonel Voss. You, dear child, must be my daughter. How do you do? Felicity, you are as beautiful as I always remember. Now, if you will excuse me I have to go. Hamlet and Othello are escorting me back to Sir Robert. King Richard waits for me. So nice to meet you... Jim, dear boy, your help of course. We have to put the horses into the shaft. Unfortunately, dear child, this is the rainy season. Were it not, I would propose a journey to the Valley of the Horses. The Place of the Legend. Maybe next year in the English winter. Or the year after. It has indeed been a pleasure seeing you again, Felicity. Indeed. Indeed... Come, dear boy. We can't keep these nice people waiting. I'm sure they have things to do."

"Are you really my father?" asked Justine in a small voice.

"Oh, yes, dear child. You look just like my mother. She was a great beauty you know. A great beauty. Well, I'll be off. Time waits for no man. Thank you Mrs Brigandshaw for your kind hospitality. It shall not be forgotten. Sir Henry. Thank you kindly old friend. Harry, dear boy. Rather, a case of hello and goodbye... Indeed. Those dogs are quite mad, you know. Poor old King Richard the Lionheart... There are some things, Felicity, that can never be repaired. This is one of them. Thank you for bringing my daughter. I shall always cherish the memory of seeing her face."

Astounded and disbelieving, and before anyone could stop him, the old man was walking away briskly in the direction of Hamlet and Othello's field. Calling each of them in turn. Jim stood rooted to the spot. Harry nodded to him grimly. Jim followed the old man. The dogs were still savaging the cannas. The children were screaming with the same excitement. Felicity Voss was crying. Justine was watching her father walk out of her life with an open mouth. Shocked.

"You must be Mrs Voss," said Emily gently, taking the woman's arm. "I'm Emily Brigandshaw, Harry's mother. I'll show you to your room. I'm sure it's been a long journey."

"The longest journey of my life," said Felicity Voss.

By the time Justine followed her mother, her father's receding back was out of sight. Only then did she start to cry, shuddering throughout her whole body.

"He didn't even kiss me," was all she could say, over and over again.

Harry had put his hand under Justine's right elbow and was guiding her into the house.

"Let him be, Justine. It was his decision. He is a great gentleman. What he did just now was the bravest thing I have ever seen in my life."

"I don't care what he looks like."

"But he does. Last time he saw your mother he was a dashing cavalry officer, back from the Boer War. He wants your mother to remember him like that. He knows better than anyone he ruined your mother's life."

"Will he take me to the Place of the Legend?"

"I don't know whether it exists."

"Does it matter?"

"To your father it matters."

"Then he'll take me."

"Maybe."

"I do want to go. I really do." She was looking over her shoulder as Harry drew her into his mother's house. The ginger cat was still fast asleep on the windowsill with his eyes wide open. The first time since Harry had got home he heard the Egyptian geese honking.

THE FOLLOWING DAY, just after breakfast, a dispatch rider on a motorcycle arrived on the farm with a telegram from Tina Pringle. Harry showed it to his mother.

"Who, might I ask, is Tina Pringle? Where is she going to stay?"

"You met Tina once, Mother, before the war. We now have a spare room in the rondavel."

"At least that's something. Those poor people from England. So embarrassing at dinner last night. And Madge is beside herself. It's just one thing after another. Nobody tells me anything."

"My dearest Mother," said Harry smiling. "Do you know how much I love you?"

"People always say they love each other. Mostly they don't mean it."

"From the bottom of my heart, Mother dear."

"What do you want, Harry?"

"Nothing but the pleasure of your company."

"You've gone all silly since that cable arrived."

"I rather think I have."

"They are down at the river again... Best to leave them alone. I thought she was your girl before the cable. Is she nice, Harry?" Harry knew his mother was referring to Tina Pringle.

"You probably won't approve."

"I've stopped judging people years ago... Come and sit on the veranda and we'll have a good talk. The cook can bring us a fresh pot of tea. I want to hear everything. You can bring me up to date on Hastings Court. It doesn't hurt any more... Your grandfather is planting the biggest tobacco crop ever this year. Did I tell you Tinus has a cold and won't wipe his nose with a handkerchief? Those children are little savages. Will Barend behave properly now he's had such a terrible fright? And he was such a nice boy."

Emily went on and on, Harry listening to every word. He knew just how lucky he had been to have this woman as his mother. He leaned across and kissed her on the cheek.

"What was that for?" asked Emily.

"For being my mother."

All thought of Mervyn Braithwaite had left their minds. In the safety of his own home Harry had left the Webley pistol in his old room.

LEN MERRYL and Jim Bowman had gone off alone into the bush before breakfast. It was Jim's job to bring back a small buck to be roasted over the open fire. With so many mouths to feed a spit roast had been decided on by Emily first thing in the morning. In the thick bush of Elephant Walk, kudu was plentiful. Mrs Brigandshaw had been quite specific.

"A young ram, Jim. Somewhere half grown. Pick your target. Take the .22 rifle and give the shotgun to your friend. If he sees any francolin, he can have a shot. One small kudu and three francolin. Never shoot more than you can eat. And by the way, I told my son the name of your English visitor last night. He thinks the police will want to see him. Harry thought he recognised the man yesterday when he arrived home. Didn't expect to find him on his own farm."

"What do the police want with Len?" Jim had said in alarm.

"The man who killed my daughter-in-law was seen by Tembo at the railway station. He thinks the man was waiting for Harry. Your Len Merryl saw what my son thinks was Mervyn Braithwaite shoot a man through the window of a Cape Town bar. If Mr Merryl can identify the man again, the Rhodesian police will send Braithwaite down to Cape Town to be tried for murder."

"Will Len have to go to Cape Town?"

"Yes, if needed but Harry will pay for any cost. What's Mr Merryl doing here?"

"Looking for a job. He doesn't want to go to sea again. He worked his passage out on the SS *Corfe Castle*."

"Harry will bring him back from Cape Town and find him a job in Rhodesia."

"Have the police caught Braithwaite?"

"No, but they know what to look for. Harry gave them a detailed description at the police station when they were waiting for the rain to stop in Salisbury. In better days Braithwaite was my son's CO in France. If you call war better days. Mr Merryl's job will be to pick him out of a line-up. There are not that many people in Rhodesia and Braithwaite has to be staying in a hotel or a boarding house."

THEY TALKED about Neston. They talked about Jenny. Or Len talked about Jenny. Jim talked about Cousin Mildred.

"You know she loves you," said Jim Bowman referring to Mildred. "When you left from Woolwich docks on your first ship she was watching from the doorway of a warehouse. What you did for Mildred when she was dying of pneumonia in London was so beautiful. She told Jenny. Jenny told me. Mildred has been hoping so much ever since you wrote to your sister about coming to settle in Rhodesia."

"Poor Mildred. The war killed more than the dead."

"You don't love her? Isn't that why you came?"

"I came to find a new life... I never gave her any ideas about love. She was my cousin and in trouble."

"She knows that. People hope. Like me. I hope to marry your sister. Get a farm of my own. This year I get a bonus. Three per cent of the crop. The government will give me land if I prove I can farm and show them enough money in the bank to grow the first crop. There's so much empty land in Rhodesia. Three more years, I can make it... I think Jenny's going to marry a Belgian. He's rich, charming and flies aeroplanes. He showed me how to build our airstrip. Mr Brigandshaw has a plane being assembled in Cape Town... There is a family of kudu on the next ridge. Stay where you are, Len."

Len heard the shot five minutes later. All the time he was thinking of

Cousin Mildred. The thought of marriage and responsibility had been the last thing on his mind. From the fevered body of Mildred Len's mind went to Teresa in the bar in Cape Town. There was blood all over her front. For a second Len thought the gunshot that killed the kudu was the gunshot that killed Willie McNam.

Breaking cover, Len went forward to help his friend with the carcass of the kudu. They were going to cut a pole and hang the carcass so they could carry it on their shoulders.

WHEN THEY got back to the family compound with the dead buck, Harry Brigandshaw was waiting for Len. They left for Salisbury with Harry driving the Austin. Len was going to report to Salisbury central police station. Deliberately, Harry had not told him the man was clean-shaven and dressed like a gentleman.

At the police station, the police said the man had not been found even though a thorough search had been made.

When they got back to Elephant Walk, Mildred and her son Johnny were gone. Jim Bowman had taken them back to a farm outside Salisbury in the horse and trap.

"ARE YOU GOING to get a farm, Jim?" Jenny asked when Jim came back alone after tea. The horse was spent having come back at a spanking trot all the way.

"That's the idea."

"I'd like that."

"What about Le Jeune?"

"He's old enough to be my father. Poor Mildred. She was hoping so much from Len... Does Len have to go to Cape Town?"

"They haven't found the man. Probably never will... Do we have an understanding, Jenny?"

"Why not, Jim? You're my class. It's better that way. We know what to expect... I have to be back at the hospital on Monday... Roast venison for supper."

"I know, I shot the buck this morning."

They were arm in arm, comfortable with each other. 'Jenny is such a practical girl,' Jim thought to himself with satisfaction.

MILDRED HAD cried all the way to Salisbury. Only the first letter from Len to his sister Jenny had given her hope. The letter had asked after her. Len was coming to Africa. Her hopes had risen. Her life had had a future.

Were it not for little Johnny she told herself, she wanted to die. She had been so silly. Who would ever want to marry a woman who had earned her living as a prostitute?

Soon after the Salvation Army had taught her the rudiments of reading and writing she had written to her cousin Jenny Merryl in Rhodesia. The old woman who taught her lessons had helped put the words onto a sheet of paper. The woman had addressed the letter so the post office could read where to send it. Her own writing was not very good. She had heard from her mother that Jenny worked at the main hospital in Salisbury. Mildred had hoped that address would be enough. Jenny was the only tenuous contact Mildred had with Len. After all, Len was Jenny's sister. Once Len had sailed from Woolwich docks he had vanished from her life. The vicar at Neston had replied on behalf of her mother. Mildred had wanted to show her mother she could now write. However badly. The bit about Jenny in the vicar's letter had just been her luck.

A PATIENT OF Jenny's had been in the Salisbury hospital for six months. He had lost both his legs and his wife when his car hit an elephant on the road between Salisbury and Bulawayo. The man had only gone thirty miles out of Salisbury. He had three young children on a farm. The children had been looked after by friends. When Mildred's barely readable letter arrived for Jenny at the hospital, the man was about to go home. The doctors had done the best they could.

The man would be able to propel himself around in a wheelchair. He would not be able to look after himself, let alone three children. With no crop planted on his farm that year and the bills from the hospital still to be paid he was almost broke. Jenny felt sorry for the man. Cousin Mildred's letter might well be a godsend.

Jenny had told the man the story of Johnny Lake killed in the war leaving her cousin Mildred with an illegitimate child. She had proposed Cousin Mildred come to Rhodesia and care for the man's family. The man could instruct his labourers on the farm from his wheelchair.

There was still enough money to bring Mildred to Rhodesia third class. The man thought any cousin of Jenny Merryl would be wonderful. Jenny had not told the man Mildred had been a whore.

When Jim Bowman dropped Mildred at the farm with her dreams of marrying Len Merryl shattered, she had been working for Cedric Bland for six months without pay. Only when the crop came in would she receive some money.

She was in such a state when Jim Bowman left that he got it all out of her. He was a patient man from sitting so long in a wheelchair. The story of Len holding her body in bed to keep her warm made him cry without shame. He had been through so much in a year he knew the meaning of pain, mental and physical. Cedric Bland understood desperation and why Mildred had become a whore.

Johnny Lake, the son of the soldier killed in the Western Front, now four years old, had gone to play with the other children the moment he was home on the farm. Little Johnny was always happy. When Mildred was sobbing in Cedric Bland's arms draped over the wheelchair he was smiling to himself over the top of her shoulder. For Cedric, Mildred was indeed a godsend.

TEN MINUTES after Tembo had recognised Mervyn Braithwaite, alias the Honourable Peyton Fitzgerald, alias John Perry, he was back in his room at Meikles Hotel packing his bags. He kept a taxi waiting outside the station for a quick escape once he had killed Harry Brigandshaw and any of his women on the platform. The part of his brain that hated Harry for calling him Fishy Braithwaite at Oxford and stealing the affection of his fiancée Sara Wentworth was as clear as crystal. As a precaution he had rented a bolthole in a private house on the wrong side of the railway track in the name of his first alias John Perry. He still had the forged passport in the name of John Perry. Coming down to a low-class accent was simple. Mrs Hill was as common as dirt.

Before anyone could begin checking the hotel registers with his description, he had paid his bill and been dropped at Mrs Hill's door.

"Thought you got lost, Mr Perry. Want a cup of tea?"

The last thing on Mervyn Braithwaite's mind was a cup of tea and conversation with Mrs Hill. He paid off the taxi and with a bag in each hand sought the refuge of the room he had yet to use. He had paid Mrs Hill in advance. He just smiled at her on the way into the wooden house.

"Pretty smart luggage for a bloke like you," said Mrs Hill before he could close the door to his room. She had followed him. Obviously his new landlady thought she had a chance of getting more than a lodger. "Did you steal them suitcases?" she giggled in what she thought was intimate laughter. To Mervyn it sounded like a cackle. "How long you staying?"

His good clothes though were the problem.

"What you up to? Don't want no criminals, I don't. A woman on her own has to be careful."

"In England," Mervyn said in his best cockney accent, "I was a gentleman's gentleman."

"Can you speak posh?"

"Of course I can," said Mervyn breaking into his normal speech.

"Oh you are a card... Sure you don't want that cup of tea, Mr Perry?"

"When I come back from shopping."

"I'll be waiting."

Mervyn bought enough food for three days so he would not have to go out of the house. He also bought the *Rhodesia Herald* as was his habit. The story of Barend Oosthuizen, the Preacher, returning to Rhodesia on the train, was headline news. Mervyn read the article without interest until the paper said the Preacher was Harry Brigandshaw's brother-in-law.

"Got you, you bastard. This time I got you. You'll meet him at the station and I'll be waiting."

His whole body was as calm as a snake lying out in the winter sun. He checked the small leather case in his bag for the gun. Then he went and took tea with Mrs Hill. Nothing was going to stop his revenge.

He was smiling all over his face when Mrs Hill poured the tea.

"There you are, ducks."

"Thank you, Mrs Hill."

"What are you doing in Rhodesia?"

He spun Mrs Hill a story of which Philip Neville would have been proud of. Not only had the newspaper told him Harry Brigandshaw was the Preacher's brother-in-law, it had told him the arrival time of the train from Johannesburg. The paper said there would be a big crowd at the station. The Preacher was going to preach. From the depths of hell a mile under the earth the paper said the Preacher had been saved. God had forgiven his sins and there were plenty of them. That part of the article made no impression on Mervyn Braithwaite.

He liked the idea of a big crowd. Of everyone being distracted. If Harry Brigandshaw was not at the railway station, he would have to go all the way to Elephant Walk to kill him. But he would be there. Mervyn felt it in his water. Brigandshaw's time had finally come.

Mrs Hill, enthralled by his story that included a gold mine that had belonged to his late employer had not even questioned the tale being told in an upper-class British accent. Nor the fact that a man with a gold mine would stay in one of her rooms.

ACROSS IN LONDON, while Tina Pringle was travelling through the arid bush of Bechuanaland in the same train carrying the Preacher, Barnaby St Clair heard of her affair with Harry Brigandshaw. The raging jealousy even frightened his brother Merlin.

They were in the Trocadero, London's supper club, and had ordered a whisky each. Merlin had not been thinking straight when, as he thought a moment too late, he let the cat out of the bag. He should have known his brother. Some things were best kept away from conversation. For Merlin, who had also received a twist in the stomach at the news, his first words were spoken without malice or forethought.

"Did you hear Harry's got a new girlfriend? Story last night I heard was they didn't go to the ship's dining room for days. Holed up in Harry's cabin. The owner's one is quite something my friend was telling me. Had a letter from his sister posted in Cape Town. His sister and mother are visiting relatives in South Africa."

"Good for Harry," Barnaby had said. "He deserves it after losing Lucinda. To be shot dead by a madman. I think of her often... Brett was far too young for Harry... *The Golden Moth* is still playing to packed houses. She's been seen all over town with Oscar Fleming, the impresario. And he really is old enough to be her father." Barnaby cackled nastily. "What makes good-looking gals go for old men? Such a waste of youth."

"Harry's new girl is not much older than Brett."

"Anyone I know?"

"Tina. Tina Pringle."

For a moment, Merlin thought his brother was going to pick up a chair and smash it over a dining table.

"I'm sorry, Barnaby. I thought."

"Shut up!"

"Don't be rude, Barnaby."

"I said shut up! After marrying our sister, how dare Harry sleep with a member of the family that has been subservient to the St Clairs for generations."

"You did."

"Discreetly. As a mistress. Not out in the open in the owner's suite for everyone to see... Who told you?"

Merlin ignored the question.

"He really is a bastard," said Barnaby.

"Maybe he'll make an honest woman out of her."

"Don't be bloody ridiculous. She's mine. She's my mistress. He's damn well not going to have her. She's always been mine."

"But he has, Barnaby."

After the first shock, Merlin was quietly smirking. For once he had something Barnaby did not have. A mistress. In a great flat. A daughter from the mistress quite devoted to him. Every time he went to see them his daughter said she loved him. The image of his daughter Genevieve floated into his mind. Contentment flowed with the thought. He was lying to himself a little. She did not say she loved him every visit.

By the time the drinks came, Barnaby was gone. To Merlin, there did not seem to be so much point to Barnaby's wealth after all. Even with his own money there was still something Barnaby could not have. Tina Pringle had obviously refused to be his mistress.

Finishing his drink, Merlin decided to go and visit Esther in the flat he rented for them in Chelsea. Outside the Trocadero, it was raining hard. The doorman looked at Merlin's back as Merlin went out the door without his overcoat. Merlin did not have an umbrella. The doorman shook his head at the strange ways of the gentry.

In the taxi, Merlin gave the driver Esther's address. He was dripping wet from all the rain and smiling to himself. He had now forgotten that once he too had mooned over Tina Pringle. He was happy. He was truly happy. He was going to visit his eight-year-old daughter who said she loved him.

17

THE TEDDY BEARS' PICNIC, NOVEMBER 1922

The train cut a straight line through the arid, flat bushveld of Bechuanaland trailing white smoke back over the top of the long carriages. Outside the window, Simon Haller had watched the herds of game, hour after hour. Elephant. Buffalo. Black rhinoceros. Zebra. Giraffe, their tall heads above the sun-baked trees. Buck. All kinds of buck. Impala. Kudu in the mean shadow of the trees. Wildebeest. Packs of wild spotted dog. A pride of lions thirty yards from the safety of his passing window. Bush, game and sun. But no people. Not even a hut to show there had been man. As if God had taken man from the landscape.

THEY HAD STOPPED at Mafeking so the passengers could stretch their legs before the long, dry haul to Bulawayo, the Place of the Killings. Bulawayo was the first town in Rhodesia where they would stretch their legs for the last part of the journey across the country to Salisbury and Simon's home.

He had tried to interview the Preacher on the platform at Mafeking station. People had gathered quickly to see the man with the flowing blonde hair, the white robe to the floor, the iron cross on his chest. Instead of an interview he and Solly Goldman the photographer had been subjected to a sermon full of passion. Solly had taken three photographs of the man with the burning slate green eyes. Simon had been unable, as he said to his editor afterwards, to get a word in edgeways. The crowd was spellbound. The railway man in the dark blue uniform and peaked hat had to go up to the Preacher and tell him to get back on the train. No one had taken any notice of the guard's whistle which he had blown furiously. Once the Preacher disappeared into the train, the passengers clambered back on board. The great metal monster of an engine blew its steam whistle with final authority and the clanking iron wheels began to turn on the iron rails and the journey north continued. The Preacher had said nothing Simon had not heard before. It was the way he said it that kept the people spellbound.

THE TRAIN PASSED over a dried-up riverbed. The bridge that spanned it was a hundred yards long. Once every five years the river was a raging torrent. Elephants dug the riverbed with their tusks, making deep holes. Muddy water seeped into the deep holes for the elephant to drink. There were three elephants below the railway bridge digging for water as they passed. Neither Simon nor Solly had spoken for hours, lost in their own thoughts. The four other passengers were either asleep or feigning sleep; they all had their eyes closed.

"Do you think he means what he says?" asked Solly. The rhythm of the train was constant. Clackety-clack. Clackety-clack.

"No man ever knows what is truly in another man's head," said Simon. "Preachers like Barend Oosthuizen and popular politicians tell us what we want to hear. We all want to live good lives and go to heaven. If we believe that during our life on earth, the reality of death doesn't matter so much. We can face our own mortality with hope rather than fear… Did you ever listen to a popular politician who wasn't committing fraud by promising to give the people what they want provided they vote for him? So they will give him that plum job in government? He knows better than the people he can never fulfil his promises. When he is in power, the people don't matter to him until the next election. Sometimes they won't give up power and turn nasty using the police and the army to further their private agenda of power and wealth."

"ARE you saying there isn't a God?"

"I don't know, Solly. Without God there's no point to anything. Why everyone was listening on the platform. They want to be reassured. They want someone to carry their burden. Provided they believe in God it will all be worthwhile in the end. People have to believe, Solly. Whether this preacher used the words of God to save his own neck from the hangman's noose, only God knows."

"So you think he's a fraud?"

"We're all frauds, Solly… One of those photographs is going on the front page of my book. The best photograph. The best one."

"Are you going to call him a fraud in your book?"

"Don't be silly. I want to sell thousands of copies. I'm going to tell my readers what they want to hear. Like the politicians. We scribes carry the burden of our own sins. Our selfish pursuits, however we dress them up for the public."

"Then you are a fraud."

"Didn't I just say that? Think of your politician. Have any of them said the truth?"

"So you want to make the Preacher famous?"

"I want to make myself famous, Solly Goldman. Fool the people but never fool yourself. Now I'm going back to sleep."

"Do you think the world will ever get better?"

Simon had closed his eyes. He ignored the question. It was oppressively hot in the carriage even with the window down. The air blowing in through the window came from the furnace of the sun. There was a place in South Africa someone had named 'Hot as Hell'. Simon understood why... He was thinking of the pretty girl who had stood close to him on the platform at Mafeking station. When he finally fell asleep, in the heat he had an erotic dream. When he woke with a start, his penis was rigid within his trouser pants. The woman who thought the Preacher wonderful was looking across with awe. Simon crossed his legs, but it made no difference. He closed his eyes again. It was too hot to worry. The girl was back again in his thoughts.

LIKE TINA PRINGLE, courtesy of her brother, Barend Oosthuizen, courtesy of the *Rhodesia Herald*, had a compartment to himself. Unlike Tina who was dreaming of her unborn child, Barend was fighting the devil. What he wanted more than anything on earth was a pint and a half of whisky followed by a brawl, followed by a whore. The need for alcohol was screaming through his body. Only the thought of ridicule and the police stopped him going down the corridor to the bar in the dining car. He had killed a man. Only when he was buried beneath the earth was it the least of his worries. The people would turn on him as quickly as they had come to his protection. They would tear a fraud apart. A people duped was worse than a woman scorned. How could he keep up the pretence was all he thought about as the train ran on towards his own destruction? Madge would see it in his eyes. Madge would forgive him as she had always forgiven him before. His children, so young, would have no idea of life's reality. His mother would hide her eyes. The dogs would run away. God, that he called to in his agony would never forgive the sin of using Him to protect his mortal skin.

God, quite rightly, would forsake him. He was the devil's work. Not God's. The devil would take him where he belonged in hell. This time there would be no escape. He would burn forever... The need for alcohol flooded his body again and made him shake. He had the tremors worse than ever before.

"God? Please help me. Please help me."

Clackety-clack. Clackety-clack. The smell of smoke. The heat pushing in through the window. Outside the bush in all its silence. Nothing moved in the noonday sun.

TINA HUGGED herself with excitement. Whether the morning sickness had been in her mind or body she had run down the corridor twice to the toilet. She hoped Harry was going to meet her train in Salisbury. Harry was going to be a father. They were going to be happy together. Forever. She looked outside at the Africa that was going to be her home. Her child's home. The home of her family. She could not wait to reach her destination. The following afternoon. First Bulawayo. Then Salisbury. Then Harry Brigandshaw.

WHILE TINA, was being sick with child and excitement for the third time, Harry was standing with Tembo overlooking the gorge with the Mazoe River flowing swiftly through the hills and into the Mazoe Valley. Elephant Walk was to the north of the valley. They had been talking about the farm all morning as Tembo brought Harry up to date with the business of Elephant Walk. They spoke in Shona, the language of Tembo's tribe, the tribe that had been decimated by decades of Matabele war parties from the south road. The Matabele had come up to Mashonaland from South Africa in the early part of the nineteenth century and flourished by stealing the Shona cattle and crops. Each year until the British chased King Lobengula out of Bulawayo, the Matabele impi took a different path of destruction. They waited for the Shona to fatten their cattle and reap their crops before cutting the Shona men to pieces with the short, Zulu stabbing spears. Mzilikazi, Lobengula's father, had been a general of King Shaka of the Zulus before he became a renegade and fled Zululand with his army.

The British were the second power in a century to subjugate the Shona. Tembo liked and respected Harry as a man while hating the English for conquering his land. Like many other people, Tembo dreamed of a Chimurenga, a war of liberation. With the power of the

Matabele broken by the British, a successful Chimurenga would return the rule of the Shona tribes to the Shona people. It was their birthright. It was their land.

Tembo was forty years old and strong as an ox. The gun he carried over his shoulder was a Lee Enfield .303 that had been made for the war in France and only found its way to Africa when the war finished. Tembo could shoot the eye of a sitting bird from fifty yards. The hunter, Sebastian Brigandshaw, the father of the man he now called baas, had taught him well.

With two thousand Lee Enfield rifles, Tembo's dream was to chase the British out of the country they dared to call Rhodesia. He would then take revenge on the Matabele. One day he would have to kill Harry and his family. There was sadness in any war. In any liberation. Inwardly he smiled knowing Harry knew nothing of his thoughts. It was a matter of tribe. There was nothing man to man.

The only problem so far with his plan was a lack of guns and ammunition. The only gun he had was the one he carried over his shoulder. He never had more than ten rounds of ammunition. Even as he listened to Harry talking of the great wall that would block the small gorge down in front of them and flood the valley on the west side of the hills, towards the town they called Salisbury after the British prime minister at the time, it dawned on him that Baas Harry was not so naïve after all. The British they told him had conquered a quarter of the world.

Grimly, he brought his mind back to the current conversation. Maybe the Chimurenga would be for his children, or his children's children. Maybe they would all have to get on with each other. Share the country. Shona, Matabele and British.

"A great dam full of fresh water," Harry was saying, now speaking in English as Harry dreamed his own dreams, "would enable us to irrigate every inch of our valley. Every inch of Elephant Walk. No more looking up at the sky for the start of the rains. No more drought-stricken crops. No more periodic starvation for your people. One crop during the rains supplemented by irrigation if the rain stops. One crop in the winter months when the rain doesn't fall, watered from last year's rains. Every drop of rain that falls on Rhodesia to be used for the people instead of running out down the Zambezi to the sea."

"What is irrigation?" Tembo had no idea what Harry was talking about.

"Pipes and pumps and sprinklers putting water on the land at will. Whenever we want, Tembo my friend."

"That is impossible."

"Tell that to the engineers in Manchester who make our machinery... Soon I'm going to fly an aeroplane from Cape Town to the farm."

"What is an aeroplane?"

"A big bird as big as a car that flies through the sky. The same engine that turns the wheels of your car, turns the propeller of the aeroplane and drags it off the ground into the sky. You and I will fly in the sky, Tembo."

"What's a propeller, baas?"

Harry just looked at him and smiled.

"When you want the car tomorrow?" said Tembo changing the subject he did not understand.

"Twelve o'clock. Train comes at four. Baas Barend is coming home... And a girl."

"Your girl, baas?"

"My girl... We are going to kill a cow. For everyone on Elephant Walk. Two days' holiday. Beer for everyone. Brown beer from Salisbury. Strong brown beer we call Castle beer. One big party to welcome Baas Barend and my girl."

Tembo was thinking how he could stay drunk for two days without bringing the wrath of his four wives down on his head. The Chimurenga would have to wait.

BACK AT THE farm homestead, Philip Neville was sitting at a small table in the rondavel happily vacated by Colonel Voss. Philip wisely had not mentioned Colonel Voss to Justine. One minute the man she said was her father was in front of them. The next minute he was gone. He had not looked anything like a father to Philip. Not of a beautiful, rich girl from London. Maybe the old man had murdered someone and fled England. Philip had heard of such things happening. Englishmen hiding away in remote parts of the world avoiding the law. Self-exile. It had happened down the centuries. Good men. Bad men.

Ever since the gnarled old man had left with his horses and the wagon, Justine and her mother had been mostly alone. The well-bred English at the meal table never mentioned a word. The subject was taboo. 'Please pass the salt'... Philip was glad. The last thing he wanted was a father probing the state of his finances which were about to reach rock bottom. However much he wanted to, he was never going to be a writer.

Soon after the old man had left the rondavel vacant, Philip had moved in a desk. He had cleaned the one large room from floor to ceiling. He had polished the surface of the table until it shone. With the great pomp and expectation he had placed ten sheets of clean white paper, one on top of the other, on the polished table. He had adjusted the high-backed chair many times before finding the right position. He had taken up his fountain pen. Checked twice that it was full of blue ink. Pulled out the cuffs of his shirt, a long-sleeved white silk shirt he had kept for the sole purpose of writing his one great book. He had written down the three perfect paragraphs that had been in his mind so long. Read them through and through to be sure they were so perfect. And waited... And waited.

Nothing happened in his head. He thought of his great-aunt. Thought of their so many talks. Played them through and through his head. Still nothing happened. He had absolutely no idea how to write the next paragraph let alone the full-length book.

After an hour of frustrated staring at the sheet of paper with its three small paragraphs, Philip sneaked out of the room and walked down to the river. All three children followed. All three were strangely silent until they reached the water's edge.

"Daddy's coming home tomorrow," said Paula.

The three children were grinning up at him. It made him feel worse. The three dogs joined the children, wagging their tails. They all had a life, a future. When he turned thirty, his income would stop. His prospects would stop.

Philip Neville standing on the bank of the Mazoe River in the middle of Africa had no idea what he was going to do with the rest of his life. He even thought of jumping in the water and ending it all. The heavy rains had made the calm waters of the river a raging torrent.

The children and the dogs wandered off downriver. Even killing himself was something he was unable to do.

For a long time alone Philip watched the flotsam of trees and islands of grass flowing fast down the middle of the river. The water was the colour of red mud. A fish eagle called to him from the opposite bank of the river. Three plaintive calls one after the other. For some reason the sound of the bird made him cry, gently, softly all to himself.

"Why can't I write a book?" he called to the bird in the depths of his despair.

The fish eagle looked back with large, predatory eyes, its hooked beak pointing at Philip as if demanding who dared to speak. Then the bird flew away leaving Philip alone with his life in ruins.

All the way back to the houses Philip was deep in thought looking for a way to make a living when his thousand pounds a year from his great-aunt's estate finished on his thirtieth birthday. He had no idea. He had never done a day's work in his life and he was now twenty-seven. The thought of poverty gave him cold shivers even in the heat. There was nothing wrong with being born an Englishman. Provided you had money.

WITH THE SOAKING rains having fallen on the ploughed lands of maize and tobacco the farm was a hive of industry. Pips of corn were pushed into the ground in straight lines a foot apart. String had been laid out and pulled taut by wooden pegs to keep the lines perfectly straight. The long markers themselves were three feet apart. With more good rain the stands of maize would grow above a man's head with three full cobs of white corn. Into the tobacco lands were going the seedlings grown in Sir Henry Manderville's seedbeds that he had watched his men water for six weeks with handheld watering cans made in Birmingham. The small plants were lying wilted in the hot sun on top of the ridges that had been heaped up by hoes. Behind the planters came the men with buckets of water. At each plant they patted the red soil around the seedlings to make a round bed and slopped on a cup of water. In the cool of the night, the roots of the plant would take hold.

Every able-bodied person was working in the lands. It was hot, back-breaking work which no one seemed to mind. They all depended on the success of the farm's crops. If the crops failed, there was nowhere else to look for food. Last year's maize had been a disaster, the drought reducing the yield to two bags of maize kernels an acre. Two hundred pounds of food an acre. The previous year's surplus stored in silos off the ground to keep the rats at bay was almost finished.

The labourers did not know Harry had bought bags of wheat up from South Africa and had them stored in a Salisbury warehouse in case the food on the farm ran out. The wheat had been paid for from the profit made by the tobacco crop, the hog heads of tobacco exported and sold in England. Harry's mind had thought through the problem before people went hungry.

THEY LEFT AT twelve o'clock in the Austin, the children kept quiet with toffees stuffed in their mouths. Having insisted on making the journey, Madge was serenely silent in the back seat surrounded by her children. Alison, Barend's mother, had come across from New Kleinfontein, on a rare visit and was sitting nearer the window with four-year-old Doris on her knees. The grandchildren barely knew their reclusive grandmother.

In the front, Tembo was driving the car. Next to him was the .303 Lee Enfield rifle which lay on the seat with its butt under the dashboard. Next to the gun, with one hand on the gun's stock to stop it jumping around on the badly rutted road after the heavy rains, sat Harry. The Webley pistol was in a leather holder on his right hip. Both guns were loaded with a bullet each in the chambers. Both guns had their safety catches pushed on.

Harry felt like he was going on his first date and could not keep the grin off his face. This time they would have the privacy to really get to know each other. Tina. Tina. Tina. Her name kept sounding in his head.

"The road is not as bad as I thought," he said turning in his seat to look at his sister. "How you feeling, Madge?"

"Excited," she said. "And you, Brother dear?"

"Like a kid. You'll like Tina. Do you remember her visit in '15?"

"I've answered that question a dozen times. I barely remember the girl. We were at New Kleinfontein, I think. All I ever thought of then was Barend."

"Not long now."

"Is he really going to be changed?"

"The paper says so."

"They say a lot of things they don't mean."

BY THE TIME they pulled into Salisbury Station there was pandemonium on the platform. Simon Haller with his head out of the window could barely believe his luck. Never before had so many people met the train from South Africa. They were of all races. Rich and poor. Pushing. Shouting above the noise of the train. Craning their necks to get a first look of the Preacher.

"Told you, Solly, come and have a look. The front of the train isn't

even into the station and there's nearly a riot. The *Rhodesia Herald* must
have sold out every day since I broke the Preacher's story. What a
book, Solly. What a book I'm going to have. I'm going to be famous.
People will remember Simon Haller when he's dead. Did you know
that's the only true way to be immortal?"

"Flash in the pan," said Solly, not sure if Simon was pulling his leg.
He rather thought so.

"Don't you believe it. Just put your head out of this window. Seeing's
believing. They're going mad. Men going to war and preachers coming
to preach. Only way to get a crowd like that on a railway station. Grab
your bags. I want to be off the train the moment it stops. If not
before."

"You'll break your neck."

"There's too much at stake to break my neck."

Solly put his head out the window to have a look for himself. He
could feel the excitement.

"That pretty girl we saw at Mafeking is also looking out of her
window," he said without looking back into the compartment. "She
seems to be looking for someone in the crowd... She's seen them.
She's waving... You know something, Simon. This time you are right.
She really is something to look at."

"Is the Preacher looking out?"

"Not yet... That girl is pretty. Don't see them that good-looking very
often... Never seen so many people in Salisbury... They must have
had plenty of rain. It's humid. Really humid. Hot and sticky."

"It always hot and sticky this time of year... Out of the way, Solly. I
want another look."

A roar had gone up from the crowd milling on the station platform.

"It's the Preacher," said Simon, his head back out of the window, "I
told you. He has the door of his compartment open and is standing on
the step. He looks magnificent. No doubt to anyone who he is. An old
woman has got to her knees believe it or not. Right down there on the
front of the platform. Get a picture, Solly."

"I can't with the train still moving."

"Biggest story I ever made," said Simon smugly.

Ignoring protocol and the woman in their third-class compartment,
Simon was the first off the train, falling into the arms of an old man.
When Simon got up from his knees, he was still somehow clutching his
overnight bag.

"Sorry," he said to the man who was ignoring him. The man was more interested in the Preacher. The train jerked to a final halt to the screaming sound of metal grinding metal.

The Preacher was not twenty yards in front of them. He was standing on the step with the carriage door swung open. His arms were up. The right hand ended in the stump. The left hand held up the iron cross to heaven. He was blessing the crowd, magnificent in his flowing white robe and blonde hair down to his shoulders.

"Now try and tell me he's a fraud," said Simon. Solly was now standing on the platform next to him surrounded by the crowd.

A man came out of the crowd, pushing through the throng. The Preacher saw the man and smiled. The two men moved towards each other and embraced. The Preacher, taking the man off his feet and turning him round in a bear hug. Simon thought the Preacher had seen something in the crowd. The man's eyes had grown big with sudden understanding. A shot rang out, followed by a second and a third. The Preacher's head exploded from the front onto the man he had protected. Both men collapsed on the platform. Everyone was screaming.

Simon looked to see where the shots had come from. By the sound of them he thought the shots had been fired from a pistol. The sound of the fourth shot came from another direction. Simon knew the sound this time for certain. A .303 army issue rifle. People were running in all directions. Simon could no longer see anything of the Preacher on the ground. The crowd was dispersing from the platform quickly. People were staring from the stationary train, too frightened to get out.

When the crowds dispersed a little, Simon could see the Preacher was lying on the platform. He was lying on top of the other man. Simon was sure both were dead. Over towards the ticket office a man with black hair was lying on his back on the ground. Simon could see he had been shot through the right eye. Without being told, Simon knew the man was dead.

"Get photographs, Solly," he said grimly, "someone may have killed my book."

While Solly held up the flashgun with the shiny metal bowl towards the bloody corpses on the platform, Simon looked around. No one in authority had yet come forward. A black man was standing in the doorway of the station waiting room, a bolt-action rifle in his hand. Simon smiled grimly to himself. He had been right. The last shot had come from a .303 fired by the black man. Simon was not sure whether to interview the black man or look at the corpses. He had never seen a dead man before.

The pretty girl from Mafeking was running down the platform screaming the name 'Harry'. Simon understood. The man under the Preacher was Harry Brigandshaw, the Preacher's brother-in-law. He wondered what the girl had to do with Harry Brigandshaw.

The girl had reached the dead men and was down on her knees, the cloche hat falling off her head onto the Preacher's back. A crowd was again forming, ringing the Preacher. Another crowd of people were gathering around the dead man with the black hair. People were getting off the train to have a look, leaving the carriage doors open in their hurry.

A policeman in a starched, sleeveless khaki shirt and leather Sam Browne across his chest was striding down the platform. Even in the African heat he wore leather puttees and brown leather boots. All the leather was highly polished. The policeman wore a peaked hat on his head. Simon doubted the man was nineteen years old. Doubted if he shaved. His face was still pink from the English climate.

With surprising authority the policeman bent down and gently pulled the Preacher off Harry Brigandshaw. Underneath, Harry Brigandshaw's face was covered in blood. The girl from the Mafeking railway platform screamed. The policeman was looking at the Preacher for any sign of life.

The man's whole forehead had exploded outwards. Simon who was five yards away understood. Somewhere he had read about soft-nosed bullets that shattered on impact causing a massive hole to the body. Simon thought someone in Geneva had tried to ban soft-nosed bullets during the war. No one would have recognised the Preacher.

To Simon's surprise, Harry Brigandshaw brought up his arm and clutched the girl who was kneeling over him. They held each other for a long time. Then they got to their feet.

Having got up Harry Brigandshaw wiped some of the Preacher's blood from his face. He was taking control of the situation despite the efforts of the young policeman. Harry Brigandshaw was waving back a younger girl who was trying to push her way through from the back of the crowd.

"Stay where you are, Madge! Don't let the children see him! Take them away for God's sake!... TEMBO! TEMBO! IS HE DEAD?"

"Yes, baas," said the man in the doorway without shouting. "One shot through the eye."

"Ask someone to get an ambulance."

"I'll do that, sir," said the policeman.

"Tina, you're covered in blood."

"Who would do this, Harry?"

"Mervyn Braithwaite. My old CO. His target was me not Barend. Barend saw him just before he fired and put himself between me and the gun."

"My name is Simon Haller from the *Rhodesia Herald*."

"I don't care who you are."

"Can I talk to you?"

"No, you bloody well can't. That's my best friend dead on the floor."

"Can I quote that?"

"You're a leech."

The young policeman had to stop Harry throwing a punch.

"I'm sorry, sir," said Simon.

"Then stop that damn man taking pictures or I'll smash his camera. To hell with all wars. The British killed this man by hanging his father for treason. The Germans killed that man over there by turning an unstable man into a killer. I hope God now lets both of them rest in peace."

"Can I quote that, Brigandshaw?"

"Yes, that you can... How'd you know my name?"

"It's my business..."

"Are you all right, Tembo?" Harry called.

"No, baas. I don't kill no one before. He trying to kill you, baas. Same man kill your wife."

"I'll want a full statement from both of you," said the policeman.

"I'm sure you will," said Harry, grimly. "Tina, take the car to Meikles. I'll come to you later... How are you?" he was trying to smile.

"I'm fine. I'm pregnant, Harry."

"God indeed does work in strange ways."

"I'm sorry, Harry."

"I'm not... Go and find Madge, her mother and the children. Tembo will help you with your luggage... Your hat is covered in blood."

"Leave it, Harry. I imagined everything when we met. Except this. What are you going to do?"

"Marry you for one thing... Now go and help my sister and her mother, Alison. That bastard just killed her husband, her son, instead of me."

"WHERE'S my daddy? WHERE is my daddy?" It was Tinus from behind the crowd.

"Please, Tina. Get the children away. They must never remember him like this or it will sear their minds for the rest of their lives... I'll have to be a father to them. Yes, that will be it. Father. I've never been a father before. No. I've never been that. Go Tina, now!"

"Are you all right, sir?" asked the policeman.

"What do you think, sonny... No. That's rude. I'm sorry."

Harry Brigandshaw was unashamedly crying when Solly Goldman got his last photograph. Then he and Simon Haller quickly melted away into the crowd. Simon was still writing in his notebook in his bad shorthand as they walked.

"What a story," he said when they found a taxi. He still had his overnight bag slung over his left shoulder.

"Do you know something, Simon, you are one callous bastard," said Solly.

"You were not thinking the rights and wrongs of it when you got that last photograph. So stop being a hypocrite. A story is a story. You know that as well as anyone... We might even get a smile out of our charming editor... Come on. We have a deadline to meet. The story will definitely syndicate... There's a whole story about Brigandshaw and his old CO from the war. A cover-up in England... I have vague memories of that story. They put the man in a lunatic asylum. Must have escaped or they let him out."

By the time they were in the taxi, Solly Goldman had stopped listening. If he knew any way else to make a living, he would change his job. They fed off other people's tragedy, and it wasn't right. He didn't like himself all of a sudden. He decided he was as bad as the rest of them. A hypocrite.

When they reached the offices of the *Rhodesia Herald*, he was hoping the last photograph would come out well. By the time they had dinner together in the dining room of Meikles Hotel, he and Simon, neither of them felt any guilt. The photographs had come out perfectly. Solly had developed them himself.

THEY TOOK BAREND to New Kleinfontein where they buried him. He was the first to lie in the Oosthuizen family cemetery. Harry was numb.

The shock of near death had reached him the following morning. They had all stayed the night at Meikles Hotel. That afternoon Len Merryl had been brought in by the police from Elephant Walk to identify the man with the black hair shot through the right eye. Len Merryl signed a statement saying the man was the same man who killed Willie McNam, splashing blood over Teresa. The fact Len stated the man then with a full beard had shouted 'I'm not a wet fish and you're dead' was final confirmation. Three people had stated they heard the man scream the same words when he shot the Preacher. There were no charges brought against Tembo. The police said it was his right to defend his baas against a killer. That if Tembo had not fired his rifle Harry Brigandshaw would also have died.

At the open graveside at New Kleinfontein, with Barend deep down in the damp red earth of Africa from where he had sprung, Harry could only see the small boy, the companion of his youth. In the way a man loved another man Harry knew he had loved Barend Oosthuizen. That he would miss him for the rest of his life. That he would always remember their lives together with joy and happiness.

Alison, Barend's mother, went back to the lonely house at New Kleinfontein and locked the doors. Harry said he would write to Katinka in the Cape. He was going to ask her to come up to Rhodesia and take her mother back with her. There were too many bad memories of New Kleinfontein. Harry would not allow his childhood nurse to become a recluse hiding with her memories. It was because of Harry she had come out to Africa in the first place. Harry thought Katinka would know what to do. There was a special bond between mothers and daughters. Alison was only fifty-five years old. Too young to end her life alone.

THREE DAYS later they buried Mervyn Braithwaite in the cemetery next to the new church in Avondale. The bishop had refused to bury a murderer next to Salisbury Cathedral. The Reverend Rex Walsh had been a padre in the trenches during the war. At the graveyard Harry was dressed in his old Royal Flying Corps uniform. It seemed the most appropriate. He had placed his own Military Cross on top of the coffin not knowing where to find the medal that had been awarded to Mervyn Braithwaite for bravery in France. Harry had arranged a military funeral. When the lone soldier from the Rhodesian army played the *Last Post*, Harry stood to attention and saluted. Harry knew then he hated war more than anything else. War corrupted all who it touched. 'Thou shall not kill' God had said, but they did. Harry gave up a silent prayer for forgiveness to the Germans he had killed during the war in France. To their families still mourning their deaths. Other than his brother George being killed by the Germans he had no idea what the war had been about. What had made England and Germany go to war with each other. He silently prayed in front of his old CO's grave that it would never happen again. That young men would never go to war again to kill each other.

HARRY HAD TOLD Tina and the rest of his family to stay on Elephant Walk. When he reached home, he saddled his horse and rode off into the bush without a word. He knew there were no answers to be found, but he hoped. By thinking, he hoped and prayed he would find an answer to the cruelties that seemed to have no point in life.

Harry stayed in the bush for three days despite the rain. He had ridden far from Elephant Walk. Once he thought he saw a glimmer of hope but it slipped out of his mind.

He rode back wet, cold and shivering. They put him into bed delirious. He had malaria again and for days had no idea what was happening. When the fever broke he woke to find Tina sitting by his bedside. He was in his old and familiar bedroom. The picture of the teddy bears' picnic was still on the wall. The family of teddy bears was sitting in an English wood, the picnic spread out on the soft green moss beneath a surrounding oak tree.

"So you're not a dream," he said to her.

"No I'm not, Harry."

"Did the others really die?"

"Yes they did."

"Tell my mother I'd like some chicken soup. I'm hungry."

Tina went to the closed door to the bedroom and put her hand out to the white round doorknob to open the door.

"Are you still pregnant?"

"I'm still pregnant."

"That's very good."

When Tina brought the hot soup back ten minutes later Harry was fast asleep. The ginger cat was sitting on the windowsill fast asleep with his eyes open. Outside the dogs were chasing each other. The children had been told their daddy had gone away again. They were shouting at each other, too young to comprehend. Madge was sitting on a wooden bench under a msasa tree trying to read a book. She had the look of a person far away. Tina watched her for a while. Madge smiled, her whole face lighting up. Then she began to cry, sobbing her heart out.

Tina sat down in the chair next to the peacefully sleeping Harry and began to eat his chicken soup. When he woke she would go and get him some more from the kitchen. Everything was going to be all right. She was sure of it. When she looked across, the cat had gone. The window was wide open. She got up and stood in front of the teddy bears' picnic to have a better look. It was difficult to imagine Harry as a small boy when she supposed his mother or father had put the picture on the wall. One day soon their own son would be looking at the bears drinking tea and eating sandwiches, the red-breasted robin in the corner waiting for the crumbs. The picture to Tina was very beautiful. The gentle, more beautiful side of life. She found herself crying silently for all of them.

18

SOLDIER OF THE QUEEN, DECEMBER 1922

A week before Christmas Tembo drove Jim Bowman into town to do his Christmas shopping. At the top of the list was an engagement ring for Jenny Merryl. Jenny had taken the day off from the hospital and was to meet Jim at twelve o'clock in Meikles Hotel lounge. They would then go to the jeweller together. Harry Brigandshaw had given him a loan against next year's bonus from the tobacco crop that was growing evenly with the good rains. They had had to only refill five per cent of the first planting where the seedlings had failed to take. In the maize lands small green spiked sentinels marched in straight lines down the lands. Jim knew the airstrip he had helped to build with Pierre Le Jeune had something to do with Harry's generosity. With the damage to the Handley Page less than expected, Harry had found a South African pilot who had flown in the war over France, to fly the plane to Elephant Walk. The pilot would then return to Cape Town by train. The wedding to Tina Pringle was scheduled for Christmas Eve and Harry had no wish to make another long journey to collect the plane himself. By Christmas Eve the marriage banns would have been read in the missionary church built by Harry's Uncle Nat, the Bishop of Westchester and hopeful future Archbishop of Canterbury. The uncle who had started what he considered his illustrious career by planting the tallest cross on a spire in southern Africa. A cross that at evening time threw a long shadow far over the virgin African bush.

After picking out a small diamond that had just surfaced deep in the big hole at Kimberley, Jim was going to take a longer way home after dropping Jenny at the hospital. The jeweller had measured her third finger and Jenny would pick up her engagement ring on the following day. Jim had paid the jeweller in cash before they left. With the rest of his purchases in the car he had two more visits to make before letting

Tembo drive them back to Elephant Walk so they arrived home before dark. There were signs of no more rain and Jim had work to do early the next morning. To maximise the nutrients in the soil around the tobacco seedlings, the lands had to be constantly cleared of weeds. Jim rose six days a week with the sun and left the lands with the gang when the sun went down, both his breakfast and lunch brought to him in the lands by a young man who looked after Jim and the new house. The boy-man was teaching Jim the Shona language, a painful process as neither of them spoke the other man's language. The gang had two hours off in the midday heat to go back to their village on the farm for lunch prepared by their wives while Jim repaired any of the machinery that had broken. There was always something broken on a farm and Jim had proved his worth as a mechanic, sometimes studying the manual by candlelight deep into the night.

The first stop was at the offices of the *Rhodesia Herald* where the idea of marrying Jenny had begun. He was going to place an announcement of the engagement in the personal column of the paper, to run for three days. There was no point in saying their respective parents wished to announce anything as the people in Rhodesia did not know either Jim or Jenny's mothers and both their fathers were dead. Nervous the whole thing would not take place, Jim had yet to write the news to his mother in Neston. Even if the mothers wanted to come to the wedding at the missionary church, there was no money to pay their passage. Not even Tina Pringle's mother and father were coming out from England for her marriage to the rich Harry Brigandshaw as there was not enough time. Jim suspected the girl was pregnant, but it was none of his business and anyway Harry was his boss. He had heard the brother and his wife had been told the date and where the marriage was taking place. The brother lived in Johannesburg. Jim remembered his first meeting with the girl with a rueful smile. It was sad that amidst all the new happiness, Madge Oosthuizen was visibly a wreck. Jim imagined she had loved the Preacher very much. There was nothing that anyone in the family was able to do to comfort her. Time would heal Jim hoped but time often went slowly in adversity. At least the children thought their father had just gone away again and none of them seemed to have known him very well. Jim had learnt not to ask delicate questions. With Jenny moving into the cottage after their wedding they were going to do as much for the three children as possible.

Jenny was going to start a small clinic on Elephant Walk and use her nursing skills to help everyone in the Mazoe Valley. Harry Brigandshaw had agreed to pay for the medicines. Jenny did not want a salary. To Jenny the number of black women and their babies dying at childbirth was appalling. She was going to make sure all that changed. Jim was pleased to see how excited Jenny was at the prospect. A wife with nothing to do on a farm was always a problem. Jim imagined a great explosion in the birth rate among the Shona in the years to come. Not only were they turning the valley into a granary, they were going to fill it with happy people. Lots of them.

The door to Simon Haller's office was closed. The girl at reception told Jim to knock and go in. Jim walked round the reception desk. He was some kind of hero after the syndication of his story around the world and imagined Simon would be delighted to write about their wedding and tell the readers they were going to live happily ever after. Like so many things in life that he had expected, Jim found out he was wrong. Simon Haller was distracted. Not in the slightest bit interested in his wedding plans.

"Stories die quickly, Jim. Keep it to yourselves."

"You and Solly want to come to the wedding?"

"We'll see what we can do."

"You do remember the big story of your fabricated war hero and the search for his girl?"

"I've fabricated more than one good story, Jim my boy."

"I'll bet you have. Anyway we owe you a big thank you. Sometimes the wrong reasons bring the right answers. We are going to be happy… What's the matter, Simon?"

"The Preacher. I had a really big story going on that one. I might yet write a book about him. Make him famous… Where are you going?"

"Have a good life, Simon Haller. Despite your dubious motive Jenny and I will always remember the part you played in our happiness. Just do me one favour. Don't get the idea of interviewing the widow or I'll kick you off the farm myself."

"What's got into you, Jim?"

"You wouldn't understand."

"My, we are uppity today."

Controlling his desire to slam the door to Simon Haller's office, Jim walked round the receptionist, let himself out of the offices of the *Rhodesia Herald* and walked into the street.

"Why are people so bloody selfish?" he said to Tembo when he got into the car with Tembo not having the slightest idea of what he was talking about. At least Jenny wanted to give and not take.

Jim hoped his next stop would turn out better, but he did not hold out a great deal of hope. Mrs Voss had taken the old man's rejection philosophically with a wan smile and a sad look. Justine, the daughter, had taken it personally and that something was wrong with her. Even the aspiring writer, Philip Neville, who Jim had imagined was her suitor as otherwise what was he doing on the farm appeared to be able to do nothing to take away Justine's despair. At a distance, Jim had twice followed her solitary walks far away from the family compound to make sure she did nothing silly. There was always a chance she might walk into a lion. The lion had a bad habit of sniffing around the farm cattle for an easy kill instead of hunting wild game which often got away. Most importantly, Jim felt responsible for bringing the old fox to the farm. He had meddled in another man's life and made everyone miserable. His mother had so often warned him to mind his own business. Why, he asked himself for the umpteenth time, was his mother once again so right. She had two words for people poking their noses into other people's affairs. 'Nosy parker'. In his case doing what he thought was the right thing had been wrong. Jim doubted it could have turned out more wrong.

Jim told Tembo to park the car half a mile from Sir Robert's yard. He did not want to spook the old man he had spent so much time with searching for the mythical Place of the Legend. He liked the old man very much. Understanding there were other ways of living a fruitful life without being conventional. Most people left their property as a summation of their lives. Colonel Voss would leave nothing but his life itself and how that life affected other people. Jim knew he would never forget the strange old man with the new boots he had met on his first arrival in Rhodesia at the railway station.

There was rain in the offing but he walked the half mile. King Richard the Lionheart was the first to recognise Jim and came bounding down the farm track leaping straight up into Jim Bowman's arms without a pause, nearly knocking Jim onto his back. For a surreal moment he was holding a large dog in his arms while the dog licked his face and thinking goodness knows what rotten food the dog had been eating. The dog's breath was foul. After a short struggle he got the dog down. Next he had a few words with Hamlet and Othello. The horses knew him right away. They were grazing the grass on the side of the road, if the farm track could be called a road. Jim nuzzled the soft noses and patted their necks before walking on towards the shack where Colonel Voss was now living if he hadn't found another young man to grubstake him on a quest and gone off again only God knew where. Then the old man opened the door.

"Dear boy, how nice of you to visit. Fact is, I have a parcel for you. I wrapped it in brown paper but I'm not very good at tying string on my own. My old friend Sir Robert died shortly after I returned. We had some pleasant laughs before he went away. I sat beside him right up to the end. He left me this shack. Now wasn't that nice of him? So it's just me and the dog. The horses mostly live a life of their own. Do you know horses spend ninety per cent of their lives eating grass? Tons of it. How are you, dear boy? How is the lovely Jenny? Come into my house and have a cup of tea. My word, you have walked a long way, and it's going to rain."

"Tembo brought me in the car."

"Where is Tembo?"

"Half a mile down the road."

"Call him. A good shout carries a long way in Africa. Not many people shouting around here. I'll go and get the parcel while you call Tembo. I like Tembo but he doesn't like us white men stealing his land. You mark my words. However friendly we all seem we'll end up in a fight. Rather like the Red Indians. Nature of man. One tribe conquering another. Been going on since man came down from the trees. No, we were probably taking a swing at each other up there in the forest canopy."

When Jim came back from calling Tembo from the top of the farm track that led to the shack, the old man was holding a brown paper parcel while puffing contentedly on his old pipe with a bowl carved in the shape of a crocodile head. There was a twinkle in Colonel Voss's eye. A smile of knowing something that was going to make Jim smile.

"Justine is devastated you ran away again."

"Oh, don't talk nonsense. What does she know? Everyone wants the wonderful father. The one in her imagination is far better than me. Look at me, dear boy. Just look at me. Next thing they'll want to take me back to England and introduce me to their friends. I just happened to be the one who gave her life when society frowned on fornication. Maybe one day society won't be so cruel to the children. We were wrong. Felicity and I. Wrong, dear boy. You can't just go around impregnating young girls when you have a legal wife. However much you think you love them at the time. Felicity feels sorry for herself all alone at her age and she's right. It is my fault. Trying to find a little comfort at the end of our lives and destroying the child is selfish. Wrong. Cruel. A disaster, dear boy. The story we concocted saved her from the viciousness of people's tongues. From those self-righteous people and their cold, miserable lives. Seeing Justine just once was more than I deserve. The picture of her beautiful face will go with me for the rest of my life, a great treasure to be treasured next to my heart... Dear, dear it's beginning to rain. We'll have tea another day or you won't get back to your farm before the rivers come up...

"Hello, Tembo! Mind the dog! Just stay in the car!"

"Are you all right here?" asked Jim. Tembo had slammed the car door in the dog's face just in time.

"Of course I am, dear boy."

"I'll visit once in a while."

"Next time we'll have tea."

"What are you living off?"

"I always find a way. Done it ever since I ran away to Africa... Oh, I nearly forgot. Please give this parcel to Justine."

"Can I tell Mrs Voss what you said?"

"Of course you can. You can say whatever you like. You and I know quite well the best thing an old codger like me can do is keep right out of their way. I am not what they think I am. Or more precisely I'm not what they want me to be. Life always has a price. You know that. Fact is, neither of us have had bad lives. Better than most. Felicity is rich in money. The African bush was all I wanted to be rich in mind. You remember the Valley of the Horses? Pure magic on earth. The great beauty of nature as planned by God."

"What's in the parcel?"

"The story of my life. The truth if there is any truth. Mostly the truth escapes us. I wrote it for both of them before Walter my son was killed in France on the Somme in 1916. I still had a friend in the army who knew I was alive despite the story of my death in the Anglo-Boer War. He knew how to get a letter into my hands. He was regular army like me. Walter was killed in the first battle of the Somme. Justine was not the only one without a father as Walter was for most of his life. I missed both of them more than you could even imagine. Like I had killed myself which I had while still alive. In that brown paper parcel is their father. Not the old man you see now. She can do what she wants with it, though if she wants to have it published someone will have to dress it up as fiction. Only we must know it is true as far as the truth can go. That way she can live with her father through the pages of a book for the rest of her life. She must understand that society could destroy her. Society always destroys anyone who doesn't conform to its rules. We call it civilisation. Maybe it's the way we have to live where there are so many of us. The only way to survive."

"You won't take her into the Valley of the Horses?"

"Of course not, dear boy. Now, if you'll go please I want to go inside and have a good cry. It usually makes me feel better. Come on King Richard our guests are leaving… Thank you for coming Jim Bowman."

When Jim got into the car and looked back at the small dwelling he could see smoke from the one chimney. The kettle would soon be boiling. There was now no sign of Colonel Voss or King Richard the Lionheart. Jim had a lump in his throat. Tembo started the car with the long cranking handle. Then they were driving back to Elephant Walk.

Halfway back the rains came down and visibility was less than twenty yards.

When they drove onto the farm, the daylight was going. Jim Bowman was glad to be home.

THE NEXT MORNING he gave the brown paper parcel with the loosely tied string to Justine Voss and left her alone with her father. No one saw her all day.

Jim told Felicity what had happened at the yard.

"We are going home on the next boat that leaves Beira for England. Am I allowed to read the book?"

"I think so. I'd be surprised if you are not one of the main characters so to speak."

"Do you think Philip should turn it into a novel?"

"Why not, I'll bet it's one hell of a story? I spent months with him looking for traces of the last Arab civilisation in Africa and I know how good his stories are. That way your love for Colonel Voss will live forever in a book and Philip will have fulfilled his great-aunt's wishes and carry on receiving his thousand pounds a year or whatever the amount is now."

"Is the book true?"

"You'll have to read it. If anyone can recognise the truth it'll be you, Mrs Voss."

"I want to go and see him for the last time."

"You can't. He's gone away again," lied Jim.

"He doesn't do trips in the rainy season. He told that to Justine."

"There was a young lad just out from England visiting Colonel Voss. The young man has a little money from his father. He and Colonel Voss are going to look for gold. The colonel has a theory that the shallow diggings left by the men who built the Great Zimbabwe ruins hide mountains of gold. More gold than on the Witwatersrand of South Africa. The colonel knows where to find the old diggings now they are overgrown by the bush. The young man is going to sink a proper mineshaft, make a fortune and go back to England to buy back the family estate."

"You should be the storyteller, Mr Bowman."

"It's the truth."

"Thank you, Jim, if I may call you by your first name. I hope you and Jenny will be happy together for the rest of your lives."

Jim walked down to the river before Mrs Voss could ask any more questions. At least no one else knew where to find Sir Robert's old house. A large crocodile was basking in the sun on the opposite bank. For a moment they eyed each other. The river was only fifty yards across. There were big vundu in the river, the size of sharks but easier to catch. Jim thought the old fellow on the other side of the river was digesting his lunch. He had his mouth wide open. A small bird was inside the open mouth picking food from the crocodile's teeth.

Jim let his mind roam out and about for a long time. When he looked back the small bird had finished picking for food, the crocodile had closed its jaws, closed its eyes and seemed to be fast asleep. Jim knew on closer inspection there would still be a slit open for the crocodile to see. He never ever trusted crocodiles.

"DID YOU GET your ten pounds back?" Jim was rudely startled out of his reverie. Tina Pringle had crept up on him. There was nothing for her to do. The preparations for Christmas were out of her hands. Harry was out in the lands even though it was Sunday. Harry Brigandshaw liked to be doing something all the time.

Jim did not answer her. She sat down on the fallen tree next to him. She was still as sexy as the first time he had seen her and Barnaby St Clair in Meikles Hotel.

"No, you didn't," she answered for him. "The moment the money was in Barnaby's pocket he forgot about you. Thank you for the lunch. He thinks people owe him a living. His presence is worth more than returning the money. In a strange way he is right. I always wanted to be with him even as a little girl. When you are with Barnaby life is exciting even when he is stealing ten pounds and a lunch from a young man who probably couldn't afford it. I'm guilty too. He used me as the bait in those days. Still would if I gave him the chance."

"Having lunch with you was worth the ten pounds."

"We are the flatterers! Thank you, Jim… My father was a railway worker. We lived close to the St Clair estate. Seeing we are going to be living close to each other until you buy your own farm I want you and Jenny to know the truth. This accent of mine is false. The product of a Miss Pinforth. Barnaby knew, of course. Which was why he would never marry me. He's a snob but I still love him. Is that wrong? Out here we are starting a whole new class of Englishmen. The colonial with estates so big they can't see the neighbours' chimney smoke. Barnaby would have been no good out here. He doesn't like real work. He likes to trick people out of their money. Scam people. He's very good at it. He is now very rich with the stock market going up every day. Yet he'd never even think of your ten pounds or buying you a lunch. You were only useful to him when he needed you. Only then did you feel the warmth of his charm… He's always been in my life. I wonder if he will ever really go away. Poor Harry. He just doesn't know what he's letting himself into."

"Don't you love Mr Brigandshaw?" Jim was never able to think of his boss by his first name.

"I'm pregnant, Jim."

"Is it Barnaby's child?"

"I'm not that bad. It's Harry's all right. We had a fling on the boat coming out."

"I wish you hadn't told me."

"I need a friend. Will you be my friend, Jim Bowman? Africa is going to be very lonely. It's so vast and so few of us. Can you imagine hot roast turkey in this heat for Christmas? Roast potatoes. Stuffing. Hot mince pies. Christmas pudding flaming on a silver tray for God's sake.

Process Date	National Insurance Number
19/10/2018	YL317528D

Deductions	Amount
PAYE Tax	220.00
National Insurance	0.00

0

is Period		Year To Date	
1192.50		Total Gross Pay TD	17728.51
1192.50		Gross for Tax TD	17728.51
1192.00		Tax paid TD	3268.80
		Earnings For NI TD	17716.00
		National Insurance TD	0.00

Net Pay	
	972.50

Don't you think we English overdo things a bit? Harry's bought Tembo a shiny black Ford motor car all the way from America for saving his life. So he can take his four wives into town. Harry is so generous. Quite the opposite of Barnaby. Oh, don't get me wrong. I'm going to make Harry Brigandshaw a very good wife. Ten children, we want. Well, maybe not quite ten. I can still see Barnaby as a small boy in my mind's eye when I first fell in love with him. We were five years old... Good Lord! Is that a crocodile on the other bank?"

"He's asleep."

"He's enormous! Can he swim over here?"

"He can but he won't. He's just had his lunch."

"How'd you know?" Tina was on her feet ready to run.

"A little bird told me."

EPILOGUE

ighteen months later, *Soldier of the Queen* was due to be published in England, fulfilling Philip Neville's obligations to the will and securing the legacy from his aunt for the rest of his life.

The family had been staying at Hope Cove. Only Philip was going up to London on the train for the launch of the book. Justine was heavily pregnant and preferred to stay behind at her mother's house where they had all been living since the spring. The launch and the baby were due at the same time. For Felicity, the thought of a grandchild had revitalised her life. Given it a purpose. Ever since Philip had found a publisher for *Soldier of the Queen*, the floodgates had opened. The first three perfect paragraphs had exploded into the fictional book he had wanted to write about his Great-aunt Constance's life. Turning the Colonel Voss story into fiction had shown him the way.

Hope Cove was a perfect place to write. Everyone was happy. All Philip wanted to do was write books and be happy with his wife for as long as he lived.

Justine thought the fact his income was secure had removed the fear of failure and made it possible to write the next book. Her job was to type the manuscript and criticise anything she did not like. The arguments had been many and fruitful. She knew how to get him going again. How to worry with him when the story wouldn't flow. They were partners.

"But you must come up to London," he said three days before the book was due out.

"There will be many more launch parties, darling. Just for the moment our son needs my attention. Mother and I will be quite all right. Enjoy yourself. You deserve a break. I'll raise a glass to your success on the day. Where are you going to stay?"

"The publisher has put me up at the Savoy."

"They must think they are going to make a lot of money."

Justine was smug at the thought of the two thousand-pound advance her husband had received from Longmans, Green and Company. The smugness was as much for her father as for her husband.

WHILE PHILIP was being praised by his peers in London, Justine gave birth to their daughter who bawled loudly, the sound carrying far out into the small bay. Frank the gardener heard the cry and smiled. Another generation. Continuity for his family. Life in the country would go on without a pause. The house was already full of flowers. He went to pick some more just in case.

"A girl, Frank," said the family doctor before getting into the car with a small Gladstone bag.

"Everything all right, Doctor?"

"Everything is fine."

IN A MAD RUSH the next morning to reach Paddington station to catch a train back to Devonshire, Philip Neville just had time to post his parcel to Jim Bowman. The telegram at the hotel after the launch party had told him he was the father of a daughter. The thought overwhelmed him. More than the launch of his book. Or just as much he told himself chuckling as he ran for the post office. Longmans had told him at the party about the Americans. In three months' time he was going to America for a book tour. Justine was going with him. Felicity would look after the baby. This time he was going to insist.

By the time the parcel reached Salisbury in Rhodesia it was agreed all four of them would tour America. Felicity did not believe a hired nurse would be good enough for her granddaughter. They were still arguing over the name which had changed five times. They were all too happy to worry about the child's confusion at being called so many names. Not that the child seemed to care.

JIM BOWMAN TOOK the parcel straight to the old shack that had first belonged to Sir Robert.

"You'd better read the dedication first."

Colonel Voss was staring at the book in his hands. The glossy cover to *Soldier of the Queen* was very grand. He opened the book and read the first page.

'This book is dedicated to my father-in-law, Colonel Lawrence Voss, also a soldier of the Queen who was killed fighting bravely in South Africa. I salute him.'

"That's very nice," said Colonel Voss. "You'd better pet that dog again. He is slavering all over the floor."

"You're a grandfather."

"That's also very nice."

"So is this."

Jim handed Colonel Voss the draft for one thousand pounds drawn on the Standard Bank in First Street, Salisbury, Rhodesia.

"My word. That's a lot of money. Luckily I still have that suit you insisted on buying me. I have a fancy for a slap-up meal in Meikles. On me, of course."

When they reached the entrance to the hotel, the Zulu doorman greeted them with his usual smile which turned to a beam. In his hand Colonel Voss had placed a pound note. They had first called at the bank across the road to draw twenty pounds in cash.

"Never been so rich in my life. Think I'll move in to the hotel. You think they'll let King Richard stay with me?"

"He can come to Elephant Walk with Othello and Hamlet."

"Wonderful, dear boy."

"In the letter... You will have half of all future royalties."

"There's more?"

"Much more."

"God bless them all... Did I tell you the time I was in China? Before the Boxer Rebellion of course..."

ENJOYED MAD DOGS AND ENGLISHMEN?

If you enjoyed reading my book, *Mad Dogs and Englishmen*, and have a moment to spare, I would really appreciate a short review at your favourite retailer. Your help in spreading the word is gratefully received.

The Brigandshaw Chronicles will return with Book 4, *To the Manor Born.*

PRINCIPAL CHARACTERS

The Brigandshaws

Emily — Harry's mother

Harry — Central character of *Elephant Walk* and *Mad Dogs and Englishmen*, as well as son of Sebastian and Emily

George — Harry's younger brother (deceased)

Lucinda — Harry's wife (deceased)

Mathilda — Harry's paternal grandmother

Nathanial and *James* — Harry's uncles

Sebastian — Central character of *Echoes from the Past* (deceased)

Sir Henry Manderville — Emily's father and Harry's grandfather

The St Clairs

Barnaby — The youngest brother of the St Clair children and Tina Pringle's love interest

Ethelbert, Seventeenth Baron St Clair — Robert, Merlin and Barnaby's father

Lady St Clair (Bess) — Robert, Merlin and Barnaby's mother

Merlin — Brother to Barnaby and Robert, a confirmed bachelor

Robert — Harry's university friend and author of the *Keeper of the Legend*

The Pringles

Albert — Tina's brother who is co-owner of Serendipity Mining and Explosives Company, Johannesburg

Julia — Albert and Sallie's daughter

Sallie — Co-owner of Serendipity Mining and Explosives Company and wife to Albert

Tina — Albert's sister and Barnaby St Clair's girlfriend

The Oosthuizens

Alison — Barend's reclusive mother

Barend — Lifelong friend of Harry Brigandshaw, a troubled man fighting his demons

Katinka — Barend's sister who lives in the Cape

Madge — Harry's long-suffering sister, and wife to Barend

Paula, Tinus and *Doris* — Madge and Barend's children

The Voss Family

Colonel Larry Voss — Eccentric old man always on the lookout for a grubstake in Rhodesia

Felicity — Colonel Voss's long-lost love

Justine — Colonel Voss and Felicity's daughter

Walter — Colonel Voss's son (deceased)

Other Principal Characters

Brett Kentrich — Harry's girlfriend, an actress

C E Porter — A devious stockbroker in the City of London

Dolly Merryl — Len and Jenny Merryl's mother

Esther — Merlin's ex-mistress from the Running Horses, Mickelham

Jenny Merryl — Jim Bowman's neighbour who lived next door but three in northern England

Jim Bowman — A new arrival from England in Rhodesia

Len Merryl — Jenny Merryl's brother

Max — C E Porter's business partner

Mervyn (Fishy) Braithwaite — CO of 33 Squadron as well as Sara Wentworth and Lucinda Brigandshaw's murderer

Mildred — Cousin to Jenny and Len Merryl

Percy Grainger — A senior manager at Colonial Shipping

Pierre Le Jeune — Son of an impoverished Belgian aristocrat

Simon Haller — Reporter for the *Rhodesia Herald*

Smithers — Merlin St Clair's manservant

Solly Goldman — Photographer for the *Rhodesia Herald*

Tembo — Harry's boyhood friend and servant on Elephant Walk

The Zulu — Doorman at the Meikles Hotel

GLOSSARY

Baas — A supervisor or employer, especially a white man in charge of coloured or black people

Grubstake — Money or other means supplied during a time of need or when starting a business enterprise

Merchant Prince —A person who has acquired sufficient wealth from trading to wield political influence

Piccaninny —A small black child; very small

Pap — Maize meal – a staple African diet

Rondavel — A westernised version of the African-style hut

Sadza — An African word for maize meal

Spruit — A small watercourse, typically dry except during the rainy season

Veld — Afrikaans word for open, uncultivated country or grassland in southern Africa

Vundu — large African freshwater fish; type of catfish

HISTORICAL NOTES

Bechuanaland — Officially known as the Bechuanaland Protectorate and ruled directly from Britain until its independence in 1966 whereupon its name was changed to Botswana.

Gu Bulawayo — Known as 'The Place of the Killings' and originally founded as Lobengula's capital in 1870. The city was to become known as Bulawayo.

Meikles Hotel — The Meikles Hotel is a 5 star hotel in Harare, Zimbabwe. It was built by Thomas Meikles and officially opened in 1915.

Rhodesia — No actual historical evidence can be attributed for Rhodesia having been named after the newspaper, the *Rhodesia Herald*.

ABOUT PETER RIMMER

PETER RIMMER was born in London, England, and grew up in the south of the city where he went to school. After the Second World War, and aged eighteen, he joined the Royal Air Force, reaching the rank of pilot officer before the age of nineteen. At the end of his national service he sailed for Africa to grow tobacco in what was then Rhodesia, now Zimbabwe.

THE YEARS went by and Peter found himself in Johannesburg, where he established an insurance brokering company. Over two percent of the companies listed on the Johannesburg Stock Exchange were clients of Rimmer Associates. He opened branches in the United States of America, Australia and Hong Kong and travelled extensively between them.

HE NOW lives a reclusive life in his beloved Africa, writing his books.

PETER BEGAN writing *Mad Dogs and Englishmen* on the 8th August 2002 and finished it on the 29th June 2003.

ALSO BY PETER RIMMER

"Cry of the Fish Eagle"

"Vultures in the Wind"

"Bend with the Wind"

The Brigandshaw Chronicles:

"Echoes from the Past" (Book 1)

"Elephant Walk" (Book 2)

CONNECT WITH PETER RIMMER

Website — http://www.peterrimmer.com

Twitter — Follow Peter on Twitter: @htcrimmer

Facebook — Like Peter at Peter Rimmer Author and visit Peter's dedicated Brigandshaw Chronicles Facebook Page

Email — Be the first to know about Peter's new releases, awesome giveaways and news by signing up for his VIP mailing list! (books@peterrimmer.com)

ACKNOWLEDGEMENTS

With grateful thanks to our *VIP First Readers* for reading *Mad Dogs and Englishmen* prior to it's official launch date. They have been fabulous in picking up errors and typos helping us to ensure that your own reading experience of *Mad Dogs and Englishmen* has been the best possible. Their time and commitment is particularly appreciated.

Alan McConnochie (South Africa)

Artur Vock (South Africa)

Felicity Barker (South Africa)

Marcellé Archer (South Africa)

Vikki Lawson (New Zealand)

Thank you.

Kamba Publishing